The Torrid Zone

Alaric Bond

Published by Old Salt Press, LLC

www.oldsaltpress.com

ISBN-10: 0988236095
ISBN-13: 978-0-9882360-9-7
E.book: 978-0-9882360-7-3

The cover shows detail from *A frigate off the coast near Rio de Janeiro, Brazil* by Michael Zeno Diemer (1867-1939)

For Rick

By the same author, and published
by Fireship Press

(www.fireshippress.com)

The Fighting Sail Series:

His Majesty's Ship

The Jackass Frigate

True Colours

Cut and Run

The Patriot's Fate

Published By Old Salt Press, LLC

(www.oldsaltpress.com)

Turn a Blind Eye

CONTENTS

The Torrid Zone

Chapter One

The storm had already lasted three days and HMS *Scylla* was starting to suffer. Timbers dried by time in the Mediterranean sun were brittle, some of her caulking had shrunk and many seams leaked, while much of the cordage supplied during the last, and far too brief, refit was reaching the end of its useful life. For some while the north east trade had been conveniently on her quarter, but the wind had backed with the bad weather. Now she was running before it, meeting the Atlantic rollers under heavily reefed topsails with a storm jib for balance, while both her commissioning pennant and the prized flag that distinguished her as carrying despatches streamed out stiff in the sodden air.

Forward of the mizzen mast, the quartermaster – a seasoned hand who had already seen and coped with just about everything the elements were capable of – was holding a steady course with only the occasional shout to the three men who assisted him whenever a significant turn of the double wheel was required. In

1

front of them was the binnacle, where a dull green glow revealed the compass, while to one side stood the oilskin-clad figure of Lieutenant Thomas King, officer of the watch, who, as he cowered with his back arched against the driving rain, was probably the most miserable person on board.

If all had gone to plan he should be on land, in England, and at home. King considered this for a moment; he supposed it was right to call the country such, even though he had hardly spent more than a couple of months there in the last eight years. King was a confirmed seaman, and his true home was whatever combination of oak, pine and canvas currently supported him. But that was no reason to think differently about the country of his birth, and the recent arrival of a wife, along with their acquisition of two rented rooms in Stock Street, Southsea, made the feeling stronger. Now he yearned to be there, and they were not the usual cravings of a sailor missing rest and physical comfort; he had a far more specific need to be with Juliana once more.

The duty marine turned the glass he had been surreptitiously tapping for some while, before sounding the ship's bell with what was definitely a harder strike on the seventh and final stroke. The noise coincided with yet another flash of lightning some way off. Half an hour to go before they were due to be relieved and King could seek the dubious comforts of a crowded gunroom. It was a place certain to be both stuffy and stale with the smell of closely packed humanity, while the warm air, uncomfortably oppressive even on an open deck, would be thick with damp, and positively guarantee a poor night's sleep. But the break would be a change at least and, when Cahill finally appeared to set the new watch, he was a welcome sight.

Below it was very much as he had expected, even if there was only one man that sat at the long dining table. King passed his oilskins to a steward and brushed back his damp hair as he approached. Fraiser, the elderly sailing master, looked up from his book, and nodded towards the chair opposite.

"You'll be needing something hot inside you," he informed King in a gruff tone that properly disguised the affection he held for the younger man, an affection that had built up over the many years they had sailed together.

"No, sleep is all I need," King replied, righting himself automatically as the ship gave a deeper lurch to larboard.

"Sit down, laddie," the older man commanded; to him it was obvious that rest alone would not be enough. "At least let yourself dry a wee bit before you turns in."

King slumped into the chair and accepted the mug of coffee that the Scotsman had poured, watching approvingly as it was sweetened with an overdose of sugar. The room was unusually empty, although sounds from sleeping bodies could still be heard. Rows of tiny cabins lined each side, and their thin walls held few secrets.

"How long will it last?" King asked, when he had taken several sips of his drink and the liquid was starting to take effect.

"The storm?" Fraiser asked. "Ach, all should be blown out by daybreak, but I wouldn't swear that it won't return." He closed his book and pushed it to one side. "At this latitude and time of year it is to be expected. Once we are passed the equator things should improve, but it will be a spell afore the clement weather truly sets in."

"They say St Helena is fair most of the year about." Powered by the ship's motion, the pewter pot was making slow but steady progress towards the side of the table. King caught hold of the handle and tipped a little more coffee into his mug, before replacing it safely within the confines of a rope fiddle.

"They do," Fraiser agreed. "Though the only time I was there it also rained cats and dogs on occasion. You have not been afore?"

King shook his head as he placed the mug down. "No. I was heading there back in 'ninety five when we met with a French battle squadron, and that rather changed our plans."

Fraiser knew the story well enough, but feigned a look of interest. Despite the storm and their overcrowded conditions, the dark and empty room was a relatively peaceful place, and the old Scot hoped King might feel inclined to talk further. But the lad would not be drawn and, after nothing more was forthcoming, Fraiser tried again.

"It's nought but a speck on the ocean," he said. "But there are few mariners who have not visited at some time and many continue to do so regular enough to call it home."

Home: there was that word again: odd how it both charmed and grated. King looked up and into the eyes of the elderly warrant officer. Had Fraiser used it specifically? And why was he watching him now, as if he was expecting something of great moment or significance? The young man picked up his mug once more and actually considered broaching the subject of Juliana, and their problems. King's small but close circle of friends were all shipmates, and it was no coincidence that every one was actually aboard *Scylla*. But only the sailing master was both present, and seemed ready to share a confidence. For a fleeting second the idea even appealed, before being firmly rejected. Fraiser was a fine man but King told himself he had more than sufficient maturity to live his life without assistance.

"It will only be a short trip, laddie," Fraiser said as if in response, although King had not spoken. "We should be there in no time and likely back in Portsmouth afore you knows it."

King smiled at the sailing master's optimism. "Aye," he agreed. "But we should be there now; I had all but promised." He actually opened his mouth to continue, only to find himself totally unable to explain the situation. Fraiser was a lifelong bachelor, and it was hard to express deep feelings to a person who had probably never missed anyone beyond his immediate family. The old man nodded, understanding more than King could ever have imagined.

When *Scylla* was diverted, every member of her crew had been disappointed. It was the second time such a thing had happened; the third if their previously interrupted refit was included. Following a hurried deployment to the Mediterranean, what was customarily known as the Blackstrap Station, all had been expecting to be sent back to their home port to complete repairs. Instead the ship followed their previous commander-in-chief to the Channel Fleet, where they spent the next nine months scraping the French coast with the inshore squadron. Only then did a parsimonious Admiralty decide that *Scylla* really had waited long enough, and she was finally sent for the much needed maintenance.

It was no great length of time since they had first left Portsmouth, but her repairs after Warren's action had not been exhaustive, and certain areas were in desperate need of further attention. Her crew also required care of one sort or another; while with what was colloquially known as the Channel Gropers, every man on board had been aware that England, along with her many comforts, lay barely over the horizon. The knowledge had caused more than a few sour faces and sharp answers: it was clear that all were as tired as their ship, and both officers and men drew a sigh of relief when *Scylla* was finally able to set her prow for home.

They even made it as far as Spithead, and had their bower firmly planted in the Solent mud when the captain received news from the port admiral that she was not to be paid off. More, it appeared, would be required of them and he was to take her back to sea almost immediately. Of course Banks had been generously compensated; half a million in East India Company gold was now safely stowed below; an amount which, when safely delivered, would earn him a tidy sum in freight money. But for the rest there was no consolation; they would have nothing other than the knowledge that their planned leave was to be postponed for what was likely to be at least six months. The news spread through the tightly packed ship like the plague, then, less than three weeks later, *Scylla* was heading south for what indeed was an island hardly bigger than a fly speck on the map.

To make matters worse, the reason for their delay was not a short cruise where the capture of a few fat merchants would earn them prize money. They were merely conveying passengers and had taken on board St Helena's replacement governor, together with his wife, two personal servants and a tribe of petty officials. These had consumed much of the available officer accommodation and seemed eager to do similar to any private gunroom stores. Consequently, rather than being with his wife and in the seclusion of their modest lodgings, King was sharing an even smaller space with the first lieutenant. He gave an ironic shrug, and drained his mug.

"If you've a problem," Fraiser said softly, "it may help to share it."

"Belike," King replied without conviction, before wiping his mouth with the back of his hand. "Or perhaps it is better to let things lay – they can do nought but improve."

"The captain gave permission for Juliana to come aboard, did he not?" Fraiser chanced, after considering him for a moment.

King lowered his eyes. "He did. But then it would have been hard to have done otherwise when his own wife had also been taken on. And of course Mrs Manning has been with us for much of the commission."

That was true. Due mainly to Lord St. Vincent's legendary disapproval of women sailing in the sole capacity of a spouse, *Scylla*'s people had been almost exclusively male. The exception was Kate Manning, the wife of their surgeon. She was with them in *Pandora*, Captain Banks' previous ship, which had also carried many of *Scylla*'s men and nearly every officer. Her abilities then, both as a competent medical assistant and temporary purser, made her a popular and important member of the crew, although latterly there was another reason why it was important that she stayed on board. But when *Scylla* embarked civilians for their current mission, two of them turned out to be female, and then it seemed only natural that Banks should bring his own wife as well. Sailing, as they were, under Admiralty orders meant that no permission was needed from any Commander-in-Chief; besides all the officers had attended the captain's wedding and were well aware that the couple had barely spent more than a few days together since.

"And did Juliana not care to come?" Fraiser asked, artfully bringing the younger man back to the question he would so much rather have avoided. "I would have thought a sea trip to be the certain cure for any unpleasantness ashore."

"She is not suffering any unpleasantness," King replied firmly. "At least none that cannot be dealt with. Many see the Dutch as our allies rather than the enemy, and Juliana herself seems anything but unpopular," he added enigmatically.

"I suppose accommodation on board would have been a problem," Fraiser mused.

King shook his head. "Michael Caulfield offered to give up his quarters to us both. He said he was quite prepared to rough it in the cockpit."

"Then why did she not come?" Fraiser persisted.

The ship rode an unexpectedly violent wave causing a crash from the pantry. The young lieutenant looked away but said nothing: why not indeed?

Fraiser sat back and pursed his lips. He had probed far deeper than he had intended, and was wise enough to know when to stop. "Well, if you ever want to talk, you know I will listen," he said. "That is, if you do not care to consult a higher authority." He looked meaningfully at the book he had been reading, which King noticed, without surprise, was a Bible. The young man shook his head.

"I thank you, master, but it is not advice I require." Standing, he pushed his chair back where it immediately began to rock in time with the heaving seas. "In truth I have never learned much from books of any sort. It is a spell ashore that will truly do the business and, as you say, it will come soon enough." He set the chair firmly against the table, stopping further movement. "Then all will be put right, one way or another."

* * *

"And a King!" Jameson said decisively, placing the final marker down on the appropriate square. Ostensibly they were playing for sport, each of the coloured wooden disks having no monetary value. But every man round the table knew the difference between a red, a blue and a plain, and each were equally aware that almost a day's wage was being risked on that single bet. Jameson, who had only been rated able a week earlier, looked up to Flint, his friend and sea daddy of many years, before throwing the three bone dice. There was a sympathetic groan from the others; he also had counters on two other squares, one marked with an anchor, another a crown. Should any dice have matched one, his stake would have been repaid. Were there two, the return must be doubled, and tripled if all faces agreed. But none had come up and Mitchell, the bearlike creature who's natural lair was the dark and mysterious recesses of the holds, smiled briefly before reaching out and sweeping away all of Jameson's counters.

"Still blowing some," Flint, commented nonchalantly as the ship took an extra heave. A trickle of water rained down onto the table, smudging three of the six chalked images that made up their game. Jameson held no hard feelings about losing money. It being a tight mess all knew that any winnings were liable to stay between themselves, and he would have plenty of opportunity to claim back the loss. Besides, money actually had limited value when they were several hundred miles from the nearest landmass. Usually the purser carried a number of small luxuries, which were offered at wildly inflated prices, but even these had not been replenished during their short stay at Spithead. It was only on sighting harbour and with the promise of shore leave that anyone started to hoard or value their coin. Had they been playing for sippers of grog, plugs of tobacco or any other commodity that acted as a far more viable currency at sea, it might have been a different matter.

"An' the old girl don't like it," Hind, who besides being a gunner was also one of the ship's painters, agreed. He wiped the surface dry with the sleeve of his shirt before drawing fresh symbols on the damp wood. "If she's leakin' like this above, there's no guessin' what'll be goin' on below. It will be pumping duty for any that can turn a handle, an' more caulkin' for those what can't."

"There's no point paying fresh pitch onto old," Jameson said with the authority his new position entitled him to. "What we needs is a proper refit."

"Listen to the cove!" Mitchell, bellowed, before laughing heartedly, thumping the table with one huge fist, and making the dice dance. As a holder Mitchell had found his level some years back, and it was well below that of a topman. "Give the lad an able rating, and we gets ourselves a chippy into the bargain!"

The larger man reached out and pulled hard at the short queue that Flint had tied only the day before, and Jameson was stupidly proud of. "You stick to your rags and string, youngster; let the real men worry about what's about below."

"Any who goes aloft in this weather is man enough," Flint said simply, as the ship rolled deeper once more. Mitchell was only just acceptable as a mess mate; his size and character meant that care must be taken at all times, and Flint had been wondering whether they should apply to have the beast moved elsewhere. There was nothing specifically bad about the man, when sober he could even be good company, but after grog or, as now, a few pints of stingo, his attitude was likely to change, and he would know neither bounds nor his own immense strength.

"Well you wouldn't catch me up there with yon fairies," Mitchell assured them. "Below, where the scent is sweet an' darkness covers much, that's my world."

And he was welcome to it, as all about the table had long ago decided, though none were foolish enough to voice such an opinion. Flint looked across at Jameson; the two had joined *Scylla* as part of a draft from the Channel Fleet, but first met over five years before, when the lad was a third-class volunteer. They had sailed together ever since and Flint was especially proud that his prodigy had finally been rated topman; the highest grade of seaman possible without the compromise of becoming a petty officer.

"Better turn in, Matt," he said. "We're under short sail, but that don't mean you won't get a call if this weather grows worse."

"It ain't the weather that worries me," Jameson all but whispered. "I reckons if we do get the shout it will be for all hands, and we won't be shortening sail."

"How's that?" Mitchell asked in a loud voice.

Jameson turned back to the mess and shrugged. "Well, it's probably nothing," he said, only a little louder, "but I thinks I caught sight of somthin' earlier on." Even Mitchell was quiet, as the men waited for him to continue. "It were an hour or so back – during the thunder."

"Man-of-war?" Flint asked. "Merchant?"

"Mermaid?" Mitchell added.

9

"Frigate," Jameson answered cautiously. "An' to the north. But it were only in the flash of lightning, and I couldn't be sure."

"Lookouts stayed mum," Hind commented, after a pause.

"And it sounds like you did an' all," Mitchell added in his customary roar.

"I told Draude," Jameson continued. "And he said to forget it. Both mastheads were well awake, an' it was their job to make a report, not ours."

The seamen nodded; that was the way of things: it didn't do to speak out of turn, and no one ever dobbed on a shipmate. If a strange sail were about then the lookouts would sight it soon enough.

"Besides, it don't mean much," Hind said, after further consideration. "Not just one ship. Not when the likelihood is she'll be British." There was a general murmur of agreement, and the tension lessened while Jameson picked up his remaining counters.

"Not going to hand over the rest?" Mitchell asked, and Jameson shook his head. The man was well into his cups; even if he won, there was little chance of being paid out.

"We'll play again tomorrow," he promised.

Mitchell began to grumble but Flint stood up with Jameson, and no one tried to stop them as they made for where their hammocks were already slung.

"That man will end up on the punishment deck," Jameson said softly. "Or he'll put someone else there."

"Never mind him," Flint urged. "Tell me again of your sightin'."

Jameson shrugged. "Weren't much more'n a glance, and even that I couldn't be sure of. Besides, as Hind says, she were probably British."

"Well whether she is or not, if another ship's out there we're both likely to have a bad night," Flint grumbled as he arranged the biscuit mattress in his hammock.

Jameson was already settled and had pulled the blanket up to his chin. "If they are French," he asked, "will there be an action in this storm?"

"Only if they catches us," Flint grunted. "An' even if then,

10

probably not. Best thing both captains can do is keep a keen watch on the other an' see who sinks first."

"So there's nothing to worry about," Jameson said quietly.

For years Flint had been the younger man's principal teacher, guide and counsellor and even now there were times when he looked to him for reassurance.

"Nay, Matt," Flint said firmly as he climbed into his own hammock. "Tain't nothing. Get some sleep an' let the officers do what they're paid for."

Jameson settled further into the folds of his blanket. Flint was right, he usually was, but still that brief image stayed with him and deep down he knew that he was not mistaken. "Only I thinks there might have been more'n one," he said finally, and almost to himself.

* * *

In the great cabin they were gambling far more openly. Banks and his current partner, the governor's lady, had won the third rubber and now the other three players sat back from the green baize-covered table while Sir Terrance Hatcher dutifully counted up the score, before passing a small pile of copper coins across to his wife.

"There, my dear." he said, greatly condescending. "You may as well have your dress allowance now as later."

Lady Hatcher, who was in her early thirties, probably less than half her husband's age, gave a raucous hoot of laughter as she clawed up the money. "Were it your generosity that I relied upon, my sweet, I would most like spend my days entirely naked!"

Banks and his wife smiled politely, each not meeting the other's eyes, although it was clear that, rather than being discomforted by the comment, the older man seemed to positively enjoy it.

"Well, that might brighten up a somewhat dismal voyage," he said daringly and his heavy cheeks reddened. Then, turning to Banks, he added: "Sure, I never knew it could be such a mistake to marry a woman with money!"

"The mistake was yours to think you would ever touch a penny!" Lady Hatcher countered swiftly as she, in turn, singled out Sarah, Banks' wife. "Never did see a man so dished as when Terrance discovered my fortune to be secure. Why, the trustees to my family's estate attend court and sit in both houses; try as he might he could not get so much as a sniff, and that's a situation I have no thought of changing!"

The captain kept his smile, and his eyes away from Sarah. Certainly these were not the easiest of guests. The woman- and Banks found the term 'lady' did not come readily to mind–was of a totally different social level to her husband. Large in frame, and with a figure that was fast filling out, she retained fragments of what must once have been stunning beauty. But now her skin was inclined to a mottled bloom come evening, and both her yellowed hair and bright, yet stunted, fingernails gave a fair warning of the coarseness that could be expected. Banks had originally assumed some financial arrangement had been behind the union, and was surprised when, quite early into the voyage, Lady Hatcher revealed her status as an heiress. With an equal lack of tact the news of her husband's own dire financial state quickly followed.

Such a situation was unusual at a time when it was customary for all of a woman's assets to be transferred to her husband upon marriage, and Banks had wondered at the foresight Lady Hatcher's advisers had shown in protecting her interests. However he soon came to realise that any business or legal ingenuity was totally down to the woman herself. Loud and brash she may be, but a shrewd brain worked behind those highly accentuated eyes, and its purpose was totally self-interest. On several occasions she had tried to tempt Banks into betraying a confidence and once even his own marriage. It was an experience that had taught him well; he now felt he knew the woman for what she was, and kept a careful guard up at all times. Such a thing was difficult, as they were sharing the same quarters, but whenever possible Banks avoided speaking with her for any great length, and never when the two of them were alone.

Of course he and Sarah had discussed the matter in some

detail over many nights, whispering in their own tiny sleeping cabin not ten feet from where the subject of their conservation lay. They had come to the conclusion that Sir Terrance was prepared to stand a modicum of coarseness in return for what he considered to be an attractive partner, while in turn he gave her far more than could ever have been achieved with money alone. As an elderly man, and of a type that many would assume to be a natural bachelor, the governor was hardly every woman's dream spouse. However, by marrying him she had secured herself a title, and would, inevitably be considered part of the aristocracy, if not now, then by the time her husband's tenancy of St Helena came to an end. And before then she seemed set to enjoy life, eating and drinking to excess, while making eyes and advances to any man she chose. Sir Terrance appeared as tolerant of her behaviour as he was the hypothetical short lead she obliged him to wear. Banks and his own wife eventually decided it must be an arrangement that suited both parties equally, even if they also agreed there was no question of love being in any way involved.

The governor had Banks' crystal decanter in his hand, and was offering to fill their glasses with the captain's brandy. Sarah placed a hand across the lip of hers. "No, thank you, Sir Terrance, I have enjoyed quite enough for one evening and must be abed." Both men rose as she went to stand, and Banks reached out to steady her. He had noticed Sarah tiring easily of late, and her usually rosy face now looked quite washed out.

"I will join you directly," Banks said, collecting his own glass that was in danger of being refilled.

"And I am also for an early bed," the governor agreed. The couple's personal servants arrived, and Sir Terrance allowed his, a smug, precocious little man that Banks had disliked at first sight, to guide him gently across the heaving deck.

"Even if he cannot claim the same excuse as you two love birds!" The governor's wife chuckled, before addressing herself more directly at Sarah, "Really, my dear, you should take more care – I don't think the walls in this boat are any thicker than paper. We hear every movement the two of you make."

"I – I really must retire," Banks said, flustered, and placing his glass down on the table. "If this storm continues it is likely I shall be called in the night."

"You think the ship is in danger?" The governor looked back as the captain and his lady followed him out of the great cabin.

Banks shook his head. "I doubt it, Sir Terrance. It is a drawn out affair, but *Scylla* has endured far worse. With luck we should find clearer skies in the morning."

Lady Hatcher watched them depart, then dismissed her own maid, leaving all the space and splendour of the great cabin to herself alone. She sat back in one of the captain's dining chairs and sipped at her full glass, highly content. These might not be the most palatial of quarters, but they were by far the grandest the ship had to offer and now, indisputably, they belonged to her alone to enjoy. That was all she required, to be as near to the top, to mastery and total dominance, as possible. However large or small the pond, she must be the biggest fish. Or if not the fish itself, at least to have control of it.

That was partly the reason she had agreed so readily to marry what was effectively a eunuch, and endure a term on St Helena as the governor's lady. As the major refuelling and replenishment point in the South Atlantic, the island had an importance far in excess of its physical size, and was a vital link in the foreign trade that seemed the only thing keeping the country solvent. Any ship travelling to or from the Far East was bound to call there and with Britain's very future relying on the riches available it would be strange if she could not see to it that some were diverted in the right direction. Terrance was a pleasant enough companion, and on occasions could actually be quite good company, although he gave no satisfaction. But then neither did he object if such were sought elsewhere while she, in turn, was prepared to ignore his apparent liking for that damned prissy manservant who always seemed to be around.

A noise startled her; it was a door opening and she swiftly returned to full consciousness. One of the captain's stewards had entered, clearly thinking the room now empty. He was young, well built and had that wonderfully worldly look that Lady Hatcher found so tantalising in all sailors. She placed her glass

14

down and set herself in readiness; the man's name was John – that had been learned several days ago when he had first caught her eye, and she whispered it softly now as he approached.

Chapter Two

Stiles was still damp from his time at the masthead and in no hurry to climb into a hammock. He had already eaten a lump of cheese, saved from his evening meal, and was now considering a slice of double shotted plum duff as he squatted on the berth deck beneath the lines of sleeping bodies. The fruit in the title was in fact raisins, but there could be no doubting the rich and heavy pudding; immensely satisfying after a spell exposed so far up and in the very teeth of a gale. He bit into the sticky lump of suet and flour; if it had been sweetened the pudding would have been known as a spotted dog, but Stiles preferred an old fashioned duff; the batter's slightly sour taste emphasised the flavour in the fruit and didn't leave him feeling as if he had been stuffed full with molasses. He ripped into the pudding now, chewing gamely with his mismatched mixture of teeth and gums and sucking out every last element of sugar from the raisins. Not for the first time Stiles was silently grateful that *Scylla* had a decent cook. Unlike most of his type, Grimley bore a full set of matching limbs, and owed his position entirely to culinary skill rather than injury. The making of duff, and other puddings, usually fell to a nominated hand in each mess, but this particular example was created by the man himself. Grimley could usually be persuaded with half a prick of tobacco; others considered it too high a price, but Stiles subscribed without hesitation. The seaman's diet, though not lacking in bulk, was inclined to the mundane and a notable pudding, such as this, could be eked out and enjoyed over a considerable period. Grimley took particular pride in his craft, and enjoyed access to the best flour available. Besides, he always soaked the fruit in water or, when he could squirrel the heel taps from a steward, the captain's wine. In fact all the food Grimley served was far superior to any Stiles had tasted in fourteen years at sea, and yet the man himself was a cantankerous old sod with a mouth as foul as any dockyard matey.

Stiles was taking his second bite of the pudding when

Draude, a fellow topman, slumped down next to him. As well as being younger, Draude was far fitter than Stiles. Currently he was rated captain of the foretop, but it was an open secret that a vacant position as boatwain's mate would soon be filled.

"Late supper?" Draude asked, after watching the depredation of Stiles' pudding for a moment or two.

"Happen," Stiles replied, taking his last proper bite. There were several dozen sleeping men within ten feet of them, but neither made any attempt to lower their voices. If the noise and motion of the storm hadn't woken them, a couple yarning wouldn't make much difference. Stiles considered the last chunk for a moment, before flipping it across to Draude, who caught and deposited it swiftly into his own mouth. There was no comment or acknowledgement from either party: Draude and Stiles might not always be the best of friends, but they did share the same watch, and such considerations were always remembered.

"You were maintop last trick," Draude said when he had finished the mouthful. Stiles, who was teasing a small lump of fruit from between his back teeth, nodded absentmindedly. "Notice anything?" Draude asked.

The other seaman stopped and stared at his companion. "If I 'ad, we'd 'ave all known about it," he said, in a voice slightly tinged with resentment. Draude nodded, and gave a pout.

"Only I were at the fore tops'l yard. It's been showin' signs of weakness and Bos'un detailed Jameson an' me to take a check. Truth is, I reckons we'll be lucky if it sees us back to Pompey, but it's 'olding well enough for now."

Stiles nodded, even though he could not remember seeing either seaman at the mast or on the yard.

"We sorted it quick enough, and weren't lookin' to stay long, but while he was there young Matt Jameson thinks he saw a Frenchie."

Now Draude had Stiles' complete attention. "A Frenchie, you say?"

"It were in the last of the lightning, and some ways off, so he couldn't be sure. Might even 'ave been two."

"Two?" Stiles was now worried. "An' French you say?"

Draude nodded. "He weren't so certain of the number, but however many, I can't see them being British – not out here, and without us knowing 'bout it."

"They don't tell us everything," Stiles said, and Draude acknowledged the understatement. "What were it anyway?"

"One looked to be another frigate; the other 'e couldn't say, and weren't even definite about the first, so I figured it best to keep mum."

"An' he thinks it were a Frenchie?"

"No, that were me talking, an' jus' a feelin'." Draude scratched at his armpit as he mused. "We were sent south in a bit of a hurry see, and the barky's well due for a refit. If they 'ad another frigate going the same way, surely they'd 'ave sent that?"

Stiles shifted uncomfortably. His one hour trick at the main masthead had come at the end of the watch; before that he was aloft and quite active for three hours. The lookout perch at the main was the highest in the ship and, in a drawn out storm such as they were experiencing, would describe a circle many feet in diameter, as the ship was tossed about amid the seas. In such conditions it would have been relatively easy to miss one small sighting, especially as any experienced seaman would make himself relatively comfortable even on such a tenuous perch. It might not be possible to actually sleep, but there was no doubting the movement could be vaguely hypnotic, and minds had been known to wander.

"Collins, at the fore, didn't say nuffin'," Stiles said, after considering the matter further.

"Collins didn't see it," Draude agreed. "An' there ain't no blame being laid here. I shimmed up an' gave the direction, but Collins couldn't make a thing, an' I didn't see nowt neither. That's the thing about lightning, you don't know when it's comin', and then the whole thing's over in a flash."

"Then it were probably Jameson's imagination," Stiles said without humour. His eyes were staring sightlessly at the spirketing opposite, and it was clear the matter had been taken very much to heart.

He was well aware that of late he had been inclined to miss

things – only the previous week, when on cook's duty, he misread the lead tag and presented another mess's meat ration, and there were times when he needed to look especially carefully to pick out bargemen in the hard tack. The fact that he had failed to notice two men on a mast barely thirty feet away was hardly reassuring, and yes, he may well have missed an entire ship in such conditions. "I didn't see it," he added finally, and with more than a trace of defiance.

"An' neither did I." Draude agreed, pressing the man gently with his fist. "As I say, there ain't no blame; the lad weren't even certain. Besides, the old Syllabub can handle any Frenchman up to twice her size." He paused, and brought his hand down as he thought. "But if there is a bunch of 'em out there, perhaps we ought to be a mite careful."

* * *

Three sharp taps on the door to his sleeping cabin and Banks was instantly awake. "What is it?" he demanded, clambering out of the bed and reaching for his watch coat. Had he been alone, the caller would no doubt have entered and spoken with him, but Sarah's presence denied such a liberty.

"Mr Caulfield's duty, sir, and there is a sighting." It was the voice of Chapman, one of the volunteers.

Banks pulled on a pair of duck trousers and thrust his bare feet into boots before pushing his way out of the door. Opposite was the second sleeping cabin that had been hurriedly constructed in the coach to house the governor and his lady. *Scylla* remained in the grips of the storm and Chapman's coat was dripping onto the deck.

"Where away?" Banks snapped as he turned to make for the companionway.

"Eastwards, and there are two ships, sir; though it may be three," the volunteer said, rushing after his captain. "Lookout can't say no more for the present, but Mr Caulfield thought you should be called."

"Who is at the masthead?" Banks was moving past the pantry

now, and the smell of morning coffee came to him. Thompson, his servant, must have the spirit stove alight; it was clearly later than he thought: probably nearly dawn.

"I–I don't know, sir," the midshipman confessed. "Jackson is the watch mid, and has been sent to join him. I was turned up earlier, sir – after the first call."

"First call?" Banks stopped and glanced at the lad. "When was the sighting made?"

"About five minutes ago, sir, though it still ain't clear; no one can say for sure what the ships are or even how many."

Anger flushed through the captain's body. An unidentified sighting had been made – at least two ships, which might well indicate a fleet – and he had been allowed to sleep peacefully while his officers argued amongst themselves over what should be done. Chapman was positively squirming under his gaze, and Banks realised he must have been glaring at the lad. He looked away and continued to make for the deck. Whatever the delay, it was not the boy's fault: the officer of the watch should have called him. A captain should know immediately if his ship was in potential danger. But as he mounted the steep steps and felt a keen draught of air from the outside world on his face Banks slowly realised exactly why he had not been called and that, if anyone was at fault, it was him.

"Good morning, sir," Caulfield called out as Banks mounted the deck and, as he looked about his ship he realised the words were very nearly true. The wind had veered but still blew hard and, though the decks were damp with spray, rain had actually ceased to fall. A rolling mist was being blown above the waves but the first stray fingers of dawn could also be seen stretching across what promised to be a clearer sky. "Sighting to the east," the first lieutenant continued. "Five mile or so off; masthead thinks it to be two ships but cannot be certain."

Banks nodded; the bearing was good news at least, whatever lay out there might not have spotted *Scylla*.

"I would have called you before, sir." The first lieutenant continued awkwardly, "But..."

"Do so in future, if you please, Mr Caulfield," Banks

interrupted. It was not the first time Sarah's presence had disrupted the proper running of the ship, and he knew inside that it would not be the last. However hard she might seek to be otherwise, there was no doubt that a captain's wife could only be a distraction to his officers and men. But that was not Caulfield's fault, nor Sarah's, come to that. The blame, and blame it must be, fell squarely on him and his weakness in thinking a wife could be anything other than a negative aspect aboard a fighting ship.

"Deck there: I have them now!" Jackson's adolescent voice sounded hollow through the speaking trumpet, but it cut through the sound of the wind in the shrouds well enough. "Two ships, less than five miles off an' a third maybe a mile or so beyond."

"Bearing, if you please, Mr Jackson!" Caulfield called back.

A pause, then the lad replied in a more considered voice.

"East nor-east, sir. Larger one appears to be a frigate, with what might be a sloop in company. The third I cannot rightly say."

"What heading?" Banks called this time.

"South, sir. Or as near as makes no difference."

So there were at least three ships off their larboard quarter; they were to windward and heading in roughly the same direction as *Scylla*. One, or even two, might be escorts to a friendly convoy although, this far outside the shipping season, that was unlikely. The second possibility was an enemy force, either merchant ships or a battle squadron; again both were improbable. Few traders would be at sea at this time of year, and France was surely too short of warships free of blockade to waste any this far south. He supposed it was possible that some devilment was being planned elsewhere; a squadron travelling so might be heading to round either the Horn or the Cape. But when he had left Spithead the rumours were of peace; besides with much of their land forces committed, and almost all naval power soundly trapped, it would be foolish of the French to waste a sizeable fleet on what must be a speculative venture. Which only left neutral shipping.

Whale ships were the most likely; many frequented the Atlantic, if only on passage to the Pacific, which would explain their presence at this time of year. Few were of a similar size to a large frigate, but it was not unknown for them to travel with an escort. In fact the longer he thought about the possibility, the more it seemed reasonable, and when Sir Terrance made an appearance on deck, dressed in the only set of tailored oilskins aboard *Scylla*, Banks was in a far better frame of mind.

"We have company, I understand, Captain," the older man said, and it showed how fast dawn was rising that Banks could see dark shadows under the governor's eyes. It was the face of a man who had not slept well.

"Indeed, Sir Terrance, although they should not be detaining us."

"I am relieved to hear it. British, are they?"

"No, neutral; I am fairly certain. But even so we will not be diverted. In addition to yourself, *Scylla* is charged with despatches, and we are under orders to raise St Helena without delay."

"Clearly you must do exactly that, Sir Richard, although I assume you will at least verify the nationality?"

At that moment Caulfield, at the binnacle, called up to the top. "Could they be merchants?"

"I'd say not, sir." Jackson replied. "The first two are hull up and have their fore courses set. Each has a deep cut roach."

As he spoke an extra shaft of light shattered the grey cloud; the low mist seemed to disappear and the first rays of true sun began to lift the gloom of morning, silhouetting the mystery ships and making them visible to those on deck.

"They are clear now." The midshipman's voice was breaking with excitement but no one paid him any further attention. All could see with deadly clarity the outline of warships as they bore down on them.

"Take her west!" Banks ordered, and Caulfield began to bellow. Within seconds the watch on deck was raised from the shelter of the half deck and gangways in order to man the braces as *Scylla* turned her prow towards the last vestiges of darkness.

"Heavy frigate." King, who had appeared without the captain's notice, was staring back at the leading ship. "And that's most likely a sloop – probably what the French would call a corvette."

Banks turned to look, and could only agree. Instinct, coloured in no small way by pride, told him that *Scylla* could deal with any equivalent enemy, or even one slightly larger. But the addition of another man-of-war meant there was no choice other than to run. Judging by her size the second would probably be armed with at least twenty great guns, and there looked to be yet one more close by.

Banks swallowed; it was still conceivable that *Scylla* had not been spotted, and his sudden turn had given them at least temporary security. *Scylla* was certainly a good ship but, when viewed dispassionately, he had to admit she was in sore need of maintenance. Her bottom had not been careened since first commissioned and, though she might still carry a bone with the wind on the quarter, she was liable to be slower than an enemy fresh from the dockyard.

He supposed it was one of the disadvantages of blockade. French ships spent much of their time in harbour and such a lack of exercise meant their crews were ill-trained and in want of experience. But the vessels themselves were likely to be in better order and have gleaming copper below the waterline; a smooth, almost frictionless surface that was free of barnacles and other growth to slow them. In addition, the French designers built for speed, rather than resilience and the hulls they fashioned were far more streamlined. Some might not be as good at withstanding the punishment of prolonged use, but most could outsail an equivalent-sized British ship with ease.

Still, Banks felt he had a few tricks up his sleeve, and was not unduly worried. His main concern was that they were being taken further from their eventual goal. The wind had been against them for some while and, after enduring three day's of storm, there was already a good distance to make up. If the suspect ships gave chase he guessed they would eventually be shaken off, probably after a day's hard sailing, but such a diversion was unlikely to bring them closer to their destination, and must be avoided.

"They're altering course," Jackson's voice cracked out again. "Steering to take us in chase, an' the frigate's making more sail."

So yes, they had been seen, and *Scylla* would have to make a run for it. The next few hours would be crucial; a fast passage had been their intention, and this was going to be anything but. However it was far better for the governor and his entourage to arrive a few days late than not at all. Then the subject of his thoughts cleared his throat, and Banks glanced round to see the elderly man's concerned face.

"Do I assume that they may not be the whalers you had anticipated, Captain?" he asked.

It was then that the frustrations of the journey so far took on an almost physical aspect. His ship was potentially in danger and Banks would need every skill he possessed to see her through the next twelve hours but, whilst doing so, he must also speak with a high ranking official who was bound to want notice and explanations of each move he made. Then, out of the corner of his eye, he noticed two of what was probably the rest of the governor's party emerge from the companionway, doubtless intent on making their first invasion of the quarterdeck that day. Lady Hatcher was likely to be included while Sarah, who had been so able in keeping them from his path earlier in the voyage, was now finding early mornings strangely troublesome, and could not be expected to join the party for some while.

"You will excuse me sir, but I have to attend to my ship," Banks snapped, before rather rudely turning his back and apparently giving all his attention to Caulfield.

"She'll take more sail," Banks said, ignoring the squeal that must have been Lady Hatcher discovering French ships close by. The topsail reefs had been shaken out some hours before, and as forecourse and topgallants were added, *Scylla* soon began to move with more purpose. At first Banks wondered if the extra canvas might even be too much, but the wind that had been a constant companion for so long was now showing signs of being eaten by a rarely seen sun, that was growing in strength as it rose into the sky.

"Do you consider us to be at war, sir?" Caulfield almost whispered, although Banks heard every syllable.

"Frankly I have no idea," he replied, equally guarded;

Hatcher was still standing close by, and he had no wish to involve him in the conversation. "If not, then matters have certainly moved fast, although I should not like to discount it."

In fact he had been concerned since Pitt's resignation; a government led by Addington was bound to look more favourably on peace with France, and so it had proved. They even seemed keen; during his brief visit to London, Banks had run into a former naval officer who now worked in the City. It seemed to be common knowledge in such circles that preliminary discussions with Otto, Bonaparte's commissary, were proving far too slow and time-consuming. Anthony Merry had been sent to France to speak directly with the French government, with the first announcement of an eventual cessation at any time. And all that had been considerably more than two months ago; Britain and France might well not be at war by now, although that would hardly explain why three French warships had been despatched to the South Atlantic, apparently bent on trouble.

Then Banks considered the matter more carefully. Even if proposals had been signed the day after he left Spithead, there would be no definite action taken for some while; plenty of time for the French to raid several East India convoys and probably harvest a fortune. In addition, considering the time news of such an event would take to reach England, their actions would have little effect on the final rounds of peace talks.

Fraiser had joined them, and was consulting his notes as the change of course was marked off on the traverse board. They were still heading south but only to a limited extent, and many degrees from the course that he and Banks would have preferred to set. The sun was climbing steadily and, though there were remnants of storm in the air, the decks had started to grow warm, and some were even steaming. Banks found himself staring, fascinated, at the images of the pursuing ships, each gaining clarity as the light rose above them. Neither flew an ensign, although the lighter colour of their sailcloth and the typical over-sparring of the frigate was as good an indication of nationality as any flag.

Scylla seemed to be maintaining her lead, and it was large enough to keep them safely out of range, but every seaman on board was aware of the current state of their tophamper. Were a spar to carry away a mast spring, or even an important stay part, speed would be lost. Then the enemy would gain and, inevitably, overtake them. Thompson had appeared with hot coffee some while previously and Banks found himself gripping the pewter mug with such force that the pain in his hand reminded him of the drink's existence.

"What do you see there?" he called, before gulping deeply. The liquid was almost stone cold; they must have been standing on the quarterdeck for some considerable while.

"No change, sir," Jackson replied. "The third sighting is still indistinct, though I think the other two might be gaining slightly."

Banks grunted, and handed the half-empty mug to Chapman. That might well be the case, but it would take a goodly time for them to make up *Scylla*'s lead. With luck he could keep the French at bay until nightfall, but still the fact that they were being diverted irritated. And the crew's morale, already dented by two broken promises of home, would hardly be improved by a day-long chase from a superior enemy.

"Forgive me, Captain, but might I ask the position?" Sir Terrance's voice, so close, so loud and so intense, almost made him jump, and Banks swung round with ill concealed annoyance. In doing so he was surprised when the governor met his stare, and even hardened his own expression slightly in response. The older man might allow himself to be bullied by his wife, and usually assumed an attitude of amused indifference in all other matters, but evidently there was harder mettle somewhere deep in his soul. "We know little of the situation, and yet it clearly causes you concern," Hatcher continued, the voice now as soft and unassuming as ever, although his look of steel remained.

Banks cleared his throat. "Indeed, sir: my apologies. The vessels in pursuit are obviously not merchants, as originally suspected, and we are putting as much distance between them and us as is practical."

"But we are still heading for St Helena?"

Heading was not quite the word Banks would have used: bound was better, but it would sound pedantic to say so. "That

26

remains our destination, sir."

The governor nodded, seemingly satisfied, but any relief that Banks might have felt was offset as Lady Hatcher, flanked by her husband's valet, pushed in on them and their conversation.

"Are they not enemy ships, Sir Richard?" she asked.

"It would seem likely, m'lady." From the start of the voyage, Sarah had been on first name terms with both the governor and his lady, but for a variety of reasons Banks did not trust himself to lapse below anything other than formal terms.

"Then why are we not fighting them?" she demanded.

"They are a superior force, Elizabeth," the governor interrupted. "Sir Richard cannot be expected to expose his ship when there is little chance of victory."

The remark nettled Banks; if the present situation were not troublesome enough it was doubly annoying having to explain everything to influential spectators, especially when they drew the wrong conclusion, or answered in his stead.

"We will certainly fight, if it becomes necessary," he told them. "But I remind you that *Scylla* is charged with making as swift a passage as is possible. Consequently, and while it is in our interest, we shall continue to run although, should the situation change in any way, I shall have no hesitation in going into action." Banks addressed the last sentence to his own men on the quarterdeck as much as the Hatchers and delivered it in a slightly louder voice.

"But are they so superior?" Lady Hatcher persisted, with more than a trace of truculence. "Surely this is a British ship? And Malcolm here says that at least one of the enemy is far smaller than us."

The podgy and effeminate manservant preened himself ostentatiously as his name was mentioned.

"One is of a similar size to *Scylla*," Banks agreed. "The other certainly appears smaller, while the third cannot be identified, and there might yet be more over the horizon. But their size is not the only consideration; just the addition of two further vessels, whatever their power, complicates matters."

"I am surprised that mere numbers should influence you,

Captain," Lady Hatcher told him. "And would have thought it a naval officer's duty to fight the Corsican Tyrant, wherever his influence may be found."

Banks felt his anger rise, but he was not going to be browbeaten by rhetoric that might have been lifted from a Gillray cartoon. "Mere numbers will not influence me, m'lady," he replied curtly. "And I will certainly bring any enemy to battle, providing I can foresee a reasonable probability of success. But to expose my ship to such odds with little hope of gain would be foolhardy in the extreme, as would be anyone who attempted to make me do so."

The speech was greeted by silence for several seconds while all on the quarterdeck, passengers and seamen alike, took in the implications. Banks supposed he might have been a little harsh, but it was almost mid morning, and he had yet to take breakfast.

"I am sure you will do whatever is necessary, Sir Richard," the governor told him in a soothing voice that actually annoyed more than it placated. "My wife and I have every confidence in you. And we are also very sensible to the fact that it must be tiresome in the extreme to have us aboard to keep abreast of the situation. Please be assured that there is no one we would rather trust to our safety, and eventual arrival at St Helena, than yourself."

* * *

"Enemies about!" King announced cheerfully as he entered the sickbay. Manning looked up from his ledger.

"So I hears – a veritable battle fleet, or is Kate mistaken?"

His wife emerged from the dispensary carrying a teapot. "I said nothing about a battle fleet," she told them both sternly. "Three ships, no more, and far enough away not to bother us, or so the word has it."

King settled himself on one of the stools. The sickbay was empty of long-term patients, as it had been for the past week or more, and morning surgery had finished over half an hour ago. He had sailed with both the surgeon and his wife for several years and was accustomed to looking in on them whenever the opportunity presented.

"You will take tea, Thomas?" Kate asked.

"That will be welcome; I am on watch in half a glass so it will set me up well."

"Should be a memorable duty," Manning mused. "With a fleet on our tail I suppose we can expect some fancy sailing?"

King sipped quickly at his drink before shaking his head. "I fear not. The leading two might have the edge on us and it is more than three years since *Scylla* was in dry, while the French are like as not fresh from the yard. But whatever the state of their copper, we shall still give them a run and can expect to keep all at arm's length, at least until night."

"And then?" Kate asked.

"Then there may be action," King agreed. "If that is really what you both crave. I'd chance the captain will give it an hour or so, before changing course. Quite what heading he chooses is more his guess than mine, but with nearly twelve hours of darkness ahead, and the possibility of further storm, I'd wager this time tomorrow will see us sailing an empty ocean."

"Then there is nothing to be excited about?" Manning's voice was tinged with feigned disappointment.

"Nothing whatsoever," King agreed. "The French may delay us and that is, of course, regrettable, but they won't stop *Scylla* reaching St Helena. Nor, I trust, getting safely back to England afterwards."

* * *

In fact the storm returned to rescue them long before nightfall. It was four bells in the afternoon watch and the topsails of the third French ship, which all agreed must be another corvette, were finally visible on deck when cloud blanked out the sun. Soon the wind rose up once more and Banks, who had not gone below since dawn, was forced to order a reduction in sail. In no time the chasing enemy was totally consumed by a darkening horizon, while *Scylla* continued under topsails alone.

"We'll keep her as she is, Mr King," he said, after a brief internal debate about having the remaining sails reefed. *Scylla's* masts and spars were not as sound as he would have liked, but her topmen had been heavily used over the past three days, and every bit of speed was vital if he wanted to keep the French at bay. "I shall return within the hour, and then we may expect to alter course and perhaps reduce sail further."

King touched his hat automatically just as the first spots of rain fell and, as the captain reached the companionway, a deluge descended.

"Goodness, is it raining once more?" Sarah said, greeting him on the half deck at the foot of the steps. Together they walked past the marine sentry and into the great cabin. Banks was about to throw off his watch coat when he remembered they were sharing their quarters and he was only wearing trousers and a nightshirt beneath.

"What of the enemy, Sir Richard?" A loud, female voice called from the depths of the great cabin.

"M'lady and Sir Terrance are taking sherry," Sarah whispered conspiratorially.

Banks rolled his eyes; he supposed he must speak with them before changing his clothes. The governor did not worry him greatly, in fact he bore the man a modicum of respect, but at that moment another barbed conversation with Lady Hatcher did not appeal. In addition to a fresh shirt he also wanted food and it was ridiculous that, as captain of the ship, he should have little control over such basic needs.

"Shall I order some eggs and ham to be set for you, my dear?" Sarah asked. "You may take them in our cabin and tell me of the watch." He smiled his thanks as they passed through the double doors from the coach. "And I dare say a pot of coffee would be welcomed," she added softly while her husband braced himself to beard the dragon.

Lady Hatcher was half-seated, half-lying on a stern locker, allowing the governor's sycophantic servant to attend to her nails while Sir Terrance sat more upright on one of Banks' own dining chairs. "So, have you run the French many miles under the horizon?" the woman asked, with more than a hint of condescension.

"I fear not, m'lady," Banks told her gruffly. "But they are no longer a danger to us, nor should they be for the foreseeable future." Despite the watch coat, his nightshirt was burning with damp, and he longed for a hot towel to chafe himself dry.

"Really?" She pulled a sour face. "I would have thought you had time enough to dispose of them. Malcolm here was telling us that British ships are so much faster than anything the French can offer."

Banks bit back the instinctive retort; little would be achieved if he argued with the governor's lady, and nothing at all by contradicting a servant.

"We shall be truly rid of them by nightfall, ma'am," he told her curtly, and made for his sleeping quarters.

"Very well, Sir Richard; just see that we are."

Banks retreated, closed the thin deal door on their frail sanctuary, and breathed out. Sarah was nowhere to be seen and he was almost glad – he had neither the strength nor the wit for conversation. It was impossible to tell if the nightshirt was damp through rain or sweat, but once he was rubbed dry, a little of his normal self began to return. Thompson slipped into the small room with a fresh shirt, britches and stockings, and set about removing his boots. They had been put on over bare feet and the leather seemed to have stuck to his skin so that it became necessary for Banks to sit on the bed, and have his man physically wrench them off. Once free the captain wriggled his toes like a child while Thompson fetched a fresh towel, and it was then that he heard the first of the commotion.

A clatter as both coach doors were thrust open was followed by Lady Hatcher's voice being raised in anger. Then the door to his own sleeping quarters was roughly drawn back, and the slight body of Middleton, who had only just been promoted to midshipman, burst into the tiny room. The boy, seeing his captain sitting on a bed and dressed in just trousers, was taken aback and stumbled, narrowly avoiding falling headlong next to him. Banks looked round in surprise and mild annoyance although any humour in the situation was instantly dissipated.

"Mr King's duty, an' you are needed, sir!" the youngster squeaked breathlessly, his cheeks vividly red against an otherwise white face. "Foretops'l yard 'as sprung, an' he's 'ad to reduce sail. The French are closing on us!"

Chapter Three

It was what Draude had been fearing, but there was no time for recriminations or self reproach. When he had checked the yard, not twelve hours back, it was basically sound. There were no cracks, no dark shakes along the grain or splinters at either arm; in fact, even though the wood was flexing like a long bow, none of the usual indications of how soon the spar would fail were evident. Fortunately he was near the foretop, and thus on hand when it finally went, and now he clambered up the topmast shrouds with his arms straight and neck bent back, so that he could assess the situation. The yard was actually still in one piece, but had sprung on the windward side of the mast, making the sail distort; it would be the devil's own job getting that canvas in safely. He glanced down. There were topmen following him and the boatswain himself had just reached the foretop, but they would need a lad or one of the younger, lighter, hands for the mess to be sorted. Someone who might mount the broken yard and ride it long enough to clue up and unbend the sail. Then the spar could be sent down easily enough using the burtons. But then there were the studding sail booms, he remembered. They would have to be triced up, and it was hardly the weather, or the time, for such an operation.

"What's the damage, Draude?"

He glanced down to see Jameson and Stiles, both reliable topmen, below. The older man, who had shared the last of his duff only a few hours before, drew level as they surveyed the problem.

"Well that looks a proper mess," Stiles said at last. "Thought you checked it during the first watch?"

"I did, 'an it were holding fine," Draude hissed.

"Can't say the same now," Stiles said, before adding, "but then a lot can happen in a few hours," with heavy diplomacy.

"Aye," Draude agreed. "A few hours ago there weren't no Frenchmen about – least none that you could see."

Stiles snorted. "Well let's just hope they don't hear about this." He glanced down and beckoned the younger Jameson to join them. "Else we really will be in the mire."

* * *

Banks dragged the watch coat over his shoulders and began buttoning it up as he ran out of his sleeping quarters, ignoring the screams of mock alarm from the governor's lady in the great cabin as he did. The steps of the companionway were wet, and his bare feet slipped, but he was up on deck, and making for the binnacle in time to hear King, who had the watch, ordering the fore staysail set and mizzen canvas taken in to balance. *Scylla* had slowed and was wallowing slightly as the quartermaster tried to hold her to the fickle wind while, ahead and above, the fore topsail billowed out like an ungainly cloud.

Banks glanced around. The wind had backed further, and King's decision to set the stay sail was exactly right; the alternative, a fore topgallant made fast to the lower foreyard, would have made the ship even more unwieldy. Even so, *Scylla* was going to be a pig to handle, and they were certainly losing speed.

"Take her two points to larboard and call all hands, Mr King," Banks said, while Thompson, who had followed him, attempted to ease one of his captain's feet into a boot. "And clear for action, if you please."

King touched the damp rim of his sou'wester as the boatswain's pipes rose up to compete against the scream of the wind. Banks cursed himself for not taking care and ordering a reef in the topsails earlier. Now, as a consequence of his failure, he had been forced to cause far more disruption. A filthy night, and in the midst of a storm; these were not the best of conditions for breaking down bulkheads and all the associated inconveniences of turning *Scylla* into a proper fighting machine. But the likelihood of engaging the enemy had just risen considerably, and he had no intention of being caught napping twice.

Ahead the boatswain and his team were still trying to contain the billowing mass of canvas that had been the fore topsail, while the broken spar hung above those on deck like some wooden sword of Damocles.

"Maintop, what do you see there?" Banks shouted just as Caulfield arrived, freeing King to go forward and attend to his cherished guns.

"No sign of the enemy, sir. Though it be precious close and we can't see much into the wind."

Banks had supposed that to be the case, even if it was damned annoying. For all he knew the French had already given up the chase and were lying peacefully hove to some way off. He might safely continue at reduced speed, or even alter course further and wait for dawn, or more clement weather, to make repairs. But then it was just as likely that *Scylla* was about to be forereached by a squadron of enemy warships. They might emerge at any moment and begin pounding her with deadly broadsides before disappearing back into the gloom. It was an impossible situation, and he had only himself, and his inattention, to blame for it. Fraiser appeared, briefly saluting, before consulting the compass and weathervane.

"She won't hold the prescribed course, sir," he shouted, even though his captain stood less than three feet from him.

Banks nodded; that was obvious; they would have to turn further south, but exactly how far? Just dropping a few more points might do the trick, but the French could expect him to do that, even without having sustained any damage. Then, despite the cold of a wet dark night, he felt the well-remembered feeling of a plan, and began to shuffle, awkwardly.

There was an idea in the back of his mind, one that he instinctively knew would work, and even turn their ill luck into advantage. Caulfield was approaching and touching his hat, but suddenly Banks had no time to speak with him. If what he intended was to succeed he needed to act quickly, although first there was the small matter of his passengers in the cabin below.

Briefly acknowledging the bemused first lieutenant, Banks made for the companionway once more, and all but tripped down the steep stairs. Below, they were still clearing for action and the great cabin was in the process of being stripped back to make an extension to the gundeck. He paused, uncertain as to where the governor and his lady might be found, then noticed that the temporary sleeping quarters built for them in the coach had not yet been dismantled. He headed there, and tapped urgently on the flimsy door.

The governor's servant opened it, apparently annoyed at the disturbance, but Banks pushed the man aside, and entered. Lady Hatcher was sitting at a tiny dressing table, while the governor lay stretched out upon their bed. Both looked at him with a mixture of surprise and, in the case of Lady Hatcher, irritation.

"Forgive the intrusion, Sir Terrance, but a matter has arisen and I must wait upon you without delay."

"Of course, Sir Richard." The governor rose and indicated the only free chair in the tiny room. "Won't you take a seat?"

Banks brushed the suggestion aside like an annoying fly. "Sir, we have sustained damage aloft and need to alter course."

"I was aware of that Captain, but fail to see..."

"On our previous heading we were likely to remain safe from the French," Banks continued, interrupting the governor. "Turning south, which we must, will take us into danger, and might mean they overtake us: with the damage encountered, we cannot make good speed."

The governor nodded.

"I intend to take us further to the east and believe they will not be expecting such a move. *Scylla* can then make better use of stay sails and jibs. With luck, such a heading should see us clear of their attentions for good."

"Then you must do so, sir."

"There is, however, the chance that we will be brought to battle. Should the French not be placed as we anticipate, such a course will see us sailing directly for them. It is extremely possible we will find ourselves in action, and against a vastly superior enemy."

"I see," the governor commented briefly.

"*Scylla* is charged with both despatches, and your own protection, sir. As captain I may act as I wish, but felt it correct to at least consult with you before making such a move."

For all his vague and indulgent attitude it was clear that the governor was blessed with a sharp mind when it was needed. "I quite understand, Sir Richard, and appreciate your concern."

Banks waited, conscious of his fingers that were almost twitching with anticipation.

"As I see it there is no decision to be made. We must make St Helena, and the presence of a hostile squadron will not improve our chances of doing so. But as you said yourself, to head directly south will not in any way avoid action, so surely it is far better to do as you intend; that way at least if we do meet them it will be upon our own terms."

"Thank you, sir," Banks said, with absolute sincerity. "Then if you will excuse me…"

"Of course, Sir Richard."

Banks turned to go, but remembered the presence of Lady Hatcher and stopped. "Forgive me, Sir Terrance – m'lady – but you cannot remain here."

The governor's wife raised an eyebrow, and something of her customary menace returned. "Indeed, Captain? It is our room after all, pray why should we choose to leave?"

"If battle is joined it will not be safe," Banks said, the urgency almost making him dance with anxiety. "This cabin itself will not exist shortly as we are clearing for action. You must take yourself below – to the orlop at the very least, though I would rather you were in a position of even greater safety; perhaps one of the holds?"

"One of the holds?" the woman positively cried out.

"It will not be for longer than a few hours, m'lady," the captain replied. "You will find my wife, and Mrs Manning on the orlop, pray speak to them and they shall make you safe." Banks turned and almost bumped into the smug face of the governor's valet. "See that she does!" he ordered curtly, before pushing past the man, and out of the cabin.

* * *

Fifteen minutes later the ship had cleared for action and was sailing to the south-east. On the gundeck, Flint and his team, most of whom were also members of his mess, had both cannon under their charge cleared away, and were gathered about the larboard piece. The gun was run out and a fair amount of spray and spume came in through the port, but the gangway that ran above provided a modicum of shelter and, as they had been stood down, most were huddled together under it. Ostensibly they had done so for warmth, although there was also an unspoken element of mutual support. The wind was now almost abeam; with all feasible staysails and jibs set, *Scylla* was back to sailing close to her potential and, despite the weather and the fact that over half of them should be asleep, her crew were in reasonable spirits. After the inevitable exhilaration of clearing for action they were now at rest, but every man seemed ready for what was to come, and there was a tension in the air that all were aware of, even though none spoke, or even moved, unless it was absolutely necessary.

The call from the masthead came a few minutes later and was enough to break the spell and stir them into action, despite the fact that few caught exactly what was said. All about the deck, men began to stand to, taking up positions without being ordered, and Flint clapped his hands and rubbed them together as he squinted down the barrel of the favoured gun that they had christened *Maggie Jane*.

"Target to larboard." King's voice rang out above the storm while Middleton, the duty midshipman, scampered along the deck, repeating the lieutenant's words. Jameson, peering out of the port, remained silent. The men looked to each other; it was frustrating in the extreme, knowing an enemy was out there, but having no idea exactly what, or where. Another call came from the maintop, and this time they were all ready to listen.

"Looks like one of the corvettes, hard on the larboard bow, an' less than two cables off!"

The men braced themselves as King shouted once more.

"We'll be altering course to cross her hawse as fine as we can. It will be individual fire, so make sure of your mark!"

The tension mounted further as, still without speaking, Flint helped himself to a burning length of slow match from the nearby tub and fitted it to a linstock. With conditions as they were, a misfire from the gunlock was far more likely, and there would not be the time for a second chance.

"Captain's a rum cove," Timmons muttered with grudging respect, as Flint blew on the glowing end of the burning twine and warmed his hand next to it. "He could not have set us fairer."

Timmons was another new arrival on board; he only joined during their brief stay at Spithead but as an experienced hand he was already integrated into both Flint's mess and gun crew.

"The Frogs might be in the right place, but them's still got the wind," Dixon countered.

"Aye, but we've position," Timmons stated loftily before taking a kick at one of the ship's mousers that was straying too close. "He's a canny bugger and no mistaking."

Flint said nothing; he was wise enough to know that, in the current conditions, luck would figure far more prominently than skill. Still it was good that the enemy was off their bow, and not across it, and the fact that *Scylla* was turning to meet them indicated space enough for a considered rake.

* * *

On the quarterdeck Banks' thoughts were travelling along a similar path. There had been no great surprise in finding the French; as soon as the idea had come to him he had somehow known they would be there. But the fact that *Scylla* had met them as she had, when it would have taken no great error of judgement to see them across her own prow, bolstered him. It was their first piece of good luck for some while; pretty much the whole voyage, in fact. The storm was still raging about them, and there was little possibility of seeing anything from the deck at that moment, but Chapman, who had relieved Jackson at the main top, was keeping them informed, and it appeared they had yet to be spotted. Caulfield was standing near by, as he had done for many years and countless actions, while Fraiser, another stalwart from the past, was by the binnacle, his folded notes clamped securely under one arm. Lieutenant King, who had joined him several years ago as a mere midshipman, was forward with the guns that he had made his own. Banks supposed there were finer officers in the service, but these were men he knew well and could trust; there were none he would rather see action alongside.

"Enemy's turning to starboard, I think we're smoked!" Chapman's voice rose above the storm again and all stiffened. Then the ghostly image of a jib boom emerged from the darkness to larboard, and a murmur that quickly grew into a cheer erupted from all about.

"Stand by your guns!" King's order came up from below, but no one needed any further encouragement. They were perfectly placed: in less than a minute *Scylla* would be crossing the corvette's bows. For the first time in what seemed like an age, Banks drew breath, and even as his ship prepared to deliver a devastating broadside, a faint smile spread across his face.

Chapter Four

The night was lit by fire from the first gun, and the brightness grew as each successive piece added their own tongue of flame to the blaze. Standing by the larboard bulwark, Banks was momentarily blinded by smoke from the nearby carronades, although the air cleared long enough for him to see the damage they were inflicting. The enemy's beakhead was being peppered with shot that also carried away the dolphin striker, and dislodged her starboard anchor. Robbed of downward tension, her jib fell slack, and the corvette turned slightly with the wind. Darkness closed in almost immediately, although a faint glow still marked the Frenchman's position as *Scylla* slinked away into a heavier patch of squall and apparent obscurity.

"Masthead!" The captain's voice rose up through the last of the shots. "What do you see there?" It would take several minutes for *Scylla*'s guns to be reloaded, and one of the other enemy vessels may be close by. There was a pause; no one replied, and he was about to shout again when an older man's voice finally responded.

"No sign of fresh shipping, sir."

Banks guessed that Chapman had been foolish enough to look directly at the broadside, and had lost his night vision. It was a mistake most only made the once, and at least the regular lookout had been a little more experienced. He crossed the deck to join the first lieutenant at the binnacle.

"Keep her as she is, Mr Caulfield." With the damage they had inflicted, the corvette was unlikely to follow, and *Scylla* was sailing sweetly enough as she was: it would be a mistake to turn if there were no further enemy in the immediate area.

"A sound broadside, sir." The first lieutenant's teeth shone white in the gloom. "And no returns!"

Banks supposed he was right, but any success they had achieved was down to luck rather than skill; they could just as easily have come across the enemy with the positions reversed. Then it would have been his ship to suffer damage, and at any time now they could expect to be descended upon in force.

"What news, Sir Richard?"

Banks swung round at the unexpected call, and saw the governor picking his way across the deck.

"You should be below, sir: it is not safe!" The storm, and his annoyance, turned Banks' shout to a roar, but he noticed the old man met it with hardly a blink.

"There are men a plenty on deck, Captain," he replied calmly, holding a hand to the brow of his sou'wester to deflect the rain. "And boys too, if it comes to it. My presence here will make little difference."

"As you will, sir." Banks had no time to waste. There were still enemy ships in the area and if the governor was determined to place himself in danger he was old enough to be allowed.

"Did you hear the gunfire, Sir Terrance?" Caulfield asked.

"Hear it, sir?" The old man's face lit up. "Why I suspect they did so in England! Did we do the enemy harm?"

"Indeed so," Caulfield replied, slightly smugly. "It were one of the smaller vessels, though they are still of a considerable size. We have damage aloft and the storm to weather, but that particular Frenchman will have work to do before he troubles us again."

"And the others?" the governor asked. "They are still a threat?"

Caulfield looked at his captain, and Banks cleared his throat. "Potentially, yes. They may well have seen the fire from our broadside. But it is a dark night, and in the current conditions we should remain safe."

"Excellent, sir; truly excellent: I must go and tell her Ladyship." Sir Terrance beamed again, then, holding his sou'wester down firmly on to his head, started back for the companionway once more. Banks drew a sigh of relief; he supposed he should ensure that the couple were suitably accommodated below, but found he cared little either way. Then Chapman's voice could be heard, shrill and urgent from the main top, and all thoughts of his passengers' safety were forgotten.

"Sail ho! Fine on our larboard bow, and set to rake us!"

The boy's screech alerted everyone on deck.

"Port the helm – take her to starboard!" Banks roared, although the quartermaster was starting to turn the wheel even as the order was given. *Scylla* baulked at the rough handling, while the afterguard slipped and stumbled on the wet deck as they tried to keep the square sails in the wind. Chapman's sighting could equally be the frigate or the second corvette, but whichever it was, all knew they were in imminent danger.

The enemy was in almost as good a position as *Scylla* had been only minutes before. Banks felt his knuckles whiten as he stared forward while the ship paid off. Were it the second corvette her broadside was bound to be lighter than that of the frigate, but even she would cause considerable damage, and with the larboard battery not fully loaded, Banks would be unable to reply.

"There she is!" Caulfield shouted, pointing forward suddenly. *Scylla* had just moved into clearer air, and all gasped as the enemy frigate was revealed. Well set up and with the wind in her favour, she was speeding into the perfect position and appeared almost beautiful in the foul night. But less attractive was the line of heavy cannon that were run out, and about to fire on *Scylla*'s own, vulnerable, bows.

Caulfield was muttering something unintelligible, and Fraiser had thoughtfully positioned himself behind the trunk of the main mast, but Banks found he could do nothing other than stare fascinated at the sight of a powerful enemy ship: so close by and so very deadly.

When it came, the broadside hit them on their larboard bow, and was not a total rake. The shots were also delivered at a measured ripple, rather than the spasmodic but considered fire that *Scylla* had dealt out upon her sister. But, despite the inferior angle, the enemy's ball did their business well enough, and shrieks of wounded men soon began to compete with the wind's monotonous scream.

"Damage report, Mr Middleton!" Banks shouted down at the midshipman on the deck below, but a ship's boy was already scampering back along the gangway.

"Mr King s-sent me, sir," the youngster – a third class volunteer whose normal duty was to carry powder to the guns – touched his forehead in a hurried salute. During the last five minutes he had heard *Scylla*'s guns fired in anger for the first time, been the target of an enemy broadside, and was now delivering an important message to his captain.

"The larboard forechains is weakened, and won't take no pressure. Wants us to reduce sail, so he does – and says to be quick about it, if you plan on seeing your mother again."

The boy started as he realised what King had actually meant, but Banks' brain was already at work.

"Port the helm – prepare to wear ship. Larboard battery fire as you are served!"

The ship heaved further to starboard, and *Scylla* was thrown round, rough and clumsy until the wind passed over her taffrail. With the foremast effectively out of use on the larboard tack to take the wind to starboard was his only option. It would mean they should have the chance of paying back their tormentor, but such a sudden move was potentially dangerous to his ship, especially as her tophamper had already proved vulnerable.

Scylla groaned at the apparent mishandling, but her larboard guns fired as she bore round, and soon she had settled on the starboard tack, heading away from the frigate that had shown herself to be so deadly and into the darkness of the storm. King himself approached, just as a fresh deluge of heavy rain began to fall.

"We've taken two direct hits to the fore channel and its mounting, sir." he said, almost inches away from his captain's ear. "Long as we stay on the starboard tack all should be well, but if we have to take the wind to larboard I doubt the mast will hold for very long."

"Can anything be done?"

"Carpenter's looking at it now, sir, but I would say it will not be a quick repair. We shall need daylight, and fine weather."

Banks stared back into the storm that currently hid both French ships. As long as they remained so, there was nothing he need fear; the storm was concealing *Scylla* well enough and he had several hours in which to truly lose them. "Daylight, and fine weather." The lieutenant's words seemed to reverberate about his brain: were there Frenchman about when King got his wish, *Scylla* would be easy pickings.

"Very well. There is no other damage?"

"Nothing substantial, sir; I'd say we got off remarkably lightly, though it is a dark night for target practice. Several men have been wounded, including the governor, or so I believe."

"Sir Terrance?" A sudden gust of wind made Banks snatch at his hat and it was with effort that he avoided swearing out loud. With a superior enemy to windward, and a ship that could not sail east, he now had to worry about an old man who was unable to keep himself out of danger. "How badly?"

"I couldn't rightly say, sir. He had been watching the larboard battery reload – they were attending to him as I was heading here."

A shout came from forward; the boatswain was rigging a preventer stay from the main chains to the foremast, and Evans, the carpenter, seemed to be tearing away part of the larboard top rail. There was still no sign of the French, but even without their attention, Banks decided he had enough to do to keep himself occupied for a good few hours. The governor could look after himself.

* * *

The next morning brought the British mixed fortune. The storm eased as dawn broke, and as the sun drew strength it was clear they had the ocean effectively to themselves. Evans and his team had made an assessment of the repairs needed to the forechains and started work as soon as the weather permitted. By mid-morning they had secured them to the extent that shrouds and stays could start to be fixed and the Welshman was confident that all would be totally set to rights by evening. Aloft, the foretop yard had been fished and correctly set, then, when the wind had backed slightly *Scylla* had been allowed to take it square on her

45

stern, and began to run south once more, and at a truly credible speed.

Other damage, sustained both from the broadside and during the storm, was also in the process of being repaired. Three men were dead, but the six who had been severely wounded were considered stable enough and expected to make a full recovery. The only blight on what would otherwise have been a perfect morning was the governor, who had been pronounced dead some hours before.

To Banks it appeared that, simply to maintain its presence, their current run of bad luck had decided Sir Terrance should be struck by a splinter no larger than a ship's biscuit. Such wounds were common, and often accounted for a large number of casualties. But in the governor's case, one that would normally have hardly caused a minor flesh wound had severed the iliac artery, and the man had bled to death within minutes.

It was a disaster of course: they had yet to raise St. Helena but, with the main reason why *Scylla* was not now safely in a Portsmouth dockyard dead, the mission had already failed. Banks might not be personally responsible for the death, but he had still allowed it to happen, and the mere fact that Hatcher died aboard his ship would not look good in the report. Robert Brooke, the previous governor of St Helena, had retired some time ago: as it was Sir Terrance would have found a good deal of catching up to do on his arrival and goodness knew how long it would take before a fresh man was appointed. There was a strong argument for *Scylla* turning back now, make for England without further delay, bringing the news, and Hatcher's body, with her. But the ship was also charged with despatches and these were obviously valuable enough not to be chanced to the Company's own packet service. Some were for onward transfer to India, and Banks could not begin to estimate their worth. Additionally there was the consignment of specie that he had privately undertaken to deliver. But the final point in favour of continuing was the enemy squadron that lay between him and Portsmouth. With every mile that *Scylla* made southwards the chances of meeting them again decreased, but to turn back would be an entirely different proposition. Three ships, properly handled, were far harder to evade than one, and a meeting with any would be liable to bring the entire French force down about their ears. For all his outward confidence Banks knew his ship was not in a fit state for such an action and, with no other Royal Navy vessel for many miles, rescue was unlikely.

No, Banks decided, he would not turn back – however large or small the other considerations as such a move was contrary to all his instincts. He would arrive in St Helena, explain the situation, and deliver the gold and despatches. With luck he may be able to off-load Lady Hatcher as well, although he supposed that might be too much to hope for. But with nothing else to keep him there, and *Scylla*'s need of the dockyard now even greater, he could be confident of setting sail for England again without undue delay. The shipping season was not due to start for a month or more, so there would be no convoy to escort; he could take on wood and water, and be homeward bound within a week. The thought cheered him, as much as anything could that morning. Then another came to replace it; one he had been carefully setting to the back of his mind since first hearing the news of Sir Terrance's death.

For reasons that he was in no way proud of, Banks had stayed on deck all night, keeping distant and, claiming the responsibilities of a captain, immersing himself in his work. But he could not go on ignoring the problem forever, and he guessed that such cowardly tactics were only making it harder for Sarah, who had no such sanctuary. The bell rang for the change of watch, and he decided that now would be as good a time as any to leave the deck, and discover for himself just how Lady Hatcher was reacting to the news of her husband's death.

* * *

In fact she was taking it remarkably well. Perched on a stern locker in the great cabin with Sarah next to her and a rummer full of gin in one hand, she was alternately sobbing and laughing, whilst expertly blocking any attempts at consolation with a soliloquy that seemed destined to last the rest of the voyage.

"It wasn't the greatest marriage but then, how many are? I'm sure you have had bad periods with the captain."

Sarah opened her mouth to reply, but the woman was firmly in train.

"All men are like hounds," Lady Hatcher said firmly, then paused, as if the statement had surprised her as much as it had the captain's wife. "I mean, there might be minor differences." She waved her glass in explanation. "Spots not exactly in the same place, and some may be fatter. Terrance was quite fat," she whispered as an aside. "But a dog is a dog and, when all is said and done, they all behave the same." Her analogy had clearly sapped a good deal of energy and Sarah thought Lady Hatcher would be quiet for a moment, but the tirade was relentless.

"And even with Terrance, and his funny little ways, – he was no different, not really. But then peers of the realm are only flesh and blood, except I don't need to tell you that, my dear – I am sure that you are only too well aware." She laughed for a moment then stopped abruptly and drank deep from her glass, only apparently surfacing to draw breath.

"And there were younger and more handsome men available – well available to one in a position such as mine," she went on to explain, while treating Sarah to a condescending look. "Some may even have proved more pleasing company but few, few had such position, or potential."

Sarah supposed that the governorship of St Helena was indeed important, and was about to say so when the flow was released once more.

"You see St Helena is a pivotal place, and in such a primary position," Lady Hatcher assured her seriously, before looking down and acknowledging the need to dab at the front of her gown with the handkerchief that actually belonged to Sarah. "Our Eastern trade depends on it. Scrimp on the supervision and all shall surely suffer." Once more the handkerchief was needed. "Yet the trade that passes through it is worth millions. Millions!" She paused yet again and a far away look appeared in her eye – the thought had clearly affected the woman greatly. Then she blew her nose.

"But such responsibility is never dependant on the skills of one man," Sarah said, grabbing the opportunity. "And I am certain another will be found to fill Sir Terrance's place – professionally that is. You must not worry: the country shall not suffer."

"I couldn't give a fig for the country," Lady Hatcher told her briskly in a voice that might just as easily have come from a Privy Garden fen. "Or some pox ridden island in the midst of nowhere, come to that."

"No, of course not," Sarah agreed, hurriedly.

"And as for the work, any damned fool could do it, that's why they have aides, isn't it?" Another gulp of her drink and some of the woman's composure was restored. "But what of the position? The influence? The opportunity?"

Sarah supposed she did not know, and was starting to doubt the actual cause of Lady Hatcher's grief when she heard sounds of her husband's approach through the double coach doors. She looked up, and flashed a warning but it was too late: Banks had already entered.

The woman focused on him slowly and a strange tension seemed to take her over. Banks tried to appear agreeable, but the look was not reflected on the face of the governor's widow.

"Yes, Captain?" she asked coldly. "May I be of service to you?"

He inclined his head slightly. "I wish only to express my condolences, m'lady," he said. "I was most sorry to hear of..."

"Sorry be damned! Sir Terrance was killed whilst under your protection and I will not listen to any such hypocrisy." She drew breath. "This ship had no business in engaging the French. Had you given more attention to the safety of your charges my husband would be alive now, and I will make sure the relevant authorities are aware of the fact. Now if there is nothing else I can assist you with, I would prefer a little privacy at this difficult time. Good day to you, sir."

Chapter Five

"To be absolutely precise, sir, we shall enter the southern hemisphere at approximately four o'clock tomorrow morning." Fraiser paused and his expression relaxed slightly. "But I don't expect the exact time is of great importance."

"Indeed not, master," Banks agreed.

The storm, along with the last sighting of the French, was almost two weeks before, and *Scylla*, her crew, and more importantly, the remainder of her passengers, were now settled somewhat. Damage to the ship had also been attended to, as far as was possible without dockyard facilities. The fished fore topmast yard had been replaced with a main yard that Evans, the carpenter, had trimmed to fit. Banks had reconciled what some might regard as the wasting of a larger spar quite easily; the fore topsail was heavily used, and however tightly any reinforcement could be bound, or 'fished', some degree of movement was inevitable. Using the larger yard gave much needed strength in a vital place and, as *Scylla* was fortunate in carrying two such spars, a further was still available should the need arise.

After the hardships of the storm, the crew were also back to their normal routine, with all but the idlers getting one full watch off out of every two along with the occasional make and mend holidays to break up the monotony. Their food had also improved: the galley fire now burned hot and long enough to provide for more than the chosen few. Once more they were enjoying two pounds of preserved beef or a pound of pork four times a week together with biscuit, cheese, oatmeal, dried fruit and peas, all washed down with half a pint of spirit daily. It was the diet they knew and infinitely superior to any the majority might expect on shore. The brief action – firing their guns in anger for the first time in over a year and, ironically, receiving enemy shot in return – had also left a positive impression. They had been reminded that, rather than being mere sailors, they were proper man-of-war's seamen: prime stuff and the pride of England. Most of *Scylla's* people had seen action before, either in her, or other ships, but now everyone was considered proven and could even be considered seasoned: baptised by the smoke and fire of true action, and undoubtedly eager to repeat the process at the earliest opportunity.

The governor's personal entourage had also come to terms with their master's death, as well as the fact that the best some could look forward to was an immediate return trip to England. Most were philosophical enough to take such an outcome well, with only a few showing more than a degree of bitterness or disappointment. But any resentment was dwarfed by that exhibited by Lady Hatcher.

From the outset it was made clear that she blamed the captain personally for the loss of her husband, and there had been stony silences at the dining table together with rapid departures from the quarterdeck whenever he had the temerity to show his face until, by unspoken agreement, her meals began to be taken in solitary splendour in the great cabin after the usual dining hour. It also became common for her late husband's servant to enquire of Thompson, the captain's steward, exactly when Sir Richard might be free of the deck, to allow her to take the air in private: an arrangement that Banks was happy to co-operate with whenever possible.

Nothing more had been said of her accusations and he felt he had disguised the fact that they continued to concern him. He had however noted that others, his officers and specifically Sarah, were not quite so blasé. Lady Hatcher clearly attracted influence as easily as she did money, and however sound Banks' reputation, mud was inclined to stick. Normally such accusations might also have been supported by the crew. The average British sailor was known for his sentimental tendencies and, when asked to choose between a blousy yet arguably attractive widow against the man who had the power to see any of their backs stripped to the bone at a grating, some undercurrent of support could be expected. But, in that respect at least, Banks, and his officers were fortunate and felt they could count upon the men's support. Lady Hatcher might be of common stock, but the adoption of a title had wiped away any loyalty she may have expected from the lower deck. Her behaviour with the cabin stewards and anyone else unfortunate enough to enter her web had also not gone unreported and, however mawkish the crew might appear at times, few could feel any great sympathy for her. To them, a supposed lady who indulged in so many of their own vices was more a subject of derision than pity.

"Was there anything else, Captain?"

Banks realised his mind had wandered, and he must have been staring aimlessly while the sailing master waited.

"No, Mr Fraiser. Thank you: that will be all."

The elderly warrant officer made as if to return below, then stopped at the mouth of the quarterdeck ladder.

"If it is of any assistance I would say the weather will hold, sir," he said. "At least until the end of the afternoon."

Banks was momentarily taken aback. "In what way will that help, Mr Fraiser?"

The sailing master lowered his head slightly. "I had assumed you were planning celebrations: for the passing of the line, sir. And I guessed that was why you sent for me."

The man was quite right: Banks had completely forgotten, so lost was he in his own thoughts. He glanced up at the sky and felt the wind on his freshly shaven cheek; the morning had certainly dawned bright and clear and, although the sun was hardly over the rim of the horizon, it was already hot.

"Why yes, master, that was exactly what I had in mind." It wasn't the first time the older man had effectively read his thoughts. "So you would say that we should go ahead with the ceremony?"

Fraiser took a step nearer his captain, and his face relaxed into what might generously be called a smile. "You'll excuse me, sir, but as a Christian man I can have little truck with such superstitions."

Banks said nothing. His own faith was far less defined than Fraiser's although, in a largely God-fearing world, it was usually better not to admit as much.

"But I accept that to some they are important, and if it has to be done, today would be as good as any."

Most of *Scylla's* people were seasoned hands, yet a good few would not have travelled south before and the ritual of crossing the line was so fixed in naval tradition that Banks knew he would have to make some concession. But to stop the ship, as was customary, and waste what would be the whole afternoon as well as both dog watches in tomfoolery went totally against the grain. And it wasn't as if the whole performance was nothing more than harmless fun; all knew that the various escapades were often used as a means for righting wrongs or getting even. Men frequently suffered minor injuries under the banner of horseplay, and there were tales aplenty of ceremonies aboard other ships that had ended in maimings and worse.

"If you are considering inviting royalty aboard, sir, I'm sure the men would appreciate some notice."

Once more the master was right, much of the morning would also be lost to the absurd preparations; Banks felt plagued with bad luck – this voyage was turning out to be one of the worst he could remember.

"Could we not simply hold a tournament of King Arthur?" he asked hopefully.

Fraiser eyed him cautiously. Such a game, which required little preparation and hardly any risk, would indeed be a far easier alternative, but unlikely to satisfy men keen on one of their few official jollies. "Do you think the people would accept that, sir?"

"I could combine it with an extra ration of beer," Banks persisted. "And call a make and mend for the following afternoon?"

"It may serve, sir, but I feel they would not take to it," Fraiser said softly. "No man chose to be sent south; all would far rather be in England at present and some might even say they had a right to be so. But as they are here, they will expect their traditions to be respected."

Banks knew Fraiser was correct, and even the presence of a hostile squadron somewhere to the north would not be excuse enough to cancel the event. He would have to abandon the day, give it over to folly and foolishness, just to appease a group of men who found pleasure in such banality. It was annoying, but a morose crew was that much worse and, despite the recent action, he had noticed certain signs of discontent which it would be prudent not to encourage. Yet again Banks was grateful to Fraiser for his guidance: the sailing master might not always be the most cheerful of company, but there was much wisdom stored in that wizened old face.

"Very well, Mr Fraiser; I shall speak to the first lieutenant, and the men can elect a King, or whatever else they wish. You have been south before, I trust?"

"Oh yes, sir," Fraiser assured him. "And yourself, sir?"

"Indeed, master: more times than I care to remember." Fraiser turned for the quarterdeck ladder once more, and it was only then that Banks remembered that it was Sarah's first deep sea voyage.

* * *

"I'll have you know I've crossed the line more times than most aboard this ship," Kate replied truculently as she shook out a freshly washed bandage and started to roll it expertly between her fingers. "And went through all that pollywog malarkey when I was but a child."

"Then you will have no reason to be involved," Manning said softly, and with some relief. His wife was very much stronger now, but he still wished to avoid stressing her unnecessarily. "It will just be a few japes in the afternoon – you may watch if you wish, though much of it can be a little coarse."

"A little coarse?" She snorted. "I should say; my father was forced to break up such ceremonies in the past, and that was in a merchant ship with far less crew. And they did not have the access to alcohol that your Royal Navy finds so essential. It may have escaped notice, Robert, but we do not have the happiest of people aboard at present."

"The men are disappointed," he replied. "Nothing more; there is no harm in them. We have both been aboard a ship where there was mutiny and I cannot say the feeling is the same."

"Oh the men respect their officers right enough, and much has improved since the action. But they were all but promised a run ashore on two previous occasions, and even dropped anchor at Spithead, only to be left swinging for the best part of a month, before sailing south."

"So, perhaps a little frivolity will ease the mood," he chanced. "Cheer them up somewhat." He glanced at his wife surreptitiously; if anyone could do with being cheered up it was her.

"*Scylla* is currently tinderbox dry," Kate continued firmly, her attention still ostensibly set on the bandages. "A bit of light heartiness is fine, but things can so easily go the other way. In fact it might equally provide the necessary spark to set her ablaze."

* * *

"It will just be a few japes in the afternoon." On the berth deck Flint was unknowingly repeating the surgeon's words. "And I reckons that as a topman, and one who can handle himself, you'll be getting off light. It's the lads what 'as to watch theirselves: them and any women what might be about."

"Who are they choosing as King Neptune?" Jameson asked, even though there only seemed to be one possible candidate.

"That would be Mitchell," Dixon, the oldest member of the mess, replied. "Though I don't believe he were chosen," he continued. "I think he chose himself."

"He's got the build for it," Flint conceded. "And the muzzle."

Certainly there was little doubting that the holder's massive frame, which was almost entirely bone and muscle, made him the ideal candidate to play a king of the ocean, and the man even sported the only beard aboard *Scylla*. Facial hair of any sort was not officially approved of but Mitchell's station, in the darker regions of the ship, kept such minor infringements far from official notice, while his temper, which was as legendary as his strength, was enough to dissuade most from taking the matter further.

"That fribble from the governor's party is going to be queen,"

Dixon continued. "Can't say I cares for him much m'self, but there's a few of that persuasion who do and, you got to admit, he comes up well enough in a frock."

"Have they chosen a Davy Jones?" Flint asked.

"Hind," Dixon told them. "He may be a painter but working so much with turpentine means he's got the cleanest hands of all, even if he don't always smell so good. There are no end of volunteers for bears. Captain was asked for a sail to be slung over the side, but that weren't allowed apparently. The ship ain't stoppin' neither."

"There's a good chance the French are still over the horizon," Flint reminded them. "An' this will be no more than a bit of fun."

"Aye, but you can't work up much excitement," Dixon grumbled. "Not in a couple of hours and with us still under sail."

"Any real women takin' part?" Flint asked: Dixon shook his head.

"None can get near the lady's maid and the only one that might have been sporting enough is Mrs Manning. But she's already a shellback several times over: anyways, she's been a cross old cat for most of this voyage, an' her husband would never agree."

"Can't say as I blame him," Jameson commented dryly.

"Nor I," Flint agreed. "Things are liable to get out of hand."

"We had a prime doxie one time," Dixon told them, sparking suddenly into life and apparently shedding several years. "In 'eighty-nine, when we was headin' for New South Wales in a transport. We'd got the wench suitably drenched, an' was starting on the shaving when her dress just started comin' adrift in our 'ands. The drab was almost fully unrigged before her flash man stepped in. It were a pity," he added sadly. "She was more'n willing."

"When do we start?" Jameson, who was beginning to feel a little uncomfortable, asked.

"Four bells in the afternoon watch," Flint told him. "An' all has to be shipshape again by 'Up Spirits'."

"So, there won't be much time for the trials," Dixon mused then, fixing his gaze on Jameson, winked broadly. "Nor the

56

punishments."

* * *

King had been delegated to supervise arrangements, and stood with Cahill, a passed midshipman who had shipped as a master's mate. Cahill had the watch and both men stood at the break of the quarterdeck. Forward, a well-used royal had been rigged from the edge of the barge to the starboard gangway netting and brim filled with seawater, which was regularly slopping down onto the gundeck below. King supposed he should order the mess to be swabbed, but there would doubtless be more to clear up later. An empty gun carriage, padded out with unrolled hammocks, was in a position of prominence on the forecastle to seat Neptune himself, and two further mess benches had been placed to either side, presumably for his cortège. Next to one stood a wooden kid, which was filled with what looked like sweepings from the manger. The muck had been mixed with a little water, and now had the consistency of stiff porridge, if not the smell. A line of twelve marines, crisp in full uniform, stamped past, blocking his view.

"All present, Mr Jarvis?" King asked the corporal who accompanied them.

"Aye, sir," the man answered, saluting smartly. "I've men detailed to the fo'c'sle and half deck, and will retain four here for the quarterdeck. Bayonets will be fixed and muskets loaded," he said, as if reciting. "We'll not 'ave no trouble."

King was glad to hear it, but still felt vaguely uncomfortable about the whole procedure. It had already been agreed that no other officer would be witnessing and all women should stay below. This was partly, King assumed, to play down the event, but it did mean that he would be in sole charge, and that was not a prospect he particularly relished.

The ship's bell rang; it was time for all to begin, and King was wondering if he should make some sort of announcement when a cheer, followed by the sound of running feet, came up from the deck below.

"Lordy, will you look at that!" Cahill was staring down, and King followed his gaze. Mitchell, the half-man half-bear who all but ran the ship's bilges, was being carried on a lighter made from two sweeps connected by canvas. He was clad in a woman's floral *robe-de-chambre* that was open to the waist and waved an iron loggerhead in his right hand as if it weighed no more than a child's toy. There was some sort of crown on his head, and his black mane, for once untied, had been dusted white with flour and flowed down the sides of his bovine face. Both shoulders were partially bare and the mighty beard, also dusted, filled the open neck in the gown, finally disappearing into the garment, or merging with the thick shag of his chest fur.

"It's something to frighten the children," King agreed. Four men carried the bier, and they manoeuvred Mitchell, not too delicately, up the forecastle ladder, before dumping their load next to the gun carriage with a thump that echoed about the ship.

Mitchell bellowed, but it was a good-natured roar, and he eased himself up, and onto the throne with remarkable dignity. Someone else, with a lavishly painted face and adorned in a decorated woman's gown, seated themselves on a bench alongside while Hind, carrying a barrel hoop that had been twisted into the shape of a razor, placed himself more awkwardly to Mitchell's left. Other seamen swarmed up the gangway and onto the forecastle, pressing themselves into place, and nudging each other for the best view. Corporal Jarvis ordered his men back to create more space, although King was pleased to note the marines remained alert and stiff-faced, despite the jovial spirit that seemed to permeate the hands.

A boatswain's mate that King knew to be illiterate stepped forward with an ornate scroll and began to apparently read. "Hear ye, pray silence for his most glorious oceanic majesty, *Neptunus Rex*, ruler of the seas and all who sail upon them!"

There were more yells of delight and Mitchell looked about with a generous beam upon his face. "Let the proceedings commence!" he boomed, his voice filling the space better than any warrant officer's, and generating a further cheer from those assembled. On the deck below a dismal band of seamen, who had

58

been identified as first timers, were marched out and made to stand under the filled sail. On being shaken by those above, this deposited a stream of water over them, to the accompaniment of screams of utter delight from the onlookers. The first, Matthew Jameson, was hauled from their midst, and dragged up to stand in front of Mitchell.

King watched with interest. He remembered Jameson well; they had served together in two previous ships, and he was pleased to note that the lad, who was no more than a boy when they first met, had progressed. Jameson was no stranger to action and, despite the fact that he had not been with *Scylla* long, was fast becoming one of her prime topmen. Within a year or so he might be considered for further promotion, and was potential junior officer material: it would be interesting to see how he fared over the next five minutes.

Jameson stood, dripping in front of the royal group.
Mitchell leaned forward with elaborate interest. "And what is this dismal specimen that has been brought before me?"

"Able seaman Jameson, your highness," the boatswain's mate informed all. "Guilty of disregarding the traditions of the sea, and taking piscatorial liberties with the subjects of your Majesty."

"Taking the what?" Mitchell boomed, and there were shrieks of laughter which, King noted, were generally good-natured. "Then he shall be punished – but first we must make him more presentable. Clean him up, and give him a shave!"

More laughter, and groans of anticipation as Jameson was dragged nearer to the wooden kid and it was then that King realised that Amphitrite, Neptune's Queen, was the late governor's manservant. Presumably he had ingratiated himself sufficiently, although from what King had seen of the valet, he was not the type to be overly popular with the lower deck. Hind was being passed an impossibly large hand brush, which looked to have been made from a length of twelve-inch cable. He dipped the frayed rope into the muck, before holding it up in front of the seaman.

"State your name!" the valet shouted, in a curiously strangled voice that was clearly intended to carry but came out thin and reedy compared with those that had been before. Jameson opened his mouth to reply, but the brush was plunged into his mouth, and there were yells of delight from all.

The prisoner shook his head, and spat to one side, but seemed to be taking everything in good heart, a fact that was noticed and given due respect by the crowd. He even accepted being covered with slime and Hind's mock scraping with the razor without flinching, and by the time he was thrown backwards to land in the waterlogged sail there was a smattering of applause.

Three more followed, and were duly tried, punished and despatched without extreme comment, then King's attention was drawn to the next man. It was Timmons, part of the draught taken on at Spithead hardly longer than a month ago. Consequently he was likely to have either been pressed, or be a product of the Quota Act and it may well have been this newcomer status that was to blame, for he also showed none of Jameson's composure, and was not greeted well. King had already noticed Timmons, primarily because he was part of Flint's mess, another hand he knew of old. Flint he liked, but there was something cold and even sinister about Timmons; such things had alerted his senses in the past and did so again now as he considered him.

Ostensibly he was just another seaman; Timmons might carry an oddly superior air, but then none of the lower deck were models of normality. No, there was something else, something difficult to define but serious enough to cause concern. King watched as those restraining the seaman struggled to keep hold; Timmons was definitely fighting far more than was usual to avoid what was really nothing more than a minor indignity. And King was not the only one to pick up on the newcomer's behaviour; reaction from the crowd was even more boisterous, with an undercurrent of venom that was subtle, but defined. When, after a particularly brutal shaving, he was finally plunged into the water no one clapped and there were several open jeers of derision. An unpopular hand was also nothing unusual, but King felt it would be wise to keep an eye on this particular one for a while to come.

The sixth was being delivered just as King heard five bells striking. There was still quite a crowd below; it would be impossible to see to them all and finish by the end of the watch. This could mean trouble, especially as 'Up Spirits' was due at that time. Even if the captain granted an extension, to continue when the men had grog inside them could only lead to disaster. King was considering intervening when the noise of someone approaching from behind startled him. He turned to see Lady Hatcher crossing the quarterdeck followed, somewhat apologetically by Jackson, one of the junior midshipmen.

"What the devil is about?" she asked, her eyes blazing at King as if he had personally insulted her. "I can accept a degree of discourtesy – this is not a John Company ship, after all, but apparently my husband's death means nothing? Where is the captain, and why is he allowing such pantomime on a ship that should surely be in mourning?"

King was reasonably certain that Banks was in his sleeping quarters, quite close to where Lady Hatcher must have emanated from, although it would hardly have been diplomatic to say so. But how exactly was he to reply? Tell her that the men's traditions were more important than the death of a minor politician? Agree, and say that none of the officers were particularly in favour of what was about? But then why was she making a fuss in the first place? It had been clear to everyone aboard that there was no actual love between the two; the governor was little more than a means to an end, as far as Lady Hatcher was concerned. And there was a final, wicked, inner voice that wanted to ask what exactly would be achieved if they were all to go about with long faces. Just because Sir Terrance had managed to get himself killed, did that mean everyone else had to stay miserable?

"Who goes there?" Mitchell's roar took them all by surprise, but Lady Hatcher had joined King and Cahill at the fife rail, and was now in full sight of the assembly.

"Another pollywog for trial?" the man asked with glee. "Bring the wench forth!"

"Wench?" she hissed, and King noticed the woman's face had grown deeper than its customary afternoon glow. Mitchell's soubriquet appeared to have angered her more than might be expected, and King could not deny feelings of both respect and pity for the man. But before she could take action, Lady Hatcher's attention switched from King Neptune to Davy Jones, and she extended her arm and pointed at the unfortunate Hind.

"My shift!" Her scream was every bit as penetrating as Mitchell's voice, and may even have carried more authority. Men, who had mounted the gangway, clearly intending on invading the holy quarterdeck to seize her, stopped, and some looked uncertainly back at their elected leader as she continued. "Why is that man wearing my shift? And you, sir," she said now pointing directly at Mitchell. "That is my robe – what do you mean by dressing so?" She swung round and glared at King. "What manner of men are these?"

King opened his mouth, but said nothing while, for probably the first time in his life, Mitchell actually blushed, and there was a slight ripple of anonymous laughter.

"And what is this performance, anyways?" Lady Hatcher now had her hands on her hips as she addressed the crowd with obvious disgust. "Is this the way of the *Royal* Navy? The service we are so proud of? The men what protects us against the Corsican tyrant – see how they behave!"

The laughter was repeated, and King realised with surprise that it came not from seamen, but the marine guard. Jarvis growled a warning but it was clear that the bounds of military discipline were being stretched, and several normally neutral faces grinned openly beneath their leather shakos.

All knew the two forces made notoriously bad shipmates: both were subject to harsh discipline but the snap commands and rigid drill of a marine would be of little use when reefing topsails during a squall or standing a trick at the wheel. The bootnecks' stiff and ungainly bearing also made them an easy target for humour; it was something every marine learned to take in his precisely measured stride although the seamen, it seemed, were not quite as phlegmatic and disliked the situation being reversed. King swallowed dryly: this was starting to turn ugly.

"Malcolm, is that you?" Lady Hatcher unintentionally broke the spell, and pointed at her late husband's manservant who was still holding the now drooping shaving brush. "Why you are wearing one of my gowns as well? Whatever do you mean by it?"

"Oh, 'e does it all the time, mum," Mitchell roared back, delighted. "It's fortunate you are both of the same size – you gets twice the use!"

The manservant turned from his mistress in shame, but the renewed laughter had empowered the seamen, and the group were once more advancing along the starboard gangway.

"I see: you think you're going to include me in your childish games, do you?" Lady Hatcher roared. "And I expect you're just going to stand and watch?" she added, turning to King.

A gruff command from Jarvis, and the four marines on the quarterdeck raised their muskets with a solid click. Seeing the line of shining bayonets the leaders stopped, but more were piling up behind, and one of them over balanced and fell into the nearby sail with a hearty splash.

No one laughed: there was no longer any humour in the situation. The marines might put up a bold display, but they were heavily outnumbered. Every officer knew there was a good deal of suppressed anger in the crew, and King guessed that it was coming to the fore and about to be released.

"Elizabeth, whatever is going on?" They turned to see the captain's wife, advancing up the deck from the companionway, and King cursed silently to himself. Now things had definitely gone too far.

"Send for the captain," he hissed at Jackson. "And raise Lieutenant Cherry; tell him to turn out the rest of his force."

But before the junior midshipman could respond a call – hurried and urgent – came from the masthead.

"Sail ho! Three to the north!"

Surely it could get no worse? King spun round and instinctively looked aft. It was foolish, of course; any sighting the main lookout had spotted would be well beyond that of the deck. But no, the man must have been more intent on the proceedings below than his duty and a cold chill ran down King's spine.

All ideas of confrontations and foolish ceremonies were instantly forgotten; there was indeed canvas to be seen: lots of it, right down to the milk-white topsails and chequered hulls that showed, all too frequently, when the oncoming ships lifted to a wave. The French were back; worse, all were under heavy canvas and making for them. Because of the absurd celebrations *Scylla* was all but drifting under topsails alone; she would have to show a fair turn of speed, and even then it might not be enough.

Chapter Six

Behind him, King knew that chaos was erupting. Boatswain's pipes screamed, orders were shouted, and there was the thunder of feet as men made for the shrouds but, now that he had put the train in motion, all he could do was stare silently at the oncoming squadron; the enemy that he had allowed to come so close. Stiles, the lookout at the main, and even Reidy at the fore were equally culpable of course, and Cahill officially had the watch, but none bore the ultimate responsibility, which was his and his alone.

"Heavens, Tom; whatever were you thinking of?" Caulfield's voice came from behind, but still King did not look round.

"I missed them," he said, pathetically, before finally turning to meet the older man's worried expression.

"Well that's as maybe," the first lieutenant said after a moment. "You were doubtless distracted, but we can speak of that later. Be ready at your guns, the captain's bound to be clearing for action presently."

It was good advice and would give him reason to quit the quarterdeck, which was probably prudent in the circumstances. King exchanged a final glance with his friend; the two had served and fought together for many years, and he had the sudden premonition that now it was all going to end.

* * *

At Flint's cannon both Jameson and Timmons were still moist from their ducking, but the former was at least clean: being the first man in what had been relatively fresh water had shown some advantage. Timmons' turn had not come until later; he was not so savoury, and still bore the marks and smell of the manger.

"Well that was quite an end to the proceedings," Flint said, joining them, and ruffling Jameson's damp mop with rough affection.

"We clearin' for action?" Dixon asked.

"Not heard nuffin'." Flint glanced about. "An' we're several short."

"Some are more'n likely still wearin' their dresses," Timmons said deliberately, and indeed both Hind and Mitchell were not to be seen.

"It were just a bit of fun," Flint replied, detecting an underlying meaning in the man's tone. "It don't do to worry over such things."

"I ain't worried," Timmons told them with strange, and somewhat cold, certainty. "It's Hind and Mitchell what wants to do the worrying."

* * *

Banks mounted the quarterdeck still buttoning his jacket. He had been asleep, fast asleep. The fact that half of the previous four nights had been spent awake and on deck meant nothing; he was a naval officer, and should have been able to cope with such a regular occurrence. He glared back at the French ships; they were sailing in a ragged line with the uncommonly mild, westerly wind abeam. And, at little more than six miles distance, they were much too close.

"Forecourse, jib and stays'ls have been ordered," Caulfield told him.

Banks nodded, and returned his premier's salute. "Very good, Mr Caulfield; take her three points to larboard."

Scylla began to pick up speed when the extra canvas took effect, then proceeded to heel slightly as her prow came round, and the full force of the wind pressed the masts down. They would stay like this for at least half an hour, Banks decided; if the wind veered he would ease her back. It was not the ideal course: every mile they made south was another east, and further from their planned destination. But it was a long time until evening, and the only way he could keep the French off their backs until then was to extract the maximum from his ship.

"Captain, I would have words with you!"

The sudden appearance of Lady Hatcher should not have surprised him; she was used to taking her exercise on the quarterdeck during the afternoon which, he had to admit, was the main reason for his own absence and even partially to blame for his being asleep.

"Madam, you cannot stay here," he snapped. "Leave the deck at once."

"In good time, sir," she continued, undeterred. "First I wish to complain in the strongest..."

"Mr Jackson, you will escort Her Ladyship below; pass her to the care of the medical department."

The boy looked aghast at the woman, then back to his captain.

"Or do I have to order a marine guard?" Banks continued.

"Sir, you shall hear more of this!" Lady Hatcher's look was filled with pure malice, and she all but spat the words, before hoisting her skirts, and walking with elaborate dignity towards the companionway.

Banks brought his mind to bear on the current problems. Men were draining a sail that had been spread over one side of the spar deck, and it was only then that he remembered the ceremony scheduled for that afternoon. Water slopped down, drenching those on the gun deck below, but also lowering *Scylla's* point of balance a little. He rocked back and forth slightly, feeling the ship through the soles of his boots, then glanced up at the wind vane.

"A point to starboard."

Once more Banks waited while the change took effect. They were showing roughly the same canvas as the French, who had already proven themselves to be faster. He might add more sail, although that would only press her lower, and even decrease their speed, and *Scylla's* hull was skimming the ocean agreeably enough as it was. The extra strain would also be noticeable on her spars, and having already sprung one yard Banks knew he must be especially cautious.

"What do you see there, Michael?" he asked. The first lieutenant had been examining the oncoming ships through the come-up glass.

"They're gaining on us, sir." Caulfield replied, looking down at the instrument and re-setting its knurled central wheel. "Not markedly, but I'd say we will be close to range within a couple of hours."

Two hours; that would be five in the afternoon. The sun set around six and there would be minimal dusk: Banks doubted he would be able to avoid the French for quite so long.

"Why was I not summoned?" he asked finally, almost whispering although the intensity in his voice carried the words perfectly. Caulfield flushed, and looked away.

"It was remiss, sir, and had nothing to do with Lady Banks," he replied. "The hands were involved with their celebrations, and I'd chance the lookouts became distracted." It was no excuse, as both knew well.

"So the French were allowed to take the jump on us?"

The first lieutenant nodded.

"Who was officer of the watch?"

"Cahill, sir," Caulfield told him, miserably. "And King was supervising the ceremony."

The captain said nothing, although he did feel a measure of relief. He had been concerned about having remained uninformed, and at least that was not due to Sarah's presence. Cahill had sat and passed his board and was only awaiting an appointment as lieutenant, while he had served with King on several commissions. Both were experienced enough; he was even fond of them and either should have been able to maintain a keen lookout. It could well be that the masthead hands were not up to their duty, in which case they could be disrated or punished in another way, but it would be far worse for those in overall charge.

He himself might have been sound asleep below, but there was no actual fault in that: he was not on duty. King and Cahill had the deck and, whatever was going on about them, should have noticed the French, or at least ensured that the lookouts were paying proper attention. Ostensibly there was no excuse and Banks was reasonably certain that, should the matter be brought to court martial, they could only be broken.

The bell sounded six times, and brought him back to matters in hand. It was an hour before 'Up Spirits' and supper; that was too long to delay clearing for action, and there was every chance that topmen and trimmers would be wanted before then.

"Mr Caulfield, the people may take their grog and be fed as soon as is practical."

The first lieutenant touched his hat, and nodded at Jackson, who had returned from his trip to the orlop. The afternoon meal would be light, probably nothing more than biscuit and cheese, so should be over relatively quickly. If they were to see action it would be better for the men to have full bellies, and a measure of grog inside them would do little harm either.

Banks turned and, deliberately ignoring the three faint images off the taffrail, began to pace the deck while below men, oddly shamed by the enemy's sudden encroachment, formed up for their food in unusual silence. This voyage was going from bad to worse, he decided. The diplomat he had been entrusted with had been allowed to die, while his widow seemed set on ruining him professionally. And even if she did not, the chances were high that his ship was about to be taken. There was no doubt that an impoverished French Government would greet the quarter million pound of gold stored below as manna from heaven, and now one of his favourite officers and most loyal followers, was likely to be dismissed the service. Then, to cap it all, Sarah, his wife had started to behave strangely.

She had been sick for almost a week, and was complaining of pains, giddiness and cramp. Banks prided himself on not being a fool; he knew well just what such symptoms might mean, and really did not think things could get any worse.

* * *

"You may stay where you are, or go to the cable tier," Kate told her firmly. "Otherwise I shall have to send word to the captain, and he will doubtless have you confined."

The surgeon, who was a reluctant witness to his wife's resolve, busied himself with the instruments and tried to stay anonymous. His medical team was moving down from the sickbay in advance of clearing for action, and he had already ordered the bulkheads struck from the midshipmen's berths.

"This is not what I am accustomed to!" Lady Hatcher informed the cockpit in general. "Why, there is no light, no air; how can you think of treating people in such conditions?"

Kate softened slightly. "It is not always easy," she confessed. "Though must be done. And when we clear for action it will be a good deal worse."

"The more I see of the Royal Navy, the more I am disgusted."

"If you wished to assist," Kate said, hoping for a fellow spirit, "it would be more than welcome. The captain's wife shall be joining us presently. She helps if there is need, and I dare say you will not find caring for the wounded so very onerous. British seamen are usually most appreciative," she continued. "And especially welcome the company of a female at such times."

Lady Hatcher fixed her with a stare that even the dim light could not diminish. "I should no sooner lower myself to such work as I would beg on the streets," she told her crisply.

"Then you had better send for your servant," Kate replied. "I shall not be looking after you, and the rats in the hold can be rather tiresome I believe."

* * *

At two bells in the first dog watch – exactly five o'clock – the first shot was fired, but fell short. *Scylla* was still heading to the south east with the westerly wind conveniently on her quarter and making just over eight knots, or so the log had informed them an hour earlier; Banks had no desire to cast the thing again. The French frigate was immediately behind and closing steadily, while both corvettes were travelling considerably faster, and creeping up to starboard on a more southerly heading. He stared at them now; they were out of range of his long guns and so were of no immediate threat, but could be expected to close at any moment. Having both of the smaller vessels attack from the same side meant that *Scylla*'s firepower would be halved, and then reduced further when the French frigate seized the windward gauge, and joined them.

He had been pacing on and off for the past two hours, and now rested, conscious of the weariness in his legs and a faint tingle of sweat that ran down his back. There had been bad times in the past, plenty of them, but none seemed quite so desperate as the fix that now presented. And with his wife below, in what might well be a delicate condition, Banks knew he had more to lose than ever.

A second ball skipped once, before disappearing off their stern. It was another ranging shot, and from the frigate's bow chaser; presumably a nine pounder or something similar. Allowing for the continental method of gauging shot, the enemy's broadside guns would throw a ball more than double that weight, and there were twenty a side, not counting the carronades on her forecastle and quarterdeck. Both corvettes would only be carrying twelve pounders, but such a ball could still penetrate *Scylla's* hull and do her serious harm. If he fought he might sink one, and cause the other severe damage, but that was about as much as could be hoped for. There was no likely victory, no drawn-out battle that could foreseeably end in triumph. Men would die; he might be among them, and even if not there was only imprisonment and possibly injury to look forward to. And, he realised with a chill, such an outcome also awaited Sarah. She might be safe below on the orlop and, if captured, could probably expect to be exchanged eventually, but *Scylla* could easily take fire or explode, and there was no guarantee the French would treat a women prisoner especially well. And if he did fight it out to the end, where would be the advantage? His ship must still be taken or sunk. Really the only sensible thing he could do now would be to surrender.

He turned aside, vaguely conscious that his present train of thought was not constructive, and was pleased to see Caulfield standing at the break of the quarterdeck, talking with King, who must have come up from the deck below. He walked to meet them, aware that the eyes of the crew were on him as he nodded a greeting.

"Still out of range, sir," the first lieutenant commented.

"Indeed, Mr Caulfield," Banks agreed. "Though it is a

situation that cannot last for much longer. Your guns are ready, Mr King?"

"Yes, sir," the lieutenant replied. "Loaded with single ball, but they may be drawn and the load changed if you require."

The young man's attitude, both keen yet strangely anticipatory, rather shocked the captain. It was the first time they had spoken since King allowed the French to close on them, and he might be anticipating punishment for his lack of care, although Banks sensed there was something else. His attention switched to Caulfield, who also appeared eager, and it suddenly occurred to him that both were expecting not only action, but eventual victory.

It came as quite a revelation, considering his recent thoughts; Banks had assumed the two men would be sharing his feelings, and glanced at both once more to assure himself that they did not. King had nothing to fight for; a future court martial would see him clear of the Navy, while Caulfield was getting too old to expect promotion to commander, and must long ago have ruled out any ambition of being made post. Yet there was a definite avidness about his officers that frankly shamed him. They had none of his misgivings, and seemed as ready to fight as if they had all to look forward to and were facing an enemy half their size.

"Very well," he said awkwardly, before glancing up at the sails, and instinctively measuring the wind for both strength and direction. "Then you had better return to your gun crews, Mr King; I think it's time that we began."

Chapter Seven

At Flint's piece the men were certainly ready, and they also had no thoughts of surrender. Both guns were run out but they were grouped about *Spitfire,* the starboard gun, as that seemed the one most likely to be in use. All had taken their grog and now had relatively full stomachs, but the effect of the rum remained with them. Mitchell, who was in charge of the small team that manhandled the gun, was humming a lewd ditty to himself, while Hind, once more clad in seamen's rig, had been relating tales of previous engagements. The only one who seemed not to be thinking of the oncoming action was Dixon, who had settled on his haunches with arms wrapped about both knees dozing quietly, as was his habit.

"Starboard battery, stand to!" King gave the command as he slid down the quarterdeck ladder. He had no idea which side would be firing first, but knew it was important to get the men up and alert. Dixon yawned deeply, and rubbed his eyes, while Hind, who had almost frightened himself with the stories he had been concocting, licked his lips in nervous anticipation. Flint glanced about the men, who appeared ready, but apprehensive. They were all aware of the odds, while some also knew this was likely to end in defeat, and that in a battle lost the chances of death or disfigurement were that much higher. Consequently there was less of the tense excitement usual at the commencement of an action, instead the men seemed almost resigned to what was to come. In fact of them all, only Timmons showed any sign of delight at the coming fight.

Flint considered him as the rest of the team checked over the gun and its equipment. The man certainly was something of an enigma; he had come aboard from the pressing tender and yet, of all those taken on in that manner at Spithead, he was the only one to show little resentment at his seizing. Quite the reverse, in fact; he appeared to welcome the chance to get away from England,

and had settled into the routine of life aboard *Scylla* faster than any. He was also an experienced seaman, yet had never travelled south of the equator before – not that there was anything terribly strange in that, but to kick up such a fuss over what was really nothing more than a little foolish horseplay went directly against what was expected of a regular hand.

Flint continued to watch the man surreptitiously as Timmons ran his fingers through the lamb's wool 'sponge' that would soon be used to extinguish any burning debris in the gun barrel. He was not exactly a firebrand, and had never actually lost his temper in the mess, but there was an intensity about him that Flint did not like. And he was reasonably sure he was not alone; even after several weeks on board Timmons had yet to find a particular friend, and was one of the few who needed to ask for help when it came to tying his queue of a Sunday morning.

And then it came to Flint in a flash of intuition; the way Timmons was holding himself now, laughing, joking and clearly looking forward to the action when all about were far more pragmatic. The latent anger he held for Mitchell and Hind, even the fact that none of the ship's cats would have anything to do with him: these and many other subtleties in his manner that made up a surprisingly complex individual. Flint had known more than a few seamen who enjoyed a fight, some to such an extent that it was almost an addiction, and he wondered now if Timmons had taken such a trait one stage further. There was a type who actively enjoyed killing; he had met a few in his years at sea, and none had endeared themselves to him, or any other member of the crew come to that. Nasty, calculating, spiteful men, who took their pleasure from other people's pain; it was just his luck to have one in the mess and also under his command on the guns. He supposed something good might come of it; Timmons could turn out to be a solid man in a scrap, even if he were more likely to be looking after himself, and care nothing for those fighting alongside. But at least he felt he now knew the man for what he was, and could make sure Jameson was equally aware. Then, with sudden clarity, he remembered; of all the men of that type he had known, every single one had come to a bad end. And most had taken others with them.

* * *

Scylla turned hard to starboard and was soon close hauled and heading for the stern of the nearest corvette. The men had responded well, and with her bowlines taut, the ship made swift progress although there was little time to consider this: all had work to do. Banks moved to the starboard side and peered out, but the pursuing frigate, which had been taken by surprise by the move, was already out of the British ship's arc of fire, and only now starting to follow. No matter, their guns would be used soon enough.

"Will we be taking them to larboard, Sir?" Caulfield asked when the captain returned.

Banks shook his head. "No, I shall be altering course once more," then, looking down to where the second lieutenant was waiting on the deck below, he shouted. "Divide your men, Mr King. Both batteries will be required, but wait upon my word."

King touched his hat in response as the men began to separate so that each team was manning both pieces under their charge. Banks looked forward. At their speed and on the current course he hoped the two smaller ships would expect *Scylla* to attempt to rake their sterns, just as Caulfield had. The move might have some merit, but it would be asking too much for the French to allow such an act and, even if they did, once more his firepower would be divided. Banks supposed that, like any good man of business, he had to get the best return from his assets, and that meant using them all, and to the greatest effect. Spray streamed back from the frigate's bows, drenching the men at the forward chasers and forecastle carronades, but none noticed or appeared to care. The corvettes had registered his move, and were turning to meet him, as he had expected. One was two cables forward, and slightly to the north of the other, and both had the wind almost directly behind them. It was all well and good; he was to be denied their vulnerable sterns, but would still be in line for what should prove a greater prize.

Banks caught the eye of the sailing master. "I shall be taking her to larboard, before correcting to our current heading, Mr Fraiser. Be ready if you please." Fraiser nodded grimly and Banks knew that, however much he might morally disapprove, the Scot had an instinctive grasp of fighting tactics.

The two forces grew closer, until the nearest enemy was fine on *Scylla*'s larboard bow. If Banks maintained the present course they would pass and exchange broadsides. Being the larger ship, it was likely that *Scylla* would do the greater damage, but she must then face the second corvette with her guns empty. He could attempt to turn later and bring his starboard battery into play, but it would be a tight manoeuvre and if *Scylla* took any damage aloft, or to her steering, one that was likely to fail. Should that happen the two smaller vessels might easily overwhelm her, even before the frigate joined the fray.

"Ready!" Banks called, holding his hand high. Then he brought it down with a flourish, and shouted: "Turn!"

Fraiser, at the binnacle, began to call out the orders while the helmsmen, primed and eager, wrenched down on the wheel until the spokes were almost a blur. The afterguard and waisters heaved back on the braces, and *Scylla* dipped her bows deep into the Atlantic, allowing more water to slop over the forward bulkwarks.

"And back to starboard!" the captain called after no more than a minute.

The ship's weight and inertia carried her round, while the yards were hurriedly reset, and *Scylla* began to aim for the tiny gap between the smaller craft.

Below, Banks could see King, strutting back and forward behind his guns as each of their individual captains peered down the barrels of their charges. Clearly the lieutenant expected to direct the fire, but he would have a poor view of the proceedings and there would be no time to waste.

"On my word, Mr King!" Banks reminded him, and received a brief salute in reply.

Smoke erupted from the first corvette; they would be firing their chase guns, and any forward mounted cannon that might bear. Something hit *Scylla* forward, and there was a whine as either a shot or some lump of debris flew past Banks' right ear, but he paid it no attention.

"Ready starboard!" he warned then, just as they passed the closest ship's jib boom: "As you will... Fire!"

The first piece was discharged a second or two later, followed by the quick staccato rumble of the other guns, and ending with the nearby quarterdeck carronades that all but made Banks jump, so intent was he in his work. The corvette replied, but to no great effect; either they had not been prepared for *Scylla*'s move, or her stuffing had been knocked out by the frigate's deadly fire. The second Frenchman was already closing fast to larboard, however, and could be expected to be better prepared.

Once again, Banks would be able to control the fire. He was gratified to see that, even though an enemy was close by, and they were about to be fired upon, the starboard gun crews paid it no attention, and concentrated every effort on reloading their pieces. The second corvette was turning slightly to open up their arc of fire, Banks acknowledged the fact, but knew it would do little to change his plans. He was already banking on his ship's timbers being stronger, and her guns the more powerful. Then there was a call from forward, and the Frenchman came into range.

They might have reduced speed slightly, or perhaps the larboard gun captains were not so positive, but this time the broadside took slightly longer. The British also received more damage in return; a French shot came in through the larboard bulwark and smashed part of the crews of two facing eighteen pounders. But *Scylla* was also scoring hits and, as they finally cleared the second ship, a cheer rose up as the enemy's mizzen tumbled down upon her tiny quarterdeck in a tangle of wood, line and canvas.

The sailing master brought them round to larboard and once more the men behaved well, following his commands that kept the ship with the wind so that little time or speed was lost, and leaving her heading back for the second enemy's starboard side. On the gun deck Banks noted that their own starboard battery was close to being ready while the larboard teams, having fired later, must still weather a broadside from the corvette before replying. It would have been far better were the situations reversed, and it was at that moment that he had an idea that verged on inspiration.

Fraiser was less than two yards away, his face set in that glum, disapproving expression he usually wore when *Scylla* was in action. As sailing master he was responsible for manoeuvring the ship, and Banks freely admitted him to be the better seaman, but if what he intended was to work, he had no time to consult and must order it himself. He collected the speaking trumpet from the binnacle, and brought it to his lips.

"Hands, prepare to wear ship. Ready starboard battery!"

The order brought forth a murmur of comment and some of those serving on the deck below looked up in concern. *Scylla* had crack gun teams, but manning both batteries reduced their efficiency, and the starboard battery needed a minute at least before it would be ready. Four pieces were still inboard, and the gun that had lost men was nowhere near to being hauled out again. But the confusion reassured Banks somewhat: if he could fool his own people he had every chance of doing the same to the enemy.

"Mr Fraiser, we will wear ship!"

The Scotsman touched his hat and began the manoeuvre as calmly as if he had been expecting the order for some time and they were in the midst of an empty sea. The wheel spun and *Scylla's* prow began to turn when the jib boom was barely inches away from the enemy. As Banks watched, the final starboard guns were run out, and all but one was ready to open fire as the ship moved through the wind and turned sharply to larboard, eventually presenting her broadside to the smaller vessel's undefended rear.

It was a classic rake, and delivered at such a distance that it must have a devastating effect. As they watched, the entire stern seemed to cave in, dissolving into fragments of wood, glass and gilding, while the heavy shot continued throughout her vitals, killing, wrecking and laying waste to all in their way. It was that broadside alone that won the engagement; once it had been delivered the corvette was robbed of much of her ability and inclination to fight, and even seemed to settle slightly as Fraiser kept *Scylla* to the wind, as she made off northwards. Had they been fighting alone there was no doubt the corvette would now strike before the British could return and wreak yet more havoc upon her, but Banks still faced two further ships, and his own was not undamaged.

The other corvette now lay some two hundred yards off their beam. She had been robbed of her mizzen, but the wreckage was mainly cleared, and the warship was under way once more, running east, under fore and main alone. It would be a simple enough task to turn and catch her but, more importantly, the enemy frigate lay behind, still close hauled and heading for them. *Scylla* now had the wind, but the presence of the smaller craft limited Banks' use of it while he was well aware that, should he engage the corvette, it would only mean him meeting with the far larger enemy with at least one battery empty.

Then, as he watched, the frigate tacked, turning hard to starboard and presenting her larboard broadside. She was still a fair distance off, and Banks was not unduly worried; the French were not known for their gunnery, and he did not suppose this ship would be any different.

"Wear ship, Mr Fraiser – turn to starboard!"

Scylla began the manoeuvre just as the frigate released her broadside but, moving target or not, the British ship was perfectly straddled and found herself peppered with heavy shot. A cloud of dust and splinters rose up from where the figurehead used to be, and the bowsprit took a sound smack at its base. The clang of metal striking metal told how their best bower was also hit, but the anchor remained fast, and the only wounded were two men at the bow chasers who were struck by the same shot. It was remarkably little damage from what had been a well aimed broadside The rest of the enemy's fire went high, but even there the British were fortunate: no spars were damaged; several of the sails did show holes, but still drew well enough and, as *Scylla* gained the wind once more, Banks could not dispel a mild feeling of guilt that they had got off particularly lightly.

"Group your men to larboard, Mr King, and prepare!" he commanded.

It was the end of any thoughts of using both batteries. The sun was starting to set behind them, and now his only concern was to strike hard at the second corvette, before seeking sanctuary in the darkness of an almost moonless equatorial night. The French frigate that had proved so deadly was making a full turn, and clearly intended to give chase, but soon the smaller ship would come between them and, ironically, protect *Scylla* from her larger colleague's fire.

King indicated that his guns were ready, and *Scylla* was now positively flying through the water. Banks glanced round the deck, the men at the nearby carronades had their pieces trained forward, and were waiting for the enemy to venture into their reach, while the marines stood grouped along the bulwarks in stiff red and white lines. It would be far too long a range for muskets to be of any use, and *Scylla* was in no danger from boarders, but their officers were clearly content for them to remain at action stations, and Banks guessed that the iron faced men would have no wish to be anywhere else.

The French frigate had completed her turn and was now passing the corvette at speed. Banks must deliver the broadside, then turn sharply to starboard if he wanted to avoid her attention, but the evening was approaching steadily and he knew that in much less than ten minutes it would be quite dark.

"Ready!" King had hoisted himself up onto the larboard gangway, and was clearly intending to direct fire from there. In an ideal world Banks would have liked to have turned while firing, but that was probably asking too much, and must surely dissipate the effect of his broadside.

"She fires!" Caulfield said, almost conversationally, and Banks looked up to see a succession of flame run along the corvette's side. The French were perhaps a mite premature, probably hoping that a sound hit on *Scylla* would reduce the barrage she was about to deliver. The whine of shots passing overhead made some men duck but, apart from the severing of one forestay and two shrouds and a hole that appeared as if by magic in the jib, they were not hurt.

"Aiming high," Caulfield commented with a wry smile as the noise of the broadside reached them. It was the French way, and might well have been successful. Had one of their masts been struck or weakened, the British would now be in a very different position. But once more they had survived and Banks' confidence grew slightly as he noticed the darkness visibly creeping towards them.

"As you will, Mr King!" he shouted, and the younger man touched his hat before bellowing the order that set *Scylla's* larboard side alight. So well positioned was the target that the British ship's fire was almost instantaneous, and Banks hesitated for a second to allow the smoke to clear before instructing Fraiser to take her to starboard. The French frigate was closer, and just clearing her consort, but *Scylla* turned quickly and would soon be totally obscured by night. He supposed that the action might be continued; he could retrace his steps in the darkness and attempt to take the Frenchman's bow, but the enemy's largest warship was totally undamaged and *Scylla* had already suffered enough. No, he would keep her as she was, and trust that the luck that had supported them so far would stretch just that little bit further. The Frenchman was still a good distance off; Banks estimated that they would probably hold their course and attempt to close with *Scylla* before darkness engulfed her. In which case the British could expect one broadside, but after that should be safe. He told himself it was not so very dreadful a prospect and at what would still be considerable range, need not worry him greatly.

Caulfield may well have been of the same opinion, and actually went to speak when a cry from forward made them all turn. The frigate was clearly not intending to come any closer, and had already turned to present her main armament. As they watched the tongues of fire stood out vividly in the dwindling light. Nothing was said and all waited for the shots to arrive, confident that such a distance, along with the Royal Navy's instinctive contempt for French gunnery, would see them safe.

And then there was chaos.

This time the enemy had obviously decided against aiming

for *Scylla*'s spars, but her hull was accurately and extensively targeted. Even at such a range the heavier metal of the frigate dug deep into her bulwarks, penetrating above, and below the waterline. The quarterdeck was suddenly alive with the rush of passing shot; one struck the barrel of a carronade, lifting and spinning the weapon round like some awful living creature, until it came to rest with crushing decisiveness on two who were unlucky enough to be standing close by. Shot and splinters also flew about the gangways and throughout the lower deck, and more men fell. The roar of orders did much to mask screams from those wounded, and the forecourse shivered and flapped above them as the larboard brace parted, adding yet another visual aspect to the carnage. Banks recovered himself, and stood to one side as a damage party began to attend to the wrecked gun. The boatswain's team soon had the errant sail under control and, as the final strands of daylight were extinguished, *Scylla* was allowed to disappear into anonymity.

"That was good shooting, sir," the first lieutenant said grimly, while brushing something unpleasant from his jacket that was mercifully hidden by the gloom. "Not the standard we usually expect of the French."

"Indeed so, Mr Caulfield," Banks agreed.

The darkness now totally encased them, and they had twelve hours of night in which to shake off any pursuit although, with two wounded companions, it was doubtful that the single frigate would continue to chase them for long. Then he remembered that only a short time ago he had been actively considering surrender, and supposed he should be pleased. They had dealt out some serious damage to two of the enemy, and were once more heading south for St Helena. But he had felt at least one of the frigate's heavy shots strike them low in the hull, and knew that *Scylla* had been severely damaged. There were no true dockyard facilities on the island and, whatever their reason, the enemy were clearly intent on travelling the same road. The enemy frigate had also proved that she could both fight and sail better than most Frenchmen; Banks may have damaged the corvettes, but the larger vessel was clearly a more worthy opponent. Her gunnery was of an exceptionally high standard, and the ship herself remained totally unharmed. Should they meet again, the British must be at a distinct disadvantage, and Banks sensed that *Scylla* would not fare well.

"Yes," he repeated, with an assumed nonchalance that he hoped would disguise the concern he felt inside. "It was good shooting indeed."

Chapter Eight

On the eighth day, and after the sun had once more risen above an empty ocean, they began to draw breath. Gone, at least for now, was any threat from a French battle squadron and specifically that crack and undamaged frigate; instead the British had the world apparently to themselves and were slowly becoming accustomed to the fact. The wind had been blowing strong and constant for the past week and with a reasonable spread of sail set, *Scylla* was heading for St Helena once more. But the absence of a visible foe did not leave Banks free of problems; there were many more waiting to plague him.

Scylla was indeed holed. One, forward of the larboard entry port, had been relatively easy to reach and patch, but the other was lower down and to the stern: just under the gunroom. A heavy shot had struck below the wales, and shattered the third futtock: a major frame in the ship's construction. Its impact had caused the second, and lower futtock, to spring and left a splintered mess of the internal spruce spirketting and outer elm strakes. The profile of *Scylla*'s hull in that area meant that a sail could not be fothered conventionally with any hope of success, and neither could the damage be properly repaired from within. Evans and his team had worked throughout the first night and for much of the time since. Now the ingress of water had been stemmed to something the ship's pumps could clear, if worked for three hours in every watch, but there could be no permanent repair until the ship was taken into dry dock. And, to make matters worse, the damage had also affected their stores.

The breadroom had been completely drenched, leaving them almost bereft of flour and biscuit, while *Scylla*'s aft magazine, which held up to a third of her powder, was partially flooded. Both areas contained commodities vital to the survival of the ship, but to Banks' eyes at least, the order of importance was not as might be expected.

Several tons of high explosive were certainly ruined and not all had been in the aft magazine; the main, although further forward, was set slightly lower and had also been affected. Most of that supply was in casks, however, and even some of the dampened cartridges might be reclaimed, if the ship were blessed with warm weather. He probably had sufficient for another sustained battle, if none were wasted on exercise, and with the men reasonably well practised, allowing the guns to lie idle for a spell would not affect them greatly. No, powder was not the problem it might have been; by chance the ship's main supply of flour, stored in the aft hold, had also been contaminated and it was actually the lack of biscuit, one of the staple elements of the crew's diet, that he considered to be the more serious of the two.

By nature seamen were conservative in their tastes; salt pork, salt beef and three Banyan days a week when no meat was served was what they were used to, and actually what they wanted. Not so long ago James Cook had offered prime fresh beef in lieu of their more familiar 'salt horse', but so certain were they that some elaborate trick was being played that the petty warrant victuals were only accepted under protest and threat of punishment. On long voyages men might be given turtle, penguin, seal, or even whale meat, but it was always on the understanding that proper food would also be available should they wish it, while to tempt a crew with fresh fish in place of stuff that might have been soaking in brine for upwards of two years, was usually impossible. Consequently, the lack of biscuit, surely the most versatile of their common foodstuffs and one that was hardly ever known to run low, was far more important. When in normal storage it outlasted any meat or vegetable, and could be replaced easily enough if flour was at hand. As an ingredient, biscuit formed the basis of many of their familiar made dishes and, when consumed on its own and in its raw state, the flint like texture made a satisfying snack, as well as doing much to improve their dental hygiene. But, like it or not, they would be without hard tack until they reached St Helena, and Banks supposed they would just have to get used to the fact. *Scylla* should pick up the south east trades at any time; the strong, steady winds would give them a measure of stability, and keep the pressure off their weakened hull, but even so it would take another ten to fourteen days before they could hope to raise the tiny island and, without biscuit, it would not be a pleasant journey.

He had been pacing the quarterdeck since dawn and now stopped at the taffrail and looked back over the empty seas. The sun was well up and the day had already grown warm. Thompson would have coffee waiting for him in their sleeping cabin but Sarah was now finding mornings increasingly uncomfortable: Banks had grown used to giving her privacy, and was in no rush to go below. Behind him came the sound of sawing; Evans and his team were at work somewhere else in the ship, a party of hands were washing out hammocks further forward and he could also hear the regular thumps of the armourer as he hammered some blameless piece of metal out of shape.

At first light the boatswain had reported their tophamper to be in reasonable order; the running rigging was already serviceable and all the damaged stays and shrouds were now replaced, even if the entire lot was really due for replacement with fresh cordage. He supposed they might attend to some while at St Helena, but really the prospect of returning to England and delivering his ship into the safe hands of his 'affectionate friends' as the dockyard commissioners quaintly termed themselves in correspondence, was far more attractive.

Then another noise, no softer but different from that usually heard on a warship, attracted his attention and he turned to see Sarah approach. She was raising the skirts of her long light-grey cotton gown slightly as the patterns that clad her feet clumped clumsily on the wet deck. Her face was as pale as the white over-bodice, but she was smiling with evident pleasure and her eyes seemed unusually alight.

"You have been up for some while," she said, releasing her skirts and taking his hands in hers.

"Indeed..." Banks always found that the innate tenderness he held for his wife did not reveal itself easily on the quarterdeck. "I felt you should be allowed time to wake," he continued awkwardly. "You are better now, I trust?"

"Very much so; thank you." Her smile deepened. "And you are as understanding as usual; indeed I think you to be the most perceptive of husbands." Their eyes met. "In which case you should have little trouble in guessing why I have been so unwell of late."

"It is something I have pondered over," he replied temporising. "But thought it better to wait until things were more certain..."

"Well, they are certain now," she said firmly. "I have been speaking with Kate Manning: we compared notes and dates and think it fair to say there will be a baby born within seven months."

His set look and silence worried her, and she continued hastily.

"Nothing is ever truly certain of course." She had dropped his hands and was trying to become far more commonplace. "Much can go wrong: it is my - our - first child after all. Kate, as you know, was due to deliver, and..."

She stopped abruptly and for a moment they simply stared at each other. Many men had little time for children and for all she knew sailors, with the life they led, might be more prone to such an attitude. Even on land the majority of husbands rejected anything even loosely connected to childbirth and families, consigning all to their wives who they regarded as being entirely responsible. And in her own particular case, so much of their married life had been spent apart that it was not a subject they had even discussed beyond vague references to possibly needing a larger house in time. She might have misunderstood, or perhaps telling him now, here, and in public, was a mistake. Her eyes fell and she felt a flush appear on her face as the world that had suddenly been so bright and wonderful now seemed doomed to endless black. Then she gave a small cry of surprise as he pulled her close and, quarterdeck protocol or not, wrapped his arms about her.

* * *

"So there you have it," Kate stated with her usual directness. "Sarah is pregnant, sure as eggs is eggs."

Manning had suspected something was amiss when Kate asked for private use of the surgery and, now that the captain's wife had left and he was once more admitted to the small room, he was not unduly surprised. "How long does she have?" he asked.

Kate sent a hard look his way. "You should know better than to ask," she told him. "Her and Sir Richard have hardly been together more'n a couple of months; I'd say it will pop in eight although she seems set on seven."

The surgeon trusted his wife's diagnosis totally; she being a former midwife after all, but still the news worried him far more than was reasonable. Sarah was a happy, healthy woman, and they should be safely back in England long before her confinement: it was Kate, and the way the news might effect her, that was his principle concern.

"And how do you feel about this?" he asked, cautiously. Again that dangerous look, although this time there was an additional element: it was as if she suspected him of trying to catch her out, and he knew he had made a mistake.

"How do I feel?" she repeated. "Why Robert, am I the patient here? It is wonderful news to be sure: it will give me something to do during the day, and must bless their marriage in the best of ways." She stopped, realising what she had said, and gave a slight choke, but carried on far too quickly for Manning to pass remark or contribute. "We must make sure she has first peck at any milk Lizzy produces, and as soon as we get to St Helena there are various things she will need. I shall make notes, many notes; the poor girl will not want for anything," Kate added with a tight smile.

"She will be lucky to have you by her," Manning said. "Both as a professional, and a friend."

"Why yes," Kate agreed readily. "As a Mother Midnight I have delivered a thousand babies in my time, and got so very close to having one of my own – really it could not be more fortunate!"

Even from across the room Manning could feel his wife's pain, but her attitude prevented him from saying anything that would either be misinterpreted or ignored. He knew this was the time when the subject could, and should, be addressed, but with such a display of pleasure and professional competence, Kate was all but impregnable.

Since they had lost their own child nothing had been said, and the subject remained steadfastly closed. Their eyes met and for a second his spirits lifted as the realisation came that this might finally be the point where some progress could be made. Then a loud tap came at the door, and they both instantly reverted to more routine matters.

"Surgery does not begin for another fifteen minutes," Kate snapped instinctively as the door began to open, finally revealing the washed-out face of Lady Hatcher.

"Never mind that," she told them thickly. "I have such a headache that my skull is fit to burst. If you refuse to treat a truly sick person I shall see you both removed at the earliest opportunity."

* * *

The captain and his missus were on deck, and the stuffed-up tart who called herself a lady was with the sawbones and had taken her maid with her, so Timmons reckoned he might have the opportunity he had been waiting for. Getting past the marine guard was simple; everyone knew that jollys had limited brains and not much better memories: his excuse of having been sent to attend to a faulty head would have been long forgotten even before the end of the sentry's trick. But, now that he was actually inside the hallowed great cabin, the stakes had risen, and he felt his heart race in a way that was oddly pleasurable. He removed the kerseymere hat that had been pulled well down over his brow and stepped quietly across the painted canvas flooring. Beneath his feet he could hear the murmur of conversation: Hatcher's cronies were accustomed to monopolising the gunroom in the late morning, and usually turned the officers' accommodation into something that closely emulated a coffee house. But Timmons had the more rarefied space above apparently to himself, and moved about in unaccustomed silence.

He knew the late governor's personal servant who had played Neptune's Queen would be there or thereabouts. The man had barely left the captain's quarters in the last week and Timmons had long since decided that he would be the first to be killed.

Healey had few friends and his working environment was also the most private, so covering up the crime should be equally simple. And if it all went horribly wrong and the deed could not be concluded, there was still little risk: Timmons was quietly confident that the word of a regular foremast jack would be believed over a glorified passenger who not only was an active pederast, but also indulged other rare and even more unusual practices.

In fact Healey had hardly been the most popular of shipmates from the start. By nature seamen were a pretty broad-minded bunch and, however much the Articles of War might seek to restrict it, a proportion of homosexual behaviour was tolerated in most ships. There were lines that could not be crossed, however, and those indulging themselves so were always in danger of a severe flogging, if not the noose, so such activity was likely to be kept private.

But Healey was different: distinctly so, and a man of his type stretched even the lower deck's boundaries of acceptance to the limit. He was also a passenger and, by his position as part of the governor's entourage, an important one. Consequently the ship's corporals were doubtful of their authority and, as many of his actions did not actually break a law, were inclined not to interfere. His habit of pressing affection on those not of his calling contravened the seamen's unwritten code though, and the frequent occasions when he paraded about the berth deck with painted face and in full feminine attire upset far more than they pleased.

In fact it had been his access to women's clothes and cosmetics that had secured him the position of Amphitrite at the crossing ceremony: that and the lower deck's innate sense of humour. Now that such usefulness was expended though, Timmons knew that everyone would be content to leave him be. Everyone but him: he had a score to settle and Timmons always made sure that any debt was paid in full.

He stopped: there was movement in the new cabin that had been erected opposite the captain's sleeping quarters. Someone was shifting things about inside and singing softly in a light, falsetto voice. For a moment Timmons wondered if one of the other women was about; possibly Lady Hatcher's maid had been sent back, or maybe the surgeon's wife was not in the sickbay. That would certainly complicate matters, but not unduly so; he had killed several women in the past and they were actually his preferred prey. But no, whoever it was broke their song to curse roundly when something fell to the deck, and Timmons knew that he had his man. More than that, his man was just where he wanted him.

The thin deal door made a high-pitched squeak when he opened it, and the sound was almost exactly emulated by Healey as he swung round to meet the intruder. He was dressed in ordinary slop chest trousers but wore a light, floral bodice above, while his face bore the marks of fresh, and inexpertly applied, rouge. He treated Timmons to a smile, one born more from fear than pleasure, and the result was truly ghastly.

"You miserable little molly," Timmons stated, not unkindly, as he advanced. The Hatcher's oversized bed was set against the bulwark and blocked any retreat: Healey fell back, almost willingly, onto it. He made a small whimpering sound as the seaman came further, and did nothing when those strong hands closed expertly about his neck.

Timmons felt the long-remembered thrill pass through his fingers; it was the killing time, the brief period of madness that kept him otherwise sane, and made the rest of his life worthwhile. Then, in a few dreadful seconds, it was done; the empty body fell limp from his grasp, and he knew there would be no further noise from that particular source.

* * *

Lady Hatcher was expected to remain with the surgeon for the remainder of the day, and the late governor's manservant could not be raised, so Banks had no compunction in holding the unofficial enquiry in the great cabin. His mind was still filled with thoughts of fatherhood, but when the masthead lookouts were dragged in under the somewhat embarrassed eyes of King, who, as luck would have it, was the divisional lieutenant for both, he found his thoughts more easy to focus.

"What the devil were you thinking of, Stiles?" Banks asked, after both men had mumbled out vague and disjointed explanations for their inattention. Reidy, at the fore, might have more excuse in that the main mast, and its associated spars, was between him and the sighting, but there surely could be no valid reason why Stiles, at the main, had said nothing. The room was almost full, in addition to King and the two seamen he had the master at arms, two ships corporals, and four uniformed marines – the latter being purely for ornamentation as the ship was currently in the middle of the Atlantic, and there was little chance of either prisoner making a successful escape. But all were silent, even Stiles, who seemed not to understand the question, and remained mute, despite the fact that his mouth had been left half open. Then finally he seemed to find inspiration, and pressed his chest forward in defiance.

"Don't know what came over me, sir," he confessed. "Must have been the distraction from the deck but one moment they weren't there, and the next they was."

"They just appeared?" Banks asked, apparently sympathetic.

"Yes, sir," Stiles agreed.

No one said anything for a moment, although Banks was reasonably certain that one of the corporals was trying to suppress some involuntary laughter. He could well understand how both men could have been distracted; ignoring what might have been going on during the ceremony, the governor's widow in a rage would have been a fascinating sight in itself, but that could be no excuse. Enemy shipping had been allowed to approach beyond the extent of the horizon and Stiles specifically had endangered his ship: it was a simple case of inattention to duty, and could not be ignored.

But how could he drum up a suitable penalty? Both men were experienced hands and had never done such a thing before. Besides, a moment's inattention was hardly a capital offence, and certainly not on a par with Banks' own thoughts when he had decided the enemy to be too strong for him to fight.

The captain's gaze naturally swept about the room. King was looking disconcerted, as well he might. In addition to being the prisoners' representative, he was very much implicated himself, and stood to lose far more than the two men that stood before them. The ship's corporal seemed to have suppressed the laughter for now, although Banks could tell by the look in his eye that it would not take much to start him off once more. It was a natural reaction in such a situation, as natural as being distracted by seamen cavorting on deck, or the widow of a government official in a frenzy, but that did not mean such action should go unpunished.

Stiles was staying stock still and saying nothing, although inside his head was whirring like a broken clock. The captain was trying him on quite unfair grounds, yet he was equally aware that, were he to say something now it would probably not be believed, and might get him into further trouble. On the afternoon in question he had been conscious of much that was going on below, and had even indulged himself by watching quite a bit, but that was not the whole story. As far as he was concerned he had been paying attention, besides having a laugh when Timmons had been held under water, and marvelling at the old bitch as she went off on one He had also swept the horizon on a regular basis, just as he had been taught. And as far as he was concerned his eyes were still the best in the ship; certainly at night there was no one to beat them, but of late he had to admit they were playing strange games.

Since the incident a few weeks back there had been several occasions when he had missed the seemingly obvious and, even when something had been pointed out to him, had found difficulty in actually locating it. And it was in daylight when the situation was most noticeable, that or sudden and extreme light. It wasn't a permanent thing however and, as the instances had been getting less frequent, he had hoped they would go completely, given time.

Banks was at a loss; both men could be disrated, and might even be given a touch of the cat, if only to serve as an example to the others. But he could not in all honesty sentence men to such a punishment, especially as the resultant action had not been as disastrous as it might have turned out. Besides, there was always the fact that a heavy penalty would only draw attention to the incident, and, glancing at King's worried face reminded him that he had his own reasons for not making more of the situation.

"Twenty eight day's suspension of grog," he said finally, taking them all by surprise. "And double that for anyone who attempts to help them. Dismiss!"

The silence was broken by a roar from the master at arms, followed by the stamp, stamp, stamp of marine boots as Stiles and Reidy were marched out of the cabin and onwards towards a month of sobriety. King was the last to leave, but Banks called him back as he turned to do so.

"I have complete jurisdiction over the people," he said softly as the room was finally emptied. "But less so over my officers."

"Yes, sir," King replied, in a voice that was little more than a whisper.

"This incident will have to be included in my report," he said. "Though I shall do my utmost not to give too much emphasis; you will understand, I am certain."

"Yes sir," King repeated. "Thank you, sir."

* * *

The new watch had been set less than ten minutes earlier, and those on deck had not even acclimatised themselves to the fresh air when there came a penetrating scream. Caulfield, who had been relieved as officer of the watch, and was about to go below to a long-awaited dinner, caught King's eye, and both men shrugged. The sound had come from directly below: the great cabin, and was far too raucous a noise to have been made by the captain's wife. A man working at a nearby carronade made some remark that caused his mates to laugh; Lady Hatcher had hardly endeared herself to the crew from the start, but after the incident at the equator she was universally and openly disliked.

"Shall I attend to that?" King asked, and the first lieutenant nodded.

"If you would be so kind, Thomas; I shall retain the watch until your return. It is probably nothing – perchance her Ladyship has come upon a spider, and at this latitude it may be poisonous."

"Then I shall see that it comes to no harm," King muttered, before setting off for the companionway.

On the deck below there was a further surprise: at the entrance to the great cabin the marine sentry had been joined by corporal Jarvis and two further privates as well as three members of the late governor's entourage.

"Follow me," King snapped at Jarvis, before thrusting the doors open in front of him and grunting "Not you," back at the civilians.

As he entered there was a further scream, softer this time, and more refined. King bounded forward, almost colliding with the captain and his lady as they emerged from the Hatcher's private quarters. Banks was stony faced, and his wife appeared in an advanced state of shock. He caught King's eye and indicated the room behind him with a tilt of his head.

"See to that, will you?" he said.

King lowered his head and entered the sleeping cabin. His eyes, accustomed to the glare of daylight, took several seconds to adjust to the darkened room but he soon made out the governor's widow, who had collapsed in a heap upon the only easy chair and was sobbing steadily, like an ill-maintained pump. He glanced about, then swore under his breath. There was Healey, apparently standing in the corner of the room, his face distorted as much by the make up as an obscene death's head grin. Then King realised the man was not supporting himself at all, but slumped from a rope tied about a cleat in the overhead beam. His body draped down, and swayed gently with the ship's motion, ending with the lower legs that trailed redundantly on the floor.

"Marine!" King shouted, as the horror rose up inside. A private appeared beside him and King continued, more controlled and almost gently: "My compliments to Mr Manning, and would he kindly attend?" Then, before the man could leave: "And the master at arms as well, if you please."

* * *

"I'd say it were self murder," the surgeon said coldly. "There is bruising about the second and third vertebrate, which would concur with being hanged from a rope, and you can see the signs of strangulation for yourself."

Healey's corpse was lying between them on a mess table with the covering sheet turned back to reveal his head and upper torso. Manning indicated a bruised area about the neck.

The captain closed his eyes and nodded. He had always detested the sight of dead bodies, and all his years fighting a war at sea had not hardened him in any way. Normally such an interview would have been taking place in the great cabin, but Lady Hatcher was monopolising the space now, so to avoid distressing Sarah further he had agreed to meet with the surgeon in his sick bay. At the time he had forgotten the likelihood of Healey's corpse being present. "And he was about the only one who could indulge himself so," Banks said, half to himself.

"By hanging? Yes, I expect that is so, sir." Manning agreed. "Though there are many other ways a man may self harm aboard *Scylla*, should he so wish."

The two men regarded each other for a moment. They had shipped together since Manning was a senior loblolly boy in the first frigate Banks commanded, but despite the period of time there was no love lost between them. At one point they had even competed for the same woman and, ironically, Banks thought he could hear Kate Manning now in the dispensary next door.

"You may be aware of the number of stories regarding his behaviour, sir," Manning continued. "That might have been a contributing factor."

"Yes, you are probably right." The captain stood up suddenly; there were indeed some odd reports about Healey, but he had no wish to discuss the distasteful habits of dead men. Besides, Sarah had been unduly upset by the discovery and he should really be with her. "I suppose there will have to be some sort of investigation," he said vaguely.

"Yes, sir." Manning replied. "An enquiry is usual in cases where death is not the direct result of enemy action."

"Well, we shall see to it on the morrow," Banks almost snapped. "The sooner it is done, the sooner we can get the body overboard. You will have your evidence prepared by then?" At any moment Manning's wife may enter the sick bay and Banks was not particularly keen to see her; the day had already been tiring enough.

"Indeed, sir. But, if you will excuse me?"

Banks waited, none too patiently.

"It is customary in cases of this nature to record the verdict as lunacy. You will understand the reasons I am sure."

"But he is to be buried at sea? There is no question of consecrated ground."

"No, sir." Manning agreed. "But the finding does have bearing on any beneficiaries. In cases of self murder the deceased's estate is appropriated by the crown."

It was a quirk of law that Banks was unfamiliar with, and he wondered slightly at Manning's apparent knowledge. "I have no idea if the man had any relatives – you may ask Lady Hatcher if you feel so inclined, but yes, I shall bear what you say in mind." He glanced at the body, which, like most, held a horrid fascination for him. Healey's face still bore the marks of rouge; the bright, bold colour contrasted dreadfully with his cold pallor. It was not a pretty sight; and if there was someone waiting for him, Banks supposed that a bending of the rules would not be so very terrible.

* * *

Timmons relaxed in the warm privacy of his hammock. It had been a good day; the molly had been dealt with and a score was settled, although even he was aware that there were other reasons for the total feeling of peace that now sated him. It had always been the same; since a lad, when his chief enjoyment had been practised on any small creature that came too close or was foolish enough to trust him. When he killed the first and experienced that oddly thrilling pain that had run through his entire body he had known it was only the start, and the passion would remain with him for as long as he was able to continue.

And he had done well, managed seven long years – it was at least that time since he had scragged his first, an elderly doxie in the upper room of a Torbay pot house. There had been no embellishments then of course, just the brief exhilaration followed by a swift and silent departure before enlistment in the first ship leaving. But the success had encouraged him, as well as emphasising how well the true focus of his life melded with his chosen profession.

For sailors are both anonymous and transitory; they dress in a homogeneous manner, stay for a while, and then depart, sometimes for long periods, frequently forever. And no one expects or requires more from them. All have like attributes: similar, weather beaten faces and, apart from the odd tattoo, are almost indistinguishable. Most drink, some chew or occasionally smoke tobacco, and apparently every single one enjoys both wenches and spending money – the two usually going hand in hand. In fact they all seem to share the same traits: apart, of course, from Timmons.

But today's little excursion had been different – it was the first time he had taken his craft to sea, and that certainly made the outcome a lot more satisfying. The risk had been greater undoubtedly; from being one in several million he had cut the odds of detection down to less than three hundred, but Timmons was quietly confident that his final flourish with the noose would see him safe. A man had been despatched with his own hands and yet, as far as anyone was aware, an entirely different crime had been committed; really it was the work of a genius.

He lay in his hammock now. It was hours later but his heart still pumped wildly from the act of private passion while he considered the future. It was eight weeks since his last kill, the pauper who had been the last of five to leave their shared room in Pompey and had so been chosen. Usually that would have been enough to keep Timmons' urges at bay for six months or more, but he had done it again, and so soon, and so successfully. They would be in St Helena before long; he'd never visited the place, of course, but understood that being both remote and contained, shore leave was regularly granted. There may well be an opportunity: possibly more than one. And then they would have the return trip: should the island prove unfruitful it would be eight or more weeks before England came into sight again. Time enough for him to organise another escapade such as that day's. He had not forgotten Mitchell or Hind – both fellows who had slighted him, and certainly deserving of his personal attention. But then, as the great cabin had been such an ideal location, he wondered if that might not be used a second time. Maybe not, for a common seamen, but there were other likely candidates; the captain for one, and then he had the choice of at least three women who might prove unintentionally accommodating; really this cruise was turning out to be the best he had ever taken.

Chapter Nine

They sighted St Helena thirteen days later. A call from the lookout at first light brought most of the officers and nearly every passenger on deck to join Fraiser, who had been present since the start of the watch. As dawn rose swiftly the harsh lines of apparently separate islands became obvious against a clear horizon, and elicited whoops of delight and a high buzz of excited talk from the civilians.

"Starboard a point," the sailing master said more soberly, and the ship's heel increased slightly as the south easterly wind was taken more on her beam. He had been fairly sure of the latitude, and just needed to make a small correction to bring them to what would otherwise have been a perfect landfall.

"Cutting it fine, weren't you, master?" King asked, as he approached. The ship had settled on her new course and was now heading for the distant land, even if she hardly made any appreciable progress. "A couple of degrees of longitude and with a slightly fairer wind, we might have run her down in the night."

"There was never a fear of that, Mr King," Fraiser replied solidly. "What you see there are only the tops of two large hills that span the island's main town. St Helena itself lies fifty mile or more beyond the horizon."

"That far?" The young lieutenant liked and respected Fraiser greatly; in many ways the elderly Scot was the closest he had to a father although, as with a father, he could rarely resist the opportunity to tease him. "But they look so close."

"They might seem that way, laddie," the sailing master agreed. "But it is usually better not to judge by appearances. St Helena is full of surprises, and her topography is only one of them. The hills near the sea are more'n fourteen hundred feet high while the tallest, further inland, is nigh on three thousand. It will take us the best part of the day to reach her; something you might wish to tell those for'ard, else they grow weary with the waiting.

The two men looked to where the passengers had gravitated to the break of the quarterdeck and were still talking animatedly. Since Hatcher's death some might not be expecting to stay long on the island, but King supposed that any landfall after such length of time was worthy of comment, even if their voyage to date had hardly been lacking in excitement.

"Oh, I think we should leave them be," he said evenly. "After all, it is the first solid ground we have sighted for some while."

"And will be the last for a spell longer," Fraiser agreed. "We are more than four hundred leagues from the nearest land – that would be Africa: the Americas are half as far again, and you may double that to reach Europe."

King shook his head. "True isolation," he said, half to himself. "How do they fare on such a place?"

"Well enough." Fraiser made a brief note in his journal, then looked up and towards the island. "St Helena is firmly in the Torrid Zone – an area the ancients believed to be uninhabitable, but the prevailing south easterly actually makes for a very pleasant climate, despite being so close to the equator."

"You spoke before of rain," King prompted.

"Aye, I did, but was unlucky in my last visit. In truth heavy rain is relatively rare, though there is a good supply of fresh spring water, and I understand it can now be brought directly to the anchorage."

"But St Helena has no harbour?"

"None. Those at anchor may ride safe enough, and the previous governor improved the wharf and constructed a landing place."

"*Scylla* will need more than that," King said gloomily. Despite repeated efforts from Evans and his team, the ship still leaked badly and was in desperate need of repair. "There are no dockyard facilities at all?"

"We shall have to see," Fraiser temporised. "It is a few years since I was ashore, and Governor Brooke sounds to have been peculiarly active in his post."

Mention of another governor set King's mind on a different track. The council on St Helena must be expecting their arrival.

Scylla would probably have been sighted already, with preparations underway to receive both her, and the important passenger she supposedly carried. He wondered what their reaction might be when, rather than a new man to take responsibility, they could only produce a corpse and excuses. It would take months for the news to reach England, and probably a year or more before another replacement was found, primed, and eventually stood in the same position as they did now. Doubtless there were capable men already in place who could carry out a governor's duties, but Brooke had retired the previous March and it was already a long enough interregnum. Even ignoring any blame the captain might incur for the governor's death, to carry such news would hardly make him the most welcome of visitors.

"If we cannot repair at St Helena, there is always the Cape," Fraiser continued, still thinking of the problems with the ship herself. "Though to my mind it would be better to return north as soon as we may, and set her to dock in England." He glanced at the younger man, expecting a response, and was surprised when none was forthcoming. He supposed it possible that some of King's previous urgency for home had been lost; or perhaps he was just getting better at hiding it. In Fraiser's experience time cured much and that which it did not usually became less apparent. Long voyages with scant chance of reliable communication were part of the seaman's lot: either they became resigned to the fact, or went mad.

"What do you think they will make of the governor's death in England?" King asked, changing the subject and surprising the sailing master yet again. The older man said nothing for a moment; it was a subject that had hardly been discussed, although every officer, and even some of the men, must have considered it at length.

"I should say that is not for the likes of you or me to speculate upon," he replied eventually, turning his head, and regarding King for a moment.

"But will the captain be blamed?" the lieutenant continued, unabashed, and completely forgetting the late governor's staff that were standing close by.

"Maybe he will, and maybe he won't," Fraiser told him evenly. "We cannot predict the ways of man, and neither should we judge them."

"But he did nothing wrong, they must see that," King said. Then, catching a look of reproach, continued in little more than a whisper: "Punishing a man for doing his duty is surely unjust."

"Unjust, you say?" The Scotsman rolled his eyes. "And there is no doubt in your mind as to that?"

King shrugged. "As far as we know, we are still at war with France. Sir Richard did not actively seek a confrontation with a superior force, but when one presented, neither did he turn away. Had he done so then yes, that would have been neglecting his duty. As it was..."

"Your loyalty does you credit, laddie," the older man conceded. "But I repeat, it is not down to the likes of us. We just have to rely upon the Lord's mercy, and the equity of our betters."

"Well I know which my money is on," King replied bitterly.

* * *

But for Banks it was not quite so straightforward. As *Scylla* rounded Munden's Point and stood in towards St Helena's main anchorage his mind sifted through the myriad responses he could use to match whatever reception he might face. They had made the private signal to the station on Sugar Loaf Point some while back and received no indication or communication from the shore since, other than a request to anchor. Now, as the sub-equatorial sun prepared to make its late afternoon plunge towards the horizon, he stood firm in immaculate full dress uniform, wearing an expression of confident anticipation that fooled every person aboard the frigate, except one.

Sarah was watching him surreptitiously as they waited by the entry port and, feeling her eyes upon him, he turned to her. "You are quite certain you feel well enough?" he asked softly.

"I was never better, thank you, Richard," she replied, while subtly reaching across and gently squeezing his hand. They had discussed the visit in low tones for most of the morning while

Scylla crept up to the island. Both were well aware that the government on St Helena may well censure the captain and, even if they did not, Lady Hatcher was quite capable of causing a scene on her own account. In either case it would do no good for them to show signs of weakness and, despite the internal misgivings she currently felt, Sarah was determined not to let her husband down.

In fact Lady Hatcher was standing close by and clad in stiff finery; the tailored and formal gown, with just enough black for decency, made her appear very much the governor's widow, and was in distinct contrast to the less modest attire she had commonly worn during the latter days aboard *Scylla*. Neither of them knew exactly what was in the woman's mind but Sarah, for one, feared the worst, and had also rehearsed likely outcomes. Sir Richard Banks might be a senior post captain; skilled in seamanship and fighting tactics, as well as a proven leader of men, but no husband is the complete hero to his wife and Sarah held few illusions about his diplomatic skills. What was correct and proper on a quarterdeck rarely met the needs of council chambers or politic discussion. She knew from experience how he could hesitate and struggle all too easily if under pressure, whereas the governor's widow was exceptionally eloquent when the need arose. As far as Sarah was concerned, Richard would have been safer accompanying a female lion ashore than Lady Hatcher.

Scylla continued to inch closer until a muttered command from Caulfield at the binnacle set off a series of actions; the mizzen topsail was backed, slowing her progress further and a crack from forward was followed by a loud splash as the best bower plunged to the sea bed, twelve fathoms below. The ship continued forward for a spell until an unseen hand checked her, and a second anchor was released. The sails were whipped up to the yards as if controlled by some hidden and high-speed mechanism, and she came to rest.

Within minutes the gig was skimming across a sea made artificially calm by the frigate's sheltering bulk, with Jackson at the tiller and the captain's coxswain already standing to receive a line from the nearby wharf.

It was, indeed, a new construction, and well made from hefty slabs of deep brown timber that looked likely to last out the rest of the new century. Banks helped Sarah up the short steps and in no time the party was assembled on the smart wooden walkway. Ahead stood a delegation of officials, one wearing a golden chain and an especially elaborate hat that he appeared uncertain of in the light wind. Most wore East India Company uniforms and there was a group of highly polished soldiers standing rigidly behind, while what must have been an entire company of troops could just be seen formed up on the parade ground beyond. Banks even thought he caught the glint of brass instruments and swallowed nervously; this was clearly intended to be a glorious occasion; one that all attending had been looking forward to since the last governor departed. And now it was about to fall embarrassingly flat.

He set off, conscious of his wife by his side, as well as Lady Hatcher, who was following close behind and constantly whispering to her maid. The official in the large hat stepped forward and seemed to be examining them as they grew closer; his smile froze as he searched their faces for one that was not there, and Banks had to resist the temptation to increase his step. Then they were almost face to face, the small guard of honour was ordered to present arms, and all uniformed officers saluted. Banks responded crisply, before proffering the same hand to what appeared to be the senior man, and introducing himself.

The official accepted the handshake and muttered something in reply that Banks did not catch, then cleared his throat and spoke in a firmer voice.

"Governor Hatcher is not with you, Sir Richard?" The man blinked. "Perhaps he is unwell?"

"My husband is dead," Lady Hatcher announced in a cold and distinct tone that was designed to carry. "Sir Richard all but killed him."

* * *

"There will be shore leave, sure as a gun," Flint told them as they leaned over the bulwark. "Mind, not that there's much to do when you get there," he continued.

"What no pot houses?" Mitchell asked, sourly.

"Oh yes, by the score, only the military calls them different." Flint replied. "They ply a decent trade; even brew their own beer. But that's about it."

"That's enough," Hind assured everyone. "All I ask is my stingo and a willin' woman, nothing else is required."

Flint gave a brief laugh. "Well, that's not what you'll get, matey."

"No doxies?" They all seemed incensed. "That ain't natural."

"It is on St Helena. This is a John Company island, and the Honourable East India Company don't provide such things for your foremast jack; least not outside the shipping season."

"But what about all them lobsters?" Mitchell asked.

"I'm not saying there's none," Flint relented slightly. "But not what you're used to, or expecting. Rumour has it the army is catered for privately, but you won't get a lot of co-operation from that quarter. There was a fine pushing school south of Jamestown that dealt with jacks last time I was here, but they closed it down as soon as the Indiamen left."

"Where there is a need, someone will supply it," Dixon said with the air of one who knows. "Throw out a fish, and the cats will always gather."

"That is assuming there are cats about," Flint persisted. "We're a long way from anywhere, remember. Woman lets out her front room and the Company don't approve, there ain't no fine – she's simply shipped off to the Cape, never to be seen again."

"Well that's no good to us," Mitchell groaned. "What's the point of takin' a cruise if there ain't no one to dock with?"

"But hold fast; there is a good side." Flint added, cheering slightly.

They waited.

"St Helena has the fewest cases of clap in the southern hemisphere."

* * *

Kate was alone: all the women had departed. Lady Hatcher with her maid, while Sarah accompanied the captain. She was probably being bored rigid right now by a tour of a barracks or some other such local delight. Robert had also gone; he used the excuse of having to present their medical certificates to accompany the shore party, along with Tom King, the couple's closest friend. Quite what the two of them might get up to if left together Kate did not care to guess but she carried few illusions about seamen of any rank, and did not expect either man to return for some while, or completely sober.

She sat in the empty sickbay, annoying her needlepoint that never seemed to grow in proportion to the effort invested. The ship was all but silent; every one of the governor's staff had departed, and those of *Scylla's* people that remained were principally on the upper deck and would doubtless be exulting over the sights of what appeared to be a very dull and uninspiring island.

Or maybe it was her? She had never been what the lower deck might refer to as a jolly dog and, since the loss of her child, had rather taken shelter behind a barrier of quiet and private contemplation: that and her dedication to work, which was boarding on the obsessive. She knew that such behaviour was hardly beneficial to Robert who, to some extent at least, had lost a child as well, but could do little to change it. On several occasions he had attempted to bring her old self out, and she responded in kind, trying hard to regain her previous subtle, if often mildly sardonic sense of humour, along with a slightly less disconsolate countenance. But every effort failed miserably, and left him just as confused and isolated as before, and her every bit as depressed.

The pain was simply too great. No matter how she dressed it up: explained to herself and others who would listen that it was the chance every expectant mother took. That nothing good came from little effort, and several attempts might be needed if they were to achieve the family they both wanted. But no matter what ruse or trick she pulled to forget the past, the fact of her loss was always there: always waiting for her to return and provide the attention it demanded. On rare occasions she had even spoken of this to Robert, and he had been as supportive and understanding as ever. There might be no medical cure for her ailment, but he was perceptive enough to recognise it as such. And patient, always so damnably patient. Sometimes Kate even wondered if it was this very tolerance that was feeding the condition; perhaps if he had behaved like most husbands; taken a stronger stance: demanded that she brought herself back to the real world, and start behaving like the wife he had every right to expect, perhaps then it might do the trick. That was not his way however, and Kate accepted that for Robert to change his personality would be every bit as difficult as she was finding changing hers.

And then, just as things were starting to improve, the captain's wife became pregnant. Of course that could not, in any way, be construed as bad news; Sarah was probably her closest female friend, and she was sincerely happy for her, if cautiously so. But Sarah was a different person and Kate already sensed would have a perfectly splendid pregnancy. Even now the initial sickness she had personally experienced throughout her term was starting to wear off, and the woman was positively glowing with wellbeing. There was not the smallest portion of Kate that wanted anything else, and nothing in her power that she would not give, or do, to ensure the couple were shortly blessed with a happy, healthy child. But still the inequity of it all could not be ignored, and she knew herself to be sinking ever deeper into the pit that had been both her refuge and prison for far too long.

The sound of approaching footsteps made her look up from her work. It was a heavy-booted tread and marked the wearer out as both adult and an officer. There was no shortage of either aboard *Scylla*, despite the absence of the shore party, but still some sixth sense made her wait, expectantly, as the sound grew nearer, and she was not in the least surprised when it stopped outside, and was replaced by a gentle knock. The door opened, admitting the sailing master. Kate was mildly intrigued; she knew Adam Fraiser well, and respected him greatly, but he was not by nature a social person and his healthy diet made him a rare caller.

"Mr Fraiser, so good to see you; come in, do," she said, rising, and dropping her needlepoint to one side. "I'm afraid Robert is off ship at present; I could take a message for his return if you wish."

The older man's face relaxed into the close approximation of a smile. "Thank you, my dear, but I wanted only to ask a favour of you."

"Of me?" This was indeed unusual.

"Or to be more accurate, your department," Fraiser clarified. "I require pure water; some will be available ashore, no doubt, but I recalled that you have access to a supply of distilled from the galley range."

"Why yes. The cook delivers a pint or so every day from his still. How much do you require?"

"Half of that will suit me admirably." he replied, as she went to one of the cupboards and removed a restraining bar that kept the larger jars in place. "It is for my Leige Barometer; it is a bit of an affectation I know but I value the accuracy and in truth the device uses remarkably little liquid, though it must always be of the very purest."

"Well, we have far more than is needed," Kate told him, fetching a flask that she proceeded to fill. "But we don't dissuade the cook in case he takes offence. Indeed Mr Grimley is not one of life's most cheerful creatures," she continued, reaching inside a drawer for a suitable stopper.

"Perchance it is a case of name, like nature?" Fraiser suggested.

"Indeed," Kate agreed, frowning deeply as she pressed the cork home. "Though I have seldom met one quite so constantly miserable; if he doesn't make a change he will remain without friends, and die a sad and solitary death."

Her eyes swept round to meet those of the fatherly sailing master. She felt a strange pang of conscience as she realised what she had said, and how her words could so easily apply to herself. Then it was as if something vital inside suddenly gave way; the tears rose up unasked, and quickly began to flow.

"Oh, my poor, wee child," Fraiser said softly, before reaching out and holding her close against his chest.

Chapter Ten

"You have certainly caught us on the hop, Sir Richard." Colonel Robson, the lieutenant governor smiled, not unkindly, and motioned Banks to a chair. It was a pleasant room, and seemed almost obscenely spacious to one used to the confines of a frigate. Both doorways were easily seven feet high, and wide enough for two to enter side by side, while the ornately moulded ceiling must have stretched all of twelve feet above their heads. But, despite its apparent opulence, the actual furnishings were not of a high standard. The governor's desk, presumably cleared and polished for a new incumbent and now apologetically reclaimed by his deputy, might be imposing but lacked the sophistication of European pieces. The top of the walnut occasional table to Banks' right was also slightly warped, and his own chair creaked alarmingly under what he assured himself was less than average weight.

"I am sorry for any inconvenience, sir," Banks said. As a senior Royal Navy post captain he outranked an HEIC lieutenant colonel, although Robson's position as acting governor made the distinction somewhat vague, and Banks' current dependency on the shore destroyed it completely.

"I suppose the death of a governor elect might be termed as such," the older man mused. "Though between ourselves and from what I can collect, you are hardly to be blamed."

Banks felt some of the tension in his breast lessen, and it was hard not to break into laughter. The scene at the quay was still fresh in his memory. A confusion of voices, with Lady Hatcher's being the most dominant. Accusations and complaints flying like grape shot, while he did his best to rebuff the more outrageous. And all the time attempting to explain to the group of confused dignitaries why their long-awaited leader was lying in a case of spirits on the orlop rather than receiving their greetings. In the end it had fallen to someone other than the lieutenant governor to rectify matters. Banks was still unsure of the man's identity, except that he was one of the members of council, and had both the good sense and authority to act quickly.

"You will take some refreshment, sir?" Colonel Robson asked, "Tea we have in abundance, and there is a remarkably good Mocha coffee that is grown on the island. Or maybe it is time for something stronger?"

Banks refused; all he wanted was to clarify the current problem, then discover what facilities were available to his ship. Once the troops had been dismissed it had not taken long for the shore party and those sent to welcome them to repair to the waiting carriages. Fortunately there were several of the latter, and the same intelligent official had seen to it that Lady Hatcher, along with her maid, were swiftly separated from the rest. Sarah was also absent, although she, like Banks, had been brought straight to Government House, an ornate building enclosed within an embrasured wall that housed the official offices. She was now with the lieutenant governor's wife, whereas Banks had no idea of Lady Hatcher's whereabouts. Last seen she was being all but pressed into a coach, and had been making a good deal of noise about it.

"I believe you mentioned Sir Terrance's death as being in action," the lieutenant governor said. "That is unfortunate. I presume a place of safety had been provided for him?"

"Yes, Colonel. He was allocated quarters in the cable tier; his wife and staff were there and remained safe."

"But Sir Terrance did not stay?"

"He came on deck upon hearing gunfire."

Robson nodded, apparently satisfied. "I did not know the man of course, but can understand such a draw. It is probably better that we say no more for now; there will doubtless be an official enquiry, but I am sure you did not take your ship to battle lightly. I am equally certain you cannot be held responsible; if a government official outside of your service chooses to place themselves in danger, well, then it must be on their own head."

Banks' feeling of relief grew; it was obvious that, despite its size and remote position, St Helena did not lack intelligent staff.

The promise of an official enquiry hardly appealed, but that was more due to the time such a procedure was likely to take.

"And the action, Sir Richard: it was conclusive?"

"I am afraid not," Banks confessed. "We ran into a battle squadron; three warships: a heavy French frigate and two corvettes. Over the space of several days I was able to severely damage the smaller craft, although the larger remains unharmed."

"And she is in the vicinity?"

"Not sighted for some while, but the squadron was definitely heading south when first encountered."

The lieutenant governor gave a brief smile. "It seems that any ship within five hundred miles will find us eventually – indeed, there is precious little elsewhere to go."

"She is a large fifth rate, Colonel," Banks told him. "But even if all three ships have survived, I doubt they could carry a sufficient force to threaten this island."

This time Robson laughed out loud. "Oh we do not fear invasion, Sir Richard," he said lightly. "There are troops a plenty hereabouts, with artillery enough for a small war. And as only one beach is suitable for a landing, and that stays protected by more metal than is carried by one of your liners, we can remain relatively secure for some while." His smile faded. "It is rather the oncoming shipping season that concerns me. Even alone, a powerful frigate would be a damnable nuisance, and three as you describe might cost us a small fortune. The Navy will sort it out, no doubt, although of late they have been inclined to rather abandon convoys further north. You could not meet her once more in your ship I suppose?"

Banks' mind went back to that final deadly broadside; in some ways it was unfortunate that the action had not continued for longer. If *Scylla* had been able to inflict even some minor damage on the enemy he would feel a good deal more confident: as it was she had received, but not delivered. It was purely psychological, of course, but that, combined with the Frenchman's rate and accuracy of fire, had instilled an almost supernatural quality onto his adversary. And if that was his impression, he dared not consider what the lower deck, with their predilection for tall tales and superstition, would be making of it. Even now legends might be forming based on what was probably just another French warship that happened to get in a couple of quick and lucky strikes. "Of course I would be happy to take my ship to battle again," he said, in as neutral a tone as he could manage. "But *Scylla* is badly damaged, and will require considerable repair before that can happen."

A tap at the side door interrupted any reply from Robson, and heralded another arrival. Banks was pleased to note it was the efficient official encountered earlier.

"Ah, Henry, so glad you were able to join us," the lieutenant governor said, standing up and indicating Banks. "I don't think I had the chance to make any official introductions before. Henry Booker, Secretary to the Council: Sir Richard Banks, Captain of his Britannic Majesty's ship, *Scylla*."

The two men greeted each other formally and Banks was impressed by Booker's straightforward look and firm handshake. He was a man of late middle age, and on a station such as St Helena, might be considered to be at the end of his career. But Booker clearly had an alert mind and had already demonstrated both his efficiency and personal authority.

"Henry has the office next door though spends much of his time in here with me. He has been indispensable since the departure of Governor Brooke," Robson explained. "Frankly we have all been putting in long days, and were rather looking forward to a rest, though it appears we shall have to continue a while longer," he added, awkwardly.

"Forgive me for not arriving sooner, I have been entertaining Lady Hatcher," Booker said, as all three sat down. "She was a mite upset, as I think you will have gathered."

"Sir Richard and I have discussed the matter briefly," Robson murmured. "I think we can save anything further for the official enquiry."

"Of course," Booker agreed. "I have settled the good lady at Plantation House. That is the governor's official country residence," he explained to Banks. "The alternative was to have her here, and some distance seemed to be preferable in the circumstances."

All were in total agreement with the last point. Even to Banks it was patent that Lady Hatcher's presence at what was clearly the centre of government for the island could only be an embarrassment. He was also impressed that Booker had acted so quickly, and without bothering Robson. "She has her maid of course and Major Morris, of the Artillery, who was related to her late husband. He is with her now and doing a good job in keeping her calm. Be assured, she will not be neglected," the secretary added with a degree of consideration, even though all were well aware that no one with such a personality as Lady Hatcher's could ever be condemned to such a fate.

"Doubtless arrangements can be made to remove her possessions from your ship in due course, Captain?" Robson asked.

"I was assuming she would be returning to England in *Scylla*," Banks said, striving once more for an impersonal tone.

"Indeed she may," Booker replied, while still apparently considering Banks' statement. "Though the shipping season is but a few weeks hence, and it might be more pleasant for her to travel back in one of the Company's Indiamen, than a warship. Besides," his strong blue eyes seemed to twinkle as he continued, "I would judge her not to be the easiest of passengers."

Once more Banks was impressed; Booker appeared as perceptive as he was quick to react, although in Lady Hatcher's case perhaps deep insight might not be required.

"I will call a meeting of Council tomorrow morning," Robson said, taking control once more. "There is much to discuss, advising the Honourable Board of Directors of Sir Terrance's death, for one. And we shall have to see about repairing your ship, Sir Richard; as well as reporting on this blasted Frenchman. What is the extent of *Scylla*'s damage?"

"Holed below the waterline, Colonel. I was to enquire of your facilities."

"We have no dock of any description, Captain," Booker told him. "But are efficient enough at carrying out repairs afloat. I shall ask the superintendent to attend tomorrow's meeting and you may speak with him."

"And afterwards, I wonder if I might entertain you and Lady Banks during your stay here?" Robson interrupted. "We were to have offered you a place at Plantation House and indeed were intending to dine there tonight. That will have to be cancelled out of respect, of course, but my own country residence is not five miles from here, and my wife and I would be delighted to accommodate you, and any of your officers you would care to name."

Banks thanked the lieutenant governor, even though he had been looking forward to returning to *Scylla* with Sarah and spending their first evening away from Lady Hatcher.

"You did intend staying ashore, I presume, Captain?" Robson asked.

Now he was taken further aback; he had assumed the invitation was for a meal, not accommodation "I, I had not considered…"

"I have a house not far from the colonel's and have already offered your surgeon and lieutenant quarters," Booker told him. "They are obviously awaiting your permission, but it really would make things so much easier if you were all on hand, as it were."

Banks' mind went back to *Scylla*. She was still leaking steadily, although the damage would be under less pressure now they had found a sheltered anchorage. Caulfield was the only commissioned officer aboard, but he should be able to deal with any immediate problems. He would organise a guard boat as a matter of course and, as she was under the protection of heavy shore batteries, the ship should be safe from even the most aggressive of seaward attacks. But still the prospect of abandoning his command did not come easily. "I have to consider the possibility of the Frenchman finding us," he said.

"Governor Brooke did much during his time here," Robson told him. "Amongst many projects he initiated a series of look-out points, and a system of signalling that seems to work adequately enough. During the day we can spot a ship up to eighty miles off, and at night there are two picket boats that patrol Chapel Valley Bay. I think you will find your ship will remain unmolested," the lieutenant governor added, with just a hint of condescension.

"The anchorage is also safe from any storms – not that one is due," Booker said. "Indeed no ship has foundered off our coast since the British took possession."

Banks found himself smiling. "My wife and I would be delighted, Colonel," he said, then, turning to the secretary "And if you are sure the presence of my men will not be too much trouble, Mr Booker?"

"None whatsoever; my daughter lives with me and grows powerful lonely outside of the shipping season. I am certain your officers will be welcomed greatly, especially if they have any news of Europe."

"Then I will leave you to make arrangements," the lieutenant governor said briskly. "Perhaps you could help Sir Richard signal his ship, Henry?"

Banks stood and followed Booker out of the office.

"I really cannot thank you enough for what you did today," Banks said awkwardly. "And for agreeing to accommodate my officers, of course."

"As I have stated, Sir Richard, I am more than happy." Then Booker's expression hardened. "Though I should perhaps add a word of caution," he continued, more guardedly. "The official enquiry would not normally present problems, but I gather Lady Hatcher does not intend to make things easy. As secretary to the council I can hardly encourage you to speak out of turn, but it might be better if we find time to discuss some of the details of her husband's death in private, and prepare for any allegations she might be intending to make."

The inner feeling of tension had all but gone, but Banks felt it return with the secretary's words. He had barely known Booker three hours, yet already felt he could be trusted. And if such a man was concerned, then there was probably every reason for him to be also.

"But St Helena is a delightful island, as I think you will find." Booker's tone lightened and he continued as if starting a fresh conversation. "For centuries it has been known as a place of sanctuary: where difficulties are solved and the sick recover. Let us hope it can work some of its magic on the present problem."

Chapter Eleven

King woke feeling strangely exposed. His bed was wide, flat and very open; there was the whisper of a draught that blew from the nearby window: apart from that everywhere seemed quite solid and almost eerily still. He moved and the rich mattress rustled beneath him, which was another thing, other than that of his bed, and his own breathing, all was deadly quiet. At any time of the day, and even when safely at anchor, *Scylla* was alive with noise. It was something King had grown accustomed to: from the creaking in the frame to the constant whine of her rigging, the frigate was never at rest. And it varied: there were muffled conversations, shouted orders, the scream of sea birds, even sudden, unexplained, laughter, or far off mysterious hammering, but never silence. Over the years he had grown used to the sounds, even if his ears automatically blanked most out. But with their absence he felt mildly disconcerted; the world was changed every bit as much as if time had been removed, or colours transposed.

He eased himself unsteadily out of the bed and allowed his gaze to sweep around the large, but impersonal, room. On the chair next to him lay his uniform jacket: it was something tangible, of real life, and stupidly reassuring. The curtains had been drawn back since the previous evening, and there was now a pewter jug and basin that he did not remember on the oversized chest of drawers. The fact that someone had entered while he was asleep did not worry him greatly; until he was made lieutenant there were few nights when he slept without someone being awake near by. But neither did it reassure him. He rose and walked in nightshirt and bare feet to the window, where a further shock awaited.

It was daylight, and the view was so obviously of England, but it was not the England that he knew. There were no smelly, narrow streets or mean, port side houses, this was the England of his dreams and, he told himself erroneously, of his childhood. His room was on the first floor; below he could see a formal garden, well kept and bright with flowers, even if some seemed unfamiliar. Beyond was a small orchard filled with apple trees and further away, divided by neat hedgerows apparently made up of blackberry bushes, a series of fields like any found in Sussex or Surrey. A herd of cows gathered to one side of the nearest and, even more distant, what might be goats were dotted about. There were no trees to be seen on their approach to St Helena, nor from the anchorage, and little had been visible on his two coach rides. During the first he had been squashed between Williams, the purser, and one of the fresh intake of HEIC staff, while the second had taken place in total darkness. But now he saw many, and not just in the formal orchard. Great forests of the things; some standing guardian over the fields while others, filling the valley in clumps and clusters, seemed to flow, unbidden, up to the bases of the nearby hills. Oak, chestnut, weeping willow; some that looked distinctly foreign and might be bamboo, as well the more familiar apple, pear and other fruit bearers. On his few return trips to England King had noted that many of the native forests were being systematically cut back, presumably for timber. Consequently this was probably the largest collection of woodland he had encountered since a lad, and his seaman's eyes gazed in wonder.

From somewhere deep in the house a clock chimed; it was eight, time enough to get moving, but still he felt an odd lethargy that was difficult to shake. On the dressing table sat a package that had been handed to him on his arrival. Clearly a fast sailing vessel from England had beaten them to the island, and carried a small amount of post for the ship. His share had consisted of the package and, as the address had been written in Juliana's distinctive hand, he had all but torn the wrapper to pieces. But inside was only a statement from his bankers and a tailor's account for six pairs of woollen stockings and two new shirts. He picked up the paper yet again and examined it; there was definitely no message from his wife: not even the briefest of notes.

He and Juliana had wed more than two years ago, and he had

supposed they were as happy as any married couple could expect to be, accepting that so little time was actually spent in the other's company. But the last brief leave, when *Scylla*'s anchors hardly settled in the Spithead mud, had not gone well. His previous concerns were that she might not be taking to living in a foreign land, especially one actively at war with her own, while he also feared that a husband who was constantly absent, fighting that very conflict, would only make matters worse. But he could not have been more mistaken; Juliana had adapted admirably.

It was the small signals he had noticed first: nothing substantial. Several invitations to parties and subscription dances, and a message, delivered by one of the Southsea street urchins, that could only be given personally to Mrs King. Then there was that parcel of letters, tightly wrapped in ribbon, that he discovered when searching for scissors in her needlework basket. Initially he was too frightened to open them and then, on summoning the courage a few days later, found they had disappeared. Taken alone each were almost insignificant but their presence alerted him to other, equally subtle, signals that Juliana herself had sent out. A reluctance to visit certain eating houses they used to favour, her monthly curse arriving so neatly as to completely fill their brief time together and once, to her immediate horror, she had even called him by another man's name. All were of small moment, or so he had tried to convince himself, but as he considered them again and for the hundredth time, there was no doubt in his mind that they were growing apart. But then even that was unfair, as they had never properly been together to begin with.

"Ahoy, Tom!" Manning's voice came from outside the room and King paused for just a moment before calling for his friend to enter.

The oversized door opened silently to reveal the surgeon, fully dressed and suitably smug. "Eight bells: better be rigged and ready," King was told. Manning wore his dark, formal uniform well, giving the impression of both maturity and medical competence, even if his face still bore the boyish grin that King remembered from when he had been a mere loblolly boy. "Mr

Booker's man said that breakfast would be served in half a glass, and I gather it a pity to be missed."

King moved back from the window and poured out a basin of water. "You're uncommonly early, Bob," he said, before sluicing his face with the cold water. "And horribly bright."

"Ah, I am not used to sleeping alone and have been up since first light exploring, along with the purser," Manning said, as he carelessly tossed King's jacket onto the bed and settled himself in its place. "This house is like a palace; friend Booker must be more of note than we surmised. I have seldom seen so large a mansion, and there seem to be servants wherever one looks."

"Most will be slaves," King replied in a matter of fact voice while feeling at his chin. He had shaved before going ashore the previous afternoon and decided it would not be necessary again until the promised meal that evening.

"Slaves or not, they seem a pretty cheerful bunch," Manning said. Then, on apparently noticing the coat for the first time: "Did your dunnage not arrive from the ship?"

"Yes, but I have yet to unpack fully," King replied, his voice muffled by a towel. "In truth it is hard to know how long we shall be ashore."

They had arrived at Booker's house in darkness and, after the briefest of meals with their host, had taken an early night.

"I dare say more will be revealed at this morning's meeting."

"You are not attending, I collect?" King pressed an arm through a shirt and pulled it over his shoulders.

"No, I have to find the hospital; it is in an area called Maldiva, apparently, though surely nothing can be so very hard to find in a place so small."

"Feeling a mite unwell are we?"

"I have to wait upon the surgeon general," Manning replied patiently. "There are the medical certificates to present and the sick bay is precious short both of laudanum and number five catgut. But we two are both invited to the dinner tonight, are we not?"

King paused in the process of pulling on his second best pair of stockings. "Indeed, tell me: what usually happens at these affairs?"

"Blessed if I knows," the surgeon answered cheerfully. "Nearest I've ever been to an official dinner is to dine at Sir Richard's London house when he was wed, and I can't say I found that particularly rousing. I would chance it 'swords be worn' and 'wine with you, sir', oh and probably endless speeches. You have sufficient to wear, I trust?" he added in a softer tone. "If not I'm certain Michael Caulfield will respond to a signal."

"Oh, I shall cope tolerably well," King said, with more confidence than he felt. "The one thing in favour of a naval uniform is that it is never out of fashion."

"I should question that they are with the latest ways on this little speck," Manning mused. "We may be ten weeks from England, but it is ten years or more behind the times. Though that might be for the better if what I witnessed in London of late is any judge."

"Ten years behind? Why that is the best I have heard for a long time," King said, his face brightening.

Manning appeared doubtful. "Why so?"

"It would mean we are no longer at war."

The heavy rumble of a gong sounded from somewhere distant, and King wrenched his britches up in sudden hurry.

"That will be breakfast," Manning grunted. "And from what I saw being prepared, it would seem to be a feast. There was bacon and kidneys a cookin' and an especially enticing smell of mutton chops."

"I have not eaten kidney in ages," King reflected, forcing both feet simultaneously into his shoes.

"Ah, and there is more to look forward to than just scrag," Manning continued. "Our host ain't the bachelor we suspected. He's married, or must have been at one time. Leastways there is a daughter, and I'd gauge you won't find a fairer wench within a thousand miles."

* * *

Banks was also anticipating a fine breakfast. He and Sarah sat opposite each other at the middle of a long, narrow table with Robson and his wife, a mature and rosy woman, at the head and foot respectively. Between them was sufficient food to feed a hungry twelve and the visitors, too long used to shipboard provisions and rationed portions, were overwhelmed.

"Sarah, dear: help yourself to some of that kedgeree, do," Mrs Robson urged. "I always think it a good start to any meal, and especially suitable for one in your condition."

Sarah blushed, and avoided her husband's eye as she busied herself with a spoon. They had agreed to say nothing of her pregnancy while ashore, but it was a secret Sarah had found impossible to keep from the lieutenant governor's wife. Mrs Robson had no aspirations or interests apart from her family, which were now all grown and gone, and had greeted the news with enthusiasm. Sarah also enjoyed the telling, as well as the numerous discussions and debates that followed. For far too long she had been burning to speak more freely and without the guilt that Kate's presence induced. Since discovering herself to be pregnant, there had been few that she could truly share her pleasure with.

"Try some of that ham, Sir Richard," Robson urged. "There is a man in town who cures it to perfection."

"You keep an extremely good table, Colonel," Banks said, dutifully spearing a slice with his fork.

"Oh, this is not our usual fare, Captain," Mrs Robson assured him, cheerfully ignoring her husband's warning look. "Much of the time it is bully beef and salted bacon, though we do well with fresh vegetables and have some truly splendid fruit."

"But all this?" Sarah waved her hand at the offered food. "Surely it is not entirely for our benefit?"

"The Company pays an allowance for entertaining guests," Robson said stiffly. "Even if precious few are received outside of the shipping season. And much of what we require can be obtained on the island. We rear beef, lamb, goats plus a few pigs, and most other provisions are found."

"Except honey," Mrs Robson interrupted, and again her husband's eyes flashed in her direction. "Wind keeps blowing the bees away," she explained in a stage whisper to Sarah.

"But getting back to the meat," Robson continued, "Jennifer is correct; much of what we ourselves eat, and all of the troops' provisions are preserved, and come from England."

"How many are there on the island, Colonel?" Banks asked.

"In military terms, slightly in excess of a battalion," Robson replied, after finishing a mouthful. "Then there is a core of artillery, a further five hundred civilians and fifteen hundred slaves."

Banks was surprised; to feed so many must be expensive both in money and material. Presumably fully provisioned store ships made regular journeys just to maintain the population, and that would be in addition to any victualling requirements from merchant vessels travelling to or from the Far East.

"The Company supplies us with salt meat at well under prime cost," the lieutenant governor continued. "It is basically sold at a loss, but far more can be made if we eke out our indigenous stock for what is a more profitable market."

"There is a ready demand from the Indiamen," Mrs Robson explained. "Fresh fruit and green stuff is always welcomed, but they seem especially keen for meat."

"Three months sailing time from Bengal," her husband agreed. "Many of the passengers are crying out for it when they reach us, and willing to pay the eleven ha'pence a pound we charge."

"We also have ways of making sure no one undercuts us, or wantonly wastes fresh," Mrs Robson continued with evident satisfaction. "No citizen is permitted to butcher even their own oxen without permission from the governor's office."

Banks chewed on his ham meditatively. As both a member of the aristocracy and a King's Officer, trade was almost an anathema to him, and he tended to look down on those who indulged in such practice. But it was clear that the East India Company were masters at the craft, and employed some highly talented people. Their empire, already vast and steadily growing, was evidently built on something other than physical force.

"So, what of today's meeting?" Robson said with an

unexpected change of tack. "You will no doubt be unfamiliar with our ways, Sir Richard; if there is anything I can clarify now, it might be the better – that is if you are not adverse to discussing business over a meal?"

Banks nodded as he swallowed; John Company officials might be experts at commerce, but as he had already noticed, they were equally keen to avoid wasting time, and apparently not against cutting a few corners. "By all means, Colonel."

"You will be worrying about the state of your ship," Robson continued. "I cannot make promises for the dockyard superintendent, but he is a man who has worked miracles in the past and I can see no reason why he should not do so again."

"That is good to hear," Banks commented. "I am also blessed with a talented carpenter, and he is well supported."

"Well, it has been daylight for a number of hours, and no report has come through of your Frenchman, so I think we can discount an enemy attack at least for the rest of the day. Is there anything else that concerns you?"

Banks was silent for a moment. There were so many ways in which that question could be answered. Booker's words about Lady Hatcher's intentions were still with him, and he was equally concerned about how the Admiralty would view his actions. The enemy frigate might not be in sight, but she was likely to be found in the area and, until his own ship was once more in a fit state to meet her, that thought would remain at the forefront of his mind. "I think we should make every effort to inform London of Sir Terrance's death," he said, finally deciding to temporise, and choose a safe option. "Your offices will also need to be aware, so that a replacement may be arranged. And doubtless there will be relatives and associates who ought to know."

Robson nodded emphatically. "Yes, that is a good thought, and one we must indeed act upon. A Company vessel arrived not three days back – one from our packet service – you may have seen her at the anchorage. She is a tidy craft, and fast; she left England after *Scylla*; her captain boasts about always making the journey in under nine weeks. I doubt that she will be with us long; five days at the most, and then be off once more."

"What does she carry?" Banks asked.

"Oh, a mixed and light cargo; this time it will be a consignment of coffee, as well as some samples of orchel; it is a lichen we have found growing hereabouts." Robson helped himself to a further slice of toasted bread. "The Board of Directors consider the dye it produces to have potential value."

Banks nodded, and followed the lieutenant governor's example. The last time he had eaten soft tack was more than two months earlier, and even biscuit had been denied him for over a fortnight.

"There are one or two Company men who were intending to travel home in her as well," Robson continued. "Although I expect your news, and the lack of a replacement governor, may have changed a few minds. Whatever, she can carry despatches; the sooner news of Hatcher's demise is received, the sooner it may be acted upon."

"Francis, really!" his wife complained. "Do we have to talk of death at the breakfast table?"

The lieutenant governor bowed his head slightly. "Forgive me, my dear, I was forgetting." Then, turning back to Banks: "But a camel is nothing more than a horse designed by a committee, as I am very fond of saying. It is far better to talk here, than about a board table, perchance much can be settled, without the need for debate or argument"

"Oh, I am more than agreeable," Banks said then, greatly daring: "I wonder if Lady Hatcher might be persuaded to return in the packet also?"

Robson snorted. "It may make matters more simple if she did," he said, half to himself. "At least on the face of it. But, even if she were persuaded, I truly wonder if it be the best option. Booker tells me she intends to make trouble, in which case it is probably better that she does so here, and during our own enquiry. I fear that involving Leadenhall Street can do little to improve your own interests, Captain," he said sadly.

"She is rumoured to be influential," Banks conceded.

"Influential?" Robson laughed. "You are putting it far too mildly, sir: why did you not know it were down to her intervention that Terrance Hatcher was appointed to the governorship in the first place?"

Banks didn't, and the façade of optimism that had appeared since his good reception began to crumble.

"No, we are dealing with a very difficult customer in Lady H," Robson reflected sadly. "Knows all the right people, and you can be certain most owe her a favour or two. If she is after your hide, chances are she'll have it, and that of any who stand with you."

Banks found the mouthful of toast was beginning to set in his mouth, and only swallowed it with a good deal of effort.

"So, do you have any further concerns?" Robson asked.

Banks almost laughed out loud – considering the fix he was in with Lady Hatcher, all else seemed to dwindle into insignificance. His father, responsible for much of his advancement in the Navy, had effectively disowned him on arranging his command of *Scylla*. He had fared well enough during Warren's action off Ireland, but since then the commission had not been spectacular and Hatcher's death, along with the mess his widow was cooking up, would hardly serve as a recommendation for further employment. But, he reminded himself, Robson was asking a sensible question, and one that deserved an answer. "Nothing immediate, Colonel; beyond provisions of course. We are eleven weeks out from England; water is low, and powder. And we are particularly short of biscuit, or could take flour if you have none to hand."

"Both biscuit and flour are available, as is powder, and Governor Brooke made special provisions for watering ships at the anchorage. But might it not be better to delay victualling until you have spoken with the dockyard superintendent, and can decide upon your repairs?"

That made perfect sense, even though it was spoken by a landsman, and Banks' opinion of the East India Company rose even further.

"In that case there is nothing more I need."

"Capital." The lieutenant governor sat back in his chair and smiled as if he had just pulled off some truly remarkable feat. "We can sort out the minor details at today's meeting; half an hour should suffice for that, if there be no other business. And I must thank you, Captain. In truth I would judge that most of what was to have been said is already covered."

* * *

King told himself he had breakfasted well and was satisfied, whereas he had eaten very little and felt anything but. He had fled to the garden as soon as was politely possible, and stood there now, gazing intently at the formal beds of manicured roses and exquisite specimen plants, although actually seeing very little. But then he had other things on his mind, and they were not the expected worries of the third in command of a wounded warship.

Manning was wrong: Booker's daughter was not outstandingly attractive. She had nice eyes to be sure and pleasant, light brown hair; worn long, in the casual manner, and ending in a slight curl just below her shoulders. Her figure was disappointing however; slim and almost boyish in shape, it lacked the curves that most deep sea sailors come to regard as essential. Neither was she deferential, or in any way reserved: both traits King automatically expected when first meeting a woman, and was disconcerted when they were so obviously absent. But she had made an impression nevertheless, and reached him in a way he had not thought likely, or even possible, once his marriage vows were taken.

The breakfast table had been loaded more heavily than any he had seen before, and included food not tasted in years, but at every opportunity King found himself staring stupidly at the woman who had been introduced all too briefly and thereafter seemed determined to ignore him. To be fair she had other things on her mind; her mother's absence was both unexplained and apparently permanent, and many of the wifely duties of hostess and landlady were on her shoulders. She, – and King was still cursing himself for having missed her name – had arranged everything from the breakfast, to their rooms and, for all he knew, was probably involved in organising the dinner that evening.

And, as she snapped out instructions to the many servants who readily responded without question, she was evidently good at her work. But there was something more about her, something he could not quantify yet seemed as important as the shape of her face or the sound of her voice. No matter how hard he might try to deny it, his recurring thought was that the two of them would have a definite empathy, if only time and circumstance would permit them to discover it.

He began to pace up and down the short stone patio, automatically turning at each end, as on the deck of a ship, instead of following the path that continued about the garden, and would have provided a far more pleasant walk. Of course, as a married man he should have no such feelings. He and Juliana had met back in 'ninety seven, when he was briefly held as a prisoner of the Batavian Republic. She had been widowed a few years earlier, after her husband chose to fight against the invading French, and King could see more clearly now that, as a British officer continuing the same struggle, his position must have held a special attraction for her. They had grown close in what had been an artificial situation, but the one he engineered later, when he arranged for the smuggler's lugger to whisk her to England, now seemed destined to force them apart once more.

Or would do, if he allowed it. On leaving Spithead he had decided his marriage was well worth the saving. That was something he could still do, if only his mind was put to it, even if an essential ingredient turned out to be his own presence. One course was to retire from the Navy; something he had done in the past when a lack of both prospects and money forced him to serve with the East India Company. It was not a time he enjoyed, and did not wish to repeat, but still he considered the option. A spell on land, with Juliana, and living as a normal married couple, might be the answer; he could find a place at the Leadenhall Street headquarters: that, or one of their regional offices. His experience at sea would also serve him well in the Preventive Service. Alternatively he could even stay with the RN and try out as a regulating officer or the Sea Fencibles, should he so choose.

But then, of course, there was the not so small matter of the captain's report. It remained distinctly possible that he would face court martial on returning home and, even if the result went entirely in his favour and he was exonerated from all responsibility for endangering his ship, a future position with a captain other than Sir Richard was unlikely. But still he felt in his bones that living in England would be a solution. A place where they could re-spark the flame first ignited in that small house off the Texel, and a degree of marital harmony regained. And then there was the woman he had met, all too briefly, at breakfast.

It was odd, but two hours earlier he had been unaware of her existence, yet already she was an important element in his life, and even seemed destined to change it. For all he knew she was spoken for, or may even be wed, although the ringless hands that he had been quick to note made such a prospect unlikely. And as a woman of position she might not take to a rather shabby junior lieutenant, especially one who was already married. But King felt fully entitled to brush aside any such possibilities. Based on an assumption that was almost completely fuelled by current dissatisfaction, he had already made up his mind that his future would be closely linked with hers. And it was an indication of his adolescent resolve that little importance was placed on the fact that the object of his attention was someone he had only just met, and whose name he was yet to learn.

* * *

Caulfield stared at the bleak outlook and shivered. He had already inspected the nearby coast with the deck glass: Jamestown, the only settlement of any size on the island, appeared totally dwarfed by the two bleak mountains that sat to either side, and was not an unimpressive sight. There was a church, and several military fortifications; apart from that, just a mixture of rather shabby houses and those appeared to be lacking proper tiled roofs. Even without setting a foot on shore he could predict the sort of place it would be, and it did not appeal.

Around him the watch on deck had been stood down and were waiting, more or less patiently, for eight bells and their first spirit ration of the day. He knew that they, as well as many of the officers, were craving shore leave but could not share their feelings. When a midshipman, or even as junior lieutenant, he would have been just as excited, but time and many disappointments had taught him that, whatever the veneer of exoticism it might have assumed, one pot house remained very much as another. He supposed there might be interesting travel further inland, but that usually involved horses, and Caulfield did not enjoy riding. In the past he had known officers who sketched or painted, while others botanised, and there had been one master's mate whose entire purpose in life was collecting exotic insects, to the dismay of those that shared his berth. But Caulfield had no such interest; his hobby lay in music, and specifically his 'cello: apart from replacing strings, and the occasional bow re-hair, there were few things he ever required, and the shore held little attraction for him. No, St Helena was basically a rock, and a small one at that. But then in all his years as a professional seaman there had been few ports that had offered him anything other than shelter or temporary rest. This was just another stop: a break in the routine of travel, but hardly an improvement.

"Shore boat pulling for us." The forecastle lookout's call lacked urgency and was almost conversational although to some extent it did lift Caulfield out of his melancholy. He took a turn or two across the deck, then paused to watch the small cutter press its way through what was actually quite a heavy sea. The sternsheets appeared crowded: probably indicating officers aboard, even if all had abandoned their hats and were wearing watch coats or cloaks. Caulfield looked about with an element of guilt but all was in order and, with the exception of one of the fore topsail braces that was currently being replaced, he had nothing to explain or reproach himself for.

The boat drew near, and one aboard replied, "*Scylla!*" to the forecastle lookout's challenge. The captain was returning, and Caulfield also thought he could see King amongst the group at the stern, which meant that some sort of activity might be expected. They were heading for the frigate's larboard side, so no official compliments or reception was required, but Caulfield straightened his stock and smoothed down his uniform as he made his way to the entry port to meet them.

The captain came off first, and shook his premier's hand almost as soon as he was on deck.

"All well here, I trust, Michael," he said.

"Indeed, sir." Caulfield's mouth opened to enquire of the shore before closing, with its job undone; there were some questions that a lieutenant could not ask of his captain, especially in full view of the watch on deck.

"You did not feel inclined to lower topmasts?" Banks asked, looking about him. "We are well protected by the shore, don't you know?"

"With the French in the area I reasoned we should remain ready to sail," Caulfield replied.

"That was probably wise." Banks eyed him carefully. "Though it must have made for an uncomfortable night in this swell."

King was on deck now, along with an unknown civilian dressed in a dark brown watch coat. "This is Mr Brady, the Jamestown dockyard superintendent," Banks explained, and Caulfield shook the new man's hard hand. "I'd be obliged if you would send for Mr Evans; we are to inspect the damage to our hull."

Caulfield glanced at the duty midshipman, who sped off in search of the carpenter.

"In the meanwhile you had better prepare for going ashore, Mr Caulfield," Banks told him. "And take enough for several days," he added. "Mr King will enlighten you further, but there is an official dinner this evening, and afterwards you will be travelling across the island, so bring appropriate clothing." The captain stopped, as if suddenly unsure of a point. "I assume you can ride a horse, Michael?"

* * *

Timmons watched them. From his vantage point on the forecastle he saw the captain lead *Scylla*'s carpenter and some official from

133

the shore down into the bowels of the ship, while King and the first lieutenant stood yarning on the half deck. The ship was in need of repair, as any fool could tell, and it needed even less intelligence to deduce that, whatever method they chose, she would have to be lightened. That might mean pumping her dry of fresh water, and even unloading some of their stores, but there was also a far more predictable side effect; the main bulk of the crew would be taken ashore.

He switched his gaze to the nearby settlement. It was small, certainly and, due to the high proportion of India Army men about, would probably be very much like Gibraltar. The prospect encouraged him greatly; Gib. was a fine town in his eyes, and one where his particular brand of mischief had prospered well, despite the vast numbers of military and naval personnel who thronged its narrow streets. He had never been to St Helena of course, but had high expectations of the place. It could be just the setting to deal with Hind and Mitchell, or there may be other prey equally suitable. Flint's talk of a lack of pushing houses did not trouble him greatly; doxies were obtainable wherever, if they were properly sought, although despatching that molly had quite woken his taste for the esoteric. He might even try for a military man – maybe a cadet; Timmons was a great admirer of the young. St Helena was also supposed to be well equipped with black folk, both slaves and free: surely one of either status was unlikely to be missed. And if all of that came to naught, there was still the possibility of an officer's wife, or one of the other civilian workers; he especially liked killing women.

The more he thought the faster the ideas came, and it was with a mixture of annoyance and fear that he noticed Jameson looking at him strangely from across the forecastle. He cleared his expression and turned away, but the prospect of further activity still left a warm feeling inside and he knew that never in his life before had he ever been quite so excited.

Chapter Twelve

"And Mr King," Booker said gruffly. "You will remember my daughter, Julia from breakfast this morning, I am certain."

King bowed politely and extended his hand, inwardly cursing: of all the names possible, why did she have to be encumbered with one so close to his wife's?

"Did you enjoy your first day on St Helena, Mr King?" she asked, as her father turned away, his mission apparently accomplished.

"It is a pretty and pleasant place," King replied, stumbling over the words. "Very much like England, in fact; I was surprised."

They moved from the entrance where Booker was continuing to greet visitors and found a quiet spot in the room that was rapidly filling with guests.

"Surprised it is pleasant," she asked seriously. "Or so much like England?"

King felt his face grow red. "Both," he said, then realising his mistake, shook his head. "No, I meant, neither..."

And so ended any ideas he might have held for intimacy, he thought bitterly, while also noticing that her figure actually looked stunning in that white, sheer gown, and how delightfully her eyes danced when she laughed.

"Well, I hope you had an agreeable time."

"Thank you, yes," he replied, blushing further.

"And you will be seeing more tomorrow, I find," she continued, brightening. "An overland trip to Sandy Bay, is that not right?"

"Indeed, we are to scout out the area in the hope of careening my ship."

"I may show you a map, if it be of any benefit, and perhaps save a day's travel."

King smiled. "We have examined a chart, but still wish to

visit." He had no reason to doubt the accuracy of an East India Cartographer, but careening a ship was a delicate process and much more investigation would be required, along with greater detail than a few random soundings.

"Well, it is our only true beach," she told him, "I spent many happy hours there as a child."

"Have you spent your whole life on St Helena?" he asked.

"Goodness, I hope not!" She was laughing again, but he had grown used to that, and actually was not sorry. At least it meant that he was pleasing her in some way, and she did have the whitest teeth he had ever encountered. "I was born in India, but we came to live here when I was but three, so can remember little of any other place."

"And have you travelled elsewhere?" He spoke slowly, choosing his words with care; to look a fool three times in the course of one conversation would probably be pushing the boundaries too far.

"No, I never have. You must remember how remote we are. Two months at least to England; one to Africa, though there is little there to see when you arrive, or so father tells me. On several occasions I have sailed with the fishing fleet and viewed the place from afar, but that is the furthest I can boast since arriving."

King shook his head in astonishment. On land many civilians lived and died within a three mile radius, but most went further; to London, or the nearest city, at least once in their adult lives.

"I don't think I have ever met someone who has never been anywhere," he replied tactlessly, before adding: "But it is no great defect," in an attempt to make amends.

"Now there I must disagree with you." He noticed with relief that she had taken his comment in the manner it had been intended. "A lack of travel is a very bad thing; and when you spoke earlier of my having spent all my life here, you were not far from the truth. Being close to the equator means the seasons are not clearly defined: we tend to live more in cycles, from one shipping season to the next. When you look back there is little difference in the years; one just seems to roll into another."

"But that is terrible." Again he felt the cold wind of a gaff. "I mean, the place is pleasant and…"

"I know exactly what you mean," she interrupted, fixing him with those serious brown eyes. "And I concur. It is a big world, Mr King, as I am sure you of all people are aware. Spending an entire life on one single spot is a waste to anyone's thinking."

"But why?" he asked and she shrugged.

"A lack of opportunity, I would gauge. I could have gone home to school – we think of England as home even though it be many miles away and may never have been visited – but I did not care to be away for what would be my entire childhood. Then my mother became ill and died when I was thirteen. Not too long after I began to take her place, accompanying my father, first to social and then official functions, until eventually I found myself running his household. It is quiet at the moment with the shipping season not yet begun, but in a month or so it will be a different matter. There are balls, and plays for the visiting fleets – sometimes we have fifty or more vessels at anchor at one time – and then I am extremely busy."

"I can imagine," King replied. "And do you enjoy it?"

"I enjoy the fresh faces." She was smiling at him especially now, or so he thought. "And there is something good about always being the host and never the guest. But still I would like to go elsewhere for a spell, if only to properly judge the difference."

"It seems such a contrary life to mine," he said. "There are times, such as blockade duty or long spells at anchor, when we see the same horizon for weeks, even months at a time. But those are easily outweighed by others, when the ship may travel a hundred miles or more in one day." He looked up from the floor where he realised he had been staring. "But you could go, surely? Your father would allow it?"

"Yes I could," she agreed. "Though sometimes I feel as much enclosed as any slave in our household. Papa would definitely not forbid my leaving, but to where? And with whom? Oh, there was once a man who wanted to take me off St Helena but, as far as I could tell, it was only to install me in his London house, which would be little different." Her eyes flashed dangerously. "And then I discovered he had a country residence as well, and that was where he kept his wife, so the plan rather fell to pieces I am afraid."

Even to his ears King's obedient laughter sounded false, but fortunately Julia Booker did not seem to notice.

"And so I shall stay," she continued. "Papa will probably retire in the next ten years or so. He talks of moving away, but I cannot believe that will happen. For a start my mother is buried here; he would be leaving her behind, along with his memories. And there are worse places, Mr King."

"You may call me Thomas, if you wish," he said. Her sadness had struck him in an indescribable way; he felt the urge to reach out and touch; to hold her against him, to reassure her as if they had been friends for many years, and not just met that morning.

"Thank you, Thomas," she replied. Her eyes were serious, and seemed to be searching into his. Or was that just his imagination?

* * *

"You have come a long way, Captain," the vicar informed him sternly. "Doubtless you, and your men will want for spiritual comfort. My church is in Jamestown, you cannot miss the spire."

"I shall advise my officers accordingly, sir," Banks replied.

"Should you consider a thanksgiving service to be in order, I am certain one may be arranged. There is a minister aboard your ship, I assume – would he be present this evening?"

"*Scylla* has no chaplain," Banks stated firmly. "As a mere fifth rate, we are not obliged to carry one."

"Not obliged, Captain," the man's tone was now cold. "But a suitable man may still be appointed, may they not?"

"Indeed, sir, though we have never felt the necessity," Banks continued, immersing himself further. "I conduct regular worship with the help of my sailing master, Adam Fraiser."

"Adam Fraiser? The name is familiar." The cleric appeared doubtful. "Though I own I cannot place it; has he religious training?"

"I do not believe so, sir." Banks sensed that the conversation was not progressing well; soon he would have to admit that *Scylla*'s regular divine service was very liable to postponement or cancellation. He looked desperately about the room; King was deep in conversation with a pretty young woman and Manning seemed to be engrossed with two surgeons that Banks had been introduced to earlier. If only Fraiser had agreed to accompany them ashore he might have been able to palm this persistent little man off on him. Then a familiar face caught his attention and, catching his eye, Colonel Robson headed across the room, with a smartly dressed artillery officer in tow.

"Well, at the very least you must allow me to visit your ship," the vicar was continuing; a look of acid disapproval now firmly fixed upon his face. "No doubt there will be much work to be done."

"Reverend, you will not mind me interrupting," Robson said, sparing Banks any need to reply. "Sir Richard, may I introduce Duncan Morris?"

Banks took in the figure of a young man, probably less than twenty-five years old. He was elegantly clad in what closer inspection revealed was obviously an expensively tailored uniform.

"Major Morris is in overall charge of the artillery on this island," Robson continued, turning his back on the vicar, and effectively excluding him from the conversation.

"Including those that are currently protecting your ship," the young officer simpered.

Banks inclined his head. "My ship is quite able to protect herself, thank you, Major," he said, evenly. "Although I do appreciate the benefit of your shore batteries, of course."

"If she were able, Sir Richard," Morris replied slowly, his words carefully chosen, "Then I am surprised that she is in quite so beat-up a state."

A chill seemed to fall upon the room, and Banks was almost certain that the general hubbub of conversation also dwindled slightly. He stared at Major Morris; neither his name, nor face meant anything, and yet the man bore an animosity that was both obvious and uncommon at a first meeting.

"My ship was damaged while fighting a squadron of three enemy warships," Banks said, just as deliberately.

"Then I suppose we should congratulate you for arriving at all," the younger man replied, unabashed. "But it is indeed a shame that you did not take greater care of my uncle."

"Dash it all, I had quite forgotten," Robson blustered, trying to drag Banks away. "Young Morris here was indeed Sir Terrance's nephew…"

"I had nothing to do with your uncle's death," Banks said, standing his ground.

"As will be shown in the enquiry I am sure, Sir Richard," Robson added soothingly. "Morris, I think the Booker girl may need rescuing; go to her, will you?"

Banks stood stony faced while the young man nodded at the lieutenant governor, glared at him, and then turned slowly on his heel to where King and Booker's daughter were deep in conversation.

"Don't mind him, old man," Robson said softly. "Bit of a firebrand, and hasn't got the manners he was born with. But a splendid officer none the less."

"If he was regular army I would report him for insubordination," Banks replied stiffly, as the sound of a gong echoed about the room.

"Well, I'm sure there is no need for that; I say, that sounds like dinner at last. And look, there is Lady Banks; come let us go through and eat."

* * *

"Won't be no provision nor need for chests where we's goin', so make sure your ditty bags is good and full, then when we leaves, it will be the easier." Draude, who was now a fully-fledged boatswain's mate, moved amongst the crowded berth deck. The first watch was freshly set; those below had been expecting to sling their hammocks and were taken aback by the change of routine. Jameson collected his canvas bag and joined Flint at the back of the disorderly queue that would eventually lead them down to the orlop.

"I'd take a fair supply of woollens with you," the older man told him. "I've known islands like this before. Don't care how near or far they is to the line, them's always got a chill in the breeze."

"How long do you suppose we'll be ashore?" Jameson asked, as they reached the head of the wide companionway.

"Blessed if I know," Flint shrugged. "But if they're gonna set the barky to rights, it'll be a while."

"How shall they fix her?"

"Now you're askin'." Flint rolled his eyes. The darkness of the orlop seemed to have been made even more apparent by many points of light provided by an unusual number of lanthorns. Both hatches were open, and work was underway in the holds. The two seamen glanced down as they shuffled past, and Jameson raised a hand to Mitchell, who was helping to manoeuvre a leaguer in his deep and private underworld.

"Might be able to rig a dry dock, though I can't see it m'self," Flint mused, as they reached the seamen's storage area. "Less the India boys have been diggin' somewhere we don't know about. Otherwise they'll just have to beach her on her beam ends, which will mean all this lot will have to go, includin' the cannon."

Jameson pulled a face; that much work was not going to be easy, and a position as topman would not excuse him in any way.

"Even beaching her won't be an easy manoeuvre; plenty have been laid down for careening what never get's up again," Flint continued morosely. "An' the barky will be dead exposed if that Frenchman comes a lookin'. Ask me it will be better to head for the Cape and see what they're capable of. But I ain't the captain," he added, as if in explanation.

The chests had been laid out in a ragged line by the holders. Flint and Jameson found the one they shared and opened it. Jameson's ditty bag only contained his sewing kit, and a spare pair of trousers. To them he added two shirts, all five of his stockings and, taking note of Flint's earlier advice, a gansey.

"When we going then, Mr Lewis?" Flint asked, as a crisply dressed warrant officer passed by.

The master's mate snorted; he and Flint went way back, and had even shared a mess when Lewis was a regular hand. "Blowed if I knows, Flint. But they're preparing to lighten ship on deck as well, so I'd say it'd be tomorrow, or the day after at the latest. Whatever, the cap'n ain't gonna waste no time, and while we're leaking like the proverbial sieve he's probably right."

* * *

Despite the young artillery officer's offensive behaviour, Banks decided he had enjoyed the meal. The food was every bit as good as he had come to expect, while the rest of the HEIC staff had demonstrated how experienced they were as hosts, and done all they could to put their guests at ease. There was, perhaps, a slight underlying tension separate from the open hostility of Major Morris, but then he supposed that was inevitable, and in reality he was being treated extremely well.

After all, the council had been expecting a new leader; someone to head their small, but efficient team. Rather than that, Banks had delivered a decidedly troublesome yet influential woman, as well as apparently leading a powerful French squadron to threaten their small enclave. Worse, there was also the not so minor liability of a Royal Navy warship in desperate need of both repair and victuals and effectively relying on their mercy. And until that particular problem could be addressed, her crew of more than two hundred must also be housed and fed. Yes, Banks decided, he was being treated extraordinarily well. He might just as easily have been shunned or politely told that, however honourable the East India Company claimed to be, they had been severely let down, and could accept no further responsibility for him, or his command.

"Did you meet Henry Booker's daughter?" Sarah asked, as she joined him in the small dressing room that was part of their quarters in Longwood House. "Quite a beauty, and has never been off the island, or so I collect."

Banks undid his stock, and pulled it free. He had indeed noticed a young woman; she stood out as almost all the other ladies present had been well into their forties.

"She is his daughter?" he asked, absent-mindedly. "I had no idea."

"Well what did you think, Richard?" Sarah pulled a face at him in the large mirror. "The girl is far too young to be his wife. Tom King was paying her particular attention, I noticed."

"King is married," Banks said firmly, and in a voice far more suited to the captain of a frigate than Sarah's husband.

"No man is married south of the equator," she replied, before pointing at her husband and adding: "except for you, of course."

"Still, I cannot believe King would be disloyal," Banks said softly. "Why he even made arrangements to have his wife collected from Holland; such an operation must have cost a small fortune."

"Maybe so, but then he is also a young man, and as prone to natural instincts as any of his type."

Banks was quiet for a moment as he thought. He had a small enough team of officers as it was, and could not afford the loss of even one to foolish affairs or romance. "If you are serious, then I must see to it that they never meet again," he said, finally.

"In that case you have not made a very good start," Sarah told him.

He turned from unbuttoning his shirt to stare at her. "What do you mean?"

"They are setting off at first light, do you not remember?" she replied, wiping the rouge from her face and adding a small dash of cream from a china pot. "Henry Booker was organising it, just as we were leaving. Horses, servants, food – quite an expedition, from what I could gather."

"He promised a guide to show Caulfield and King Sandy Bay," Banks said, confused. It had actually been agreed at the morning's meeting: Booker was merely confirming the next day's itinerary at the end of the evening. Sandy Bay was the only area of the island that had a beach anything like suitable for careening a ship of *Scylla*'s size. All of the governing body were of the opinion it would still not be appropriate, but Banks wanted his own officers to confirm the fact. "I must confess at the time I failed to see why they needed such a party," he said. "And certainly not horses, not on an island this size."

"Well if you had listened beyond the horses you might have heard mention of his daughter acting as guide."

Banks shook his head; he had not heard. The day had been especially taxing which made it roughly the same as so many others that preceded it.

"I suppose I could send Fraiser instead," he mused, reaching for the nightshirt that was conveniently laid out for him and had clearly been laundered since the previous night. "Or perhaps a master's mate?"

"Oh, I should not concern yourself," Sarah said, leaving the small room, and heading next door for the oversized bed. "They cannot get into so much trouble in one day."

"Besides, Caulfield will be with them," he grunted, joining her.

"Yes, Michael will be there," she agreed. "And even Tom King might find his youthful instincts dulled somewhat if he is sitting on a horse."

Chapter Thirteen

In fact the provision of horses turned out to be eminently sensible. The road to Sandy Bay wound up and down some of the steepest hills King had ever encountered, and the short, stocky animal he rode, actually more of a mule than a horse, hardly missed a step despite the loose ground and some genuinely memorable gradients. But by midday, when they had been travelling for over four hours, he was starting to tire; both his back and belly were far more used to keeping balance on a heaving deck, and ached from the erratic motion of the horse, while his rump felt as raw as ten-day-old mutton. Ahead, Caulfield and Julia were deep in conversation, something that should have caused him concern, but somehow King could not summon the energy to worry. He might be a widower and ostensibly free, but the first lieutenant was also considerably older, and a dry old stick at the best of times. He did not think Julia would be swayed by his charms, not when King had all but monopolised her company for most of that morning.

She had turned out to be just as captivating as he had sensed: a bright, witty mind, with just the right degree of humour. In turn King felt he had finally made a good impression, and such a thing was not easy when they were on her home ground and she was very much the guide. Their conversation only ended when Caulfield tumbled from his mount. It was not a bad fall; poor old Michael had more or less rolled off, landing sideways on the dense and forgiving turf. The action had amused everyone however, including the three servants who were following on foot, and even evoked open astonishment from his horse. Julia had gone to the first lieutenant's aid, helped the older man back up, and stayed with him ever since. But by then the sun was up and King, who had been growing increasingly hot for a while, was not sorry. He knew that his conversation was starting to flag; to his mind it was far better that she should be bored by the balding, and slightly portly Caulfield for a while. Besides, there would be plenty of time for him to be with her later: he had already discovered she kept her own set of rooms in Booker's house, and more or less arranged to visit her there.

"We're just passing over Sandy Bay Ridge." King looked up as Julia's voice broke into his thoughts. The couple had stopped a little way ahead, and she was turning on her saddle to shout to him. Bringing himself back to the real world was something of an effort, and King spurred his mount on in an attempt to appear more wide awake than he felt.

"It's not far now," she continued, as he neared. On the left there is Diana's Peak; the highest point on the island. Just behind it is Mount Actaeon, and shortly we'll be passing Cuckold's Point."

Cuckold's Point. It was not the best of omens for such an outing, but King nodded, and tried to look intelligent, even if the sun was extremely hot, and he so longed for a chance to get off the damned animal. Something of this must have conveyed itself to the girl, and she smiled when he finally reached her.

"Poor Tom; you look entirely washed out. What say we stop under those trees and rest up for a spell?"

King didn't appreciate the fact the she had noticed him wilting, but the small copse of what looked like mimosa appeared far too inviting to ignore, and he followed when she and Caulfield turned their horses off the path.

It was certainly cooler under the flowery canopy; King dismounted stiffly and stretched his legs that seemed determined to make him look as if he had been struck with rickets. Midshipman Jackson, who had been the back marker as suited his lowly status, followed, and also reined in his horse, before nonchalantly dismounting in such an expert manner that King was both annoyed and grudgingly impressed.

"Haven't been for a proper ride in years," the lad told the lieutenant, the novel surroundings, and relative distance from all things nautical apparently giving him licence to speak casually. One of Julia's servants, a young black man with broad shoulders and a gentle countenance, came and collected both horses, leading them away to where the others were being watered. Another, an older woman with a white and broad smile, unloaded the wicker basket she had been carrying on her head for the entire journey, and began to sort through the contents with a girl who may well have been her daughter.

"There is nothing substantial for luncheon," Julia said as she and Caulfield wandered across. "Cold pie, and some fruit. Father thinks there should be time sufficient for you to do your work, and be back for supper, but we have made good time and can still take a half hour's break now."

She was wearing a long, grey dress, and sported a straw hat, not dissimilar to those worn by many of *Scylla*'s regular hands in hot weather. The low brim emphasised her deep brown eyes and, as she sat down and arranged herself elegantly on the turf, King felt a sensation of desire that was very nearly painful. Caulfield planted himself next to her with an air of proprietorship, and King was quick to move in to the other side before Jackson could claim the spot. The younger female servant appeared with a large pewter jug, from which she poured something clear into beakers. Drinks were duly passed out, with the girl smiling not too subtly into the midshipman's eyes; an act that was promptly repaid by a reddening in Jackson's complexion.

"Lemonade," Julia said, taking hers, and sniffing appreciatively. "We have been blessed with a good harvest this year," she said. "And not just lemons, all seem to have done especially well."

"I noticed a lot of fruit trees on the way up," Caulfield said. "It looks so much like England."

"So I understand," Julia replied. "Though strangely St Helena is not quite as hot, nor as cold as home. We get two crops of apples a year, and some are truly enormous. And there are the blackberries of course; they were introduced a few years ago, but have grown to be rather a nuisance. I understand that peaches used to be quite prolific as well – so much so that people would feed them to their pigs. But of late they have started to be attacked by some sort of fly. Now they are hard to grow, but delicious when they do."

King was struck again by the whiteness of her teeth when she spoke; in fact all the usual signs were there and, when combined with such magical and slightly surreal surroundings, he knew for sure that he was firmly on the downward path to destruction.

"There is a hen and ham pie," she said, taking a proffered plate from the older servant. "Thomas, will I cut you a slice?"

King accepted readily, although his reaction would have been identical if she were offering something far less appealing. He sipped at his lemonade, and looked about. The scenery had changed once more. Caulfield was right, it had appeared very English on the ascent, but now exotic trees and wild ferns had taken over from the traditional oak and willow; there were brightly coloured shrubs that King could not begin to identify, as well as long spindly trees almost bereft of foliage. He knew that what Julia had blithely referred to as mountains were in reality hardly more than steep and ambitious hills, but even they had a distinct shape that marked them out. Some large houses were set precariously into their steep slopes; apparently summer residences for Company officers and factors. And at other times he had noticed small idyllic cottages surrounded by their own land and seemingly intent on enticing him with a magical way of life, far removed from the normal stresses of fighting a war. Even the insects that buzzed, unseen, in the undergrowth added something bewitching to the place, and the contrasting scent of gum tree and fresh heather rounded off the impression nicely. It was all so very different from the bleak and barren prospect they first sighted from the sea.

"We only should take half an hour," Julia prompted, and King hurriedly paid attention to the untouched pie on his plate. Jackson had finished his, and accepted another chunk, which he consumed with a lad's appetite, although Caulfield seemed strangely reticent, and hardly nibbled at his piece.

"Could you stand an impertinent question?" the first lieutenant asked while the remains of their meal were being taken away by the women, and the manservant had gone to fetch the horses.

"That rather depends on the subject, Mr Caulfield," Julia

replied, suddenly coltish.

"It is the servants," the older man, now serious, continued. "They are slaves I assume?"

"They are," Julia agreed. "Though at times I have to remind myself of the fact." She looked more closely at his face. "You are shocked, clearly."

"Not shocked so very greatly," Caulfield confessed; he had already found himself growing fond of Miss Booker, and had no wish to crush her in argument. "I have come across such labour before, and they seem far more content than others; certainly those I met on the American plantations."

"That is probably the case," Julia reflected. "Most have lived on this island for several generations and I think are as satisfied as any in domestic service. They are well fed and provided for, with a full day off in every seven – more than their counterparts in England receive, I am told."

"Their counterparts are not slaves," Caulfield reminded her gently.

"Maybe not," Julia agreed. "But all must work: surely there is little difference how they were recruited?"

"The difference is choice," Caulfield persisted.

"And you are saying that an English servant has choice? Why yes, I suppose you are correct – they can choose whether they work, or starve."

There was polite laughter from Jackson and King, but Julia was well into her stride.

"None of our people are forced into labour; we are not inclined to use the whips or battens common in some countries, and if they were severely unhappy I am certain papa would organise a transfer, or even return them to their home country, assuming one could be identified. But even then they might not find life any the better; there are few of us who can survive for long without some form of labour and for most their home might turn out to be as foreign to them as England would be to me."

"But slavery is morally wrong," Caulfield said, with rather less conviction.

"Oh, I entirely agree with you," Julia replied instantly. "And things are changing, on St Helena, at least: there have been no new slaves imported for almost ten years – no other British settlement can say the same. My father pays a small allowance to those he employs, and they receive both medical attention and accommodation. Most marry and raise families, and if it is that their children grow up to work in the same manner, is that so very different from the system of family trades common throughout Europe and the Americas?"

Caulfield nodded his head gravely. "What you say is true, and this is not a perfect world, but still I cannot justify abducting a man and forcing him into labour: it is against the laws of nature."

"Indeed?" she asked innocently. "And are there other Englishmen who share your views?"

"A growing band," he confirmed with obvious pride. "I do not say we will be successful straight away; but in time the world shall come to see and acknowledge the error."

"So a man should not be forced to work, even though it might ultimately mean his survival?" She said the words slowly, as if they were being learned and committed to memory. King grew suspicious, but Caulfield clearly sensed he was on the edge of a conversion.

"I believe it is his right to choose," he said emphatically. "And no one should do so for him."

"And you would never be a party to such a thing?" she enquired.

"On the contrary, I should do all I could to prevent it," Caulfield confirmed, with perhaps slightly too much self-righteousness.

"Well then, I must express my surprise," Julia said after a short pause. "For, as far as I was aware, the Royal Navy is still abducting men, and forcing them to sea. I wonder that you have none on board your own ship, Mr Caulfield?"

Jackson coughed, King snorted, but the first lieutenant only went a slightly darker shade of pink. "You are talking about pressing a man for the king's service," he objected. "That is a different matter entirely."

"Why so?" Julia asked. "Because someone in government has

decided it to be the case? I see no variation; indeed your method of slavery is surely far worse. A victim of the press gang is forced to work, if he does not he will certainly be beaten – should he try to escape he may very well be hanged and, even if he accepts his fate, the chances of his dying either of disease, drowning, or in battle are extremely high."

"It is not the same," Caulfield said, shaking his head sadly.

"Maybe not, Michael," Julia agreed in a softer tone. "But there is a similarity, you must allow?"

The horses were ready, and even though he was still uncomfortably stiff, King rose first and made for them. Julia's words had impressed him in several ways. There were certain unwritten rules of social etiquette and one effectively forbade any woman from arguing with a man. Exceptions occurred, of course: intimate friends or close relatives might surely bicker, although King had been brought up expecting a husband's word to always be respected. But Julia had not only argued, she had done so well: setting the first lieutenant up perfectly, and then delivering the *coup de grâce* with all the skill of a seasoned debater. Perhaps it was the isolated world that she lived in? Maybe a lack of polite society meant that she was one of those modern females who took little heed of protocol, and actually had the effrontery to make up her own mind? Kate was one but even she, King decided, would not be so direct with her thoughts, nor as clinical in the way they were presented. It was a decidedly radical stance in what was, after all, a man's world, and one he was not sure if he approved of. But at least he could discount any threat of Caulfield becoming a potential suitor. That possibility had now been firmly removed.

* * *

It would be bearding the lioness in her den and may well come to nothing, but when Booker suggested visiting Lady Hatcher at the governor's country home, Banks supposed the idea had some merit. But it was not a visit he was prepared to undertake alone, not through any physical or psychological fear of the woman, but nearly three months cooped up in a ship of war had taught him a little of her ways. Throughout that time she had never been one to hold her tongue and, if she were to repeat any of the threats or allegations made towards the end of their voyage, he would rather she did so in the presence of a witness.

Booker was the ideal person, being not only a Company man but, having no prior knowledge of either party before their arrival on the island, might legitimately be presented as neutral, should he be called to a court of enquiry. The man was not altogether keen however, causing Banks to wonder if he were concerned about Hatcher's political power reaching even such a far flung outpost as St Helena. But then, as the suggestion had originally come from him, he could hardly refuse.

"You are late," an obviously rejuvenated Lady Hatcher informed them upon their being shown into her presence. Not only was she wearing different, and far smarter clothes, but her skin and hair had been attended to. The face appeared younger, and it was even conceivable that she had lost a little weight, but there was no disguising the cold tone in her voice, or the hard direct stare that was used without restraint. Banks had privately hoped a few days on the island might have mollified the woman. She had gone through the trauma of losing her husband, after all, and *Scylla* was no palace; some time away, enjoying magnificent countryside, eating good, fresh food and taking reasonable exercise might have made a change, although that was clearly not to be.

"My fault entirely," Booker said, with nonchalant gallantry. "The government coach made good time, but we were inconvenienced by a flock of sheep that blocked the road by Steer's Common and proved unusually stubborn."

If Booker had hoped the tale and his telling of it would lighten the atmosphere or even induce humour he was mistaken, and hurriedly cleared his throat in reaction to the woman's set stare.

"Well, if we have to meet we can do so in the library," she said, leading them into a side room where a uniformed man stood up from his seat. "You both know my late husband's nephew, I believe." Morris nodded briefly at Booker, but declined to acknowledge Banks in any way, and no handshakes were exchanged. "I assumed you would be bringing a witness, Sir Richard, so there will be no objections to Duncan being present; and you won't be requiring tea, I am certain."

"I am here in my capacity of host, Lady Hatcher," Booker said smoothly. "It is clear that there has been some disagreement between you and Captain Banks; if I, and Major Morris, can sort matters out, then that would be much for the better. And I am sure that is what we all would like," he added, with slightly more emphasis.

"I fail to see how my late husband's death, caused as it was by this fellow's incompetence, can be talked away with a few sugared phrases," Lady Hatcher snapped.

"I gave orders and made arrangements for your entourage to be kept in safety," Banks said firmly. "That your husband ignored them was his concern, not mine."

"Well frankly, sir, I am surprised that you should have chosen to bring the enemy to action at all," Morris said. "Your ship was charged with despatches, was she not? Does that mean for nothing in the Royal Navy? The Dear knows that frigate captains are renowned for their inability to turn down a fight, but surely carrying such important passengers should have persuaded you to be slightly less foolhardy?"

Banks had not expected such an outright assault, but was mildly relieved that the young officer's accusations could be so easily wiped aside.

"All captains, be they frigate or otherwise, are allowed a degree of discretion, as far as carrying despatches are concerned," he said stiffly. "And, although such a thing was more out of courtesy than obligation, I did approach the governor before engaging the enemy, and he gave his full and wholehearted support."

"And where did such an interview take place?" Morris asked.

"In the governor's cabin," Banks replied, as a chill feeling of concern began to make itself known within his stomach. "Lady Hatcher was also present, as was her husband's manservant."

"I can recall no such meeting," the woman replied haughtily.

"And you will have a good deal of trouble finding anyone else to back up your story; both Terrance and Malcolm are now dead: died upon your ship, and while in your care."

In the face of barefaced lying Banks found himself taken aback. He felt his face grow hot and went to speak, but on catching the eye of Lady Hatcher, thought better of it. Fortunately Booker guessed the problem, and stepped in.

"If there is any discrepancy here I am sure it can be disregarded," he said. "As Captain Banks has made clear, he was under no obligation to speak with your late husband in the first place."

"Well I would say that is for a court of enquiry to decide," Morris said with an air of finality. "You can bandy words and rules about as much as you wish, but the Board of Directors may not be so easily hoodwinked."

"There is no attempt to hoodwink, Major Morris," Booker retorted. "Indeed I would caution you against making such an accusation." The young man swallowed, but said nothing. "But we had hoped that such formalities might be avoided. Indeed it would seem to be a waste of Company time and effort. And to suggest that the Board of Directors are to be involved can only..."

"The Board of Directors will surely be involved," Lady Hatcher interrupted. "And I dare say the Admiralty shall also be interested in Captain Banks' conduct. Indeed I should be surprised if he is not called to answer at court martial." She paused, and set her eyes firmly on the captain, her smile filled with an evil intensity. "In fact I am certain of it."

Chapter Fourteen

"Shore boat approaching, sir," the midshipman told him, and Banks turned back from the open grating that seemed to have been claiming his attention for most of the morning. Whether *Scylla* was careened in Sandy Bay, or some other method was found of reaching her damage, she would have to be lightened and they had already made a good start. The holds were now empty of just about everything, apart from two week's supply of preserved meat. Even their fresh water which, after several months in storage, was anything but, had been pumped over the side. Two new casks from St Helena had been taken aboard and, with the sun unusually hot overhead and no restriction having been placed upon drinking, one was already almost empty. All agreed that the local product, made even tastier by being transferred from its source through several miles of lead piping, was far superior to even that found on the Isle of Wight.

The forecastle lookout hailed the boat, and Banks moved across to be by the larboard entry port when his visitors arrived.

Henry Booker was up first, followed by Brady from the dockyard, who had already made the journey three times that morning. Banks greeted them warmly; *Scylla*'s people had done well, but their efforts were more than matched by the Company's men, who had taken to lightening the stricken ship with a will.

"Thought I should come aboard and blacken my nose a little, Sir Richard," Booker told him. "That is if I am not in your way?"

"No, I am pleased to see you," Banks replied. "And would be happy to show our progress if you wish it."

"Brady has kept me informed, but yes, I should like to see for myself."

Banks led them back towards the open grating. "As you can observe, all but the lowest tier of beef and pork has been cleared," he said, staring down into the black void below. "We should not wish to go further until news is heard from Sandy Bay," he explained. "And still have topmasts set up, as you have doubtless noted."

Whether or not Henry Booker knew enough about nautical matters to recognise the fact was not revealed, but he nodded seriously.

Brady, the dockyard superintendent, spoke.

"All the preserved meat you have sent ashore is safely stored, Captain. We have more if you wish to supplement, but that will have to be arranged with Mr Stubbs, the store keeper."

"Who has already been instructed to provide everything you require," Booker interrupted. "There was some question of rope, and other boatswain's stores, I believe?"

That was another reason why topmasts were still in place. Banks had hoped to start re-rigging the ship as soon as was feasible. Having access to what was an apparently endless supply of fresh cordage would make this possible.

"Thank you, I shall send a party with our requirements."

It was likely that anything supplied by an HEIC island depot would not come cheaply, but Banks had worries enough in other quarters. If he were to meet that Frenchman it was not just *Scylla's* hull that must be sound; reliable standing and running rigging was equally necessary. Should Lady Hatcher make the trouble he was already anticipating, quite how much was spent on providing the line was of no great concern to him.

"The ship is riding several strakes higher already, sir." Brady again. "But still I doubt her damage can be reached successfully."

"The guns have yet to be moved," Banks replied. "Though I should have to wait until more is learned by the shore party before such measures are taken."

The idea of stripping his ship of her ordinance went totally against the grain. It would probably be necessary, and while they lay within the protection of the shore batteries, it need not cause him concern. Still, he had already decided that the cannon would be the last to be removed and, while there was a chance that *Scylla* would have to sail to the south of the island, he had every reason for them to be retained.

Brady shook his head. "You won't find any good news from

that quarter, sir," he said. "Sandy Bay ain't right for what you have in mind; the prevailing wind is contrary and you'll find the bottom far too cluttered with rocks for a safe beddin'. Besides, what cannon we 'as there ain't powerful enough to cover a vessel of this size."

Banks had heard the same from other sources, but still felt that no one knew his ship, and what could be done with her, as well as his officers. Brady would be used to the confines of a dockyard and probably lacked the lateral mind necessary for serving at sea, while, as for advising on artillery protection, that was well out of his domain. King and Caulfield were far more informed sources and had also been eager to go, although why they could not have taken a cutter, and done the journey by sea was quite beyond him. Sarah had her theories, of course, but he preferred not to consider those at that moment.

"If it is so, do you have camels available?" Banks asked.

Booker seemed surprised by the question, while Brady appeared to understand, but looked doubtful. Camels were a possible solution: a pair of barges that could be flooded, then strapped to either side of the hull. In theory, when the water was pumped out the ship would be raised. Her damage might still not be accessible however, and *Scylla* would be vulnerable to a strong wind, but it remained a last resort.

"Not as such, Captain." the dockyard superintendent replied. "We've a heavy barge, larger than most, that might lift one side if you wished to lay her over; but that would inevitably obstruct the damaged futtock, and we don't have two."

"Two might not be needed," Banks said quickly as inspiration struck. He was feeling a rush of blood run through his veins as if he were going into battle. Hearing that at least one suitable barge was on hand had started the thought process, and he began to speak even before a logical conclusion was reached. "What say we just use one?"

Both men now appeared equally confused.

"Use the one," Banks repeated, thinking still. "And simply lift the stern?"

"Lie it crossways under her counter do you mean?" Brady's

eyes came alive as he caught Banks' thread. "We should have to remove the rudder of course, but there is no difficulty in that…"

"Could it be raised sufficiently?" Booker asked, not totally following Banks' thinking, but knowing enough to get the gist.

"If we shifted the sternmost guns for'ard," Banks added, the energy flowing through him still. "I'd say we might even lift her clear of the water."

"Careening her would definitely be a safer, and more conventional option." Brady was speaking slowly, and possibly regretting his earlier enthusiasm. "And if there is more to attend to on the hull…"

"Three or more years of growth," Banks answered. "Yet we may also clear some of that, if it can be reached," he added quickly. The novel method might not be ideal, but any option was preferable to *Scylla* having to set sail and bring the Frenchman to battle with a crank hull.

But Brady was clearly not one who came to decisions lightly, and continued to consider the proposition as he spoke. "If Sandy Bay is unsuitable, as I fear it may be, then I should say it worth the trying," he said at last. "We still have to fix the barge in some way, and there is the added complication of keeping the bows from going under," His eyes cleared suddenly, and he seemed decided. "But I should say it may work – if nothing better comes to mind," he added, to cover himself.

"Well, we shall know for certain before long," Banks said, relief that a solution – any solution – might have been found, evident in his voice. "You are expecting them by nightfall, I believe?"

Booker nodded. "By six at the latest, Sir Richard. It will not take them long, and my daughter is well acquainted with the roads, such as they are. I shouldn't think they will run into any trouble."

* * *

Trouble was also on Timmons' mind, although in his case he was not trying to avoid it. Both watches had been active since first light, with only a brief spell for breakfast and, despite the novelty of their surroundings and the work, which was both tiring, and monotonous, he was starting to feel some well remembered sensations deep inside.

It was probably the recent kill that had sparked everything. Knocking off the molly had got his blood up and the anticipation of shore leave, with so much further potential, only served to maintain the pressure. And it was strange that physical work, such as he was now undertaking with the hoist, did little to quell any passion within him, the very reverse in fact. He was one of the team manning the falls, and with each cask of meat that rose slowly from the hold it was as if he was cranking up his own personal cargo. Possibly it did not help that Mitchell was working directly beneath. It would not take much, just the parting of a line or a slight slip by a loader, and the barrel in motion would come tumbling down upon his head. Such a thing might even be engineered easily enough, if Timmons could only replace one of the men guiding the barrels up. So much preserved meat landing on him from a height would do Mitchell no good whatsoever, and to be crushed by something heavier must be a fitting end for the big bear. It was simply a shame that Timmons had been detailed to the falls, but impatience was not one of his faults. The ideal opportunity would come, just as it had with Healey. He only had to wait for the right time and place to present itself.

Strangely, as he considered this, there was no longer any animosity towards Mitchell. The man had crossed him, and would be accounted for; Timmons knew that, and the knowledge nullified his previous ill feeling. But the intent remained – nothing was going to take that away.

* * *

All that had been said about Sandy Bay was correct; it was useless. The beach, a brief stretch of black, volcanic sand, might have been acceptable were it not for the profusion of jagged rocks that were too large and numerous to be moved and, although there was a reasonable ridge above and to the east that would provide placement for a sizeable shore battery, only light cannon could be moved across such a rocky road. They might achieve something with the ship's own ordinance, but the task would take far too long to be considered viable. The final point was the one that had worried both King and Caulfield when studying the chart. There were twin, extended headlands that seemed specifically designed to make manoeuvring difficult; when combined with the prevailing south easterly wind, they were likely to see the ship wrecked, if not on beaching then when putting to sea once more. Neither officer had felt the need to cancel the trip however and, to some extent the day had not been wasted although, on finally seeing the area for themselves, both knew there was scant purpose in remaining any longer.

"Will you be taking measurements?" Julia asked innocently, as she joined them.

"I think we can see all that is needed," King replied. "What say you, Michael?"

Caulfield pursed his lips and nodded gravely. "Aye, it will not take her," he said. "Any repair must be undertaken at the anchorage, unless..." his eyes swept round to meet Julia's in hope. "Unless you know of another likely prospect?"

"I fear not," she replied. "This island is known for its uninviting coast; it is possibly one of the reasons we have kept possession for so long, though strangely no ship has been lost off it, and few are ever wind bound."

"Then it shall have to be the anchorage," King confirmed. "Even if the repair will not be as sound."

"If it be achievable at all," Caulfield added gloomily, as concern for their ship finally overpowered any feelings each may have held for the girl.

"Then there is nothing more to be said," she stated with an air of finality. "We must make haste if the journey is to be completed in daylight; there is a way to go, as you are both fully aware."

They turned with her, and all three began to trudge back up the empty beach to where Jackson was waiting with the servants. And it was when they were almost halfway back that the girl pushed her hands through both men's arms, linking them as one in both hope and disappointment.

* * *

They began just before first light the following morning, when all the ship's boats were lowered, and her topmasts finally struck. Anchored nearby, the Company packet, a well-built, square-rigged, affair was also due out that day, so the dockyard was sufficiently occupied supplying her last minute needs. But Brady was as good as his word, and a heavy barge was being towed out to *Scylla* as the sun began to rise.

"That's the last of the quarterdeck carronades removed, sir," Caulfield informed Banks, while shouts and the occasional hammering from the stern signalled that work with un-shipping the rudder was also in process. "If you'll excuse me, I'd like to check on their stowage. We can't afford to have any go adrift should the wind rise."

Scylla's anchorage was actually well sheltered, but it was not entirely unknown for the steady south easterly to shift, and the first lieutenant was right to take every precaution.

"Very well, then you may begin sending ashore those men that are not required," Banks said. "Make certain there are marines in every boat, and please remind Mr Cherry, Mr Lewis and all accompanying midshipmen of my instructions regarding the men's behaviour."

Caulfield saluted smartly before disappearing forward. They had discussed the berthing arrangements the previous evening as soon as he and King returned with news of Sandy Bay. Booker had already allocated three block houses in the Jamestown barracks and Cherry, the marine lieutenant, along with his men and a handful of warrant officers, were fully primed with instructions and appropriate punishments if any of the hands proved unruly.

But even without *Scylla*'s marines watching their every move, Banks was not really expecting trouble. British seamen were known for their ability to conjure both drink and women seemingly from thin air but, with substantial stone walls separating them from the town, and upwards of a thousand East India Army officers and men also present, he felt that even they might find such circumstances hard to overcome.

"How is her trim, Mr Fraiser?" Banks asked, turning to the sailing master who, he noticed, was standing by the bulwark and apparently staring morosely at the shore.

"She is well up by the stern, sir," the Scot said, his attention returning instantly to the matter in hand. "There are still the long eighteens in your quarters, and those on the half deck, but I think we may have sufficient as it is. Besides, it would be better not to take her higher until we are certain of support from the barge."

"Very good," Banks replied. He began to pace the deck, noting as he did that the leg towards the taffrail was now decidedly uphill. A wrenching noise, similar to that of a small tree being felled, came from the stern. King and the carpenter were clearly making progress with the rudder, and Banks could only trust that the device would be as easy to replace later.

Next the dockyard superintendent appeared at the entry port and climbed cautiously up the quarterdeck ladder. Banks stopped his pacing and swung round to address him directly. "Well, Mr Brady?"

"We've started to flood the barge, sir," he said, clearly taken by surprise and touching his forehead awkwardly. Noticing the gesture Banks decided that he had been wrong about the man not having sea experience: such an instinctive reaction indicated time spent in the Royal Navy. Just why he had left was a mystery of course; he may have been laid off, or might conceivably be a deserter; but whatever his reasons, Brady definitely lacked the mildly contemptuous attitude that many of his profession adopted when dealing with a post captain, especially one so dependant upon him. His deference might be down to something else, however. What they were about to attempt could so very easily end in disaster, in which case it would be better for him to be on good terms with Banks.

"I set the men to fixing additional cleats last night," Brady continued hastily. "There are plenty enough now, as well as chocking points, if they be needed. And the barge is as sound as a bell – she were hauled out an' filled with water yesterday evenin'."

"You have done more than could have been expected," Banks told him. "Especially when there are other vessels under your charge."

The superintendent gave a brief laugh and seemed to relax. "Oh, we'd far rather be dealing with you than Cap'n Walker's little lot at present," he added in an outburst of familiarity. "They got a female passenger aboard who's askin' for the world with ribbons on. Makin' 'em run about like headless chickens, she is; I wouldn't want to spend the next few weeks with that as company."

Banks was in two minds about the news that Lady Hatcher had decided to return to England in the packet. On one hand he was delighted to be rid of her. As far as he was aware, she had hardly set foot outside of the governor's country house, but even so her vague presence had shed an uncomfortable shadow over the whole island. Her absence also effectively ruled out any possibility of a court of enquiry on St Helena itself. But that did not mean that a future investigation would not take place at all; indeed, it was far more likely the Board of Directors in London would insist upon it. And even if he were exonerated, there was also the small matter of a threatened court martial. He could not be sure what influence the woman wielded at the Admiralty but, without his father's support, he himself had very little. She might not even need to be successful; just by stirring matters up his name would be blackened sufficiently with those in authority, causing considerable harm to any future naval career.

There was a movement from the stern that diverted Banks' thoughts just when they were in danger of becoming morbid. He looked back to see the carpenter's head appear over the taffrail. In a few agile movements the man swung himself over, before standing on the quarterdeck and smacking the dust from his hands.

"Mr King sent me to tell you the rudder's free, sir!" he said, beaming broadly at Banks and Brady.

The deck was at an angle, half her guns had been moved, and now warrant officers were springing over the side like monkeys;

163

Scylla was turning into something between a construction site and a circus, but there was no doubting the positive attitude, and Banks knew only too well that such a thing could move mountains.

"Very good, then you may begin to secure the barge, Mr Brady," he said, before continuing to pace uphill once more.

* * *

"You may as well transfer to the shore," Manning said cautiously, there being some doubt in his mind that she would want to join him. "They will be a week or more working on the ship and, if anything, this accursed angle shall only increase."

"Ashore?" Kate asked. "Would that be permitted?"

"I am the surgeon, and in overall charge of the medical team," Manning reminded her without humour. "It is for me to say, and I think you will be the better for some time on land."

"You make it sound as though I am ill," she said then, realising there was to be no reply, added: "And probably you have every reason to think so."

Manning studied her for a moment. There was, perhaps, a slight change in her countenance; a hint, no more, that the dark veil she had worn for far too long might finally be lifting. Perhaps, but he could not be certain.

"I have splendid quarters, which Mr Booker is happy for us to share," he said at last. "And believe you will get on well with his daughter."

"Then that sounds very nice; thank you, Robert," she replied crisply. "And will Sir Richard and Sarah be there?"

"They are staying a few miles off with the lieutenant governor," Manning told her. He knew that Kate and the captain's wife had been good friends for the entire voyage. And even afterwards, when Lady Banks had discovered herself pregnant, she had not apparently been affected although her petulance had certainly increased. But then Kate had changed in so many ways since they had lost their own child that he could no longer be certain of anything. Except, of course, that the woman who stood in front of him now was not the same person he had married.

She had definitely grown more severe in her manner, and was also far more irritable. Never one to suffer fools gladly, her reaction to minor annoyances were liable to become even more extreme of late. And yet, on other occasions, a far more major set back might be ridden out with almost inappropriate good humour. He wondered which was to be the case now and outwardly regarded her with more than a little care, while deep inside mourning the loss of the woman he had loved.

"I should be allowed to see her, though?" There was a strange, yet familiar glint in her eye, and Manning was suddenly hopeful.

"The captain's wife? Why yes, I see no reason why not. I'm sure she would appreciate your company."

"Well I would understand if it were to be otherwise," Kate replied instantly. "She must feel uncomfortable, having me around; almost as if I might be an omen of ill luck." He went to speak, but she stopped him. "Oh, and don't think that Sarah is in anyway to blame; I have said all the right things, of course and tried to play the part of friend and nurse. And I sincerely want nothing but the best for them both," She looked at him intently, her eyes imploring his belief. "But she must know that I cannot help but resent their happiness deeply."

"It is natural that you would," he said. Then, greatly daring: "and natural that you may have been not quite yourself of late."

Her eyes rested on him. "Robert, have I been so very much the bore?" she asked.

"Perhaps not always the easiest to deal with," he confessed. "Yet you had every reason to be so and no one has cast blame, of that I am certain."

"Yet Sarah has picked up on it," she said, almost to herself. "And there must be others."

"Everyone who matters knows what you have been through, and all understand."

"And you; you must understand better than any of them; especially as it was your child that was lost as well as mine."

"I am not a mother," he shrugged. "It is different."

She shook her head. "There was still no excuse, and I am sincerely sorry."

Without speaking the two drew close, and soon she was in his arms again, and they embraced properly for the first time since the child had died. A loud and ominous creak sounded from somewhere deep inside the bowels of the ship and as they drew apart the deck took on a slightly deeper angle.

"Heavens, listen to that," she said smiling more sweetly now, and still holding his upper arms in her hands. "We must be away, else the ship starts breaking apart about us."

"You are sure you wish to go?" he asked.

"Oh yes, I had thought us to be moving, so have already packed my bag. We can collect it from our cabin on the way."

She leant forward and pecked him quickly on the cheek. "I am sorry for what has been," she said. "And how I behaved."

"There is nothing to apologise for," he told her gently. "You were in mourning; indeed we both were, and will be for some time to come."

"That is it exactly; it was a shared thing, yet I was taking everything on myself, and almost punishing you."

He reached up and placed his finger across her still quivering lip. "No more for now," he told her. "It is good that we have spoken, and indeed I think we should do so again, but first let us depart."

As he turned she naturally took his arm and, for the first time in what seemed like an age, the two walked out of the sick bay truly as a couple.

Chapter Fifteen

Three days later, when Banks and King stood on the small wharf looking back at *Scylla*, their precious ship was not in the most elegant of positions. Brady's barge had proved ideal for the work: pumped dry, and secured under her transom, the warship's stern was now raised by several feet. However the extra buoyancy, together with her emptied holds and a selective movement of ordinance forward gave the frigate a dramatically prow-heavy attitude. The bows were pretty much submerged to the hawse holes, while her rear was proffered up in a most inelegant manner. Her lie would offend the rawest of seamen, whilst even a casual observer would have to look twice to be sure she was not in the act of sinking. But however extreme the measures taken, there was one major redeeming factor: the damage below the waterline was now accessible. It might not be possible to replace the entire wounded futtock frame, but additional strengthening timber was already bolted alongside, and soon a proper job would be made of her scantlings and spirketting. The carpenter and his team had been at work almost continually and a deep void was now visible to one side, exposing the frigate's innards, and adding further to her indignities. There was no way of telling how much longer the business would take, but Evans had risen to the challenge with all the energy and commitment a captain might have wished for, and Banks was content that no one could see the job finished sooner.

"Michael Caulfield seemed strangely eager to stay aboard." The captain's voice was low and his tone informal; it was hard to maintain quarterdeck authority when their ship was little more than a wreck; besides, he and the young lieutenant had been shipmates for many years.

"Perchance he is more content there than ashore," King replied neutrally. It had been agreed that each of *Scylla*'s three commissioned officers would take turns to remain with the ship at night, but Caulfield had volunteered for the first trick, and was apparently content to remain. Even after that day's excitement, when the French frigate had been spotted offshore, and remained visible for some while, backing and filling in the stiff offshore breeze, he had shown no reluctance to be left. *Scylla* was safe enough under the protection of the shore batteries: a full moon would rise shortly after dark and the watch keepers on land were confident of sighting even the smallest vessel by its light. Still, each evening Banks and King had been loath to depart, and on this occasion it was harder still. Stripped of most of her crew and set at such an extreme angle, the ship felt a strange and dangerous place: not somewhere to leave a friend for the dark hours, especially when an enemy lurked near by. And King's reluctance was always tempered by the fact that he was secretly spending his time ashore in Julia's private rooms, and had every intention of doing the same again that very evening.

His relationship with the young woman had panned out in almost exactly the manner he had predicted, although that did not stop him from keeping an eye on his superior, as far as her affections were concerned. Caulfield might be older, and far more crusty in his ways but, as the executive officer of a frigate, he had a good deal more status than any junior lieutenant. And it was obvious to him that, on the rare occasions they had been together since the trip to Sandy Bay, she enjoyed Caulfield's company, even if they disagreed on certain points.

There were no such differences between King and Julia however; they got along together splendidly. As a sailor, he was used to forming quick relationships, and she had proved equally adept. Even after so short a time, King felt a strong bond was forming between them. In the last few days they had talked much, laughed often and would soon, his young mind blithely predicted, become lovers. He didn't seriously think that an older, and slightly balding widower who held mildly radical views would take her away from him, although still felt a guilty relief that Caulfield had once more chosen to remain aboard.

Strangely King did not regard his own marital status as a disadvantage. A foreign wife who lived well over five thousand miles away and had already shown herself to be independent of him need not be an obstacle. He had no knowledge of the intricacies of such procedures, and it was not something he could enquire of Fraiser, Manning or any of his other usual advisers, but in his naïvety it seemed obvious that there would be ways by which the marriage could be annulled, and the term 'deed of separation' came readily to mind. And even if not, he thought Julia would be content to stay on the island as his mistress. Such an arrangement was not uncommon, besides someone in her position could hardly be shunned from local society when for so long she had been an important part of it. King would be quite prepared to make allowances himself, of course – he could not expect Julia to make all the sacrifices. The first step would be to resign his commission, then once more apply for employment with the East India Company. It might not be the best of career moves for an active young man, but with the threat of court martial hanging over his head, the option was certainly worth considering. Given time, luck, and the right connections he could eventually progress to take Julia's father's post, live in the house where he now lodged, and spend the rest of his life on the island that had won his heart as much as any young woman. It was a future that appealed and, in his current mood, seemed well within reach.

"Do you think we will see any more of the Frenchman today?" King asked, breaking the silence that had lasted for some while.

"I doubt it, and the anchorage is well protected if we do," Banks grunted. "What worries me more are the other vessels."

"The corvettes?" King was surprised; the two accompanying ships had stayed further out to sea, but must be of little danger to *Scylla*, compared to a heavy frigate. "You surely are not contemplating an attack by fireship?" he asked finally. Such a ruse was not unknown, but normally would only be used against a mass of moored shipping. Apart from *Scylla*, there were only small craft and fishing vessels at the anchorage.

Banks shook his head. "No, but I secretly wonder if they are what we think. You remember the action? One was left pretty much a wreck, yet this morning two were sighted, and both seemed to be sailing sprightly enough."

"The second was indistinct," the younger man reminded him.

"And stayed further out to sea," Banks agreed. "Yet the other came in almost as close as the frigate, and both were annoying the shore batteries for some while."

"Is that so unusual?" King asked. "They seemed to be sounding out the island's outer defences; surely that is pretty standard practice when dealing with unknown gun emplacements?"

"So why did the French not use all three vessels?"

King said nothing; it was a question he had not even considered. The third ship might certainly have been weakened in the earlier action, and ordered to stay on the horizon although, as the captain had stated, she seemed to be sailing quick enough.

"How about if she were unarmed?" Banks suggested.

"Unarmed?"

"Unarmed, and not, in fact a warship. I should say the badly damaged corvette was either sent back for repair, or sunk after the action."

King was about to ask of the other when the answer came to him like the cold wave of sudden sickness. "And you think the far off sighting might have been the Company packet?" he asked, appalled.

"I do; it is strange that those on watch did not recognise her, but she were a long way off, and thought to be several hundred miles north of here."

That was quite true; the service vessel had left more than three days before. She was fast and reputed to be well handled, but some mixture of ill luck and timing might easily have led her to be taken.

"So the French may well hold Lady Hatcher," King said slowly, his voice notably free of concern.

Banks nodded; for the last few months the governor's widow had been a blight on his very existence and even now, when she had officially left the scene, the woman continued to haunt him. Silently he wondered if he would ever be free of her.

Thoughts of the capture had led him to consider other

implications. For a ship as fast as the packet to be caught implied an element of surprise, in which case the transport's captain could easily have been remiss in ditching the confidential papers. So, in addition to his nemesis, the French might also have his carefully worded report. There was nothing so terribly damaging there, but news of Sir Terrance's death would inevitably be delayed for even longer, and that would hardly improve its eventual reception in London.

On the other hand he had been given time and, in theory at least, a golden opportunity to put matters right. He need only take *Scylla* to sea and defeat the French to make all well again, although that would be no easy task. A single French frigate would be problem enough; the presence of another armed corvette must add to his worries considerably while a captured transport, especially one likely to be carrying the widow of an important government official, could only confuse matters further.

The first of many lanthorns was being lit aboard *Scylla*. Time was still very much the enemy, and work would continue throughout the night, with the carpenter's team, as well as those hands who had associated skills, standing double tides until it was completed. But the fact that dusk was falling brought a slight chill to the air and, without reference to the other, both men turned to begin the long walk back to the town proper.

There was no doubting the departure of Lady Hatcher had made the island a far friendlier place. Like King, Banks had worries in England and he was also developing a strange affection for this tiny community set in the middle of nowhere. Knowing that a child was due, and family life would soon begin, had altered his own thinking considerably. For the first time in his naval career he wondered if being a man-of-war's captain was really the correct occupation for one with other responsibilities. Unlike King, he could not imagine spending his days in a place so isolated, though the reminder that normal, domestic life did exist, and could even be open to one such as him, was timely indeed.

The two walked through the archway at the end of the drawbridge as the light started to fade, and by the time they were crossing the parade ground it was quite dark. The change from day to night came suddenly; however long each spent in a land less than a thousand miles from the equator, the transition would probably always come as a shock. Then the harsh staccato sound of a far off signal gun cut into their thoughts, to be followed, ten seconds later, by another and almost immediately afterwards a bugle began to be blown hurriedly and quite close by. Presumably a parade or some form of evening inspection was being called, but such a thing was of no concern to them, and both continued to walk without mentioning the matter, or considering it further.

Then a lamp, shining high up on one of the two massive hills that dwarfed the town, caught their attention. The light was shielded and revealed several times in a seemingly random manner, presumably a signal, although the code was not obvious. This time Banks did turn to King and was about to comment when a group of uniformed men came hurrying out of the night and across the empty ground towards them. Their lack of order and obvious haste was disconcerting and as they passed Banks stopped one who appeared to be in charge. The man undoubtedly resented being delayed and gave a sharp reply.

"It's the battery," he said, adding a grudging "sir," after a glance at the bullion on Banks' tunic. "The gunners are being called to duty."

"Is your artillery not usually manned?" King asked, surprised.

"Only with a skeleton crew," the man replied, clearly eager to follow his men. "Enough remain on hand to maintain the equipment and carry out saluting duties, but the full compliment are officially designated for field service and only summoned when there is cause."

"And there is cause now?" Banks asked.

"Indeed, sir," the man almost snapped back. "Did you not notice the signal?"

Neither officer replied and the man continued at little more respectfully.

"The watch on Diana's Point has sighted an unknown vessel," he explained. "And those on Ladder Hill confirm that a raider is in sight to the north; probably one of the warships that was

172

bothering us this afternoon. It is a common enough occurrence during the shipping season and can cause a nuisance. Fortunately Captain Walker's vessel has already sailed, so there is only the fishing fleet to worry about. That and the wrecked Navy frigate, of course, but she is hardly our problem."

A rocket rose up from the roof of Government House, illuminating the surrounding area. By its light the man seemed to focus on their uniforms, apparently recognising them for the first time. "And if you are anything to do with it, gentlemen, I would return there forthwith," he added, before disappearing into the night.

* * *

But both men had no thought of turning back to *Scylla*; poorly manned, and with scant armament, their presence aboard could do little good. Instead Banks and King rushed after the artillery men as they made for the batteries. As sea officers they were unaccustomed to running any great distances, and tired easily, but a further signal from Ladder Hill, together with what sounded like far off cannon fire made them hasten their step. As it was they arrived at the entrance to the small fortress, only to find themselves halted by a sentry who held his musket firmly across their path.

"There will be no entry to the casemate during an action," the man said, as if reciting the words from a book.

Banks was too used to being in command and felt his anger rise as he gasped for breath. Fortunately King interposed.

"We are king's officers," he explained. "Kindly alert whoever is in charge to our presence."

The sentry eyed them suspiciously before finally calling out. The duty sergeant duly appeared and was followed, after a slight pause, by another figure that Banks immediately recognised.

"Sir Richard, or should it be Captain Banks?" Major Morris asked, a supercilious smile upon his face as he emerged from the darkness. "Are you here in an official capacity, or is this merely a social visit?"

"My ship is in danger," Banks said; the words were still coming in gasps but his face was now red as much from the young man's attitude as any recent exertions. "I demand you let me through."

"Demand, is it?" the major asked, just as another distant barrage of artillery was heard. "I hardly think you in a position to make even a request." His smile increased. "But then my uncle's widow will be well on her way to England by now, so there should be no harm in your at least witnessing what is about to happen."

He nodded at the sentry, and Banks and King followed him under a low stone doorway. "However you must remember that we are the experts here," Morris cautioned. "You will not interfere with anything we do, and if I find your presence in the least annoying, you will be removed. Do I make myself clear?"

* * *

Caulfield had also seen the signal from Ladder Hill and was equally in the dark about its meaning but, when viewed from the quarterdeck of an immovable ship that was on the verge of sinking, he took it even more seriously. *Scylla* had struck her topmasts, so the highest viewing platform was her maintop, less than a hundred feet above deck, but still he sent a midshipman up to supplement the lookout in the hope of seeing what was about. Darkness was complete and the moon had yet to rise; nothing could be seen to seaward, although on land things were far more active.

Lights were appearing on the wharf and about the town entrance that must be silhouetting *Scylla* beautifully, while there seemed to be a deal of activity at Munden's Point, the far eastern headland. But both of the two main batteries that protected him to the south remained apparently deserted. It was on them that the frigate's safety depended, and Caulfield was starting to worry.

* * *

On the main eastern battery it was indeed dark. Banks stumbled after Major Morris as he sped down a stone staircase that led to what was clearly the main gunnery level. Still there were no lanterns, but all around men were active, and enough reflected light came from over the low parapet for King and Banks to make out a line of heavy cannon that were in the process of being served. From the headland to the east there came a series of bright pinpricks of light, too large for musket fire but not in the same league as the heavy monsters that surrounded them.

"Field pieces," Banks said, half to himself.

"And too far off to be a real danger to shipping," King agreed. Noise of the barrage reached them; the sound was high pitched – it was indeed small calibre shot, hardly likely to damage a determined enemy bent on entering the anchorage and destroying anything within.

Both officers peered out into the darkness. The fire from the far off guns had left their eyes slightly dazed but, if there were an enemy out there, surely it would be in sight by now?

A blinding flash seemed to erupt from the sea itself and illuminate the bay; King actually went to raise both hands to his face, so sudden was the shock.

"The Frenchman," Banks murmured, as the simultaneous broadside landed on the edge of the anchorage. The target was unclear; possibly the battery on the eastern headland or perhaps one of the small clusters of fishing boats that lay beneath. But the intense light was etched on their retinas for several seconds, while thoughts of what might be to come remained with them far longer.

"She's travelling east to west," King added urgently, as the image of a ship slowly became clear. It was indeed a frigate, and almost certainly the same one they had met at the equator. And she was passing, close hauled, on the larboard tack: sweeping in towards where *Scylla* lay, anchored and vulnerable.

"That would explain the field fire," Banks said. "They probably have a temporary battery established there." Both men immediately peered at the eight heavy guns that lay in the gloom before them. Their range must be sufficient to reach the enemy ship and the modern carriages would give an arc of fire more than wide enough to find it even now. In fact a lucky shot might well damage the Frenchman; delaying would make the job more certain, admittedly but must also risk hitting *Scylla*. Banks looked about for Morris, who seemed to have disappeared.

"Where is your officer?" he snapped at one of the nearby gunners.

"Sergeant's here, sir, but Major Morris and Captain Hamilton will be in the guard 'ouse, more'n likely." The man indicated a small brick room that could just be discerned at the far end of the line of guns. Banks bounded towards it in the dark, tripping over a wooden crate, and all but colliding with another of the gunners as he went. He pounded on the door and when a voice came from inside, he entered.

* * *

"Shut that bloody door, you oaf!" Morris was sitting at a table with another officer. Both were drinking what smelt like spirit and the other man was holding up his hat, in an attempt to shield the small lantern that sat on the table between them.

"An enemy ship is entering the harbour, and yet your men are making no move to even lay their weapons on it. When do you intend to open fire?" Banks demanded.

"We probably won't have to," the other officer, younger than Morris, responded cheerfully. "Not if you insist on signalling the battery's position to them."

Banks looked from one to the other. Ignoring the fact that they were of a different service, he outranked them both, and yet they were treating him like an annoying stranger.

"You will address me as sir," he said, enunciating each word distinctly.

"We shall call you anything we wish," Morris informed him blithely. "Inter-service courtesy is exactly that: courtesy: something I will not waste upon the man who killed my uncle."

Banks snorted with disgust; in the current excitement he had quite forgotten the relationship to Hatcher. But they were in action: his ship was in danger – this was hardly the time to bring up old quarrels.

"I do not care who your relations are, or were; if you do not defend my ship I shall have your hide," he said with feeling.

"Oh, we shall be opening fire shortly," the major conceded. "But even I know enough about wind and speed to guess it will be fifteen minutes or more before such a thing will be necessary. And I am far more informed about land-based artillery than you, Captain Banks. So if you wish to watch the remains of the action from the emplacement, you will kindly leave us now."

"But waiting will endanger my ship, and when you do finally open fire she may be hit by your guns!"

Both men looked to the other and laughed. "When last seen your command was all set to take a final dive into the deep," Morris said with obvious satisfaction. "Although I do intend to destroy that Frenchman, which is something that you have proved incapable of. Should your ship be damaged further in the process, then it is of little concern to me, and frankly I fail to see the problem."

"You might be in direct charge of the battery, but I intend to make a report, and your attitude and performance will not impress." Banks said; he was properly angry now and could feel the blood fairly rushing through his veins. He longed for some physical activity to purge the energy inside, but was only faced by amused and contemptuous looks from the two young officers.

Morris placed the glass down from which he had been sipping and sighed. "Captain Banks, let me explain the situation in words even a sailor might understand. Both of our main batteries were constructed in the last few months and, as far as we know, the French are unaware of the existence of either. With luck they should consider that those on the eastern headland they were trying this afternoon are all we possess, which is why we have only been firing the lighter cannon. It was a ruse to lure them into our trap, and one that has apparently worked. Now, contrary to what you might require, we would like them to continue deeper into the bay, where we should be able to destroy them completely. Consequently I will be delaying my main fire until the Frenchman is comfortably within range. Better than that, a moving target is never the easiest to hit, especially at night, so I will wait until she stops, which she should do when she comes alongside your own vessel. Once that occurs I shall have no hesitation in ordering my guns to open up and, with luck, may even sink her: a feat that you have proved woefully unable to achieve. I am sorry if that sounds too far fetched to your ears, but assure you it will read well enough at any subsequent enquiry."

Banks felt his fury rise still further.

"Now in the interest of keeping our position secure, I will shield this lantern," Morris continued. "I expect you to be gone, and the door closed behind you, by the time the light is revealed once more. If you are not, I shall have no hesitation in seeing you removed, and held in custody – for your own protection, of course. Indeed it is a pity you did not extend the same courtesy to my uncle." He picked up the cap and held it against the light. But Banks had heard enough and stormed out of the small room, and back into the darkness outside.

Chapter Sixteen

Six eighteen pounders, housed in what had been the captain's quarters, were still in position, and Caulfield ordered them cleared away as soon as it become obvious that an enemy ship was close by. Such a paltry broadside would do little damage to a heavy frigate, and may even disrupt the delicate balance of barge, anchors and steadying cables that was currently keeping *Scylla* upright, but some reply was necessary, if only to give the forty or so men still aboard a degree of hope.

The French had already fired one broadside, but the target had been a light battery on the eastern headland, and the angle at which they continued to approach meant that none of their main armament could reach them. Only one nine-pound shot, probably from a chase piece, had hit the British ship, and partially penetrated the starboard bulwark, but there had been no significant damage or casualties. Several minutes had passed since then, though, plenty of time for the French to reload. The moon was also rising in the east and the frigate could now be seen relatively easily against its warm glow. She was steadily altering course to starboard and, rather than being held on the very edge of a luff, was now on a comfortable broad reach under topsails and jib, while all the time inching inexorably closer to where the British ship lay.

Watching, Caulfield could not fail but be impressed; by his estimation the frigate would continue the turn until she drew level with *Scylla*. Then it would just be a question of time before she came down upon their starboard side. She should pass close enough to touch, and would be able to deliver a massive broadside close to and at her leisure. Whether or not she spilled her wind, and continued to fire, or moved on, leaving the harbour with the wind conveniently on her quarter, it would make no difference. Exposed, as she was, and almost unarmed, *Scylla* would probably never recover from that initial hit, and there was very little he could do about it.

* * *

As Banks returned to the parapet he noticed that King had been joined by both the lieutenant governor and Henry Booker, as well as another man he did not recognise. There was enough light from the rising moon for faces to be seen. Robson introduced the stranger as one of his staff; he appeared to have been taking notes, and kept peering hard at the watch he held in his left hand so Banks assumed him to be some sort of personal assistant. At the anchorage *Scylla* was in plain sight; her foreshortened masts and extraordinary attitude making what once had been a proud warship appear even more vulnerable as the elegantly rigged Frenchman bore down on her in the fresh breeze.

"These guns will be waiting until the enemy closes," Banks said, in a tone that betrayed the disgust he felt. In apparent reaction to his words, the secretary began to scribble on his pad: clearly a report was being complied and Banks made a more private note to guard his tongue in future.

"This battery has only recently been extended," Robson said without emotion. "As has that to the west," he continued, indicating apparently nothing but darkness on his left. "Neither have shown any light and it is likely the French will either not know of their existence, or if they do, what they are now capable of." He paused and looked Banks directly in the eye. "All things considered, Sir Richard, I would say Major Morris is playing a very close hand."

Reluctantly Banks could only agree, and actually saw matters as clearly from the Company's position as his own. *Scylla*, to them, was nothing more than a liability, and one that was taking up almost all the resources of their small dockyard. In time they might be able to restore her to fighting fitness, but to do so would take a good deal of effort, and even then there was no guarantee she would deal with the current problem. But as bait for a trap, one that would lure that same menace into the grip of their brand new heavy guns, she was indispensable. A few well-sighted broadsides and any future threat to the Company's precious island, as well as their visiting merchant ships, would be wiped clear. And if a Royal Naval warship was also lost in the process it would be of little concern to them; and considered nothing more than collateral damage. In their position he would have no hesitation in mirroring Morris' actions – it was just unfortunate that the man had connections with the late governor, and was also a prig of the first water.

"I understand all that you say, Colonel," Banks said, trying for an even tone. "But would suggest that opening fire now might still wound the Frenchman sufficiently, without endangering one of his Majesty's ships."

Once more the assistant began to scratch frantically.

"I am sure you are concerned for the welfare of your command, Sir Richard," Robson replied soothingly. "As are we all. But our prime worry must be the destruction of that enemy raider. The first fleet from China will have received the Grand Chop by now – it is a strange expression, I know," he explained. "But in essence simply means that the Hoppo will have permitted them to sail. They can be expected within the month, and a powerful raider such as we see before us now could do untold damage, were she to encounter them."

"Will they not have protection?" Banks asked.

"Oh, yes," Booker replied. "The Company has an extensive fleet of armed ships that can sail with their fleet when the Royal Navy is unable to assist. They have been successful on numerous occasions, usually against pirates and small privateers, but none are larger than what you would term a sixth rate, and even those merchants that carry guns would be no match for a professional warship of such a size. You must understand, Sir Richard; our primary concern has to be the destruction of that frigate."

That was the trouble; he did understand; he understood all too clearly. But he could also see his own ship was likely to be destroyed in the attempt – indeed he would shortly be witnessing exactly that.

* * *

181

Caulfield also understood. From his position on the sloping quarterdeck of *Scylla*, he had the most to lose, and already guessed why the batteries that lay not three hundred yards off were still shielded in darkness, their guns cold and silent. Beside him the midshipman, Middleton, was shifting his weight from one foot to another as if eager for action of any sort, or desperate to answer some urgent call of nature. But he was merely a boy, whereas Caulfield remained the product of an older Navy: he had been taught about controlling emotions and was far more composed. The Frenchman was less than three cables off and sailing sweetly in the offshore breeze. She need only continue for a short while longer; extend the sweeping turn that he grudgingly admitted was a graceful curve, to bring her broadside to bear on them at a truly deadly range. *Scylla* would reply, of course: on the deck below men were ready now, and should not miss a target that large. But whatever damage the British were able to dole out would be repaid several times over by the enemy when they drew alongside.

Caulfield wondered at the result. *Scylla* might be knocked off her precarious perch, and, with the gaping wound to larboard, was certain to sink, right there at the anchorage. But even if such a thing were avoided, with the rear half of her hull almost clear of the water she was as open and vulnerable as any ship could be. Most of the shot would be taken effectively below her waterline, calling for truly extensive repairs or, more likely, *Scylla* would just have to be towed out to sea and scuttled.

But the enemy still had to reach them and, as he watched, an extra manoeuvre was being carried out aboard her. The anchorage was reasonably constant at ten to fifteen fathoms, but he remembered a slight area of shoal just about where the frigate now lay. It shelved, but not extensively, probably down to eight fathoms. Nowhere near enough to ground her, but possibly sufficient to cause a measure of alarm should the French be taking soundings, or if their charts were not completely accurate.

Caulfield's attitude of calm started to waver, and he found himself begin to twitch slightly. Even as he watched the enemy turned more sharply to starboard. Deep water would be found almost immediately, but now the Frenchman was positioned slightly further out into the bay, and at a less advantageous angle. She would not be able to close on *Scylla* without further manoeuvres and must continue towards them, almost head on, and then make a last minute turn, in order to lay herself alongside.

His foot began to tap as an idea formed in his mind, and soon he was every bit as restless as the midshipman next to him. Cahill was in charge of the guns below; he was a capable enough fellow, and one who held the respect of all the hands, but Caulfield wondered if he would also have the sense to direct their fire to where it would do the most damage. He decided there was only one way to be certain.

"Stay here," he snapped at the boy. "If the French make it alongside secure the men. I shall endeavour to return should they try to board."

The child looked doubtful, but Caulfield was already heading for the officers' companionway. To desert the quarterdeck in the face of an oncoming enemy might be considered bad form, but there was a chance, just a slight one, that what he had in mind might cause damage enough to mitigate the danger.

On the lower deck men were gathered about the three guns that were run out to starboard. The ship was cleared for action, so no bulkheads or partitions of any sort lay between them, and the crews were openly discussing the oncoming enemy, while Cahill paced back and forth behind them.

"How are you loaded?" Caulfield demanded as he approached.

"Single round, sir," Cahill replied quickly. "But I was about to order a dose of grape into the bargain." He seemed surprised, but not sorry that the senior officer had joined them.

"Belay that, but retain the round," Caulfield snapped. "And hold your fire."

"They are almost in range," the master's mate protested. "Hind's pretty much got sight of her prow, an' the others aren't that far behind," he continued, as the men stared back at Caulfield in disbelief. "We was thinking to get two, maybe three shots in before they reached us."

"Hold your fire!" the first lieutenant repeated, as he bounded up the sloping deck towards them. "I have an idea."

* * *

The seamen had arrived on the wharf several minutes before, and now spilled out so that each could get a clear view of the action. They consisted of the starboard watch, who were due shore leave that evening, together with any idlers and those of the larboard who had expressed an interest in seeing the battle, and all were under the supervision of Lieutenant Cherry. The marine officer was in overall charge of *Scylla*'s crew billeted ashore and had seen little wrong in allowing most of the men out of their barracks at once, even though he accepted that some might not return by the prescribed time. There was nothing they could physically do to save their ship, but Cherry reasoned that to continue relying on second hand news from HEIC soldiers and other such sources would create more tension, and possibly lead to greater trouble, than trusting the men to behave themselves. Still, his entire force of marines was accompanying them, and he had spoken with Lewis before selecting those of the larboard watch who would effectively be given extra leave. Strangely, Timmons was included in the latter. His behaviour, which was not normally of the finest, had improved considerably of late and the master's mate considered him worthy of the risk.

And so he was proving. Most had filed obediently through the streets of Jamestown with only a few attempting to deviate into one of the punch houses, and finally allowed themselves to be herded over the drawbridge to where they now watched, spellbound. They were standing in a ragged line as the Frenchman, only dimly visible from that level, headed relentlessly for their own stricken ship. Some were making ribald comments with differing levels of humour that ranged from expert opinion to wild speculation, but all followed the developments with professional interest and Timmons, it seemed, was no exception.

They stood in groups that were roughly defined by their allocated messes: he had engineered a place next to Mitchell, the heavily built holder, and seemed to be getting along with him surprisingly well. No mention had ever been made of the bigger man's behaviour during the line crossing ceremony; such trivial matters would have been wiped from Mitchell's mind long ago, and most of Flint's mess were unaware that one of their number still held a grudge. Something far more interesting was taking place in the anchorage before them, and Timmons seemed as fixed on the fate of their ship as any.

But Timmons had not forgotten; neither would he. And, however much he may play the part of a genial messmate, nod wisely at the big oaf's inane comments, and make the odd supportive suggestion, his mind was actually on another tack and prospect completely.

He could not care less about *Scylla*. One ship was very much the same as another to him, and those who attached personalities and even plied affection on what was really no more than a floating prison were entitled to sympathy or derision as far as he was concerned. But he was still apparently watching, and from his attitude and general countenance, no one would have guessed that the fate of his former home was not at the forefront of his mind.

"And what damned good would that be?" Mitchell demanded loudly, in response to Flint's assertion that a spring was needed on the anchor cable. "They ain't hardly any guns mounted, so there's no point in moving the barky about."

"They still got a few at the stern," Flint replied evenly.

"And could have kept more on the forecastle rigged, if only they'd 'ad the sense." Dixon added for good measure.

"A few ain't gonna stop a Frog that size," Timmons replied. He wasn't usually one for shouting out in public but had his own reasons for wanting to support the holder: Hind was his other intended target but, being a painter, he was aboard *Scylla*. Consequently Timmons was planning to make it Mitchell's lucky night.

"Even if they'd got the guns, they're not going to do much

firing," another added, further up the line. "Way she's rigged it wouldn't take more than a few rounds from an eighteen to see the barky off the barge; then she'll go straight to the bottom without any help from the French."

"Ask me the best thing they could do is abandon her now," Timmons again; to him the idea of being stranded on a Company island appealed to him greatly. They might be there for months while the Navy decided what to do with them, and he could get up to quite a bit of mischief in that time.

"Still, if they got the guns, they should be usin' them," Flint persisted. "One or two shots might not cause much 'arm, yet it would only take a lucky hit to make all the difference.

* * *

Several hundred yards to the east and fifty feet up, Banks was also starting to wonder why *Scylla's* meagre armament was not in use. The Frenchman must be within her arc by now; surely they could start taking pot shots at her bows, and yet even the few guns the British frigate still mounted stayed silent. The sound of a door closing to his right made him turn, and he could just make out the forms of Morris and the other gunnery officer as they strode down the rampart behind the backs of the HEIC gunners.

"She's firing again, sir," King prompted, and Banks looked back to see the last glimmer of light from the Frenchman's twin bow chasers. Despite the deviation, the frigate had regained a good position, confirming his assessment of the enemy captain's ability. The French could continue now, and then turn once more just as they were closing with *Scylla*. Set, as she was, the British ship was clearly poorly armed, so there would be little risk to the Frenchman's vulnerable prow; even if all of *Scylla's* remaining guns fired on her hull, they would do little damage. But, once she had completed her turn, the enemy could come alongside and pound his ship into a total wreck. And being so close meant that, when Morris did decide to use his guns, it would be all but impossible for them to miss *Scylla*. In fact, placed as she was, she was probably more liable to be hit than the Frenchman. For the hundredth time he told himself the strategy made sense, but to watch his command be systematically blown to pieces, and by both enemy and friendly fire alike, felt like more than he could possibly stand.

* * *

Hind's cannon was to be first. He was used to serving although had never actually captained a piece before but, as he squinted down the barrel with all the aplomb of a seasoned gunner, no one would have guessed. His right hand was raised, and the servers proceeded to heave the massive lump to one side. Hind knew that both of Flint's cannon had the habit of firing to the left. This particular gun was unknown to him, but it would probably be similar in performance, and he made a small allowance for the tendency. It would have been much easier to simply aim at the oncoming ship's bows; a large and inviting target that Hind felt he could have hit nine times out of ten, but the first lieutenant had called for a far harder mark. The enemy would soon turn and was already slowing slightly, so he took a second or two to be certain. Then, standing to one side and glancing quickly at Caulfield, he pulled the firing line.

The gun spoke before flying back and rearing up slightly, the forward carriage wheels actually leaving the deck as her motion was checked by the breach rope. *Scylla's* very fabric shook, and Caulfield could not be certain if her angle had altered, but there was no point in worrying over such a detail. Hind shouted to his servers who had rushed to the gun port to see the result. Whether he had hit or not made little difference; with luck they might still get one more shot in before the enemy blew them apart.

Davis was next, and had already lined up his gun and was preparing to fire when the news of Hind's miss came from those at the third gun.

"Couldn't see no sight, nor passage," one of the loaders told them mournfully. Caulfield took a turn about the deck to disguise his disappointment. For an untrained gunner to hit a moving foremast with a strange cannon was a lot to ask, but still he had secretly hoped for more.

The second gun was duly discharged, and the servers hurried to reload. Those at Hind's gun were still in the process of clearing their piece and the third, captained by Jehu, was waiting to fire. With all otherwise occupied, Caulfield himself went forward to an empty port and peered out at the Frenchman.

She was completely undamaged, and had closed considerably. As he watched the wind caught her sails and she began to pick up speed. Caulfield knew only too well that, once she turned, it would take no more than three or four minutes for her main broadside guns to have *Scylla* in their sights. Hind might get another shot in, and possibly Davis, but Jehu seemed to be taking an unbelievably long time to fire his, and it was likely to be the only chance he would get.

The gun finally erupted in a cacophony of sound just as Hind's men signalled their piece ready. Caulfield was still peering through the empty port, and noted a small hole appear by the leech of the enemy's topsail; that was poor shooting; despite his care, Jehu must have totally misjudged the gun's performance, and effectively wasted the shot. Hind was squaring his piece, but soon it would be too late and, even as he watched the enemy opened fire once more with her two forward-mounted chasers.

"Left a little." Hind was still lining up, but now the enemy frigate was starting to turn and would become harder to keep a bead on than ever. "A little more…"

Caulfield drew back from the port; even if they hit her, it was unlikely to stop the Frenchman, and he really should be considering returning to the upper deck. It would be futile to offer further resistance; the best that could be done for his men was organise an evacuation. They had the long boat and a cutter moored off *Scylla*'s larboard side; the two would be large enough to take all those still aboard. Then Hind's cannon spoke for a second time, and the result was greeted with a roar from all about.

* * *

The Frenchman had been hit just above the foretop; the entire topmast instantly began to crumble and topple in a confusion of canvas and line while the ship, thrown off balance by the loss of forward pressure, slowed and all but came to a stop, her tattered canvas fluttering in the wind.

"You have your stationary target, Major!" Banks roared, caring little if the whole damn world heard. Being forced to witness his command so exposed and so soon to be destroyed was akin to watching a much-loved child about to be bullied. The sight of *Scylla* finally striking back, and doing so effectively, thrilled him in a way he could never have anticipated.

A shrill whistle cut through the night, followed by Morris' cold words: "B battery, prepare to fire." The gunners had been following the course of the Frenchman and little adjustment was necessary. "On my word: three, two, one – shoot!"

When heard from behind a parapet made of brick and stone, the broadside sounded sharper than any either of the two naval officers had known aboard ship. But, painful or not, the noise was like the sweetest music to their dulled ears. From what Banks could see, the enemy frigate had been neatly straddled, but there was no time wasted on congratulation and, still working in almost complete darkness, the gunners served their pieces with commendable speed. But before they could be run out once more, another barrage came from the westward battery.

This was more dangerously sited, as far as *Scylla* was concerned; the angle meant they must effectively fire past the British frigate to hit the Frenchman. The greater distance did mean that their light was not so blinding however, so the effect of the shots could be viewed more easily. Banks drew a quick intake of breath; despite the fact that this was their opening barrage, the enemy ship was hit at least twice while no shot apparently went close to *Scylla*. And now the guns next to him were ready, and almost immediately fired off once more. King had moved forward and was staring down at the Frenchman with his hand held up against his eyes to retain some degree of night sight.

"Main t'gallant's gone," he reported with ill- concealed glee. "An' I'd say the rest of her top-hamper has taken a pounding."

"And another, lads! Let's show them we don't care!" The

voice of Robson almost made Banks jump: he had forgotten all about the lieutenant governor's presence on the parapet, and was surprised that the man stood so close.

"The standard of gunnery does you credit, Colonel," he said, despite himself. Seeing the enemy hit, and hit decisively, while his ship remained undamaged had done much to restore his humour.

Robson bowed slightly. "Thank you, Sir Richard; we take such things rather seriously. You will forgive me but there are none of your Admiralty's beggarly doling out of powder in the HEIC; all practice weekly for just such an occasion, and when one occurs, are suitably ready."

Banks nodded, but said nothing; he was in no mood to defend his service, especially after such an eloquent demonstration of marksmanship: he had seldom seen better.

"In situations such as this, damage to spars is far more valuable than any hit on her hull," Booker added, his tone strangely conversational amid the furore of heavy guns being served. "The French do not have access to the supplies we carry, so subsequent repair is far more difficult. And the target may even be dismasted; in which case we can sink her at our leisure."

Still Banks remained silent, even though what the man said made sense.

"Frenchie's back on the wind," King reported. Sure enough, even from his position Banks could see that much had been done to stabilise her rig and the frigate was starting to limp away, with the wind at her tail. The forecourse had been quickly set, and she was under better control, although a shadow of the tidy craft that had sailed so gracefully only a few minutes before. She was still a danger to *Scylla* of course; her broadside would be fired dangerously close to the British frigate's side, but Banks trusted that even a crack crew would have enough to do in controlling their ship, and so it proved.

A ripple of flame ran down the Frenchman's hull, but the timing was erratic, and some splashes appeared extremely wild. *Scylla* may well have been hit, and there might be more damage for them to repair than before, but she would survive to see the work carried out. And Banks was relatively certain that particular

Frenchman would give the anchorage a wider berth in future.

* * *

By two o'clock much of the excitement had subsided. The Frenchman was long gone and *Scylla*, only marginally injured by the intruder, had licked her fresh wounds sufficiently until daybreak. The HEIC gunners were also stood down, while their officers enjoyed a late supper. Banks and Robson had retired to Longwood while King lay in his own room and bed, but disappointedly alone, at Booker's house. Only Lieutenant Cherry was up and active, as were his junior officers and men.

As he had predicted, the temptation of a town had proved too much for some of *Scylla*'s crew; most had been spotted, and taken back smartly enough, but two still remained at large. Consequently all the marines were currently patrolling the darkened streets, stamping along the narrow lanes in a way that both expended their frustration and actually lengthened their night's work. But Cherry was not unduly worried; no one could go far on an island and most casual deserters were taken back within a few hours. Either they found remorse with daybreak, or unintentionally gave themselves up in stupor. The whole thing was a small time annoyance, nothing more, and would probably end with a black mark on a charge sheet followed by some minor punishment for the miscreants when they were, inevitably, caught. It wasn't as if anyone was likely to get hurt.

Chapter Seventeen

"He really is a most thoughtful and kind man," Kate told them earnestly, as their small cart wound along the unmade track. "Despite his Christian beliefs."

Julia resisted the instinct to laugh out loud as she could see the captain's wife was taking Kate's comments in all seriousness. Neither of the women were particularly well known to her, and she had yet to fully experience Mrs Manning's direct way with words. As the newcomer, she could not know that Sarah was simply pleased to have her friend back in something approaching her previous humour.

"Frankly, I would have never expected a bachelor to be so wise," the surgeon's wife continued.

This time Julia's smile did break through. "Why, they can't all be so very foolish, surely?" she asked.

"Perhaps not," Kate conceded. "But Mr Fraiser has a wisdom you would not expect of a normal sailing master."

"Richard values his skills most highly." Sarah said, still relieved beyond measure to be having a proper conversation with the woman once more. Since they had left England, Kate had been her closest friend. Despite their differences in station – the wife of a captain who is also a peer of the realm would usually be on a very different social level to a former midwife – they had got on famously. Kate was probably the more serious of the two; after having lost her mother at an early age the rest of her life had been lived in the predominantly male world of merchant ships and, latterly, men of war. This had imbued her with a mildly sardonic streak that could very easily turn sour, but on the whole she was good company. Sarah, on the other hand, was the daughter of an Irish magistrate. During the recent troubles she had fled to England, although not before much of her family's home and possessions had been destroyed. Both women had found comfort in their marriages, and it was especially upsetting for Sarah when news of her own pregnancy seemed to act as a chock between their continued friendship. But now that had changed and Mr Fraiser, of all people, appeared to have been the catalyst although, as the sun shone down and the small open carriage moved slowly along the rutted path, Sarah couldn't have cared less for the reason. It was a glorious day, with the prospect of many more to come; she would shortly be starting a family, and St Helena really was the most wonderful of islands.

"The Clarkeson's house is still a good way off, you are not tiring?" Julia asked. She had remained quiet for most of Kate's monologue, sensing its importance to the two women, and knowing there was much that she would never understand, even if the name, Adam Fraiser, was one that she knew well, and had special reason to interest her.

"Oh, I should never tire of this," Sarah said positively, glancing about at the scenery. "Indeed it was a splendid idea of yours."

"It felt right to show you a little more of St Helena," Julia told them, clearly pleased. "And with the men so busy with their boat, I felt this to be the perfect trip. The road is wider and far better than that which leads to Sandy Bay and the Swanley and Thompson Valleys are so pretty – much is just like England, or so I am told. And if we get the chance there are some lovely islands, just off the coast."

"But we are expected for lunch, are we not?" Sarah asked; she had her own reasons for wishing to find a house before long, and the bumpy cart ride was hardly helping.

"Oh yes, I sent word last night. The Clarkeson's are wonderful people, and will be overjoyed at seeing English folk and hearing of home."

"What part are they from?" Kate enquired.

"Oh, neither have visited, at least not to my knowledge," she assured them.

Then they were quiet for a while, each content in their own thoughts. Julia wondered vaguely about asking more about the officer who had proved so helpful, but Kate had apparently said all she wished to on the subject and for several minutes the only sound was the steady trot of the horse, interrupted by an occasional murmur of encouragement from David, its heavily set driver. The scenery was everything Julia had promised; wherever they looked lush vegetation seemed to drip as if painted with an eternal brush, giving an unusually healthy cast to the air, and contrasting beautifully with the occasional fissures of savage blue volcanic rock. The road they travelled was mainly set along a ridge that afforded breathtaking views of the deep dark ocean, but still there were areas when it would wind suddenly downhill, plunging them into the gloom and chill of a damp forest that might never before have been penetrated. And it was just after one of those occasions, when a slight incline slowed the horse to an even more ponderous walk, and a merciful sun was just threatening to break through that Julia asked a question that had been very much on her mind for the past week.

"Tell me," she said, finally breaking the silence and still wondering if the wives of both the British frigate's captain and surgeon were really the right people to address. "What do you know of Thomas King?"

* * *

Timmons had been living on his wits and very little else for the past two days, and the hen he had just eaten, warm and raw, did much to revive him. He brushed the blood and feathers from his hands, then returned to the small stream that had been his guide for most of the morning to wash properly. He was, so he reckoned, a good five miles from Jamestown. It was a fair distance, and far enough to risk stealing the poultry. For the first day he had avoided even the heavily laden fruit trees and blackberry bushes, so concerned was he that his escape would be complete and permanent.

Killing Mitchell had been the easy part. The old fool agreed far too readily to a diversion, just before they were due to be marched back to the barracks. And getting away had been almost as simple – wait for the next time the battery released a broadside, then slip off quietly. Once over the drawbridge they were on the main street and then into the tangle of side roads and lanes. No one had seen them go, not even their messmates, it was perfect.

Both agreed they should get as far away as possible from the dock, but for Timmons the lure of what the natives called punch houses was dubious. They found one eventually of course, and Mitchell laid into his beer as if the daily half pint of strong spirit he was accustomed to was never issued. Timmons kept pace as much as he could, but remained totally sober throughout. There was far too much on his mind to succumb to alcohol; something a lot more potent drove his brain.

And then afterwards, in the street, when both of them were apparently disorientated, leading the big man into a dark enough alley was both simple and satisfying. It was late by then, and Timmons knew there would be bootnecks out searching for them. Consequently he could not afford any noise and, when Mitchell had shown signs of wanting to sing, the time had effectively been chosen for him. A swift crack on the side of the skull with his cosh, and the holder had dropped to the ground like any of the sacks he so regularly manhandled. And then a further blow, this time with a heavy stone which might have been placed there specifically for the purpose. Timmons actually felt Mitchell's skull crack and it was as if the broken bone itself released the feelings of relief and satisfaction he had been craving.

He could not enjoy the moment for long, though. Alone, and now far more mobile, he skipped through the darkened streets as if they had been familiar to him all his life. His intention had been to allow himself to be detected nearer the barracks, deny all knowledge of having been with the old mule, and take his punishment for slipping off just like any jolly Jack Tar caught out on a cruise. That was the first of his setbacks: there had been more to follow.

Immediately after despatching Mitchell he almost ran straight into Corporal Jarvis and a file of marines marching towards him. There had been no alternative, he was forced to double back, pass Mitchell's body, and continue on down the alley. He knew he was in danger of becoming truly disorientated and had stopped and looked up as soon as he could. The town sat between two huge hills that towered above: he could just make out their ghostly peaks in the moonlight. Both would be impossible to climb without being spotted, but he knew that if he kept them to either side he must head for either the dock or the country. Then a shout told him that the dead holder had been found, and he immediately began to sprint for what he hoped would be the former.

It was his second piece of ill luck. As soon as he noticed the ground begin to rise Timmons knew he was heading further inland. By that time a hue and cry had been raised, and twice he needed to dodge patrols of HEIC soldiers. Knowing that the Company's men were after him as well added an extra edge, and he continued to run for most of the night, only stopping when the sun sprang up with its customary haste.

By then he was in thick countryside, but there were still houses about, and suddenly people. In fact they seemed to be everywhere; riding horses, herding cattle, driving sheep, or simply walking aimlessly about to annoy him. He spent most of that day in a copse hardly large enough for the name, and only moved when darkness descended once more.

A day had passed since then and things were finally beginning to look up. Food had been found and he knew from cautious experience that more should be relatively easily to come by. He was still on the run, and this was not an ideal situation, but certainly one that bettered the dull monotony of the barrack huts. It was strange, he had more space, and sleeping in a bed was certainly a novelty, but his wooden shed felt far more claustrophobic than any crowded berth deck. Even the lack of movement seemed disconcerting.

And so he had resigned himself to making the best of things. Timmons knew he would be caught eventually; nothing could change that and, equally fixed, was his excuse. He had not been with Mitchell, not set eyes on the man since the wharf; no one had seen him on the street, and his present adventure could be easily portrayed as nothing more than a game attempt to desert. It would be up to them to prove otherwise, and not an easy task.

A sound caught his attention and he instantly froze. There

had been no trace of human activity for some while, and yet here was conversation; several voices could be heard above the clatter of a light carriage. He moved away from the stream and took cover behind a nearby blackberry bush. Some sort of vehicle was certainly approaching, and the figures in it were women. His heart suddenly beat faster: this was turning out far better than he could have hoped. Admittedly there was one male present: a young and well-set Negro driver, but he would only be a servant. Besides that almost added spice: women were usually his victim of choice, but he had never killed a black man before, and the concept appealed to him greatly.

* * *

"A wife?" Julia asked in disbelief.

Kate and Sarah seemed no less surprised although in their case it was not by King's marital status, but rather the girl's apparent ignorance of it.

"She is Dutch," Sarah said, as if in explanation.

"And very pretty," Kate added, to no noticeable benefit.

"He failed to mention a wife," Julia told them sadly, and in a slightly softer tone.

"Perhaps it just didn't come up?" Kate asked brightly, and then changed her expression as she caught a particularly harsh look from the captain's wife.

"You can hardly know him." Sarah reached out to the young girl who seemed to be close to a state of shock. The carriage was still clumping along the rough path, but suddenly its passengers had no eyes for the beautiful countryside.

"No – no, you are quite right," Julia agreed, composing herself, and even adding a cheery smile for good measure. "I hardly know him at all."

* * *

Work on the lower larboard hull was complete and the paint, though still tender, felt dry enough for what they had in mind.

Banks strode to the taffrail and looked down to where the dockyard superintendent was perched on the side of the barge. "Very good, Mr Brady, you may begin to open the seacocks."

The man gave a wave in response, and his team turned the three long handles attached to brass valves set deep in the bottom of the barge. A series of fountains spurted up, but soon the flow ebbed, and then seemed to stop completely as the incoming water smothered it. But *Scylla* was certainly on the move, and her deck's unnatural cant immediately began to correct.

"Once she is level again we can begin to move most of the guns aft," Banks told Caulfield and King, as he rejoined them by the break of the quarterdeck. "It should be a simple matter to remount the barge on the forward section and pump it dry; then we can set to work there."

They had previously decided that the extra couple of days it would take to raise the frigate's bows was worthwhile. By reversing the cant, and cleaning that part of her hull, much of the ship's bottom could be cleared. Being fully coppered, *Scylla* would not suffer any material damage from the build up of marine growth, but removing it would give her a fresh turn of speed; something that could be a vital factor in the coming action.

"The caulkers and pitchmen are ready to start on the half and quarterdecks," Caulfield announced. "And I think we can risk painting the forecastle, despite her being on the camel."

"If the recoil from an eighteen pounder didn't shake her off, a few painters are hardly likely to make any difference," Banks agreed. "And then the stores can be taken on once more." He looked about: the mention of lading reminded him he had not seen the sailing master for some time. "Mr Fraiser is ashore, I assume?"

King shook his head. "Below, sir. He has not left the ship since we arrived."

Banks was surprised. For a man to shun every chance of exploring a foreign port was almost unheard of. But then there was much about the sailing master that he did not know or understand.

"Shall I send for him, sir?" King asked.

"No, leave him be." The captain sighed. "It will be a day or two before we begin lading; there will be time enough."

"And then, do we put to sea once more, sir?" Caulfield enquired cautiously. The ship would certainly be able; his question really should have been, what were Banks' intentions? They might return home, and could expect to raise England well within three months, but that was ignoring another obstacle that needed to be overcome first.

The French frigate had been spotted on several occasions since the attack at the Jamestown anchorage. Usually she was accompanied by a corvette, but once a third vessel had also been sighted, and this time there was no dispute: it was the East India Company packet. That she had been captured was sufficiently bad news, but it also made facing the French force even more imperative. Banks had every confidence that Lady Hatcher could hold her own, even when in enemy hands. She would doubtless be released at the first opportunity, as was the custom, but being in enemy hands could hardly be a pleasant experience. Were he to sail off, abandoning the Company's Island and leaving their first fleet in from the East to be ravaged by a powerful French raider, he would upset many important people. But to allow Lady Hatcher to remain a prisoner when, in theory at least, he had the power to release her, would certainly never do. She might be openly planning his professional destruction, but to head home apparently without a thought for her welfare would only strengthen the woman's hand, and must certainly finish his career.

And he had no reason to avoid a fight. With a clean hull, fresh cordage, new canvas and what would be full magazines of powder, there were no material grounds why *Scylla* might not acquit herself credibly enough. Having to face more than one ship was going to make the job harder, but even then, with a full and practised crew, no British naval captain should be disconcerted by such a prospect. More to the point, the Royal Navy had acquired the habit of victory against high odds, so much so as to make it commonplace. His fellow officers and the public in general would look unfavourably on a naval officer who lost such an action; it would be almost as bad as if he were to simply avoid it completely. Should the French prove victorious, and somehow he managed to survive and be exchanged, it would matter little what other damage had been done to him professionally, he would never command a King's ship again.

But the fact remained that there was something about this particular enemy that had affected Banks in a subtle but important way. The French captain was clearly no fool; he had consistently handled his ship with flair and ability, while proving himself to be a determined and wily opponent. His ship was also obviously well-manned: the seamanship needed to clear that anchorage with a damaged rig had been exemplary, especially as it was undertaken whilst under fire from powerful shore batteries, while her gunnery was superior to any Banks had encountered in a foreign vessel. Banks guessed that the entire crew would have been hand-picked especially for such a mission; he was to face the best of the best, and it was a daunting prospect.

Of course he had met such odds and worse in the past, so why now was he feeling the pre-fight nerves of a raw recruit? Perhaps it was having Sarah with him? He had never fought a battle in a similar situation; she would not be physically on board but, even with her ashore, he feared there was little chance of the single mindedness he always relied on in action. Or maybe it was his own people: the officers and men he had come to know and trust for what might well prove to be a little too long. There could be no doubt of their efficiency – seldom had he sailed with such well-trained and reliable men. But they were all in desperate need of a rest, and the odd evening of shore leave on what was effectively a military installation was by no means sufficient. A couple had already run, one of which to be later discovered murdered. The two events might be connected but that would remain uncertain until the other deserter was finally caught. Banks was still unwilling to believe that a member of *Scylla*'s crew would wantonly take another's life, and was harbouring a private hope that the killing may yet turn out the work of a Company soldier or civilian. But even accepting that there was a bad one amongst his people, the vast majority were sound enough. All they lacked was a spell of rest in a proper English harbour, and that was the one thing he could not supply.

He noticed that Caulfield and King were regarding him strangely, and remembered that he had been asked a question. "Yes, we shall sail as soon as we are able," he replied, trying hard to make the words sound more positive than his thoughts. "We shall have to work the men up of course; they have been idle for far too long. But with the powder and shot promised, I see no reason why all should not be back to full fighting fitness before the end of the week."

It was clear that his words had inspired them, and both men nodded approvingly. But however long they had known him, and whatever the trust that lay between the three, Banks knew they were being fooled, and felt guilty as a consequence.

* * *

The horse had been showing signs of discomfort for some while and David, the driver, had already rested him twice. But it was now less than two miles to the Clarkeson's estate, and mainly downhill, so they decided to continue. Then, as they were entering yet another area of forest, he stopped once more, and began to cough terribly.

"Oh leave him be," Julia told the servant, who was trying to persuade the animal off the path. "It is not so terribly far; we shall just have to complete the journey on foot."

"That would be fine," Kate said. "It is a splendid day for a walk, but I am concerned about our charge," she added, looking directly at Sarah. "Do you feel up to some exercise, my dear? In your condition it might not be the best of activities."

"I am happy to walk, but would wish to take some necessary time first," she replied, blushing slightly. "It is early in my confinement for such a thing to be a problem, I own."

"Well, what say David here goes on to the Clarkeson's," Julia suggested, clambering out of the vehicle. "He can set off now, and return with another cart and animal. We shall follow in our own time and meet him on the way. Would that suit, David?"

The man, who had been comforting the horse, turned back to

the women and smiled readily. "That would be fine, Miss Julia." he said. "Rufus here, ain't so bad, but he's in no mood for more pullin'. I should have known before we took him."

"Never mind," Kate said, determined that nothing further would spoil the day. "You go on ahead to the Clarkeson's. Take some water if you wish, there are two bottles in addition to that for the animal. We shall meet again shortly; the horse will do well enough here."

"You do not wish me to stay with you, Miss Julia?" the black man asked.

"Lord no, David!" his mistress laughed. "Little can happen to us hereabouts, and if it does, well, there are three of us: we can more than look after ourselves!"

* * *

Timmons watched him go. From his vantage point less than a hundred yards off, he had even caught snatches of their conversation, and was in no confusion as to what was happening. He also knew that time would be needed before the servant was properly out of hearing, and time was something he had plenty of. The women would not make as fast a progress as the servant; he reckoned on half an hour, and there would be a good mile or more distance between the two groups. Then he would just have to wait for a modicum of cover.

But when one suddenly jumped down from the carriage and broke away from the other two his mind began to recalculate. She seemed to be heading straight for him; that, or the massive oak he was hiding behind. Timmons began to grow concerned; he did not think he had been spotted, but such positive action raised doubts, and he lowered himself further into the thick vegetation.

He had been following them for some while, keeping track of the buggy as it crept along the rough track. Through open areas he would stay back in the last of forest cover, then sprint forward when they reached another patch of vegetation. Such stalking was easy, especially when the quarry was oblivious and otherwise distracted. Even now, the thicket where he hid was surely dense enough, and his clothing blended perfectly with the dry bracken and rough gorse. The woman came on, though, and was apparently making directly for where he stood: his body tensed further.

He might have been seen, or even sensed: such things were known to have happened before even if her expression, which was getting clearer by the second, was completely blank, and not of a person expecting to discover another near by. There was something vaguely familiar in the face, but Timmons' brain was fully set on what was about to take place. She had closed to within ten feet, and he was just getting ready to run when, totally without warning, she took a sweeping glance about before hitching up her skirts, and squatting down in the midst of a small clearing.

His heart continued to pound as he watched, and slowly emotions emerged that would have been far better controlled. His prey, so perfectly presented, was half facing him, but clearly distracted and, as he stole out from behind his cover, did not look up. The well-remembered thrill was now passing through his body, and driving him on as effectively as any conscious intention. He pulled the heavy, sand-filled cosh from his pocket and wrapped the lanyard about his wrist, already knowing that this was going to be easy.

* * *

"Gracious, whatever was that?" Julia said, after the single and suddenly curtailed scream echoed about the small forest. She looked to Kate who had been trying to persuade the horse to take some water, but the woman was already charging off through the undergrowth in roughly the direction that Sarah had taken. Julia followed; both were wearing long dresses and, with no defined path, their progress was slow. There was movement up ahead, however, and soon the shape of a figure standing next to a large oak tree could be made out. It was a man. He had certainly not been the cause of the noise, although he may well have instigated it.

Kate slowed and put one hand out to stop Julia, who dutifully came to a panting halt next to her.

"Wait here," she hissed. "If there is any trouble, make for the road, and try and catch your servant."

Julia's face was now white. "What are you going to do?" she asked, but Kate was already moving off.

"Sarah?" she shouted. "Sarah, are you there?"

* * *

Timmons ducked down at the first shout. In front of him, what he now recognised as the captain's wife lay sprawled on the ground. Her limbs were thrown out like a tossed rag doll and a small trail of blood was starting to flow from the side of her head. The shout came again but, even if he cursed silently to himself, his ire was indisputably up and there was little he did not feel capable of. The cosh was still in his hand, and he spun it round in the air as a second woman entered the clearing and looked directly at him.

"Timmons!" she shouted, and he felt a moment of acute panic. It was the surgeon's wife; probably the last person he had expected to see. From a distance he had not recognised any of the faces, neither had he tried: faces actually meant little to him. But Mrs Manning was known to be a tough old bird, and he might have thought twice about making a move had he known she was about. "Whatever are you doing here, Timmons?" she continued, still pinning him with her expression. "And what have you done to Lady Banks?"

Now immature guilt replaced his initial fear. It was as if he had been caught in a mildly immoral act, not having just taken a swipe at the captain's wife. The woman lay before him now, her legs obscenely bared almost as high as the knees. He spun the cosh in the air again, more in bravado than any attempt to intimidate or threaten, and was surprised when Mrs Manning immediately drew back. Then he began to grow confident.

He stepped forward, over the body, and towards her. She retreated further and Timmons knew again that there would be no problem. She had turned and was trying to run almost as he reached her, and there was a scream from further off as his left hand closed upon the woman's arm. The third could wait; he was suitably occupied for the time being, and nothing was going to stop him.

His cosh came up, and Mrs Manning went to fend it off, with an ineffectual wave of her right hand. But he was far too good for her, far too strong, far too experienced: he was in total control.

The third woman screamed again, although it was doubtful if Timmons even heard. The sand filled cosh swung once, but the surgeon's wife ducked and it found empty air. The weapon even hurt him slightly as it rebounded off his own leg, and then he was properly angry. He took another stroke, this time hitting Mrs Manning soundly on the shoulder. She tried to back away as he moved forward, but fell instead, and he towered over her in a most pleasing manner. She was whimpering, and doing so because of his presence; the knowledge empowered him further, and he was just deciding to take longer over this one when an unexpected blow sent him to one side, and Timmons went sprawling into the nearby undergrowth.

It was the black man; he had returned, but was unarmed. Despite the shock, Timmons knew this need not present a problem: the man had clearly been running, and was probably nothing more than a slave anyway. He pushed himself up from the ground, regained his feet and swaggered slightly as he advanced, swinging the cosh threateningly.

One of the women screamed again, and it was just the distraction Timmons was looking for. The black man glanced to one side and Timmons launched himself into the attack, whipping the cosh sideways as he did and landing a pearler to the side of the servant's skull. The man reeled, and blood started to flow down his dark, glistening face, although Timmons was only just getting into his stride. Another strike, downwards this time, and carrying with it all his seaman's strength. The blow was dodged, and landed ineffectually on the servant's heavily muscled arm. Timmons drew breath. He had known a pause would give his opponent the chance to move, but was still surprised when he did so with such speed.

The fist was thrown with confidence and expertise. It caught Timmons on the corner of his jaw, hardly a prime hit but the pain and shock were enough to disorientate him for a second. He shook his head, then assessed the situation afresh. This was to be no walkover, but Timmons had fought harder men in the past and was certainly no coward.

He raised the cosh once more, but before any strike could be made a huge black hand shot forward and caught his wrist, encompassing it and closing with enormous strength. One hard shake and the weapon fell from Timmons' grasp slipping down his arm on the lanyard. Timmons grunted with pain; his wrist was locked firm in the servant's grip and, being so, he could not manoeuvre in any way. Then he found himself being dragged forward and could see the look of victory breaking out on the other man's face. The black man was smiling; his teeth gleamed white against dark lips and Timmons knew then that it had all come to an end. He was finally beaten.

Chapter Eighteen

Timmons would hang; Colonel Robson had been in no doubt of that. Banks skipped down the steps of Government House and strode purposefully across the empty parade ground, his mind determinedly set upon the most recent interview, and not that at the hospital which had preceded it.

It seemed that, by repeated charters from the Crown of Great Britain, the island had been assigned in perpetual property to the East India Company as Lords' Proprietors. With the supreme and executive authority vested in the governor, or anyone acting in that position so, even without the meeting of the full council, Robson had every right to exercise the powers of captain-general. Alternatively, should a civil route be chosen, there were magistrates a-plenty on the island, and the evidence would seem to be as conclusive as it was damning.

Of course Banks could dispute the matter, claim Timmons was a member of *Scylla*'s crew, and entitled to trial by court martial. There was also the unexplained murder of the other night; what was his name Michael? No, Mitchell, Banks reminded himself as he made for the drawbridge that spanned an inner moat. If Timmons was involved, as seemed overwhelmingly likely, it was only right and just that he should be punished.

But then what was right and just? The attempted murder of two women was more than enough to see the man hanged; adding a killing to the charge would do little good to the first victim whilst not changing the final outcome a jot. And as far as Banks was aware, the lower deck had accepted Mitchell's death as just another hazard of shore leave; it was even possible that actual harm might be caused if one of their own were shown to be responsible. Besides, if he really was determined to summon a court martial, such a route would necessitate the presence of at least five Royal Naval post captains. In almost any other British port that would hardly present a problem, but this was St Helena, and at that moment it was doubtful if so many could be found within a thousand miles. Timmons might be taken back to England, of course, but did he really want a man waiting to meet the noose as a passenger?

No, let them use their rope – Banks was more than happy to turn Sarah's assailant over to the HEIC. He had already been impressed by the Company's speed and efficiency in other matters, and was sure they would put the miserable little man to death in just such a way. Robson seemed confident that the thing could be done within the month, and if it were not; if some lenient magistrate took pity, or the prisoner's friend brought up a strange and unusual defence, Banks would just have to bend some rules and see the matter through another way.

With the realisation that Timmons' future was effectively settled, he finally slowed what had been a frantic pace, and allowed his mind to rest on a far more attractive subject. The military physician had pronounced the baby safe, and Sarah's wound to be superficial, with only rest and time required to produce a full recovery. Banks was doubtful of the man's experience in dealing with perinatal problems, or those of women in general, come to that but, as an HEIC Major there was no one more senior to hand, and he did not feel inclined to challenge what had been an excellent prognosis. The pleasant memory caused him to slow his step further, and then stop completely as he allowed it to be replaced by yet another.

He especially recalled Sarah's eyes, the moment they had let him into the room. Soft and strangely trusting, like a young animal's, they were one of the things he had noticed at their first meeting, and again when *Scylla* returned from her deployment with the Channel Fleet. He supposed it odd that, after only a little time together, their beauty seemed to fade, or at least lost some of its impact. The eyes were still lovely of course: a true insight into the soul of the woman he loved, but that initial surge of attraction definitely dulled after a short time.

But it had been back that afternoon: seeing Sarah so small, so vulnerable and so totally dependant on others, it was as if all the emotion he had ever felt for her was delivered in one mighty dose.

She must have experienced something similar and wept as freely as any wounded child. And when he took her cold hand in his and whispered those foolish reassurances it had been hard for him to maintain the expected persona of a senior post captain.

Hard, but not impossible; Henry Booker's daughter had been there, as well as Kate Manning; little would have been served if he had followed his wife's example, and he especially wanted to retain his resolve in front of the surgeon's wife. And so he had taken a grip and forced his mind towards dealing with Sarah's future, just as he had with that of her assailant.

She was to be transferred to Henry Booker's country residence. The two women seemed keen to rescue her from the more masculine atmosphere of the military hospital, and Banks supposed it was good they were both so determined to take total responsibility, even if he was left feeling slightly out of place. The surgeon's wife had also been bruised by Timmons, but was carrying her wound lightly, like the stoical creature she had become. He had been told in no uncertain terms that, besides rest, what Sarah most needed was to be back in England. The first would be provided, and he grudgingly accepted that the second was totally in his own hands.

The thought spurred him into action once more, and soon he felt the chill of a faint breeze as he rounded the sea wall and stepped onto the wharf. Ahead, he could see his ship; comfortably at anchor now, with a sound enough hull and bright new paint to her topsides. There remained much to be done but the sight of her, almost unexpectedly solid, forced him to an acceptance that he had been postponing for far too long.

She was all but ready for sea, and Banks knew there was little preventing him from meeting with the French once more. They should finish lading on the morrow and could set up topmasts; the boatswain had asked for a further day to replace essential cordage: then he could set sail whenever he wished.

Both enemy warships had been spotted on several occasions about the island, and the packet, which presumably still held Lady Hatcher, had also been in company twice. Banks had no idea how to face them; St Helena rarely experienced unusual weather conditions, and the only shipping due was that vulnerable first convoy in from the East. He knew it might be expected in under a month and so had that time: three, maybe four weeks, to work his crew back into shape, and bring the enemy to battle. They must be sunk, taken or at least damaged enough to make future interference with the trade ships impossible, and if *Scylla*, undeniably the weaker force, were destroyed in the process, then so be it, but the attempt still must be made.

However, seeing her now in the late afternoon sunshine he felt there was more than a chance they would succeed. No captain can be confident of his command when she is little more than a wreck and dependant on the goodwill of another service for her survival. But now she was whole: a viable fighting force and, even though inferior to the enemy she was to meet, he felt the common pride that any worthwhile master has in his charge. She had never disappointed him in the past, and he felt she would not do so this time. When – if – she made it back to England, *Scylla* was due for a major refit, and it was unlikely he would ever sail in her again, but the frigate had carried him thus far, and he knew, just as certainly, she could take him a little way further.

Banks' only concern was for his own performance. In the past few months so much had happened to wear him down, that he wondered if he were equal to her, and could actually raise the fire inside to win another battle. He told himself that Sarah alone was a strong enough reason, and nothing could be done to truly help her until the French were defeated, but still he could not summon sufficient energy and the actual will to fight was strangely missing. But of one thing he was certain; no purpose would be served by remaining on St Helena. The island might appear a small oasis of order and strength but in reality it offered nothing more than a claustrophobic and unnatural existence and, for probably the first time since arriving, he longed to be free of it.

* * *

The peacefulness of Julia's private rooms was in distinct contrast to both their worlds for the past few days. King had spent much of his time engaged in *Scylla*'s final lading, while she was still in a state of shock following the incident at White Ram Hill. The journey back had been dreadful; the captain's wife slept fitfully but Julia had been very much awake while that awful man just sat there staring with those powerful eyes that seemed to look right through and to her inner self. And even before then, there had been the shock of discovering King to be married. It was something that dwindled into insignificance following the rest of the day's adventures, but once she was back safe and in her home Julia had sent for him and now, as he sat in front of her, the importance returned.

He seemed to have sensed something in her manner, and came right to the point. The two of them were ideally suited – it was apparently something King had decided upon at their first meeting and, now that they had spent some time together, he felt no need to reconsider.

Such arrogance would normally have simply annoyed her, but for some reason Julia found herself being carried along for at least part of the way. On the face of it what he offered was what she claimed to want, and even when reminded of his marital status, there still remained a faint longing that could not be denied. But the reality of his marriage remained, and with a strength that took them both by surprise, she had coldly asked him how his wife might react to such a situation.

To be fair, he had not attempted to deny her existence. Neither did he try to explain how easily a separation might be obtained, or even asked if there was not another way that they could be together. And finally his lost expression, coupled with the tenderness she could not help but feel, softened her approach and she found herself telling him far more than she had originally intended.

But King, it seemed, did not wish to hear more and, even though her presence was still compulsive, he hardly listened. His fragile world, so hastily erected, was lying in tatters about his feet. Part of him was keen to leave, to quit the room, the house if he could; return to *Scylla* and never set foot on St Helena again. Part of him, but not all, and he stayed.

"I recall what I said before, about never leaving the island," she was saying. "There is something else you should know."

He waited.

"My mother was born and died here – oh I know she spent some time in India; papa took her there after they were married, but it was only for a few years. In those days he was a Company factor; they met when his ship stopped to victual, and were married within the month."

"A quick courtship," King murmured, although at that moment he cared little for her genealogy.

"Yes, I gather it was just after she turned down another in marriage, though mother died before I was old enough to ask, and it is not the sort of thing I could ever discuss with papa. Those about at the time have told me more, and I guessed the rest. Almost as soon as they were wed, the two of them continued on to his house in Bombay with the next convoy, and that was where I was born."

King supposed her story was leading somewhere, but he had other concerns on his mind at that moment. Then she began again.

"You see, mother was in roughly the same position as I find myself now. She had never left St Helena and, once they were married, I don't believe either of them really wanted to live anywhere else. They only stayed in Bombay a few years – I was three when they returned, and by all accounts mother was pleased to do so. But I also hear she was never the same again. People who knew her as a single woman say how gay and bright she had been, yet I remember a far sadder person. It was as if leaving the island had taken something from her and, once it had gone, she could never get it back."

"Or it could have been her first love," King said, interested despite himself. Julia looked at him enquiringly and he continued. "The one she broke up with, before she met your father. If she really was in love, the separation would have been far more catastrophic than simply moving house, or even getting married."

"Yes, I have occasionally wondered that." Her eyes returned to him. "Tom, I think you are the first person I have spoken to of this."

He shrugged, and silently supposed it something of a compliment.

"And would chance you to be right," she continued, still thinking. "Losing something can indeed cause far more pain than the happiness experienced when it was first obtained. I should say you are remarkably astute."

"Do you know anything of this man?" he asked, conscious that her praise had brought colour back to his cheeks.

"Just that he was with your Royal Navy," she replied, now smiling. "It was one of the things that cautioned me of you when we first met."

"And was he married?" King enquired more coldly.

"No, I believe he was not. And I think she did love him rather. He was a master's mate - that is not a very superior position, is it?"

"It is a warrant rank," King told her. "But an essential post, and not without prospects."

"Well, it were hardly good enough for my grandparents," Julia said sadly. "So the dashing Mr Fraiser had to be declined."

"Fraiser?" King asked, his senses now alert.

"Yes, Adam Fraiser. You may know of him," she chanced. "Earlier Kate spoke of a man named so in your ship and I do wonder if he be the same."

King shrugged. "Both are common enough names," he replied evenly, although so much was falling into place within his mind.

"I understand he was Scottish," Julia continued, further confirming King's suspicions. "It was another thing that grandmother took exception to apparently. But then he was also religious, so one probably balanced the other. Whatever happened, Mr Fraiser sailed off in his warship, and papa arrived almost immediately afterwards in an Indiaman; otherwise, of course, I would not be here," she said simply. The light was now returning to her eyes.

King smiled for what felt like the first time in ages. Yes, it all made sense; Fraiser's reluctance to go ashore, the fact that he was still unmarried, even the old man's remarkable insight into human nature and relationships could now be explained. Of course, as far as the sailing master knew, Julia's mother was still alive, and may even be living on the island, which accounted for his staying aboard the ship. Had she been half as attractive and alluring as her daughter, King wondered at his self control, and could easily understand how such a woman might change a man's life forever. But he could waste no more time thinking of the old Scot; Julia was speaking again.

"So you can see how it is, I am sure: married, or not, I could never leave here with you, Tom. Nor could I with anyone else, if I am totally honest. I may complain about seeing nought other than these few square miles, but in reality they are all I need. You know they call inhabitants of St Helena, Saints, I suppose?"

King nodded briefly.

"Well that is me, I am a Saint, and will probably die one."

"And were I to stay here with you?" he asked, playing his last and most valuable card.

She paused, and seemed to look at him afresh. "I have been employed by the East India Company before," he added quickly. "Perchance they would look kindly on my reappointment."

"I do not think that would work, Tom." Her words came more slowly, and were not without regret.

"But you do not know," he protested. "You cannot."

"I know you are proposing to leave your wife," she said with an air of finality. "So why not a mistress?"

* * *

HMS *Scylla* was finally ready for sea and most aboard were glad. Those who had been billeted in the HEIC barracks were comfortably back in their familiar berths, with reassuringly cramped hammock space and the well-remembered smells of a hard-worn ship. Some might be missing the regular shore leave but in reality even the island brewed beer had been but a minor pleasure. And though they might grouse at having to content themselves with just the daily half pint of high potency issued spirit, there had been remarkably little to actually do in the small town. All would have preferred a proper English port, with the things that St Helena so noticeably lacked, even if these included a better than even chance of the pox. It was common knowledge that on returning to England the ship would be paid off and, though the likelihood was that most would immediately be turned over into another vessel and could be asea again within hours of releasing *Scylla*'s hook, all were eager to be home.

And it meant little that the home they pined for – the perfect and accommodating England – had never existed beyond their imagination. The wives of those who were married might still remember them and offer a genuine welcome but, for the rest, there would only be doxies, either previously known or yet to be discovered. Both time and distance turned them into ripe, rich women who would smell sweet and surely treat them like royalty, and a few might even go some way towards fitting such a pattern. But there were also those, the majority, who would fall short, and expertly relieve their temporary husbands of all they had earned, leaving behind nothing more than memories and maybe an annoying itch.

That their betters shared the lower deck's longing for home, rest and women was not surprising. More unusual was the unspoken fact that three of *Scylla*'s senior officers could confine their interest in women to the same one, even if it were for subtly different reasons. Were the captain aware of the extent that Julia Booker had altered their morale and general temperament he would have been concerned. As it was he remained in ignorance, even though she had quite unintentionally created a series of whirlpools that affected them all. These were subtle, private changes but, when taken as a whole, might easily have weakened the effectiveness of the ship had those concerned not been provided with a first rate distraction in the form of their duty. For all were seamen first, and biological males a good way second. Julia Booker might have upset them in differing ways, but each reacted in an identical fashion, by concentrating hard on the many tasks that made up their complex world to the exclusion of all else. It was only when there came a lull, such as now, when there was literally nothing for them to do, that the memories returned, and their thoughts went back to the tiny island that they had known for less than a month and would shortly be leaving forever.

Certainly Caulfield, standing by the binnacle and waiting while they singled up to the bower anchor, had seen all he wanted of St Helena, and there was no doubting that Julia Booker was to blame. Initially he had been attracted to her; even to the point of nurturing insane ideas that she might one day agree to be his second wife. But it soon became obvious they held wildly differing views, so he decided, not for the first time, that the brief spell of married life he had already enjoyed was enough, and he would remain a widower for the rest of his days. He had long ago convinced himself that such a state of affairs was not unusual for a seaman, and might even be the most sensible arrangement. When those of his fellow officers who took a wife might not be with her for more than one day in a hundred was there really any need to bother? The recent incident had been nothing but a brief flash of light in an artificially darkened world: by staying aboard ship and determinedly wiping the memories from his mind he had almost regained his previous assumed disinterest as far as the opposite sex was concerned.

Meanwhile King was on the forecastle and supposedly supervising experienced men as they carried out work that could have been done in their sleep: so, for the last few minutes, he was also inclined to day dream. He had no intention of returning to the shore, not if it could be avoided. Despite an almost idyllic climate and terrain, St Helena was just too cut off for a man of action. Such small communities bred narrow-minded people; not Julia, of course; he could still think only good of her, but the combination of working for the HEIC, and spending what would probably turn out to be the rest of his life in such an isolated place would never do, not for the likes of him. Soon they would be free to sail for England: even without further damage *Scylla* was due an extensive refit, and shore leave for the officers was bound to be available. Then, at last, he might finally address the problems of his own marriage.

But, possibly due to the length of time, or maybe his affection for Julia, King was now not so confident of a successful outcome as he had been. However he did have a greater understanding of the situation, for there was no denying that, at soon as he suspected Juliana of perfidious behaviour, he had found no difficulty in seeking out a suitable replacement. Admittedly the affair had come to naught, but he had been tempted and, if such a thing could happen so easily to him, could he really condemn his wife for behaving in a similar manner?

He had already decided that two or three weeks on shore should do the business. In that time they would either sort their differences out, or call an end. But first, of course, there was the not so small matter of an enemy frigate, and that was not going to be an easy obstacle to overcome.

The Frenchman had been sighted twice in the last four days, and was undoubtedly keeping watch on the island. She may simply be waiting to pounce on the first juicy Indiaman, but an eastern convoy was a large affair and, with two other vessels to assist, could as easily be found several miles out to sea as by effectively blockading the anchorage. No, all knew that she was waiting for *Scylla*, and the knowledge that their enemy was so keen for combat had disconcerted almost every man on board.

Almost, but not all. Fraiser could not have cared less about any physical enemy nor, if he was honest, the island that still remained unvisited, even though it lay less than three hundred yards from where he stood. Of them all he was the only one to be affected by the young Miss Booker, and had yet to actually meet the woman.

When King had asked leave to speak with him he had naturally assumed there to be personal matters the lad wished to discuss, and never for a moment guessed they might relate to himself. And now, now that he knew the one woman who had ever meant anything to him was dead, while her daughter who, from King's description, sounded so similar was very much alive, he cursed himself for neglecting so many chances to have met with her. But all was not lost; the captain's wife was still ashore; should their encounter with the French end well, she must be collected before *Scylla* finally set course for England. He supposed an opportunity to seek the young lady out might yet be found, but on what grounds? That he was an old friend of her mother? Even that was hardly true; they had spent some brief time together nearly thirty years ago. That he missed her now, and had thought of her every day since that time? Oh, how lame, how lovesick that sounded; she would think him a fool, and an old one at that. Besides, how would he react if he happened to meet her father, the man who had effectively taken the woman from him? Fraiser knew his place, and it was not pursuing the progenies of lost loves. If the Lord had meant him to marry Kitty Davies, Fraiser would have done so. And if, after spending so many days within a few yards of her daughter, it had been intended for them to meet, that would have been arranged also. No, whatever happened the sailing master decided he would stay aboard *Scylla*; it was where he had been placed, where he belonged, and where he would stay.

Below, Banks lay on the firm leather upholstery of the stern locker. Of them all he had been least affected by Julia Booker, although she still retained some bearing on his life. And he was equally unusual in leaving something far more tangible behind than mere dashed hopes and unfulfilled ambition. His wife was recovering well, but not to be risked aboard *Scylla* when the ship was very likely to see action. They did, however, require their surgeon's mate so Kate Manning was once more aboard, while Sarah convalesced at Henry Booker's house where his daughter was caring for her. Should all fare well, he would be back to collect Sarah within the month: that was him or his ship, he hurriedly reminded himself, for however much he might consider himself to be immortal, it was by no means a fact. And if both he and *Scylla* were lost, Sarah would be well cared for; probably returning home with the next convoy: she might even see England in time for the baby to be born.

The image of Sarah giving birth without his support was far too painful and Banks determinedly moved on to other matters, yet still his mind returned to her frail, washed-out face and the child she carried. He knew, or at least hoped, that when battle were joined his skills as a commander would return to the fore, but in these doldrum days of doubt and indecision even the thought of her as a widow was preferable to the spectre of an indestructible enemy.

Eight bells began to strike: four o'clock in the afternoon: the time he had set for them to raise the final anchor and set sail. They would have approximately two hours of daylight before darkness descended. Much of the night could be spent in exercise; it would not take long to bring experienced men back to their previous high state of effectiveness, then *Scylla* might set out in earnest to hunt for the French ships.

Banks heaved himself up from his resting place while the bell was still sounding and, by the time the last note had been struck, there was a call from the marine sentry, followed by one of the midshipmen knocking at the cabin door. He smiled to himself; his officers were clearly up to the mark. All would be concentrating hard on the job ahead, without the distractions of complications ashore, or future problems in England. He envied them their single mindedness, and only wished his own life were even half so simple.

* * *

"Ready for you now, me hearty," the guard told Timmons, not unkindly, as he and three of his fellows entered the cold stone room. The seaman stood and allowed his hands to be secured behind his back. The faces he knew well enough, even though Timmons had spent less than a week in the small cell, for hardly any of the time was he left alone. There always seemed to be one of them about – casually – as if they had nowhere else to go, and they would play cards when he wished, share a meal with him, or talk.

Their conversations had been mainly one-sided, however; Timmons was never one who felt the need for chitchat, but instead drew wicked pleasure from their intercourse by continually introducing the one subject they would not address.

But the time was soon spent, and his trial had been equally brief, hardly a morning taken while his divisional lieutenant and midshipman identified him. The former spoke in his favour, although Timmons could tell his heart was not behind the words and, even if something that might mitigate or explain his crime was said, he would have had none of it. His time had come, as he always knew it must; he was heading for home and frankly would sooner be on his way than attempt any useless prevaricating.

And now, he supposed, this was the end of the journey. The men started out of the door and into the light of the parade ground outside. A prod from behind set him in motion and he realised with an odd feeling of loss that he would never sit, lie, run or even move his hands freely for the rest of his life. But that made only a minor impression on him. He was outside now, and looked about. There were a few officers and men of the India Army, but no sign of anyone from his ship, although Timmons did not care to look too closely; none of *Scylla*'s people had any special meaning for him, except perhaps Hind, the one man with which he had yet to settle his score, and seeing him would only spoil the moment.

A plain wooden gallows lay directly ahead, and Timmons supposed it was as good a way to go as any, certainly preferable to being hoisted up to a fore yard in front of an entire ship's company. He made for it without any encouragement, and mounted the wooden platform almost eagerly. A man dressed in black began to read from a Bible but Timmons had no interest in him or his words. There was a noose hung out of direct sight, secured to the cross beam by a strand of cotton; Timmons guessed it had been hidden in an act of clemency. A sack was pulled roughly over his head, but there was equally no need for that. He had no fear of dying; indeed the act had always rather fascinated him and, towards the end, even become the focus of his life. And he had always known it would come to this; there was never any future in his calling; in fact he felt he had done surprisingly well, and certainly far better than most. The rope was about his neck now: he could feel its roughness through the canvas that shut out the last of any light. Someone pushed him forward, the noose tightened and he took a step but, just before he did, the thrill came back, and with far greater force than he had ever known before.

It was just as when he was in the act of killing; a vibrant

sensation that rushed through his entire body, making both fingers and toes quiver and, ironically, seeming to breathe actual life into his frame. But this was far better than he had previously experienced, and it was all for him.

Chapter Nineteen

"When last sighted the enemy frigate was off Dry Gut Bay," Banks said, stabbing the chart with his finger at the eastern edge of the island. "That was two days ago. Since then she could be anywhere but, given that they have looked in at the Jamestown anchorage every three days, she might be expected to do so again at any time."

"And will we meet her?" Caulfield asked. Banks shook his head. Contrary to most captains, he encouraged discussion at such meetings, and the first lieutenant's comment was an example of how positive such an attitude could be. "No, but our presence may well be anticipated," he replied. "In truth, I believe the French will expect exactly that. Consequently I propose another course: one that might not be foreseen."

Banks' glance swept round the small group as they waited. All the officers present had served with him for many years, and trusted each other totally. A spell on shore was always difficult; he supposed it possible that their recent interlude at St Helena might have affected some in subtle ways, but any trite emotional entanglements could be forgotten now. These were professional men: King's officers, and there was a job to do.

"On previous occasions the enemy frigate was often accompanied by one or other of her consorts," Banks continued. "But these sightings were always when she was to the south of the island. Whenever she looked in at Jamestown itself she was alone."

That was quite correct, although the significance was lost on the other three.

"It is my contention that, as she is expected to the north once more, the remaining two will be further out to sea, and somewhere to the west of the island."

"Keeping watch for a homebound convoy?" Caulfield asked, filling in the spaces.

"Exactly," Banks agreed. "The frigate is accompanied when she is to the south, as they can run west easily enough with the wind on their tails, but when to the north, both smaller vessels are better employed elsewhere."

The three men nodded; even if not guaranteed, that was a hypothesis worth working on.

"At the moment I estimate the frigate to be here," he said, indicating a spot just north of Flagstaff Bay, "And steering west, in order to look into Jamestown at first light. With luck she will not have heard that we left yesterday. There are three hours of darkness left: I intend taking *Scylla* to the west." Banks pointed to the chart again. "In order to seek out the smaller craft. If they can be located we might take one, or even both, and settle the odds a little more in our favour."

King could see the wisdom in the words, but it was one thing to find the smaller vessels, and quite another to catch them. *Scylla*'s performance would be improved by her recent repairs, but she was still likely to be slower than the corvette, while a well-found packet might run her under the horizon in a morning.

"Mr Caulfield, I know you were hoping for further time exercising the hands aloft, but I feel we must make maximum speed, you will understand, I am certain."

"Indeed, sir." The first lieutenant was positive. "Though all were at a high standard prior to our repairs, and I feel the attitude amongst the people is much improved of late."

"I would agree." All eyes looked toward Fraiser, as the older man made a rare contribution. "The lower deck are keen to see England once more."

"They are also ready for a fight," King added. "And have no need for extensive practice."

"Very good." Banks' tone was level and totally matter-of-fact; no one could have guessed how closely he empathised with the men. "But there is no reason why we cannot exercise the gunners, Mr King. I would like as many drills as possible, and they can be round the clock: in fact the hands should be especially practised at night. Clear for action after the second dog, although hammocks may continue to be slung on the berth deck and the galley stove relit each morning. In essence I want us at the maximum state of readiness; there is no telling when we will meet the enemy, only that we shall. And when we do, we must be ready."

King nodded; there were few things he enjoyed more than exercising the great guns and he totally agreed with the captain's comments regarding time; more could be learned from working in dark than light.

"Then I shall thank you gentlemen, and not detain you further." They had obviously finished and, as he rested back on his chair, Banks suddenly felt immensely tired. Clearing for action would effectively rob him of his sleeping cabin and all privacy, but he cared not. The thing had to be done, and the quicker it was, the better; only then might they return home, and he could see Sarah safe. The other officers were rising to leave and, as he stood he also found himself moving stiffly, in just the same way as his father. Maybe he was getting old? Perhaps his fighting days were over, and really a respectable retirement from the Navy should be considered? It would certainly be better than suffering any disgrace at the hands of Lady Hatcher and her cronies.

But he was made of stronger stuff than that, and when he was alone once more Banks did not slump back into the chair, but rather moved away from the table and strode briskly round the room. Many were relying on him – Sarah above all: she had not married an elderly man who would run from the thought of danger. No, he would meet the Frenchman, face him broadside to broadside if necessary, and then, when he was victorious, take *Scylla* back to England and brazen out whatever was to come. The movement and his determination eased his joints and, as Thompson entered to announce his meal ready to be served, Banks answered in a strong and positive voice. Yes, Sarah was reason enough to confront any enemy, and seeing her safe more than justification for what he was about to do. He began to spoon beef stew onto his plate even before the vegetables had been delivered, and was half way through the meal when the servant hurriedly retired. With luck they would find the enemy within the next few days – this time next week they might be heading for Spithead once more. The idea pleased him, and he was finished and calling for his pudding in record time. It was certainly a change for the better, and one he was determined to retain. But at no point did Banks actually credit the cause of his change to the right quarter, and acknowledge that his present mood was actually due to the actions of an habitual murderer, and his unintentional contribution to the war effort.

* * *

Stiles was once more installed at his favourite post on the maintop, and frankly could not have been happier. He had been one of those billeted ashore at the Company barracks, and none particularly enjoyed the experience. In theory their blockhouse was a marked improvement on the frigate's berth deck; there had been beds with rich pillows, blankets and more than enough room to move about, despite the fact that most seamen tend to remain motionless when asleep. There was even a pair of iron braziers filled with coal that could have been lit, if anyone had felt the need. But despite its space, warmth, clean clear air, and the fact that the room remained reliably stable, the place lacked the close-packed intimacy that all were used to. Being allowed to explore the town on alternate nights had also been pleasant enough, but even that novelty started to wane before long. There were only three decent pot houses in the town, and those were always packed out with Company soldiers. The beer was good and strong, a local brew, but there had been no visit from the paymaster during their stay in Pompey and, as most were owed for the past two years and more, they were effectively penniless.

Movement came from below; Draude, the boatswain's mate and young Jameson, one of the newer topmen, were currently hanging precariously below the main crosstrees. They seemed to be adjusting the backstays, and working in concert with a team on deck. It was common enough in new line; however fine the quality all stretched to some extent, and their efforts were affecting Stiles' current post on the topgallant yard in a most disagreeable way. He was a seasoned hand, and well used to the wide arc the main mast could describe at its extremities, but the sudden jerks and jolts were far harder to anticipate, and just starting to annoy.

But it would be dawn soon, he told himself, and four bells almost immediately afterwards: the time when his particular trick at the masthead would end. There was still a further two hours of duty to follow, but he had spoken to Grimley, the cook, the previous evening, and there should be a prime duff awaiting him when his actual watch did finish. The thought of a good breakfast encouraged him and, even though the work beneath continued, he determinedly retained his usual cheerful disposition.

He took another wide sweep across the forward arc then, realising the sun was about to rise, clambered up until he was standing on the yard proper, enabling him to more easily monitor the entire horizon as soon as it was revealed. *Scylla* was sailing almost exactly due west, with the south easterly wind comfortably on her quarter. The captain was in no rush and, with their current sail pattern, she must be making no more than six knots, which meant that they should have covered nearly fifteen miles since the morning watch began. Stiles had no idea what the wind had been doing for the previous four hours, but during the first watch it had been blowing strong; the likelihood was high that dawn would find them in the midst of a clear ocean, with St Helena to their stern and well out of sight.

Yes, here it came: he was growing used to the rapid rise of the sun, and braced himself to sweep the surrounding area, just as Jameson began to shin up the topgallant mast to join him.

"You getting tired of hangin' about like a bat, then?" Stiles asked, as the young man made himself firm to the other side of the yard.

"Aye, the blood rushes to your head after a while," Jameson agreed laconically. "Back stays are regular now though, so I thought I'd join you and see what the morning was to bring. You're expectin' a convoy, is that right?"

Stiles shook his head. "Convoy's comin' from the south east, but they al'ays overshoot and end up west of the island. They're s'pposed to be a way off, though," he said. "It's the French we got to look for. Frigate an' two smaller. But anything you see, sing

226

out," he added as an afterthought.

Since missing two sightings in the past few weeks, Stiles had become increasingly cautious of his own reliability. There had also been other, less important, incidents when items in clear view to everyone else were inexplicably overlooked. He could see detail well enough, and still had eyes better than most, or so he told himself, but sometimes quite large objects could be effectively invisible to him. Until, that was, they were pointed out. This did not happen all the time, and the sighting need not necessarily be far off: just in the wrong area. And sometimes if he looked at it directly the thing would almost disappear; the trick he had found was to catch it to one side. Should the condition continue it would have to be reported of course, but Stiles enjoyed masthead duty far too much and, being as how the problem came and went, he was content to see if it would simply cure itself.

The sun came up almost directly behind them, chasing a shadow that, when viewed from their height, seemed to race across the ocean's misty surface, almost faster than could be followed. Stiles glanced back, purposefully not looking at the brilliant orb that was quickly establishing itself, then round to where the steaming dark waters were rapidly being revealed. Within seconds the light had spread as far as the western horizon, and he drew a sigh of relief as he noticed all was clear. He turned and went to speak to Jameson, but the young man's attention was fixed on something far closer to the ship. Stiles followed his gaze, but saw nothing. Then, by altering his focus slightly, an object did appear.

It was a small square rigged vessel – the one they had anchored alongside in Chapel Valley Bay, and had later been taken by the French. She was almost directly ahead and, as he looked at her, Stiles became uncomfortably aware that the enemy corvette was also emerging from out of the rapidly clearing mist a mile or so beyond.

"Sail ho!" he yelled, his voice only trembling slightly as he went on to make a full report. Both would be in clear sight of the deck and the packet lay comfortably within range of *Scylla*'s guns, but it was Stiles' duty to report any sighting, and he was painfully aware that he had been prompted to do so only because Jameson had been there.

Below there was a mass of activity, someone was bellowing orders; guns, already cleared away, were being run out, while a midshipman with a glass slung over his shoulder was starting the long climb up the main to join them. And it was all because of Stiles; him and his sighting. In the past such power would have thrilled, and was one of the reasons he especially enjoyed lookout duty, but something inside told him that his time at the maintop was about to come to an end.

* * *

"Open fire, Mr King!" Banks ordered, and the first of the bow chasers erupted less than a second later. The packet must have spotted *Scylla* first, as she was already turning to take the wind full on her quarter as well as hoisting an additional jib. But the range was so close that escape would be impossible; all the British frigate had to do was bear away and she could blow the smaller vessel out of the water with a single broadside. It was a tactic Banks would prefer to avoid, even without the possibility that Lady Hatcher was still aboard. Taking the packet intact would give him an additional craft; she may be of little use in action, but as an extra eye, or even a means of communication, her presence could be highly beneficial.

The shot landed less than twenty feet from the packet's prow, causing the helmsman to momentarily allow her to fall off.

"And again, Mr King," Banks roared, adding: "This time you may aim for a hit."

The second nine pounder was duly fired, but the shot went undetected. Banks waited at the break of the quarterdeck. The first chase gun would be ready in under a minute; time enough for another try, even though the packet was now moving rapidly. If the third attempt had no effect he would have little option other than to put the helm over and use his broadside guns.

"Ready, sir!" King called out from the forecastle, but before the order could be given a cheer rose up from the British seamen.

Banks glanced up to the enemy; she was turning into the wind and her sails were shivering in the breeze; the French had struck.

"We shall shortly be heaving to, Mr Fraiser," Banks said steadily. "Mr Caulfield, the red cutter, if you please. Prepare an armed boarding party, and have a detachment of marines accompany them."

Chances were high that the packet was not over manned, but Banks was taking no risks at this late stage. Supplying a prize crew would take at least fifteen of his prime seamen, as well as two junior officers, but recapturing the Company's vessel would go down especially well with those on St Helena. In addition, he might shortly be releasing Lady Hatcher from the clutches of the French. Banks snorted silently to himself as he took a turn across the deck. On the last point he was uncertain. Of course he must make every effort to set a captured English lady free, but this particular one would be a lot less trouble if she were still held prisoner.

He stopped pacing and his eyes fell on a master's mate, standing conveniently nearby. "Mr Lewis, you shall take command," he said. It would have been preferable to send a lieutenant, especially as the governor's widow might be present, but he could not spare either Caulfield or King. "Take a junior mid. with you," he continued. "Your choice, but make sure he is familiar with signals."

Lewis beamed as he touched his hat, and Banks knew instinctively he had made the right decision. The man was young and agile enough for the work, and had both the experience and confidence to command. He was also a first rate navigator, which might be a useful asset in the coming days.

But what of the corvette? Banks switched his mind from the problems of supplying a prize crew to that of the other enemy, still some distance off their larboard bow. She was holding steady three miles away, a mute witness to her consort's capture. In the past both the smaller French warships had the heels of the more lubberly *Scylla*; some improvement might have been made with her recent repairs, but Banks decided that she was still likely to be the slower craft.

The packet was coming into their lee now; Fraiser called for the mizzen topsail to be backed and soon one of *Scylla*'s cutters was crossing the short distance between them.

"Lewis' first experience of command," Caulfield said in little more than a whisper, adding: "And he started out a regular hand, as I collect."

"I consider him ready," Banks commented, equally softly. "And we shall not be far off, if there be trouble."

"He has men enough to quell any chance of re-capture," Caulfield said, surprised that the captain should even consider such a possibility.

Banks turned to begin pacing again. "I was thinking more of Lady Hatcher," he replied.

* * *

By mid-afternoon they were underway once more, and heading east. Any hopes of rescuing the governor's widow had proved fruitless; the woman was not there, having apparently been transferred to the French frigate upon capture. Several hands from the original crew of the packet were present however, and their release had allowed Lewis to return five of *Scylla*'s own, along with her marines. Once the transfer was completed Banks sent the packet off to windward, where she was now keeping station with them on the very edge of the horizon. Before long she should raise St Helena, and be able to exchange signals again shortly afterwards. The island may have had sight of the frigate but, even if not, Robson and his fellows would at least be aware that their packet was back in British hands. The French corvette was shadowing them on their larboard quarter, although Banks cared little for that. Perhaps, if the enemy frigate were encountered to windward, *Scylla* would not be in the best of places, but at present he could think of no alternative. When they came upon the Frenchman he trusted his fighting brain to begin considering the options more carefully. To do so now, with no knowledge of the enemy's position, was entirely futile; such thinking required the spur of action.

The bell rang seven times; it was half an hour before the end of the watch and the second spirit issue of the day. Most of the hands would still be mildly befuddled from their noontime allocation, even though they had since eaten their main meal, and taken part in a two-hour gun drill. But the daily rum ration was sacred to the lower deck, and Banks knew he could only postpone or cancel it at his peril. Then a call from the masthead wiped all such thoughts from his mind, and the ship itself seemed to take on a far more urgent air.

"Packet's altering course!" The shout cut through the normal shipboard sounds, quelling any chatter in an instant. "She's turning to leeward, and coming down on us with the wind."

Banks looked towards Middleton, the signal midshipman, but the lad was already making for the deck glass, and would soon be heading aloft. Lewis must have spotted something, simply turning back to relay a signal from St Helena would not have caused him to manoeuvre in such a dramatic fashion.

It was strange how quickly Banks' earlier prediction was confirmed: already his brain had started working out the relative distances and speed in order to place *Scylla* in the optimum position. For the packet to have made contact with the French frigate meant the enemy was to the east, and probably not more than a few miles over their own horizon. He turned to the sailing master, who had come on deck early for the setting of the new watch and was currently studying the traverse board.

"Take her as far to starboard as she will manage, if you please, Mr Fraiser. And set t'gallants and stays'ls, if you think fit."

The increase in speed and extreme change of heading could only frustrate Lewis, who must now alter course again if he wanted to close with them. The enemy corvette would also be alerted, but Banks was determined to gain as much sea room as possible and even try to claim that all important windward gauge, if it were in his power.

The sailing master manoeuvred them with his customary competence and soon *Scylla* was close hauled with the wind on the very edge of the luff. Lewis had not changed course and was now signalling, although his windward position meant the flags were currently unreadable.

Caulfield cursed, but Banks remain unmoved; there was little the master's mate could tell him he had not already guessed. In his mind he could see the enemy, eastwards and probably slightly to the south. They would undoubtedly have sighted the packet, and guessed she was no longer in their employ. More than that, her sudden turn would give a fair indication of *Scylla's* position. Still such concessions were worth making if it meant they could finally meet the enemy with the wind in their favour, and as his ship cut through the dark Atlantic, Banks felt his confidence grow.

Scylla was performing wonderfully; he had not seen her create such spray since their time in the Med. and the last gunnery practice had also been impressive. The men seemed to have benefited far more from their spell on the island than he had anticipated, either that or they were as eager as he was to see England again. It was a shame the drill had not been finished with a few rounds of live fire; nothing compensated for ninety minutes of backbreaking dumb play better than finally allowing the guns to speak, but even that might be remedied within the next hour or so.

"Enemy sighted sou-sou east, steering west!" Middleton's squeal came from the main top, and Banks' heart skipped a beat before he realised the lad was simply relaying the signal Lewis was making. The master's mate had shown sense in keeping to his original heading and continuing at maximum speed; *Scylla* was now making definite progress south, and they could finally read the tattered bunting that had been flying from the packet's main for some while. Such an action would have sailed the enemy frigate under their horizon, however, and it was vital they regained contact as soon as possible.

"Acknowledge, and order them to return and shadow," Banks said. If Lewes continued for much longer he was in very real danger of running in with the enemy corvette. The packet swung round, almost within her own length, and was soon bearing away from *Scylla* once more with a veritable bone in her teeth.

"How far are we away from the island?" Banks called out to

Fraiser.

"Nigh on seventy miles to the nearest point," the older man replied without hesitation. Banks nodded; then there was little chance of involving any of the shore batteries, but at least sanctuary was not so very far off, should the need arise and some consolation lay in knowing that future movements would probably be visible from the island's main lookout point. The ship's bell rang eight times; was it really all of half an hour ago that he had been anticipating the end of the watch?

"You may pipe 'Up Spirits' then send the hands to supper, Mr Caulfield," Banks said. "But retain the watch below; I want every man back and ready to beat to quarters within fifteen minutes – do I make myself clear?"

Caulfield touched his hat and turned away to bellow down at the waist. It was fortunate that the men would be going into action with full bellies. Supper was normally nothing more than a scratch meal, and consisted of little other than cheese and hard tack, although the tot of rum would give them far more than mere sustenance. But that was assuming *Scylla* came up with the frigate while there was adequate light. The evening chill was already descending, and Banks rubbed his hands together as he thought. It was now less than two hours until night, and with the moon still too new to make much difference they would be chasing about in the dark for a good twelve hours. He knew that such conditions would affect the enemy as much as them: it was simply a question of who could make the best of such a situation. Who could make the best, he reminded himself, and who would come off worst.

* * *

By the beginning of the second dog watch the dark had indeed arrived, and they were no more the wiser. In the brief time before sunset Banks had altered course twice, once to the east, and again as much as they could to the south, but the French frigate would not be found, and all his efforts had achieved was to shake off the corvette. On several occasions they had also lost sight of the

233

packet, but that was only temporary, and caused by Lewis using his vessel to the fullest extent, dipping over the horizon in an attempt to locate the enemy, before hurrying back with nothing to report. Now the two vessels lay within a few cables of the other, Banks not wishing to risk his consort being snapped up in the absolute night that had descended upon them. There was little point in remaining on deck, and he had gone below to the expanse of space that had been the great cabin, where he and Caulfield now stood peering over a chart that showed their estimated location and, for want of a suitable table, was laid over the barrel of an eighteen pounder.

"I should say they will not wish to stray too far from the island, if only to verify their position," Banks said, and the first lieutenant nodded in agreement. They had already decided that the two enemy ships were not likely to be in company. It would have been hard for them to meet up, or even closed to within signalling distance before nightfall without one of the British vessels detecting them. Since then a particularly dark night had descended, with thick, rain- filled cloud that effectively cloaked the ocean. Despite the India packet being close by, a feeling of isolation hung about *Scylla*, and any long distance observation was quite impossible. Only exceptional luck could have brought the two French ships together in such conditions, and Banks could not deny the feeling that, if the enemy were to benefit from such good fortune, there seemed no point in his pursuing the matter further.

"So, do we stay hove to, in what we hope will be to windward of them?" Banks continued, finally asking the question that both had been trying to avoid. "Or venture north, and attempt to seek them out?"

"Finding even two ships in such weather will be no easy task," Caulfield grunted. "And at least we are relatively certain to be between them and the island."

"Or so we think," Banks reminded him. "It would have taken very little to have passed us a few hours back. They might have turned to the west, and be seeking out the homebound convoy, or headed east and be standing off Jamestown as we speak."

"We might attempt to raise the island and enquire," Caulfield mused. "Though at night any signal would betray our own position and be of little benefit unless the enemy were in sight."

"Indeed, that is the crux of it," Banks grudgingly agreed. "Sight is what we need, and sight is something we do not have."

* * *

Sight was also a commodity that Stiles apparently lacked. He had reported the problem to Middleton, his divisional midshipman, who immediately removed his name from those detailed to masthead duties. He had also been sent to the surgeon, but there was nothing that could be done. Mr Manning had peered at his eyes, and shone lanterns with various coloured lenses, but apart from muttering a few nonsense words and making Stiles feel mildly sick, no conclusion was reached. And now, at a time when he should have been comfortable and aloof in his lofty perch, he was sheltering under the starboard gangway next to one of the guns that had been allocated to him. Stiles was happy enough as a gunner, and actually enjoyed his first drill with Flint's team, where he had handled Mitchell's rammer as if he were born to the task. Yet, even though the men were pleasant enough, he would still have preferred to be alone, and at the masthead.

"Getting used to having your feet on the deck are you?" Jameson asked.

Stiles snorted, but said nothing. It was all very well for him. Even though he was officially gun crew, the lad was still rated topman, and could be aloft at any time, were there the need.

"Wouldn't make much difference if you was up there now," Flint added philosophically. "No one can see in this weather – we might put a blind man on watch, and not notice the difference."

"I ain't blind!" Stiles snapped. "I can see perfectly well – it's just a passing thing – the sawbones said so."

"The surgeon stood you down," Flint reminded him more firmly. "An' said you were to have nothing to do with lookout duty."

"Said you were a danger to us all as well, I don't doubt,"

Dixon added. "So he sent you down here to be a gunner, where you couldn't do no harm."

The rest of the men laughed good-naturedly, but Stiles stood up and stomped off towards the forecastle ladder in disgust.

If he were honest, the knowledge that he was losing his sight had been with him for some while. It was not a pleasant companion, and he had kept it to himself, hoping that the condition might somehow resolve itself. At the moment it was worse during the day – at night he still felt he had remarkably good vision, in certain areas. But, accepting that it would deteriorate further, Stiles could only predict a bleak future. Today he had been stood down from lookout duties, in a month he might not see much at all, and be unable to even earn his place as a gunner. *Scylla* was due for a refit; within a few months they could be at peace, with all paid off and no one needing a blind sailor. By this time next year he could be begging on the streets: it was not a pleasant prospect.

"It may pass." Flint's voice startled him slightly, and he turned as the man appeared from out of the gloom and continued. "Maybe a rest is all you need?"

"There is nothing wrong at night," Stiles insisted rather pathetically, his voice and tone now low. "Just sometimes, in bright lights..." He looked across to where the packet was hove to and wallowing in the broad Atlantic swell. "There is Lewis next to the helm," he said. "Can you see him?"

Flint peered through the blackness and rain. With negligible moon it was hard enough to make out the packet in any great detail, and actually spotting individuals on her deck a total impossibility.

"You mean you can?" he asked, surprised.

"Not when I looks direct," Stiles confessed. "But if I catch him to the side of my eye, he comes through clear as day. They got a small patch of light near the forecastle – like someone hasn't blacked out below correctly, can you see that?"

Flint shook his head, impressed despite a measure of doubt. To him the packet's prow merged into the gloom, but then for all he knew Stiles was talking humbug, and could see nothing at all.

"And beyond her, to for'ard – there is somethin' else," the seaman continued, his voice now rising slightly and gaining urgency. "Something's out there in the dark."

Flint raised his head and peered forward, but could see nothing. "Where away?" he asked.

"There!" Stiles voice was far louder now, and he stabbed his finger out over their starboard bow insistently. "It's another ship, and she is also hove to, but drifting more to leeward – I can see her jib!"

Flint looked again, then shook his head. "There's nothing to be seen, matey," he said sadly.

"Yes there is!" Stiles all but shouted. "It's the French!"

He turned from the forecastle and began to run along the gangway to the quarterdeck. King was at the conn, and looked surprised and almost annoyed as the seaman rushed up to him.

"I can see the Frenchie!" Stiles spluttered. "She's about half a mile off our starboard bow, but fadin' fast!"

King moved across to the starboard bulwark and peered forward, but all he could make out was the vast blackness of ocean and sky, with no discernible division between. "Send for the captain!" he snapped, and heard the duty midshipman scurry off. King made for the binnacle and brought out the night glass. He focused and swept the brass tube about for more than a minute before lowering it once more. "Take a look," he said, handing the telescope to Stiles. "There's nothing to be seen."

The seaman brushed the glass aside in contempt. "Never could use them things, and surely can't now. But I could see a ship clear enough, and she'll be gone in no time lest we do somethin' about it."

Chapter Twenty

Banks arrived almost simultaneously with Robert Manning, who King had decided would also be needed. The latter was still dressed in his nightshirt and seemed somewhat bemused, but answered readily enough when the captain interrogated him.

"Stiles, yes I examined the man this morning. A prominent mydriatic dilation of the pupils, combined with an inability to compensate for strong light: the two are closely linked, sir," he said. "No sign of tumour or infection; the first can be an indicant of cranial haemorrhage, but there are no supporting symptoms."

"And your prognosis?" Banks demanded.

"I'm no physician, sir." Manning shrugged; as a surgeon he could pop cataracts or remove a splinter but there any expertise regarding eyes pretty much ended. In fact the information he had given was actually the product of private study. "It may pass off, or could be an early signal of something more sinister. I would not care to speculate."

The captain turned away, and stared out into the darkness once more. "There was nothing from the masthead?" he snapped.

"Nothing, sir," King confirmed.

"You are certain?" Banks was centring on Stiles, who lowered himself slightly under the great man's inspection.

"I'm as certain as I can be, sir," he mumbled. "It sure looked like a ship to me."

"But you cannot see it now?"

"No, sir," Stiles confessed miserably. "That I cannot."

Banks was starting to fume; the ghost of a sighting was far worse than none at all. They might move to investigate, but that meant abandoning their valuable position to windward. And, even if the French were out there, on such a night no one could guarantee they would be found. He glared about, hoping for something that might give him inspiration, and naturally his gaze fell on the officer of the watch.

"What do you know of this man?" he demanded of King.

238

"Has he proven reliable in the past?"

The lieutenant hesitated. "He was in error before, sir. During the crossing ceremony."

Banks swung around and directed his full attention back at Stiles, who was now looking particularly wretched.

"Yes, it was you; I remember," the captain said. "Let them close unreported as I recall."

"It might have been a mistake, sir," the seamen muttered. He was certain as ever of the sighting but had been addressed by his captain in such a manner once before and felt no need for a reminder.

"You there, Middleton," Banks barked at the nearest midshipman. "Take a glass to the masthead and tell me what you see. If there is a ship, do not call out; use a backstay."

The lad was off, eager to be free of the confrontation as anything, and they waited while he skimmed up the shrouds. For more than a minute he was out of sight then, with the sound like that of rushing water, a body was finally seen flowing down the taught line, and the midshipman bounced nimbly back onto the deck.

"Well?" Banks demanded. They all held their breaths, but the lad shook his head.

"Nothing I can see, sir. And Piper is at the masthead; he is certain no ship passed him by."

"Piper couldn't spot the nose in front of his face," Stiles murmured, then stopped suddenly as he remembered where he was, and who could hear.

"And you can do better?" Banks demanded. "You who was too distracted to see an enemy squadron in broad daylight, and only today reported problems with your own eyesight?"

Stiles lowered his head further but said nothing while Banks all but stamped his foot on the deck in frustration.

"Is it possible, medically, I mean?" he asked Manning.

"The pupils are constantly dilated," the surgeon replied. "So in theory his night vision is unaffected and may even be improved. Yet such a condition would undoubtedly present problems during the day, or in bright lights. As to the cause, sir, I could not hazard a guess."

Banks cared little for the reason, but what Manning said made a modicum of sense. And as Stiles was trained for such duty, his eyesight should normally be of the highest order.

"Call all hands and bring her to the wind – topsails and forecourse," Banks snapped, suddenly coming to a decision. "Make no signal to the packet, if she follows, so much the better. But I will not have unnecessary lights, with luck we will find her once more at dawn."

The watch on deck seemed to shatter into fragments of silent activity as they attended the sails, while those who had been below for little more than two hours came tumbling up, rosy and steaming, from their hammocks. Stiles gratefully retreated from the quarterdeck and went to find his gun, where Flint and his mates were bound to be waiting for him. When rated as lookout he was used to starting a deal of action, but never before had there been such a situation, and never before was he so unsure of himself. But then what did he have to lose? If his eyesight really was failing he had no future as a seaman, and may as well go down causing a stir as not. He was still stubbornly convinced of what he had seen; the enemy were definitely out there, although finding them was going to be an entirely different matter.

"Blimey, Stiles – you really are in the suds this time," Dixon told him, with more than a hint of respect. "You certain you saw that Frenchie, are you?"

Stiles rubbed at his eyes, which had now caused him far more trouble than they were worth.

"Reckon I am," he said.

* * *

The ship herself awoke with the minimum of fuss, and began to creep forward, only the groaning of timbers and an occasional squeal from her tackle betraying the fact that she was once more a living creature. The gunners, now divided between both batteries, squatted patiently next to their allotted pieces, while most of the midshipmen were assembled on the forecastle, the foretop and the main crosstrees, each eager to be the first to spot a hidden enemy. The rain was now falling heavily, and all were thoroughly soaked, although it was doubtful if any noticed, so tense had the atmosphere become. Everyone was silent, as they had been ordered to be but Banks, standing by the binnacle, was especially so and felt as if he had been cast from stone. His body was rigid and his eyes set forward, apparently unblinking, despite the atrocious weather. Sense and reason told him that this was a waste of time; the man, Stiles, had already proven himself to be unreliable; they were simply giving up their hard won advantage on the whim of a fool. Yet there was another inner feeling that said otherwise, something in the seaman's hauteur and the fact that he bothered to alert his betters and then stick to his story until only universal doubt and intimidation finally wore him down. Such a stance might carry the blame for a thousand other similar ventures: armies being raised by what came down to the intuition of one sentry, a ship changing course because the officer of the watch sensed an uncharted rock, or a lad that thought he saw the flash of breakers. There was every reason to believe the enemy did lie ahead of course, but in a crew of nearly three hundred the fact that only one had eyes sharp enough to see them was a wild enough conjecture to begin with, without including the man's medical condition and past history of unreliability. Still, Banks felt in his bones that Stiles was right, and was already steeling himself to act when news of the enemy's position came through.

But at the end of quarter of an hour, in which time they had sighted nothing other than a further bank of heavy rain, even he began to grow restless. The hands at the quarterdeck guns were whispering softly to one another, and there was the start of what might become laughter from further forward. Banks felt himself unbend; the pain in his joints was telling him just how much he needed sleep, and his annoyance at having been robbed of the much-needed rest had grown to the extent that he was finally raising his arms to stretch, when there came a ripple of interest from the forecastle.

Caulfield and Fraiser exchanged glances; the lads grouped forward were certainly excited about something, and there was what might have been a small cry. Then one of the young gentlemen, a volunteer who had only joined them at Spithead, broke away from the others and began to scamper along the sodden starboard gangway.

"It's them, the French," he spluttered as he tripped at the break of the quarterdeck, and almost slipped on the soaked planks.

"Make your report, if you please, Mr Steven," Caulfield said firmly, and the lad seemed to take stock, before addressing the captain in a far more formal manner.

"Frenchman sighted off the starboard bow, sir," he said, his voice quavering slightly. "We're comin' up on her stern; there's a small light on deck, so them's certain."

"Which ship is she?" Banks asked.

The lad shook his head. "No way of knowing, to be sure, sir," he said, before adding in a more confidential tone. "There's quite an argument goin' on amongst the oldsters."

All could appreciate the difficulties – the vaguest outline of a hull, probably barely glimpsed and then only for a few seconds, would be almost impossible to identify.

"She's hove to, an' there's not much to judge her by," the lad continued. "If it's the frigate she's further off, or it could be the corvette, and not so far," he added lamely.

Or a different ship entirely, and they were on a goose chase, Banks finished for the lad. But he had not voiced his thoughts and, to be fair, the likelihood of another vessel of any size being in such a position was slight. Even if they had found one of the Eastern fleet she would hardly be hove to so close to her destination.

"Very well, Mr Steven. Return to the forecastle, but keep me informed," Banks ordered, then looked towards Caulfield and Fraiser. "We shall behave as if it is the frigate that has been located," he told them, while the messenger skidded off. "Bring her a point to starboard for now, but prepare to take us further upon my word."

Fraiser touched his hat, and muttered to the quartermaster, "Mr Middleton, my compliments to Mr King, and can he man the larboard battery – larboard, you have that?" The boy nodded eagerly. "Tell him to wait until we turn, I shall attempt to rake. There will be no need for broadsides; he may order independent fire as soon as a suitable target presents."

Now the stakes really had risen, and it was all any of the officers could do to not break into conversation, while the nearby hands were whispering intently to each other as they took up their positions. Cherry had assembled his marines along the larboard bulwark. The uniformed men were in the process of fixing bayonets when there was further excitement from the forecastle.

"She's seen us!" a voice rang out from the darkness. "Seen us and is taking the wind."

That, Banks supposed, was inevitable but however much she might try, *Scylla* was already in motion and must be making a good five knots.

"What ship is she?" Caulfield's shout brought no immediate answer, then a cautious voice replied."

"We think it the frigate, sir; least, most of us do. She is still more'n a cable off, so it is impossible to be certain."

That was far closer than any of the officers had anticipated. If it did turn out to be the larger ship, and they were able to get in a decent rake for their opening gambit, much of the fight would be knocked out of her. The corvette, on the other hand, could even be sunk, but in her case a broadside would signal their presence, and probably bring the frigate down upon them.

Caulfield had moved to the larboard bulwark and was leaning out precariously, his hat wedged tightly under one arm, and the rain streaming down his head, making him look almost entirely bald.

"I have her!" he shouted back. "And she is less than a cable away – but it's the corvette and she is starting to move to larboard."

So much the better, Banks thought. Such a manoeuvre would actually place the Frenchman in even greater danger when *Scylla* took her starboard turn, although he would still have wished it to be the larger ship.

"We're close on her now, sir!" Caulfield called back anxiously, and Banks nodded to Fraiser.

Scylla heeled slightly as the helm was pulled back. Braces were adjusted to keep pace with the wind, and all talking stopped as the gunners stood to. The turn was tight and savage, and Banks almost gasped as the lines of the French warship could finally be seen over the larboard bulwarks. From somewhere forward King's voice rang out as he spoke to his gunners, but no other order was necessary; all knew their duty well enough. A flash split the night, and was followed almost immediately by another, and soon the sound of heavy artillery echoed all about them. It was as if some terrible and unfairly captured beast had escaped and was set on wreaking revenge.

"Splendid, sir, splendid!" Caulfield screamed above the din, and Banks felt drawn to join him by the ship's side. The enemy was certainly badly damaged; a fire had started inside the corvette's great cabin, and by its light her wrecked stern could be seen. Then, almost as they watched, the flames crept through to her upper deck, and she began to fall off the wind, her rudder apparently broken or destroyed. It was clear to all that the ship could be of little danger to them now but, on the downside, the fire must draw the other warship in, were she in sight. Banks looked up at his own command. Her canvas, stretched tight and drawing beautifully, stood out as clear as any signal in the light from the flames: they would have to move a considerable distance before darkness could save them.

"Masthead, what do you see there?" he bellowed. A midshipman's voice came back to him faintly.
"Nothing else in sight, sir."

Banks grunted to himself – that may well be the case, but he would hardly have trusted the most seasoned lookout to have kept his night sight while the corvette's funeral pyre was burning so close by. He was half considering sending Stiles back up to his old station; whatever the problem with the man's eyes, it was obvious it did not affect his vision in the dark, but before he could come to a decision the current lookout's voice rang out.

"Deck there, sail to leeward!" All on the quarterdeck waited; even the sounds of guns being let off indiscriminately in the stricken corvette were ignored. "She's close hauled off our larboard beam, and steering to cut us off."

"Keep her as she is!" Banks positively roared, so anxious was he that they did not give up their valuable position. *Scylla* had picked up speed after her turn, and was now making good progress with the wind almost abeam.

"How far off?" Caulfield prompted.

"A mile, no more and probably less. She should be in plain sight of the deck in this light."

"I have her!" King's voice came from forward, and Banks realised that he must be the hatless officer whose body was picked out in the light as it hung from the main shrouds. The larboard battery was likely to be in use again at any moment; Banks looked down, and was pleased to see that most of the guns were already reloaded. Reassured, his attention returned to the bulwark where Caulfield was staring out.

"Off our bow, sir," the first lieutenant said, pointing into the dark.

Banks looked, and sure enough the outline of a ship could be seen by the flickering light of the corvette's flames. He had known the distance but to see her so close, bowlines tight and making a good speed, still surprised him. This was the moment he had dreaded, when the sight of his nemesis, well-managed and seemingly heading for an advantage, would wipe any confidence he had in his own ship and men. But there were no such faithless thoughts, and Banks had time to curse himself forever worrying that there might have been. His enemy was a seaman, just as he was; there was nothing magical about him or his ship: both would be as vulnerable to fire or shot, as Banks was determined to prove.

"Starboard two points," he shouted back at Fraiser. The move would slow them, but he would far rather receive this particular adversary with a full broadside than meet her bowsprit to bowsprit.

Banks and Caulfield continued to watch, the sight of a powerful and potent enemy charging down on them being far too fascinating to ignore. Despite *Scylla*'s change of course there was no possibility of the Frenchman taking the lead and crossing her bows: if Banks had been the other ship's captain he would even have allowed his vessel to fall off a point or two. He went to comment as much to Caulfield, then noticed that his opponent was doing exactly that, and his estimation of the other man's skill was once more confirmed. But the two ships were closing by the second; it was a question of who would blink first.

The closer they were when they did finally release a broadside, the greater the chance of significant damage to the other vessel, but that must be outweighed by the potentially longer time taken to serve the guns when they themselves were hit. Banks continued to watch, his hands gripping the top rail hard enough to cause actual pain; then, as the first spark of the enemy's fire was seen, he bellowed for his own guns to reply.

Scylla's broadside was as close to instantaneous as could have been planned, and both ships rolled back under the combined forces of recoil and barrage. An area of bulwark almost next to where Banks and Caulfield stood exploded under the impact of a heavy shot that struck just above the level of the deck and the resultant cloud of splinters cut a swath through men serving the nearby carronade. Screams and shouted orders merged into one horrendous din as blocks began to fall from *Scylla*'s tophamper. One of the mizzen backstays was suddenly set free, and whipped about the deck, knocking a midshipman down in its travel. A helmsmen apparently disappeared as if he had never existed, but the wheel remained undamaged and the man's place was taken without the need for any order. Banks' gaze switched to the French frigate, and he was disappointed to notice no change in her appearance. *Scylla*'s shots had certainly hit, and yet the enemy seemed untouched as she ploughed on through the dark waters. He turned back, disappointed, to notice something else amiss by their own binnacle. He had to look twice before realising that the sailing master, whose stolid form seemed to have become a permanent fixture, was now unaccountably missing. He glanced up and down the deck, but could not see the man, then noticed a body, clad in an old black watch coat, which lay crumpled on the deck.

"Foretopmast is hit above the top," a voice shouted, almost into the captain's ear, and brought him back to the more immediate problem of his ship's safety.

"Will it hold?" Banks asked, tearing his attention away from the fallen sailing master and addressing the man, who he then realised was the boatswain.

"I've a party sent to investigate," the warrant officer replied, "'though it might be better if the rig ain't placed under no strain until we can tell."

The enemy shot had been divided between spars and hull, and all appeared well placed. Banks crossed the deck, purposefully ignoring the party attending to Fraiser. He looked forward; most of the larboard guns were in the process of being reloaded, although a few had reduced crews, and an eighteen pounder was tipped to one side and lay useless, its carriage smashed and barrel resting on two men who had been serving it.

"What of the enemy?" he demanded, as the first lieutenant joined him.

"Our shots told well, sir, though there is no visible damage," Caulfield replied. "Oh, and I gather Fraiser is hit."

Banks nodded, but consciously blanked his mind from following the thought further. *Scylla* was not badly hurt, but the injury to the foremast would have to be taken into consideration, even if it was pronounced solid, while Caulfield's view of the Frenchman annoyingly confirmed his own assessment and only went to enforce his previous illusion of his adversary's strength and invulnerability.

The enemy frigate was far closer now; he could see her quite clearly. She was maintaining her course, and seemed to have even gained; perhaps the damage to *Scylla*'s rig had slowed them more than he had guessed? Whatever, there was now a very real chance of the Frenchman closing on their bows, and that was something he simply could not allow.

"Johnston says the mast is damaged but will hold!" a voice called from the larboard gangway. Banks acknowledged the information with an unconscious wave of his hand, while his mind continued to calculate what might be achieved. The wind was slightly forward of their beam. To take the ship further to starboard would only increase the pressure on the mast, which, even if it was considered sound, must surely have been weakened;

247

besides the manoeuvre would slow them further. No, he really only had one option: with the starboard battery loaded and complete, he would turn to larboard. Such action meant abandoning the windward gauge, but it was really the only sensible thing to do in such a situation.

"Starboard the helm, lay her four points to larboard!" he bellowed to the quartermaster, Fraiser not being present to assist. "Mr King, prepare the starboard battery!"

The ship turned wonderfully fast, with only a few seconds of tension while her bows were exposed to the enemy. Fortunately the move was quick enough; only two shots were released on their vulnerable prow, and neither hit. *Scylla's* speed increased with the change of course, and she was soon heading for a point just beyond the other ship's counter. But both vessels were drawing away from the burning corvette and, with the night remaining as dark as ever, vision would become increasingly difficult. It was not a problem shared however; with *Scylla* between the flames and the Frenchman, Banks knew they must be silhouetted against the light, while his target was inconveniently shadowed, and fast disappearing into the gloom.

"A point to starboard!" he shouted, and the braces were adjusted again as his ship turned in towards the enemy frigate. They would close in two, maybe three minutes; Banks tensed, knowing the Frenchman could not tack successfully in such a time, but must surely be in line for a severe raking. Then there was a cry from forward and, still straining to see through the total blackness, he realised his opponent had yet another trick to play.

The enemy frigate's canvas seemed to alter with the wave of a hand: one moment she was close hauled on the starboard tack, the next she fell off to leeward and appeared to throw herself into the very teeth of the pursuing British ship. Banks' initial reaction was to take *Scylla* to windward once more, but there was simply not the time or room, even ignoring the fact that it was their starboard battery that was currently manned. Instead he ordered the helm further round, then ran forward to ensure King held his fire, just as the first shots of the Frenchman's broadside began to rain down upon the British ship's bows.

Scylla took the punishment well, several shots dug deep into her tender prow, but she rode out even those, as well as the majority that met the relative strength of her whales. What carnage had been caused below was yet to be told, of course, but they continued forward, now aiming at the Frenchman's own bows.

"Two points to larboard!"

The enemy frigate had flung everything into that last move and was still not under proper control, but her hull was being blown to leeward, forcing Banks to correct once more. He wanted to just skim her jib boom, pass as close as he could to let his gunners do their work, before turning still further with the wind before, hopefully, avoiding the enemy's potent starboard battery.

"As you will, Mr King!" he bellowed, when the frigate's prow emerged from the gloom and began to take shape. It was almost perfect timing; they might suffer damage from the Frenchman's outstretched spar as it thrust towards *Scylla*'s rigging, but that was nothing to what the British would return in the form of a full and thorough broadside.

The first gun spat flame as soon as it was level with enemy's stem, and each continued as their turn came, with the Frenchman's bowsprit missing *Scylla*'s standing rigging by mere inches. The British could not know what harm they were doing, but no ship survives such treatment without severe internal damage. Her fabric would have suffered, to say nothing to the loss of life and morale. But there was no time to reflect on their success; *Scylla* must be turned, and turned sharp, if she was to avoid the same fate falling upon her stern. Banks bellowed out the order, his voice cracking with effort as he attempted to raise it above the dull ringing deafness they were all experiencing. *Scylla* responded, but either she was not fast enough or, despite their recent wounding, the French had found the impetus to surge forward sufficiently, and were steadily moving into a prime position to catch the British ship's rump.

Scylla was actually caught midway through the turn, with their larboard quarter angled towards the enemy's guns and at a range that was considerably closer than the textbook definition of point blank. Through the soles of his boots Banks could feel the shots enter his ship; indeed none seemed to rise any higher than the level beneath him, and all about on the quarterdeck and forecastle remained undamaged. But there would be slaughter below, of that he was in no doubt. Such a drubbing may well have taken out a third of his men, to say nothing of the wounds to *Scylla*'s hull. Then a cry from the quartermaster brought his attention to the wheel and he saw the spokes run impossibly freely through the hands of the bemused helmsmen. They had lost steerage, and with the enemy so close there would be no time or space to improvise any other method of controlling the ship. He felt his fingernails dig deep into the palms of his hands, and he started to accept that *Scylla* was likely to be taken.

Chapter Twenty-One

She had either lost her rudder, or the means of controlling it, but the essential point was *Scylla* continued turning to larboard and, with the Frenchman slowing but still moving forward, the two ships were destined to collide. The British larboard battery was primed and, though it lacked men and serviceable pieces in several places, could still create a fair amount of mischief were the chance given. Taking the initiative, King ordered the spent starboard cannon to be abandoned and every fit man who was able took up position on the opposite battery, where the guns needed just to be fired.

Jameson, Stiles, Dixon and Flint were the only members of their gun's crew who had survived, although they were being supplemented by two from number four whose own piece had been wrecked earlier. The six men stood by as *Scylla* edged closer to the Frenchman, driven on only by what sails remained, and a whim of fate that might equally be for good or bad. *Maggie Jane* was loaded, primed and ready to speak; there would be no time wasted in aiming, the enemy being so close that damage must be caused wherever she were pointed. The servers also knew there was little for them to do once the gun had been secured; all fighting from that point would be on a far more personal basis. With this in mind, most had collected weapons from the nearest arms chest and were now waiting for the next and probably final stage of the action to begin.

"You know how to use that?" Dixon asked doubtfully, as Stiles fingered a wicked looking tomahawk broodingly.

"I done so before," the man snapped back. "It don't take a deal of eyesight to knock down a Frenchman."

"You have to make sure he truly *is* a Frenchman," Dixon replied. Usually boarders were ordered to adopt some simple form of identification – a turn of line or cloth about the shoulder; even a blackened or pipe-clayed face, which was a popular ruse that had the added benefit of instilling fear into the enemy. But this was a desperate action; much would depend on every man selecting an opponent and Dixon was right, someone with doubtful eyesight might be more of a liability than an asset.

"An' there's nout wrong with my peepers," Stiles maintained. "It's down to me that we found the first ship at all, remember?"

"Aye, I remember, well enough," Dixon conceded, as the enemy drew closer. "An' suppose we all should be a thankin' you for it."

"Stand by, larboard battery!" King's voice, now almost hoarse from shouting, cut through and brought a measure of order to what was in danger of becoming an argument. The British frigate was still set on a collision course but, with the French broadside spent, there was no immediate rush: the two ships could meet at any time in the next few minutes without a major response from the enemy. But *Scylla*, it seemed, was in no mood to wait and within seconds the yardarms were touching, then beginning to tangle. The two hulls crunched together shortly afterwards with a series of grinding thumps that ended in a stunned silence as both sides took in what had occurred.

"Wait for the broadside!" Caulfield's bellow echoed from the quarterdeck.

The line of marines and nominated boarders reached from the taffrail to the forecastle head, and would be augmented by any other seaman who was reckless enough to join them.

"Fire!" King's voice rang out and *Scylla*'s guns erupted in a series of separated explosions with each seemingly being felt individually by the enemy ship. Then, as the last carronade delivered its deadly measure of canister, they boarded.

It was done with a shared cheer that bolstered the British as much as it disorientated their foe. Caulfield was amongst the first, leaping from the mizzen chains as if the four feet of black, empty space between was nothing more than a footstep, and landing almost astride the Frenchman's side netting. Three came with him: one, a marine, still carrying his musket that, even after firing, made an excellent fighting tool. The nearby corvette was now totally ablaze and the towering flames gave an unearthly cast to the scene. But the light was useful enough, and with its help Caulfield scrambled down, before glancing about the enemy quarterdeck. A group of officers stood just behind the mizzen mast and became his natural target. He made for them, passing, and hardly noticing, the crews from the quarterdeck cannon who rose up to meet the bulk of *Scylla*'s boarders as they followed.

It was obvious that the French were not prepared for such a sudden physical action, and most were armed with ramrods, crows of iron or any other improvised weapon that lay to hand. The two groups met with a furore more akin to a pot house brawl than any organised attack, but the subsequent wave of boarders were mainly seamen, and spoiling for a fight. Years of blockade, frustration and unfulfilled promises now came to the fore in a way that none could ever have foreseen. They dug deep, hacking into their opponents in waves of anger and unrefined tactics that swept all before them, leaving an area of deck wiped clear of standing opponents, and allowing space for still more to pour over the side and join them.

But Caulfield was ahead of them and still very much in danger. As he advanced one of the officers separated from those grouped about the binnacle, and made for him. He was a young man, sporting a wide moustache that seemed to connect both ears. He held a long, thin blade at the guard, while his left arm was tucked neatly behind the back, as if he were about to give a fencing demonstration in some fashionable drawing room. Caulfield attacked without hesitation or finesse; his sword swept up, knocking away the blade, but the man was fast and the lighter weapon described a full half circle, before whipping back at the British lieutenant, and cutting deep into the material of his tunic.

Caulfield could feel the trickle of warm blood as it started down his chest, but he gave the wound scant thought as he saw an opportunity and brought his own sword down, striking deep into the Frenchman's unprotected shoulder. The body dropped to the deck, but Caulfield was already seeking another target. What had been a tight group of officers had dispersed; one of its number was currently engaged with a marine private who was patiently holding him at bay with his presumably unloaded Bess; another fought what looked to be a losing battle with a blond haired seaman, desperately fending off the regular strokes of the British boarding cutlass with his own rather less substantial weapon. Caulfield's breath was beginning to come in gasps; he was possibly too old and rather overweight for such exercise, but his mind could still work and he forced it to think. The quarterdeck was effectively taken, but there would be plenty more to be done elsewhere. Further down the ship he could make out what appeared to be an absolute melee; the British were on the enemy's deck but, from the apparent confusion aboard *Scylla*, it appeared that the French had also boarded.

"Below!" he shouted vaguely to any free men beside him. Certainly if there was no enemy to fight he should seek one out, and enough of *Scylla*'s own were on hand to make a match for those in the waist. Stumbling forward, he approached the quarterdeck companionway, and stared down. The deck beneath was deadly dark causing him to hesitate; boarding an enemy ship was one thing: descending a staircase into enclosed and hostile territory seemed far more dangerous and surely not for the likes of him. Logic predicted more than an even chance that the first down would not come out smiling. The pause lasted a fraction longer than it should, but others had heard his call and were forming up behind. Realising he had no choice, Caulfield gave out one loud bellow that owed as much to fright as bravado, before throwing himself down the steep steps and into the depths beneath.

* * *

Banks watched the first boarders go before nodding to Marine Lieutenant Cherry, who had already drawn his sword and was clearly eager to set off forward. As captain, Banks had done his job to the letter; the fact that his ship was now alongside the enemy was partially due to luck of course, but his skill as commander had also been a major contributing factor. There would now be a period of relative chaos; this was almost expected, and something that need not concern him. The Frenchman was being boarded efficiently enough, and though most in *Scylla* were trained fighters, only a few could command: a captain's duty lay in remaining alive long enough to take control once the bedlam had ended. There might be younger men with smaller, saucy little ships who would have thrown themselves into the fray, seeking to inspire others by example. In Banks' opinion they were playing two games: the commander and the commanded. He was in no way avoiding action and was more than prepared to draw the ornate five ball sword that hung from his waist to fight any enemy who chanced too close. But as to mixing it in hand-to-hand combat, that was something he no longer indulged in.

* * *

Further forward, Flint's men were apparently in a queue. *Maggie Jane* had done her job competently enough and been secured; now, with *Scylla*'s boarders swarming over the enemy's decks, there was nothing left for them to do, other than follow. But the gangway above was already crowded and it appeared his team would be amongst the last to go. Then, just as they were about to clamber up the quarterdeck steps, a shout from the forecastle drew their attention. That area was furthest away from the corvette's flames and in the shadow of sail, rigging and tophamper from both ships, but even in the darkness they could make out a positive swarm of Frenchmen grouping about *Scylla*'s foremast.

"The Frogs 'ave boarded!" Stiles shouted, before turning away from the steps and heading back along the line of empty cannon. Flint and the others followed, as did more from the larboard gangway, but the rest of *Scylla*'s men were in the act of boarding themselves, and their attention was set solely on that task. Flint took stock as he and a few others gathered below the break of the forecastle; there were less than fifteen British to face the intruders: the enemy had the upper hand in more ways than one.

"They got the drop on us!" Dixon grunted, looking at the crowd that seemed to fill the upper deck to overflowing. "Can't get there to join them, lest we use the ladders, an' they'll cut us down if we do, sure as a gun."

Indeed the situation appeared desperate, but movement from behind caught their attention, and they looked back to see Lieutenant Cherry, sword raised and bellowing like a bull, charging along the starboard gangway at the head of a mob of seamen and marines.

The British seemed to throw themselves at the enemy in one solid mass, and enough space was cleared at the mouth of the starboard forecastle steps for Flint and the others to join them. Their arrival was in the nick of time; despite initial success, the marine lieutenant's party was soon showing signs of being overwhelmed. Cherry himself had fallen, having succumbed to the cutlass of a desperate enemy and, seeing their leader wounded, the rest were hesitating, allowing the French both time and space to press them back.

"At them!" Stiles roared, taking the initiative and bursting through the retreating British pack before laying into the fray with wild strikes of his axe. Having a physical enemy to fight was almost a relief, and being at the fore also the ideal position; there being no need to worry about discerning friend from foe. Any man who faced him was an enemy, and all seemed only too willing to be cut or smashed to the deck with his weapon. Jameson and Flint, following behind, found themselves all but redundant until a lucky lunge from a Frenchman's pike brought Stiles' brief rampage to a deadly halt, and his body slumped down upon the deck, its purpose served.

Styles' efforts had won back the valuable deck space, and even added to it; but for such a gain to be maintained, someone must take his place. Jameson leapt wildly over his body and with a single slash of his cutlass, calmly took down the man who had caused his shipmate to fall. Flint was next to him, pressing his own blade into the face of another who had made the fatal error of pausing for a second. Dixon followed, swearing and spitting as he laid into the enemy with a lunatic's strength. His pistol had been fired some seconds before, but now he used the warm weapon to great effect as an improvised club. Almost immediately the French began to falter and before long were indisputably being pressed back. The cautious retreat soon turned into a rout and, even though the two ships had begun to drift apart, the British swept the deck clear and reclaimed their forecastle.

* * *

But things were not so rosy to the Frenchman's stern. The companionway that led to what must be the great cabin was both narrow and steep, with two side rails that would restrict the use of his sword. Caulfield had taken a step down before slipping his hanger back into its scabbard and reaching forward for the deck beam at the mouth of the hatchway. There were, he decided, some advantages in being slightly below average height: the wood felt round and polished under his fingers as, jumping clear of the treads, he launched himself forward. His body started to swing like the pendulum of a clock, but the grip was soon released and he dropped down and into the dark mysteries beneath.

Before they could reach the deck, his boots connected with something far softer that let out a muffled cry before being knocked to one side. Caulfield stumbled, but mercifully regained his balance as he glanced at the young officer he had unintentionally kicked in the face, and was now apparently unconscious. He drew his sword again; all was sparsely lit by the battle lanterns hanging between the heavy cannon that lined each side. Their dim light revealed many living shapes lurking in the shadows but, whether it be from surprise or the violence of his entry, none seemed eager to meet him. Caulfield was momentarily at a loss; his own men were tumbling down the companionway after him, and would soon present a reasonable fighting force although, with the French holding back, there was effectively an impasse. Then the flare of a pistol erupted from out of the darkness and one of the British marines crumpled to his knees. The simple act was taken as a rallying cry, and the enemy rose up from the depths in one solid mass.

Then there was fighting on all sides, with the British working almost back to back as they fended off continued and fierce attacks. Caulfield, standing furthest from the companionway, knew that it could not last for long; however well they fought, the boarding party would inevitably be worn down, until the last few remaining were finally forced to surrender. He had no way of knowing the position in other parts of the ship; when last seen the French were also boarding and, for all he knew, *Scylla* might even have been taken. His right arm ached, the wound in his chest was throbbing, and breath came in hurried snatches; it may be better to stand down now, while most of his men were still alive. But those were the thoughts of fools, children, and old men, he told himself; he must continue as if his were the only battle being fought, and it had to be won without considering any other.

His current assailant was a burly, bald-headed man armed with a wooden rammer that was being used both as a club and a quarterstaff. Caulfield could keep him at bay with his outstretched hanger, but it was all but stalemate until the brute struck an overhead beam when trying for a downward blow, and the weapon spun from his grasp. Seizing the opportunity, Caulfield advanced, and slashed down on the man before realising that he had also stepped free of the deadly ring. He turned to his left and engaged the nearest Frenchman who was more than occupied sparring with a cutlass-wielding waister. Caulfield took the man down with the minimum of effort; it was the breakthrough they needed. After having made such an inroad, the boarding party was able to beat a measured retreat, moving past the companionway, and making for the relative space of the nearby half deck. All knew they would undoubtedly meet with further opposition, but at least the confines of the great cabin were being left behind.

They had made it as far as the outer room of the captain's quarters when more French did appear. This time the number seemed far greater and the British looked likely to be swamped. Caulfield's heart was now pounding and his head swam with exhaustion. It was clear the opposition was much too fierce; his party was certain to be overwhelmed and he was actually in the act of calling his men to stand down when there came a blinding shock. The world was suddenly made light and all combat temporarily ceased as eyes too used to peering through mist and gloom were dazzled by a deep and sudden brightness. Every man paused to wonder while the deep-throated roar of a massive explosion began to rumble across the water towards them in a gathering crescendo. For a terrible second Caulfield thought *Scylla* had blown, before remembering the burning corvette. The deadly flames must have found her magazine, but their effect was also being felt elsewhere.

By the unexpected light Caulfield was able to make out the red coats of more British marines beyond what he now saw was actually a relatively small group of French seaman. And that surely was a hatless King, standing at the entrance to the half deck, a bloodied cutlass in his hand. For an instant their eyes met, then both simultaneously realised that many of the Frenchman were already beaten and their position was not as bad as they had feared.

"Forward, Scyllas!" Despite exhaustion, Caulfield's voice rang out strong, and his shout was copied by King, whose more croaking bellow quickly became overpowered by the many others who also picked up the call. Soon all the boarders were positively screaming their ship's name in exaltation and relief, the racket almost covering that of the fighting. Light from the burning corvette was now fading significantly, and many had blurred or bleary vision, but the British had seen the true situation and knew that victory was perilously close. Simply being aware that others lay beyond had heartened them, and the battle was taken up with even greater effort.

Then the two parties began to meet: *Scylla's* seamen and marines confronted their own; friends and familiar faces were dimly recognised, and there was a clamour of greetings, randomly hurled insults and more than one case of hysterical laughter. The confusion slowly dissolved as the French began to accept defeat and, before long, some degree of normality and even order returned to the frigate's deck.

"Well met, Michael," King panted, as he finally sheathed his sword and rested his hand on the older man's shoulder. "Though it were a worrying time for a spell."

Some of the French were attempting to make for the stern, and sharp calls and the sound of fists on bone could be heard, but in general peace had been established and those of the enemy that remained were swiftly disarmed. Any not wounded soon found themselves gathered in small groups to the larboard side where Corporal Jarvis and eight of *Scylla*'s marines watched over them, while the injured lay heaped without distinction to await eventual medical attention.

"Those that have run cannot get far," King continued, as he supervised the arrangements.

Caulfield nodded but was too exhausted to reply. He knew that his words would be indistinct and could still feel his heart beating wildly, but the wound was not giving him quite so much pain. "We can deal with them," he gasped at last, examining the spot, and being mildly surprised to find it little more than a deep scratch. "But first we must check the fo'c'sle."

"Joe Cherry should be there," King said peering forward into the darkness. "He was moving to address that very matter when I boarded and from the lack of activity, I would say he has been successful."

A shout, followed by what sounded like a cheer seemed to confirm this. Then a herd of French seamen could be seen being driven into the relative light of the spar deck. Midshipman Jackson, white faced and with a smudge of blood upon one cheek, accompanied them, stumbling forward and apparently moving as if in a daze.

"We have them," he said, reaching the two lieutenants. "What ain't surrendered is dead or wounded." His childlike voice quavered slightly and it was clear that either tears or laughter were not so very far away.

"Where is Mr Cherry?" King asked.

The lad shrugged.

"He never came across; I followed Cahill an' Thompson; they fought like tigers, though Thompson was hurt in the chest and we think him dead," he added, his voice sounding particularly naïve, considering the message it carried. "Some of Flint's men were there as well; Stiles is gone, an' Dixon 'as been cut about something dire."

"Very good," King said, oblivious to the irony. "Return to *Scylla* and report. Advise the captain that the upper deck is secure, and we are about to clear below. Any hands he can spare would be welcomed."

"Mr Jarvis, form a party to round up those on the berth and orlop," Caulfield was more in control of himself now and addressed the marine corporal who appeared almost casual in ripped tunic and lacking a hat. "Any that don't drop their weapons at your call, assume to be hostile; there are to be no second chances – do I make myself clear?" In a vessel with only one full gun deck, most of the combatants should already be captured, but there may be more lurking below, and the only time a seized ship can be truly considered taken is when she has been emptied of her crew.

"And you had better be on the lookout for any female prisoners," King said, stopping the marine as he remembered the likelihood of Lady Hatcher being aboard.

"Aye, Lady Hatcher and her maid; expect them to be in a place of safety; the cable tier or perhaps the cockpit," Caulfield added. "But do not waste any effort; securing the ship is your first priority."

"Very good," Jarvis replied, rolling his eyes and grimacing slightly at the mention of the woman's name. "And no second chances it is, sir."

* * *

"Mr Fraiser!" Kate said when the body was dumped, not harshly, but certainly without ceremony on the canvas-covered deck of *Scylla*'s cockpit. She hastily lowered the lad she was attending to: a third class volunteer struck on the head by a falling block. The boy had drunk a healthy measure of her lemonade, and seemed easier now, and even ready for sleep. She placed the pewter jug down and moved carefully across to where the wounded sailing master lay.

There was a small amount of blood oozing from the area

about his lower legs and for a moment she was hopeful. But a brief inspection told her that a tourniquet had been applied to the old man's left thigh; the limb below was severely injured and would most likely have to be removed. "You will take some drink?" she asked briskly, repeating the phrase that had greeted every fresh patient since action commenced.

"I think not, my dear," Fraiser said weakly. "If I am to meet with your husband I would rather do so with a clear head."

"Why, I would not offer you spirit!" Kate responded, apparently appalled. "Robert may prescribe laudanum, but that is for him to decide; until then you may take a sip of lemonade, or water if that is preferred, but you will get nothing stronger – not while in my care!"

Fraiser's face relaxed at her tirade and a slight smile played upon his face. "Then a sip of water would be most agreeable," he said. "If it will not inconvenience you greatly."

Chapter Twenty-Two

It took an inordinately long time for the British to make the short distance to St Helena, although one full day was spent securing the two ships and dividing their prisoners. The captured French were sullenly philosophical in defeat; all senior officers had been killed or seriously wounded and those that remained allowed themselves to be contained without undue protest. Some were needed at the pumps; both frigates leaked badly and there were simply not enough able British hands for the work. It was not a popular duty, and required the supervision of a marine guard, with loaded muskets and bayonets fixed, but the prisoners proved more willing to assist Grimley in providing food for so many. The French medics also worked every bit as hard as Manning's team in repairing the carnage that both sides had managed to wreak.

They finally rounded Ladder Hill Point and entered Chapel Valley Bay in the late morning of the third day, when the bad weather was nothing more than a memory and an innocent sun beat down on land that might never before have seen rain. Since dawn, when they first closed with the northern coast of the island, the small convoy had been assailed by distant shouts and cheers from random groups ashore. Some even did their best to follow the battered vessels as they came in, with *Scylla*, under jury rudder, holding a broad reach comfortably enough, even if her progress was slow.

On passing the battery near Lemon Valley Bay the British were mildly disconcerted by cannon fire, although this was finally accepted as celebratory. Then, when the Frenchman's anchor was released, and what had been an enemy was formally presented with British colours proudly dominating her national ensign, the crowded wharf showed the island's true feelings without ambiguity. Muskets were fired, apparently indiscriminately, and several signal rockets released from the vantage point on Ladder Hill, while lines of Company employees and off duty soldiers erupted into good-natured shouts and cheering. Only the two heavy batteries that looked out on the bay remained silent and apparently deserted, but no one aboard *Scylla* or her vanquished foe could have cared less. None had slept since fighting what had been a desperate and close won battle, and relief at finally knowing their ordeal over was sufficient.

The packet, with an anxious Lewis in command, anchored next. His vessel was also laden with prisoners; apart from the French prize crew there were those from the burning corvette that had been plucked from the water: the vessel itself was lucky to have survived the subsequent explosion with only minor damage to her rig and sails.

Two boats were already on their way to *Scylla* as her first anchor finally ran free and the ship began to swing in the faint current. On the quarterdeck Banks stood in clothes not changed since the fight and knew he was not in a fit condition, either mentally or cosmetically, to greet visitors. It would probably be Robson, and already he could guess at the many questions the lieutenant governor would ask. However the man may also be bringing news of Sarah, and his need for that was far greater than any reluctance to relate the recent action.

But in fact it was Henry Booker who first clambered through *Scylla's* battered entry port and, even more unexpectedly, he was followed by his daughter, as well as a heavily built black man who seemed at once nervous and oddly proud.

"You have fared well I see, Sir Richard," Booker said beaming, and shaking the captain's hand. "Not just the Frenchie, but taken back the packet into the bargain. What of the other ship, is she still free?"

"No, sir, the corvette has been accounted for, she will not trouble us further."

"And Lady Hatcher?" he asked, the smile now fixed and his eyes wide in anticipation.

"Milady is below and unhurt," Banks told him flatly. "Though I regret, not in the best of tempers."

Indeed the woman had been incandescent with rage, especially after being unceremoniously bundled out of the captured

Frenchman and back into *Scylla*, where circumstances demanded that she must be effectively left to her own devices for the rest of that night. But Banks found he cared little for the lady now, or her opinion. She might huff and puff all she wished, his defeat of three enemy warships could only be seen as a substantial victory, and certainly sufficient to colour any mischief she might attempt to make regarding his earlier actions. Besides, had he not won back her freedom? How would she look when dubious accusations were cast? Both parliament and the public were equally predictable, and accustomed to inflating victory as readily as condemning failure. Banks was no expert in such matters but guessed he would be regarded as a hero, and any attempt to besmirch his name would have to be extremely well- founded in order to sway general opinion. The Admiralty also lauded success; he might not be given a replacement ship immediately, but one would come soon enough, and this time there would be no doubt he had earned it himself, and not been forced to rely on his father's interest. His actions in preventing future attacks on the merchant convoys must also put him in good stead with the HEIC, as well as the City insurers who would have been saved a fortune. And the government should now be at the later stage of peace negotiations; even a minor British triumph must strengthen their hand and be welcomed.

But Banks was finding that, like so many crises that dwindle to nothing as soon as they are solved, all this seemed to be of surprisingly little moment. Once more his ship required extensive repairs and they may even have to await the first India convoy to raise enough fit men to see *Scylla*, and the captured Frenchman, safely home. But before then he had a greater concern, and one he simply must address, even though it hardly rated highly in military significance.

"My wife, is she well?" he asked, and was relieved when Booker's delighted expression did not falter.

"Lady Banks is indeed extremely bonny, and has been asking about you daily. As soon as you can leave your ship a fast carriage can have you with her inside the hour. I shall see to it that one is laid on for such an eventuality."

"Thank you," Banks said, as the exhaustion finally seemed likely to take him over. "Thank you indeed."

* * *

"Gentlemen, I trust I am not disturbing you," Julia said cautiously as she approached King and Caulfield, who stood nearby. "I have someone I would wish you to meet."

Both officers followed her glance, and the black man, dressed simply but well and carrying a small canvas bag, lowered his head slightly at their attention.

"David here was a member of my father's household, as I think you are both aware," she said, not looking directly at either of them. "I can say without hesitation that he probably saved my life, as well as those of Lady Banks and Mrs Manning."

"Indeed, sir. I hears you fought extremely bravely," Caulfield said, extending his hand. "And have our thanks, although I believe a more significant reward is in preparation."

"That is kind of you," the man spoke softly. "Though in truth I was hoping you would give me leave to serve in your ship."

"My father has granted David his freedom," Julia interrupted, her face flushing only slightly. "It seems I was in error and he does crave for something more than we can provide on the island."

"Do you have any skills as a seaman?" King asked.

"Precious few at present, sir, though I am eager to learn," the man replied. "I am trained as a valet, and can cook and serve at table, as well as having a fair hand at needlework."

King glanced across at Caulfield and received a subtle nod and a smile. "Thompson, the captain's man, is killed, but even if Sir Richard does not require another servant, I am certain there will be a place for any with such skills," he said.

"I own that this goes rather against what I spoke of a week or so back." Julia was now more directly regarding the first lieutenant.

"Not as such," Caulfield answered, his gaze not meeting hers. "Some would say your man is simply exchanging one form of

266

bondage for another. But I do consider it good that he has been given the choice," he continued, before their eyes did finally meet. "And right; I think that also."

"Miss Booker, I wonder if I might have your attention?" King was conscious that his question had broken something of a spell between the two and, when she turned to him with an expression of caution and reluctance, he felt his heart drop down to his boots. "I-it is of a private nature," he continued, stammering slightly. "Would you be so kind as to accompany me below?"

* * *

"There is someone to see you, Mr Fraiser," Kate whispered softly into the old man's ear, and his eyes opened. A young girl stood before him, but he could say no more; she seemed in no way familiar, although the light in the sickbay was bad and he remained heavily sedated following the operation. "This is Julia Booker," the surgeon's wife continued. "She is the daughter of one of St Helena's officials, and Mr King here was especially keen that you should speak with her."

The sailing master's eyes flashed up as the young lieutenant entered and stood behind, then back to the woman herself. Julia Booker: the name meant nothing to him and, now that he was fully awake, his leg had begun to hurt once more.

"I believe you knew my mother," the girl said, drawing closer and lowering herself to his level. "Her name was Kitty Davies; she spoke of you often, and I did so want to meet you."

The name sparked a reaction, as it would have whatever the depth of pain or drug that plagued him. Fraiser actually tried to raise himself from the fixed berth, but Mrs Manning pressed a hand against his breast and breathed calm, reassuring words that were totally ignored.

"Kitty, yes; I do remember," he said urgently and staring at her more closely.

"I was so sorry to hear that you are wounded," the girl continued. "And hope you to be well by and by. Perhaps you may benefit from being on shore for a spell?"

267

Fraiser blinked, uncomprehending, then looked to Mrs Manning who was still resolutely by his side as she seemed to have been since her husband operated.

"Lady Banks is currently at Julia's house where she is being cared for," Kate explained. "You would be able to go there and be well looked after, although there is also a military hospital should you prefer."

"What of the ship?" Fraiser asked, and received a smile and a shake of the head in reply.

"The ship won't be going anywhere for a good while, master," King explained softly. "And even when she does, you need not be with her."

This time he understood completely. He knew what had been done to his leg. Even though the sensation of movement and feeling remained strong in his foot and toes, no one would need a crippled sailing master and, at his age, it might be better to bow out with dignity. Retirement was something he had considered taking for some while, although the lack of a suitable place in which to settle had always prevented it. Throughout his long life a steadily increasing faith had given him as strong a grounding as he could have wished for, but a physical home was another matter entirely, and something he had always lacked. Now, and in the company of the young woman whose features were starting to become more distinct by the second, he sensed he might finally have found one.

Author's note

This book is set in the time between two actual governors of St Helena: Robert Brooke, (retired March 1800), and Robert Patton who arrived two years later. During the interregnum, Colonel Francis Robson FSA, an eminently capable man who had served with distinction in Madras, did indeed act as governor, although Sir Terrance Hatcher, and his charming lady, are figments of my imagination. My only excuse in introducing this fiction is that when such an important outpost as St Helena is left effectively unattended for so long, the opportunity is just too good to pass by.

The previous governor, Robert Brooke (1744-1811), would have been a hard act for Hatcher to follow, and was actually a fascinating man who properly deserves an entire book of his own. He was born in Ireland and first joined the HEIC as an aspirant officer in his early twenties. Following a period of illness, Brooke moved back to his homeland where he established Prosperous, an industrial town in County Kildare, to serve the cotton industry. It was an ambitious project and received generous government support but proved far too expensive and soon consumed all of his personal fortune. At its height Brooke effectively employed over three thousand people, although the venture ultimately failed. His property was sold, and Brooke was left not only bankrupt but rumoured to be owing an amount close to that of Britain's national debt.

Undeterred, he reapplied for service with the East India Company and, after initial rejection, (he had previously outstayed his leave) was finally accepted. Then, almost immediately afterwards, he found himself somewhat bizarrely appointed governor of St Helena, replacing Daniel Cornelille, and in control of one of the most important bases in Britain's burgeoning empire.

Despite his somewhat disastrous record in business, Brooke was to become one of the most successful governors of the island. St Helena's defences were improved to no small degree while under his control; he also instituted a better method of signalling, and extended the harbour installations that were judged to be both inadequate and dangerous, saving several lives each year. The disaster at Prosperous clearly had not dulled his enthusiasm for enterprise any; his plan for irrigating the island involved many miles of pipes, gullies and open streams, and was heavily opposed, but Brooke had the determination to see it through and, on completion, fresh water was distributed to some parts of the island for the first time. Suddenly visiting fleets could be served in a reasonable time, while the Company's considerable herds of cattle were not only able to survive the occasional drought, but also increased by 20%.

During his tenure Brooke also did much to improve the lot of the common soldier. The 'miscreant's mess' was a particular case in point; until that time military discipline rested almost entirely on corporal punishment and did little to actually modify bad behaviour. Brooke decided that regular floggings promoted an ethos of bravado amongst the men, some came to regard such punishment as a sign of masculinity while others, he suspected, actively enjoyed it. Instead he ordered offenders to be removed from the rank and file and grouped together, where they were provided with poor accommodation and victuals, while being employed in a variety of laborious and mundane tasks. This evoked an element of social disgrace that made the punishment truly corrective, and also provided St Helena with the many gardens and military installations that can still be seen today.

In 1795, and based on news received from a visiting warship, Brooke initiated an expedition using HEIC ships and corps to reinforce General Craig's recently captured Dutch colony at the Cape of Good Hope. Brooke's force also assisted in the taking of a fleet of valuable Dutch Indiamen, an act that won him praise, promotion and a considerable increase in salary.

At a time when slavery was generally accepted in British colonies, Brooke was one of the first to bring in legislation to improve matters, making the importing of new slaves illegal, and introducing harsh penalties for any found abusing their charges. His measures effectively raised the status of such labour to something nearer to that of serfdom, but by no means ended the atrocity: it would be another forty years or so before St Helena's last 800 slaves began a programme of phased emancipation. That was still ahead of any government ban, however, and Brooke's efforts certainly signalled the start of the later war against slavery that the British were to take up with all the gusto of reformed sinners.

The island itself deserves rather more explanation than I was able to give, and some of St Helena's latter history might also be related. Almost since its discovery in 1502, St Helena has been known as a place with therapeutic powers. Access to a plentiful supply of good, fresh water as well as fruit, vegetables and meat are obviously contributing factors, as is the prevailing south easterly trade wind which keeps the island healthy and the climate pleasant, despite its proximity to the equator. Consequently many members of the military that were discharged from Far Eastern service due to illness found their health miraculously restored after even a brief stay. The majority went on to either re-enlist in the garrison or volunteer for militia service, giving an unusually large force of seasoned men that could be called upon. Such strength, when added to the island's natural defences and extensive fortifications, ensured that St Helena remained immune from invasion. One plan, proposed in 1804, ironically on the orders of Napoleon Bonaparte, did come close to being adopted. The French minister, Decres, even allocated eight ships and fifteen hundred men for the task, but the expedition was abandoned at the last moment, with the force subsequently being sent to Surinam.

Then, in 1815, when a remote and impenetrable prison was required to detain the defeated emperor, St Helena became the natural choice, and accommodated Napoleon and his staff in relative comfort. His first home was at Briar's Pavilion, a beautiful estate just south of Jamestown. Then, following its rebuilding, Longwood House, the Lieutenant Governor's country residence mentioned in my story. During Bonaparte's residency the island was fortified still further, and housed an unprecedented military force, much of which was removed following his death in 1821.

As with the passing of many famous people, Bonaparte's demise is not without conspiracy theories, some of which are gloriously far fetched. The original autopsy report of stomach cancer has been regularly disputed, with St Helena itself being named as a suspect on occasion. It appears that high quantities of arsenic were used in the paint and wallpaper when renovating Longwood House, and traces of the drug have been found in remaining samples of the late emperor's hair. But such is the manna of those who enjoy this kind of tale, and it is hoped that one of the world's greatest soldiers did not die at the hands of his interior decorator.

Thirteen years after Napoleon's death control passed from the East India Company, and St Helena became a Crown Colony. Within ten years a substantial naval base was established to combat the African slave trade and for some while St Helena remained a favoured refuelling and replenishing station. However, with the opening of the Suez Canal in 1870 the island's value diminished dramatically and, apart from brief periods during major and minor wars, it has not figured significantly in British history since.

Today the island is a British Dependant Territory, although the islanders, who currently number roughly four thousand, have no right of abode in Britain, and are mainly reliant on a Royal Mail Ship for supplies and personal transport. Despite, or possibly because of, the island's isolation, St Helena remains a fascinating and breathtakingly beautiful place, with a predominantly friendly population who are loyal to the crown and genuinely welcome visitors. An airport is due to open in 2016 and will inevitably bring change: some may argue that such development can only harm what is almost a unique environment, although that should surely be for those more directly affected to decide. Certainly a regular air link can only encourage travel, while also bringing much needed finance and trade to what has become something of a backwater. Most of all it will make an island that so excels in both beauty and historical significance far more accessible, while hopefully retaining more than a small amount of St Helena's inherent mystery.

Alaric Bond
Herstmonceux 2014

Glossary

Able Seaman	One who can hand, reef and steer and is well-acquainted with the duties of a seaman.
Amphitrite	Neptune's wife or consort (in Roman mythology).
Back	Wind change; anticlockwise.
Backed sail	One set in the direction for the opposite tack to slow a ship.
Backstays	Similar to shrouds in function, except that they run from the hounds of the topmast, or topgallant, all the way to the deck. (Also a useful/spectacular way to return to deck for a topman.)
Backstays, running	A less permanent backstay, rigged with a tackle to allow it to be slacked to clear a gaff or boom.
Bargemen	*(Slang)* Weevils commonly found in hard tack.
Barky	*(Slang)* Seamen's affectionate name for their vessel.
Belaying pins	Pins set into racks at the side of a ship. Lines are secured to these, allowing instant release by their removal.
Binnacle	Cabinet on the quarterdeck that houses compasses, the deck log, traverse board, lead lines, telescope, speaking trumpet, *etc.*
Bitts	Stout horizontal pieces of timber, supported by strong verticals, that extend deep into the ship. These hold the anchor cable when the ship is at anchor.

Block	Article of rigging that allows pressure to be diverted or, when used with others, increased. Consists of a pulley wheel, made of *lignum vitae*, encased in a wooden shell. Blocks can be single, double (fiddle block), triple or quadruple. The main suppliers were Taylors, of Southampton.
Board	Before being promoted to lieutenant, midshipmen would be tested for competence by a board of post captains. Should they prove able they will be known as passed midshipmen, but could not assume the rank of lieutenant until they were appointed as such.
Boatswain	(*Pronounced Bosun*) The warrant officer superintending sails, rigging, canvas, colours, anchors, cables and cordage *etc.*, committed to his charge.
Boom	Lower spar to which the bottom of a gaff sail is attached.
Braces	Lines used to adjust the angle between the yards, and the fore and aft line of the ship. Mizzen braces, and braces of a brig lead forward.
Brig	Two-masted vessel, square-rigged on both masts.
Bulkhead	A partition within the hull of a ship.
Bulwark	The planking or wood-work about a vessel above her deck.
Canister	Type of shot, also known as case. Small iron balls packed into a cylindrical case.

Careening	The act of beaching a vessel and laying her over so that repairs, and maintenance to the hull can be carried out.
Carronade	Short cannon firing a heavy shot. Invented by Melville, Gascoigne and Miller in late 1770's and adopted from 1779. Often used on the upper deck of larger ships, or as the main armament of smaller.
Cascabel	Part of the breach of a cannon.
Caulk	(Slang) To sleep. Also caulking, a process to seal the seams between strakes.
Channel	Projecting ledge that holds deadeyes from shrouds and backstays, originally chain-whales.
Channel Gropers	(Slang) The Channel Fleet.
Chippy	(Slang) A carpenter. Originally from the ship builders who were allowed to carry out small lumps of wood, or chips, and the end of their shift.
Close hauled	Sailing as near as possible into the wind.
Coaming	A ridged frame about hatches to prevent water on deck from getting below.
Come-up glass	A device using prisms and lenses that can detect the speed at which another vessel is gaining or falling back.
Companionway	A staircase or passageway.
Counter	The lower part of a vessel's stern.
Course	A large square lower sail, hung from a yard, with sheets controlling and securing it.
Crown and Anchor	Naval board game.

Crows of iron	Crow bars used to move a gun or heavy object.
Cutter	Fast, small, single-masted vessel with a sloop rig. Also a seaworthy ship's boat.
Deadeyes	A round, flattish wooden block with three holes through which a lanyard is reeved. Used to tension shrouds and backstays.
Ditty bag	(*Slang*) A seaman's bag. Derives its name from the dittis or 'Manchester stuff' of which it was once made.
Driver	Large sail set on the mizzen in light winds. The foot is extended by means of a boom.
Dunnage	Officially the packaging around cargo. Also (*slang*) seaman's baggage or possessions.
Fall	The free end of a lifting tackle on which the men haul.
Fetch	To arrive at, or reach a destination. Also the distance the wind blows across the water. The longer the fetch the bigger the waves.
Fen	(*Slang*) Common prostitute.
Flash man	One who provides an element of security in a bawdy house.
Futtock	A lower frame in the hull of a ship (similar to a rib). Futtock shrouds run down from the edge of a top to the mast.
Forereach	To gain upon, or pass by another ship when sailing in a similar direction.

Forestay	Stay supporting the masts running forward, serving the opposite function of the backstay. Runs from each mast at an angle of about 45 degrees to meet another mast, the deck or the bowsprit.
Fribble	(*Slang*) A fool.
Gansey	A seaman's knitted woollen sweater.
Glass	Telescope. Also, hourglass: an instrument for measuring time (and hence, as slang, a period of time). Also a barometer.
Go-about	To alter course, changing from one tack to the other.
Halyards	Lines which raise yards, sails, signals *etc*.
Hanger	A fighting sword, similar to a cutlass.
Hard tack	Ship's biscuit.
Hawse	Area in bows where holes are cut to allow the anchor cables to pass through. Also used as general term for bows.
Hawser	Heavy cable used for hauling, towing or mooring.
Headway	The amount a vessel is moved forward (rather than leeway: the amount a vessel is moved sideways) when the wind is not directly behind.
Heave to	Keeping a ship relatively stationary by backing certain sails in a seaway.
HEIC	Honourable East India Company.
Holder	One aboard ship who spends much of his time moving stores in the hold.
Hoppo	Chinese custom house officers.

Humbug	(*Slang*) To deceive or fool someone with a story or device.
Idler	A man who, through his duty or position, does not stand a watch, but (usually) works during the day and sleeps at night.
Interest	Backing from a superior officer or one in authority, useful when looking for promotion.
Jib-boom	Boom run out from the extremity of the bowsprit, braced by means of a martingale stay, which passes through the dolphin striker.
John Company	(*Slang*) The East India Company.
Jolly	(*Slang*) Marine. (One of many such terms.)
Junk	Old line used to make wads, etc.
Jury mast/rig	Temporary measure used to restore a vessel's sailing ability.
Kerseymere	Woollen cloth.
King Arthur	A game often played as an alternative to the traditional crossing the line ceremony. A nominated 'King Arthur' sits on the side of a half cask of water, and each player takes a turn in pouring a bucket of water over him. But should the player laugh or smile (something that is greatly encouraged by royalty), he becomes King in his place.
Landsman	The rating of one who has no experience at sea.
Lanthorn	Lantern.

Larboard	Left side of the ship when facing forward. Later replaced by 'port', which had previously been used for helm orders.
Leaguer	A long cask with a capacity of 127 imperial gallons, normally used to hold water.
Leeward	The downwind side of a vessel.
Leeway	The amount a vessel is pushed sideways by the wind (as opposed to headway, the forward movement, when the wind is directly behind).
Leige Barometer	Also known as a Dutch Weather Glass. A simple and slightly outdated instrument, although remarkably accurate.
Liner	*(Slang)* Ship of the line (of battle). A third rate or above.
Linstock	A forked staff to hold a lighted slowmatch. Using a linstock enables a gun captain to fire his weapon from a distance, without the aid of a gunlock.
Lobster	*(Slang)* Soldier.
Lubber/lubberly	*(Slang)* Unseamanlike behaviour; as a landsman.
Luff	Intentionally sail closer to the wind, perhaps to allow work aloft. Also the flapping of sails when brought too close to the wind. The side of a fore and aft sail laced to the mast.
Manger	Area aboard ship where livestock are kept.
Martingale stay	Line that braces the jib-boom, passing from the end through the dolphin striker to the ship.

Molly	(*Slang*) General term used to cover homosexuals; from the Latin meaning soft or sissy. Also used to describe prostitutes, many of whom were from Ireland (and were often called Molly).
Mother Midnight	(*Slang*)A midwife.
Packet / Packet Service	The HEIC maintained a number of fast sailing vessels to maintain communications and carry light cargo.
Pipeclay	Compound used to polish and whiten leatherwork.
Point blank	The range of a cannon when fired flat. (For a 32 pounder this would be roughly 1000 feet.)
Pollywog	Officially a tadpole, but used to denote any that had not crossed to the southern hemisphere.
Preventive Service	The customs (or excise) service; at the time both acted independently.
Privy Garden	(*Slang*) Privy Garden was a disreputable part of London particularly associated with prostitutes. It is now known as Whitehall.
Pushing School	(*Slang*) A brothel.
Punch House	Military term for a Pot House, or public bar.
Quarterdeck	In larger ships the deck forward of the poop, but at a lower level. The preserve of officers.
Queue	A pigtail. Often tied by a seaman's best friend (his tie mate).

Ratlines	Lighter lines, untarred and tied horizontally across the shrouds at regular intervals, to act as rungs and allow men to climb aloft.
Reef	A portion of sail that can be taken in to reduce the size of the whole.
Reefing points	Light line on large sails, which can be tied up to reduce the sail area in heavy weather.
Reefing tackle	Line that leads from the end of the yard to the reefing cringles set in the edges of the sail. It is used to haul up the upper part of the sail when reefing.
Rigging	Tophamper; made up of standing (static) and running (moveable) rigging, blocks etc. Also (slang) Clothes.
Rummer	Large drinking glass originating in Holland.
Running	Sailing before the wind.
Sawbones	(Slang) A surgeon or physician.
Schooner	Small craft with two or three masts.
Scran	(Slang) Food.
Scupper	Waterway that allows deck drainage.
Sea Fencibles	A naval militia protecting the mainland of Great Britain during invasion.
Sheet	A line that controls the foot of a sail.
Shrouds	Lines supporting the masts athwart ship (from side to side) which run from the hounds (just below the top) to the channels on the side of the hull.
Soft tack	Bread.
Specie	Gold, either coin or bullion.

Spirketting	The interior lining or panelling of a ship.
Spring	Hawser attached to a fixed object that can be tensioned to move the position of a ship fore and aft along a dock, often when setting out to sea. Breast lines control position perpendicular to the dock.
Sprit sail	A square sail hung from the bowsprit yards, less used by 1793 as the function had been taken over by the jibs although the rigging of their yards helps to brace the bowsprit against sideways pressure.
Stay sail	A quadrilateral or triangular sail with parallel lines, usually hung from under a stay.
Stern sheets	Part of a ship's boat between the stern and the first rowing thwart and used for passengers.
Stingo	(Slang) Beer.
Strake	A plank.
Suds (in the)	(Slang) To be in trouble.
Tack	To turn a ship, moving her bows through the wind. Also a leg of a journey relating to the direction of the wind. If from starboard, a ship is on the starboard tack. Also the part of a fore and aft loose-footed sail where the sheet is attached, or a line leading forward on a square course to hold the lower part of the sail forward.
Taffrail	Rail around the stern of a vessel.

Tophamper	Literally any weight either on a ship's decks or about her tops and rigging, but often used loosely to refer to spars and rigging.
Torrid Zone	The central latitude zone of the earth that separates the Tropic of Cancer and the Tropic of Capricorn. Thinking that any area so close to the equator would be too hot for habitation, Aristotle first named the region. (The only area he considered liveable was the Temperate Zone, lying between the Frigid Zone, from the Arctic Circle to the pole, and the Torrid.)
Trick	(Slang) A period of duty.
Veer	Wind change, clockwise.
Waist	Area of main deck between the quarterdeck and forecastle.
Watch	Period of four (or in case of dog watch, two) hour duty. Also describes the two or three divisions of a crew.
Watch list	List of men and stations, usually carried by lieutenants and divisional officers.
Wearing	To change the direction of a square rigged ship across the wind by putting its stern through the eye of the wind. Also jibe – more common in a fore and aft rig.
Windward	The side of a ship exposed to the wind.

About the author

Alaric Bond was born in Surrey, and now lives in Herstmonceux, East Sussex. He has been writing professionally for over twenty years.

His interests include the British Navy, 1793-1815, and the RNVR during WWII. He is also a keen collector of old or unusual musical instruments, and 78 rpm records.

Alaric Bond is a member of various historical societies and regularly gives talks to groups and organisations.

www.alaricbond.com

About Old Salt Press

Old Salt Press is an independent press catering to those who love books about ships and the sea. We are an association of writers working together to produce the very best of nautical and maritime fiction and non-fiction. We invite you to join us as we go down to the sea in books.

www.oldsaltpress.com

More Great Reading from Old Salt Press

A fifth Wiki Coffin mystery

"Combining historical and nautical accuracy with a fast paced mystery thriller has produced a marvelous book which is highly recommended." — David Hayes, Historic Naval Fiction

The Beckoning Ice finds the U. S. Exploring Expedition off Cape Horn, a grim outpost made still more threatening by the report of a corpse on a drifting iceberg, closely followed by a gruesome death on board. Was it suicide, or a particularly brutal murder? Wiki investigates, only to find himself fighting desperately for his own life.

ISBN 978-0-9922588-3-2

Thrilling yarn
from the last days of the square-riggers

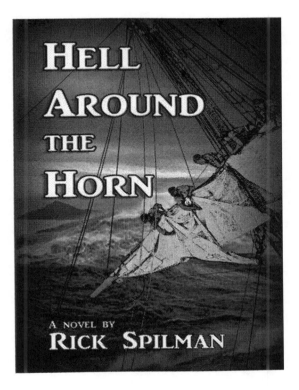

In 1905, a young ship's captain and his family set sail on the windjammer, *Lady Rebecca*, from Cardiff, Wales with a cargo of coal bound for Chile, by way of Cape Horn. Before they reach the Southern Ocean, the cargo catches fire, the mate threatens mutiny and one of the crew may be going mad. The greatest challenge, however, will prove to be surviving the vicious westerly winds and mountainous seas of the worst Cape Horn winter in memory. Told from the perspective of the Captain, his wife, a first year apprentice and an American sailor before the mast, *Hell Around the Horn* is a story of survival and the human spirit in the last days of the great age of sail.

ISBN 978-0-9882360-1-1

Another gripping saga from the author of the Fighting Sail series

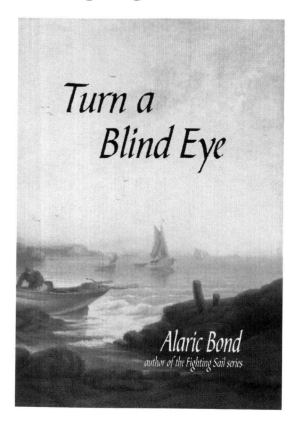

Newly appointed to the local revenue cutter, Commander Griffin is determined to make his mark, and defeat a major gang of smugglers. But the country is still at war with France and it is an unequal struggle; can he depend on support from the local community, or are they yet another enemy for him to fight? With dramatic action on land and at sea, *Turn a Blind Eye* exposes the private war against the treasury with gripping fact and fascinating detail.

ISBN 978-0-9882360-3-5

A romantic adventure from the days of wooden ships and iron men

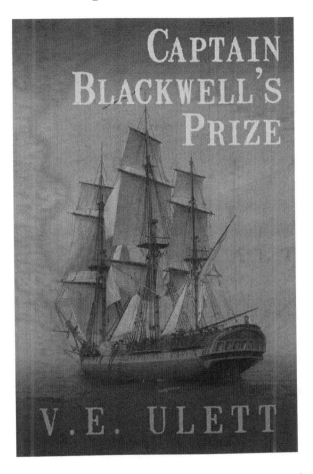

A small, audacious British frigate does battle against a large but ungainly Spanish ship. British Captain James Blackwell intercepts the Spanish *La Trinidad*, outmaneuvers and outguns the treasure ship and boards her. Fighting alongside the Spanish captain, sword in hand, is a beautiful woman. The battle is quickly over. The Spanish captain is killed in the fray and his ship damaged beyond repair. Its survivors and treasure are taken aboard the British ship, *Inconstant*.

ISBN 978-0-9882360-6-6

"Not for the faint hearted – Captain Blackwell pulls no punches!" - Alaric Bond

The repercussions of a court martial and the ill-will of powerful men at the Admiralty pursue Royal Navy Captain James Blackwell into the Pacific, where danger lurks around every coral reef. Even if Captain Blackwell and Mercedes survive the venture into the world of early nineteenth century exploration, can they emerge unchanged with their love intact. The mission to the Great South Sea will test their loyalties and strength, and define the characters of Captain Blackwell and his lady in *Blackwell's Paradise*. ISBN 978-0-9882360-5-9